The
Terranus
Affair

FRANK SALTER

Published by

MELROSE
BOOKS

An Imprint of Melrose Press Limited
St Thomas Place, Ely
Cambridgeshire
CB7 4GG, UK
www.melrosebooks.co.uk

FIRST EDITION

Cover designed by Jeremy Kay

ISBN 978-1-907732-76-8

Printed and bound in Great Britain by:
CPI Group (UK) Ltd, Croydon, CR0 4YY

FSC
www.fsc.org
MIX
Paper from
responsible sources
FSC® C013604

ABOUT THE AUTHOR

Frank Salter is a retired engineering designer, born in Dorset and now living in Hampshire, England. He has a keen interest in science and engineering and a personal vision of the future; the concept of this story has been in the making for four years. Frank is a new author and now has the time to concentrate on his writing.

In terms of genre, there is no precedent for this novel. Frank has created a Sci-fi Romance, perhaps the first of its kind. The novel centres on the blossoming romance between Lisa Macdonald, a veterinarian in the Scottish highlands and Richard Varnicus, a renowned composer. Their relationship however takes on a completely new level when Richard reveals to Lisa a talking spaceship, Horace and confesses that her father is in fact from another planet. There is a whole stack of revelations in store for Lisa. She visits the moon, and discovers that Richard is the son of the First Lady of the planet Terranus, a planet populated by homo-sapiens who have for thousands of years been colonising Earth.

The science fiction elements of the novel have been handled exceptionally well. We encounter synthetic humans, a cure for cancer, alien mammals and of course the charming Horace, a space ship with synthetic intelligence, and a fascinating interior and dynamics. Lisa's discovery that she possesses latent telepathic capabilities due to her unusual lineage also adds to the intensity of the romantic element of the novel. There is something particularly life-affirming and comforting in the development of their romance in the face of so many profound revelations. Another refreshing element of the work is its lack of any dystopian vision that is unusual in current science fiction. The novel is filled with hope for humanity, a belief that time and technology can and will create a balanced society. Human life span has extended with a more peaceful, organic society put in place.

PREFACE

Dr. Lisa Macdonald is a beautiful and qualified veterinarian. She used to work at a government research establishment, but after a bad marriage decided to return to her homeland on the west coast of Scotland. She meets Richard, a famous musician, and falls in love with him; it is a binding love that she had never experienced before. However, she finds that the whirlwind relationship is far from normal and discovers that Richard harbours secrets that question the truth about our existence on planet Earth.

ARE WE ALONE IN THE UNIVERSE?

CHAPTER I

I suppose it all started late Thursday morning. I had to go on a special errand. I did not know that my life was going to change on an astronomical level.

The morning surgery was over. My last patient was an overweight guinea pig who was losing its fur. This was no wonder when I found out what food it had been eating. The practice seems to specialise in over-indulged pets. I do not often come across a non self-inflicted problem. However, I must not complain. The salary is good and it is better than working for a government research laboratory. I just could not stand experimenting on live animals. You would not believe what goes on in the interest of medical advancement. It is so much nicer being back on the west coast of Scotland after experiencing the people pollution of London.

My colleague had just brought me a coffee so it was time for a break. He is a nice lad, just 25 years old and very keen. He always looks after me and is full of questions. Maybe he fancies me a bit, but as I am ten years older, I wouldn't want to lead him on.

I was quietly enjoying my coffee when my boss burst in through the door on one of his rare visits to see me.

"Good morning Doctor Macdonald. How is my most beautiful veterinarian this morning?" he said with an unusual but excited smile.

I like Hamish in a rather strange way despite the fact that he is a snob in mid life crisis. He is a wee bit overweight and thinning on top but he is a good vet and has a head for business. I am used to his sexist comments and innuendos.

"Good morning Hamish," I said with an air of indifference. "I haven't seen you in my surgery for a while."

"Oh I thought I'd see how my favourite vet is doing," he said as his eyes lit up. "I've just had a phone call from Richard Varnicus up at Cannock Brae." He raised his dark bushy eyebrows and scratched his bald forehead. "Do you have any idea who he is?"

"Yes I do," I said, "he is a composer with a strange name who has just had a West End musical hit."

"Aye, that's the fellow and he has scores of hit songs under his belt," Hamish continued with gathering enthusiasm. "Do you know, I was watching him on the Parkinson show just the other night. Damned if I knew he lives just up the road from here. He must have a bob or two to his name."

I could already see where Hamish was going with this. To have a rich client was like a red rag to a bull.

"Cannock Brae is not just up the road, it's forty miles from here," I said impatiently.

"Never mind that," he said, "he could be a good client and I'd like you to follow this one up."

"Follow what up?" I said.

"Apparently his dog has got caught up in some barbed wire and they are unable to free it. He said that the animal is in some degree of pain. I have already said I would send you out straight away. I see you don't have many calls to make this afternoon. I would do it myself but the strange thing is he asked for you in person." Hamish wrung his hands together and pulled a silly querying face.

"Asked for me in person? That is very odd. I have never met him," I said with a mixture of intrigue and curiosity.

"Aye, he asked for you by name and urgently wants you to go and visit him. I just spoke with him."

"Well I suppose I had better go right away."

"You're a sweetheart. I've written his address and phone number on this piece of paper." Hamish gingerly placed the

2

paper on the desk and shuffled out of the room before I could change my mind.

I popped into the loo and decided to put on a bit of make-up. I had long shoulder length hair that looked a mess, so I tied it back into a ponytail. I think I was quietly excited about going out to Cannock Brae to meet this man. I remember reading some articles about him in a woman's magazine. He is definitely a man who likes to keep to himself. Why did he ask for me in person?

I bundled my black bag into the back of the Volvo and set off up the coast road. It was a fair day. I always enjoyed the spectacular views of the sea lochs along the route. It did not seem long before my navigation thingy told me to turn left. I swung onto the single-track road that led down to the coast. Cannock Brae is a 400-acre peninsula of wild heath land and wooded areas dotted with rocky outcrops. I always wondered whether anybody lived here. The only access is by a road that follows a narrow causeway with the sea on both sides. Eventually the landscape widened out and I was confronted by a gatehouse flanked by high stone walls on either side. The peninsula was practically an island creating a perfect isolated retreat. I pulled up in front of the closed wrought-iron gates and wondered what to do next. I stopped the engine and got out. There was an intercom on the wall with a green button. I tentatively pushed it. It immediately glowed and within seconds a male voice addressed me.

"Are you the veterinarian?" it said in a strong Australian accent.

"Yes, I'm Lisa Macdonald from the Oban practice," I replied.

There was a security camera above me mounted on the wall. It made a buzzing noise and ominously started to turn towards me. It stopped for a moment and hesitated then went back the other way.

I wondered whether to say something into the intercom, but the camera finally turned to face me. I felt embarrassed, so I waved at it.

"Bonza!" the intercom finally replied. "Sorry to mess you about, can't work this blasted thing. I'll open the gates. Could ya drive right up to the house?"

The gates started whirring so I jumped into the car and started the engine. I followed the driveway, which wound its way through mature oak and beech trees and beautiful flowering rhododendrons.

There was a five-mile an hour speed limit sign and then, to my surprise, a triangular warning sign with a picture of a steam loco-motive. I crossed what appeared to be a narrow gauge railway complete with white crossing gates. *What fun* I thought as the tyres bumped over the rails. Soon the trees gave way to a huge lawn area, which had been immaculately mown. I could smell the fragrant cut grass. The house was in view now and the drive swept round to a grand front portico supported by four Roman style columns. The house itself was large, built from dressed stone, with big symmetrical sash windows. *Very impressive*, I thought, as I got out of the Volvo and collected my bag.

While I walked up to the front door, there was a man coming towards me from round the side of the house. He was tall with thick dark hair; he was rather handsome, despite the fact he was wearing very tatty, oil-soaked jeans and an even worse tee shirt that may have been white at some stage. He walked towards me with his arm outstretched and we shook hands.

"I'm very pleased to finally meet you, Doctor Macdonald," he said with a kindly smile. "Thank you for coming out so promptly. I am Richard Varnicus."

"Er … yes, hello," I replied awkwardly. "Please call me Lisa; I understand you have a dog in distress."

He outstretched his arm and beckoned me to walk with him.

"It's my housekeeper's dog," he said, "very young and hyper-active. It is from the animal rescue centre. The dog has managed to get its head stuck in a roll of rusty barbed wire up in the woods. I have tried to cut it free but it struggles and yelps and it is all a

4

bit distressing."

"What breed of dog is it?" I said, trying to sound professional.

"A cocker spaniel," he replied, "it has got its ears in an awful tangle."

We walked round the side of the house into a courtyard with a row of garages. Parked in the middle was a very tatty, beaten-up old Land Rover pick-up. He opened the door for me.

"It's about half a mile away up a rough track; I hope you don't mind going in this," he said.

I climbed in and balanced my bag on my knees. There was a strong smell of oil and diesel fumes. We rattled down a gravel road and over the railway line. I could see down the line. There was a little station with a platform and bench seating.

I wanted to ask him about it but the noise in the Land Rover was deafening so we clattered up the hill without saying a word. We travelled through a beautiful forest, which consisted mainly of old oak trees interspersed with rocks draped in a thick carpet of moss.

We came to a clearing further up. I could see a derelict stone cottage that was nothing more than a shell. The stone walls were overgrown with ferns and grass and any signs of the roof were long gone. We rattled to a halt just outside what was once the front door and climbed out. There were two figures crouched down by the old stone fireplace, which was now completely overgrown with moss.

"How are you doing?" Richard hailed them.

A slight, wiry man with grey hair and chiselled features stood up; he was holding a pair of wire cutters.

"I've managed to cut most of the wire off," he said with a satisfied grin. I recognised his accent from the voice at the gatehouse. I think it was Australian.

"I have Doctor Macdonald with me," Richard said, turning to me. "This is Jack Theaton, my handyman, and this is Thelma, my housekeeper."

I shook hands with Jack and turned to the figure crouching on the ground. Mrs Theaton was beside herself with tears running down her chubby round face. She looked up and forced a smile in greeting.

"This is Bruce," she said as she clutched the cocker spaniel that was lying on the ground. It looked quite calm apart from peering up at me with rather wild eyes.

Most of the wire had been cut away. The dog did not look badly hurt at all. I put my case down and took out a pair of surgical scissors.

"We'll have him free in a jiffy," I reassured Thelma. I proceeded to cut the tangled ear fur gently from the barbed wire. The long hairy ears have always been a problem for Spaniels. Why do we have to mess about with their genetics? It was not long before I got the dog free.

"Thank you, doctor," Thelma whimpered.

I gave him a good check-up and listened to his heart and he only had a few superficial scratches. I gave the now relieved Thelma some advice on inoculations and told her to bring him in to the surgery if she had any problems. Bruce looked up at me and furiously wagged his docked tail; he seemed quite happy. I wondered whether they really needed me at all and decided I had done my job. Richard had been very quiet. During the whole procedure I could feel him looking at me. It was quite unnerving.

"Will you three be alright going back on your own while I take Doctor Macdonald back to the house?" he said.

They nodded in agreement and thanked me. I advised them to keep Bruce on a lead.

We climbed back into the smelly Land Rover and clattered back down the hill. When we arrived back in the courtyard, Richard turned off the engine and smiled at me.

"I feel a bit guilty dragging you out all this way. Would you like to come inside and have a coffee and something to eat?" he said with his hand casually resting on the steering wheel.

He had a lovely smile and I must admit I can never pass up the opportunity to nose around someone's house. My next appointment wasn't until half past four so I graciously accepted.

He led me through a door into an annex on the side of the house. It was a large room with a gabled ceiling and a polished pine floor. He told me this was his music studio and I could see why. The room was full of equipment. There was a mixing desk and computer, two keyboards, rows of shelving with CDs, records and stacks of sheet music. He had amplifiers, speakers and a whole array of musical instruments including a full drum kit. I was mesmerised by it but not allowed to linger. He put his hand on my shoulder and ushered me through a door. We entered an impressive hall with a polished floor and oak-panelled walls. The whole area was light and airy with a slight smell of furniture polish and there was a wide carpeted staircase with an ornamental balustrade. He soon guided me down a corridor and into an impressive dining room with a large central rectangular table featuring a beautiful floral centrepiece. The table, with twelve chairs arranged around it, was quite modern; it reminded me more of a boardroom.

Richard apologised for looking so scruffy and explained that he was doing something mechanical in his barn. He pulled out a chair and told me to make myself comfortable. We agreed to have coffee and the sandwiches that his housekeeper had made earlier. Having not had any proper food all day I thanked him. He disappeared through some swing doors and left me alone to look around. Realising that I was still holding my heavy medical bag and my arm was aching from the strain, I popped it under the table and took a tour around the room.

It was once again oak-panelled with a lovely array of light oak ceiling beams and cornices. At one end there was a large bay window that overlooked the garden and at the other, a highly polished grand piano. The room had several large paintings of Scottish mountain scenery. Over the piano there was a spectacular painting depicting a cosmic view of three beautiful planets. The planets had their own moons with a distant sun. They were definitely not of our own solar system. I think it had been painted in oils but there was something about it that made me think it was a clever photograph. The colours were very vivid and you definitely had to stand well back to appreciate it.

Feeling mystified, I looked to the left and there was a triple set of French doors opening onto the garden. I walked towards them and realised it wasn't the garden at all. It was a huge internal courtyard filled with exotic tropical plants, some of which I had not seen before. Glass and timber covered the whole area with a beamed ceiling and Roman-style supporting columns symmetrically arranged along its length. The far end had floor to ceiling glass panels and there was a fantastic blue rectangular swimming pool. The pool was constructed from white marble slabs and flanked by columns and archways. It was an incredible area and reminded me of Roman baths.

I was about to try the door and take a closer look when Mr Varnicus came in backwards through the swing doors carrying a large tray of food. He walked to the table and put the tray down.

"Mrs T looks after me very well," he said. "She has made a huge plate of sandwiches and a chocolate cake."

"They look very nice," I replied feeling overwhelmed.

"Please take a seat," he said while pulling out a chair for me. I sat down awkwardly and felt very self-conscious. There was something about this man that made me feel very strange; his dark brown eyes seemed to be probing my very soul.

"Do you live in this big house all on your own?" I rudely asked without thinking.

"Yes, I'm afraid I have rattled around in this house on my own since my parents left. You see this is a family house. I was born and raised in this house and so was my father."

"And you haven't married and had children of your own?"

I replied with my foot in my mouth. I don't know what came over me saying that and I could feel myself blushing. Richard smiled at me and turned his attention to pouring the coffee. He handed me a plate and offered me a sandwich.

"I lead a very busy life and guess I just haven't met the right woman yet. What about you?"

"I'm sorry, I didn't mean to sound rude. I'm divorced actually," I said while the perspiration started to break out on my forehead.

He handed me a cup of coffee. I looked onto the tray for some sugar. He immediately picked up the sugar bowl and passed it to me.

"How do you stay so slim and beautiful?" he said, with his smile broadening. He looked at my heavily sweetened coffee cup. I laughed awkwardly and nibbled on my sandwich while trying to think of something sensible to say.

"I get a lot of exercise," I said after an awkward pause. "Where are your parents now?" I asked as if out of control.

"Oh, they emigrated to Australia about ten years ago; they are both retired now. My father was an engineer and my mother is a solicitor. They always wanted to live in Australia."

"That's a coincidence," I said, "my mother was in the legal profession also. Do you get to see them much?"

"Er ... yes, I see them as often as I can." I could oddly sense that Richard was feeling uncomfortable about talking about his parents so I thought I had better drop the subject.

"I was admiring your house. It is absolutely beautiful, especially the paintings. I love the space picture over there." I waved my hand in the general direction of the piano and popped the rest of my sandwich into my mouth.

"Thank you," he said, "most of these pictures were painted by my grandfather. He had a passion for art, especially landscapes."

"And your passion is definitely music."

"Yes, I love all forms of music and I am very lucky to make a good living out of it as well. It helps pay for my other passion that is anything mechanical, especially if it is driven by steam power."

"Oh yes," I remembered, "I meant to ask you about the railway line I crossed when driving up to your house."

"Yes, that is something my father started to build; he too has a keen interest in steam engines. I spent a lot of time finishing off his project and now the railway runs all the way round the island. It is really just playing trains but on a bigger scale. I have also got a full sized steam traction engine."

"I would be fascinated to see it sometime; I love historic things like that. I remember my parents taking me to a steam fair when I was a child. I had never seen a steam engine before and I'll never forget it."

"I'd love to show you. In fact you can drive it." Richard's eyes lit up with excitement; I could sense his enthusiasm.

We had been chatting for quite some time when there was a noise coming from the swing doors. I could hear Bruce barking furiously on the other side. The door opened and in came Mrs T with Bruce frantically skidding across the polished floor to greet us.

"Everything alright Mrs T?" Richard asked.

"We're all fine, thanks to Doctor Macdonald," she said beaming.

I looked at my watch and realised I was going to be late for my next appointment. I stood up in a panic.

"I really must be going. I have another call. Thanks very much for the coffee and sandwiches."

Richard showed me to the front door. It crossed my mind that I never had a chance to try the chocolate cake. Oh well, never mind. We said goodbye and I drove off. When I got to the gates they were shut and I wondered what I should do. I then realised that I did not have my medical bag. I must have left it under the table. Cursing, I turned the car around and drove back to the house, totally ignoring the speed limit sign. I pulled up at the front portico facing the wide lawn. I jumped out of the car and noticed Richard running towards me across the lawn with my bag in one hand and a sandwich box in the other.

"I noticed you forgot your bag," he said, out of breath. "I left the gates shut and thought I might catch you up. There is some chocolate cake in this container in case you get peckish later on."

"Thank you," I said, "that's really sweet of you."

"I only wish you had more time to enjoy it with me," he said.

"Perhaps another time. I have to dash. I've got some cows to look at and I'm already late. Thank you for the cake."

I drove off waving goodbye and hoped I had not forgotten anything else. How nice of him to give me the chocolate cake. I think he must have guessed I have a sweet tooth.

CHAPTER 2

It had been quite an afternoon and after checking out Cameron's cows I was glad to finally get home and relax in a lovely warm bath. My thoughts kept returning to my meeting with Richard. Brief though it was, he had made a big impression on me. My mind kept going over the afternoon's events. OK, so he is very eligible, he is successful, with a beautiful house and money and I had felt very relaxed in his company. But I can't help being very wary of men since the break-up of my marriage. In fact, I have to admit that I haven't had a boyfriend for nearly two years now. My ex-husband turned out to be an over-sexed, lying philanderer and yet, when I married him, I thought he was wonderful. The marriage only lasted two years. The last straw was when he raped me whilst in a fit of rage. I don't think I can be a very good judge of character. With some people, I can immediately feel comfortable in their presence and I should use that sensation as a benchmark of whether they are nice to know or not. I felt comfortable in Richard's company and I was very attracted to him, but there was something strange that I couldn't put my finger on.

Anyway, my experience of living in the overcrowded city of London was not very pleasant and moving back to my home ground was the best thing I had ever done. I was starting to prune up so I decided to get out of my now cold bath. Wrapped in a towel I went downstairs to pour myself a glass of wine. I was just about to take a sip when the phone rang.

"Hello."

"Hello darling." It was my mother.

"How are you Mum?"

"I'm not too bad, but I have had a strange letter in the post this morning. I thought I must tell you."

"What letter is that Mum?"

"Well, it's from the SIS."

"Who is the SIS?" I said, hoping we weren't going on a wild goose chase.

"You know, it's the Secret Intelligence Service."

"That's MI6 isn't it?" I said with my voice rising in pitch. "What on earth do they want?"

"Well it seems they want to interview me on a matter of national security. They say I am not to be concerned; they just want to ask routine questions. They asked me to telephone them to arrange a convenient time for them to call at my house."

"That is all very odd," I said with doubt creeping up on me. "Are you sure that it's genuine and not someone wanting to sell you something?"

"Don't be silly darling," she said. "The letter has the official coat of arms. In any case I have already arranged the meeting."

My mother used to be a successful barrister. She had to retire a year ago due to bad health so I suppose she ought to know.

"The reason I phoned you darling," she continued, "is I've arranged to see them tomorrow afternoon at three o'clock. I really hoped that you could be there too. I'm a bit worried about seeing them on my own."

"You're in luck Mum. I don't have any clients tomorrow afternoon; I can be round at lunchtime."

"Thank you darling. I hoped you could. I'll prepare a meal for you. Love you. I'll see you tomorrow."

She put the phone down and I wondered what it could be about. I used to work for a government research establishment and I have abided by the Official Secrets Act so it can't be my fault. I took a large slurp of my wine and decided to put a frozen fish pie in the oven with the chocolate cake as a dessert. I think that I will have an early night tonight.

The next morning it was very hot and sunny. I went to work wearing the lightest cotton dress I could find but with my white coat on as well it was sweltering. The so-called animal lovers were harping on about global warming but still I have to treat dogs that have been left in hot cars. I was glad surgery was over. I was just about to leave when the phone rang. To my surprise, it was Richard.

"Hello Lisa, I hope you don't mind me ringing you at work." His voice sounded really pleasant and cheerful. "I just wanted to thank you for helping Mrs T with her dog yesterday."

"That's alright," I said, "its all in a day's work. Thank you for your hospitality; the chocolate cake was delicious."

"Glad you enjoyed it. Lisa, I hope you don't think I'm being presumptuous but I would be honoured if you would allow me to take you out to dinner. I know a great restaurant where they have won awards for chocolate cake." My god, I thought, how could I refuse?

"Thank you very much," I said, "I'd love to."

"Would tonight be alright? I can pick you up from your house about seven."

I quickly had to think. I could be back from Mum's by about six so it should give me enough time to get ready.

"Make it half past seven and you have got yourself a date. I'll give you my address."

"Don't worry. I took the liberty of finding out where you live, so I'll look forward to seeing you then."

Well, I thought, *he certainly doesn't mess about; he really must be interested in me. He even managed to find out my address; that briefly struck me as odd, but hell, this is my first proper date in a long time.*

I left the surgery and drove down to Mum's in a happy frame of mind. It's Friday and I don't have to go to work until Monday morning. I have a date tonight. Life could not be sweeter.

I swung into my mother's driveway and pulled up outside her front door. I used my key to get in and found her in the kitchen tossing a bowl of green salad.

"Hi Mum, you're looking well; how are you feeling?"

"Lisa darling, you sound uncommonly cheerful and I'm fine."

"Is that a new wig you're wearing? It makes you look ten years younger."

"I ordered it on the Internet and it came this morning. I'm very pleased with it."

I should explain, my mother has had a mastectomy and the chemotherapy has left its mark. My mother always likes to look smart, unlike her daughter who prefers the tatty jeans look. In any case, being a vet is a filthy job and it doesn't pay to wear your best clothes.

We had a light lunch of ham slices, salad and some lovely 'bake them yourself' bread rolls. Mother always insists that you should have the smell of baked bread in the house when people come to call on you. We chatted over coffee about the state of the world, the Home Office fiasco and the high level of immigrants invading our country. Mum also showed me the MI6 letter, which looked official enough.

A thought occurred to me. My father was killed in Australia about five years ago. He used to be a professor of geology at Edinburgh University and was on a field trip with a colleague when the light aircraft they were travelling in came down and crashed in the Australian desert. Apparently an eyewitness saw the plane come down and burst into flames but they never found the wreckage or any bodies. We always wondered whether there was some sort of conspiracy behind it; the mystery remains unresolved to this day. My father was always very secretive and spent a lot of time abroad; I must admit that I never really got close to him. I asked Mum if this meeting might have something to do with it but she got quite angry and didn't want to bring up the subject so I let it lie.

The doorbell rang. Mum was doing the washing up so I went to answer the door. Standing side by side at the door there were two men identically dressed in black suits and grey ties. They both had dark hair but the shorter man was going bald on top. He wore thick rimmed glasses and was clutching a black briefcase. It reminded me of the film 'Men in Black'. The taller man spoke.

"Good afternoon," he said in his best BBC English, "my name is Jenkins and this is my colleague Mr Wilkins. We represent the Secret Intelligence Service and have an appointment to see Mrs Macdonald."

He produced a black leather identity wallet from his inside pocket and opened it up for me to see it. It seemed official enough although I wouldn't know what I was looking for.

"I'm Mrs Macdonald's daughter. We have been expecting you. Please come in," I said while stepping aside.

I showed them into the front drawing room and seated them. They declined a cup of tea so I excused myself and went off to find my mother. She was in the kitchen checking out her wig in the mirror. We went into the drawing room and I introduced my mother to them; they both stood up and shook hands courteously. My mother and I both sat on the sofa opposite them.

"Mrs Macdonald," the tall one addressed my mother as his accomplice took out a large notepad from his briefcase. "I'm afraid I must insist that the meeting with you be conducted alone."

"I'm her daughter; we don't have any secrets," I protested.

"I'm terribly sorry Miss Macdonald, but protocol dictates that the interview be conducted with your mother alone."

"OK," I said turning to my mother. "I know when I'm not wanted; I'll be in the kitchen if you need me."

I left the room in a huff and went to make myself a cup of tea. Half an hour later my mother came into the kitchen and started routing about in the sideboard drawer. She produced a family photo album. She told me they were asking all sorts of awkward questions about Dad's family. She told me not to worry and rushed off to the front room again.

I knew it, I thought to myself. *This must be about his disappearance, but it happened over five years ago. Why would they be investigating him after all this time?* Another half hour went by and I heard the front door close. Mum came back into the kitchen looking very flustered.

"Well," she said, "that was very strange. They wanted to know everything I knew about Dad's family and they have borrowed some of the family photographs. They gave me a receipt, but I doubt if I will see the pictures again."

"You alright Mum?" I said, holding her hand. "You don't think Dad was up to something dodgy; do you? He did travel a lot; perhaps they think he was a spy."

"Don't be silly Lisa; your father wouldn't do anything like that. Moreover, if he did, he certainly kept it quiet. Anyway, the two men seemed very happy with the answers."

"Look, I really must dash; I have a date tonight, with a man," I said looking at my watch.

"That's alright darling. I feel tired. I'm going to have a little lie down. You go and have fun."

I don't think Mum was listening so I thought I would leave her to have her snooze. I kissed her goodbye and drove off home. It was time to tart myself up.

CHAPTER 3

After taking a bath, I was ready in plenty of time. I put on full make-up and because it was so hot I decided to wear my slinky black dress with the low cut open back, and no bra. I was dressed to kill and was beginning to wonder whether I had overdone it. Too late! As I looked out of the window, a very smart metallic green Jaguar sports car pulled up outside. It was he; right on time. The adrenalin kicked in, and in a panic I nearly fell down the stairs. I must remember that I'm not used to wearing high heels. The doorbell rang and trying to regain my balance, I fumbled with the lock. Richard was wearing a light grey summer suit with a white open neck shirt. Considering the state he was in the last time we met I have to admit he cleans up very well.

"Hello Lisa," he said with a grin. I felt his eyes running up and down my figure. "You look absolutely stunning."

"Hello again." I felt my face flush with embarrassment. "Thank you, um … I'm nearly ready, come in, I'll just be two ticks."

I wobbled into the kitchen to find my bag and decided to take the white silk scarf that my mother had given to me last Christmas; it could be useful seeing that Richard's car was open top. Richard stood in the narrow hallway with his eyes fixed on me.

"You found my house alright," I said, trying to make conversation. "I am a bit tucked away down this country lane."

"No problem at all, it was an enjoyable drive here and we

couldn't ask for a nicer evening."

I miraculously found my feet and walked sensibly out into the hall, wrapping the scarf over my bare shoulders.

"OK, I'm ready, shall we go?"

I ushered him out through the front door and could smell expensive aftershave wafting behind him, much nicer than the diesel oil from our previous meeting. He opened my front gate and allowed me to go first. I stood by the car wondering what to do; he promptly opened the door for me. The interior of the Jaguar was all polished walnut and plush light tan leather. I managed to get in gracefully without flashing my knickers. I felt like a million dollars.

"A lovely car," I said, running my hand over the soft leather.

"Thank you; it's one of my favourites." I wondered how many favourites he owned.

Richard slid in beside me and unbuttoned his jacket.

"I've booked a table at the Royal Hotel; it's just down the coast from Oban, about half an hour's drive. I haven't been there for a while but last time the food was very good. The restaurant overlooks the sea loch with the Isle of Mull in the distance; there should be a spectacular sunset this evening. I do hope you like it."

"It sounds absolutely perfect," I said, smiling as lusciously as possible.

He started the engine and the V8 roared into life. I was pushed back into the soft seat as we accelerated down the road. I felt a wave of exhilaration wash over me. We turned onto the main road and as we gathered speed the warm evening air started to blow my hair around. My hair was shoulder length, thick and straight. My mother always said that I had a lot of my father's genes and there was definitely oriental blood in his family. I decided to bunch it up and tie my scarf around the back just in case I ended up looking like a frightened floor mop by the end of the journey. Richard looked at me and smiled.

"I can put the hood up if the wind is a problem."

"You don't need to, I've fixed it. I love being in an open top car, and the scenery is beautiful."

I was actually having a ball and was now resisting the urge to put my hand on his knee.

"How long have you been living in Dalmally?" he said, taking his eyes off the road whilst driving at what seemed to be break-neck speed.

"I've only been living in my cottage for about a year, but I was born in Perth and have lived here most of my life. I also spent about six years working in London."

"How did you find living in London?" he said casually with only one hand dangerously resting on the wheel.

"I hated it; it was the worst time of my life. There were too many people and too much noise."

"I'm the same; I have to go to London about six times a year on business. I spent six months there when we were producing the stage show. It was dreadful. You can't have a proper conversation with so many busy people around you. I'm always glad to get back to the tranquillity of this area."

We rounded a corner and the sea was in sight. I could smell the sweet cooler air. We turned off onto a B-road and maintained a more comfortable speed.

"I hear your show is a huge success. I have to admit that I haven't been able to see it but I was reading some great reviews in a magazine. You must be very proud of it."

"Producing a show is not really my scene. I wouldn't bother to go and see it. I had more fun writing the words and music. I can let you have a CD of the sound track if you like."

He reached over and opened the glove box in front of me. The close proximity made the hairs on the back of my neck tingle. He produced a CD complete with cellophane wrapping and gave it to me.

"Thanks," I said. "I shall look forward to listening to that."

"If we had more time you could hear it now but we are nearly there. I hope you're not a vegetarian; they do a lovely Aberdeen Angus steak here."

We turned down a tarmac drive. The hotel lay before us. It was a large sprawling building with too many flat roof extensions but was nicely situated on the edge of the loch. The large gravel car park was nearly full. The hotel was obviously busy with the summer trade so we pulled into one of the last few remaining spaces. While Richard got out of the car and walked round to my door, I untied my hair and shook my head the way they do in the shampoo adverts. My hair just popped back into shape as if by magic. Richard opened the car door for me and I gracefully slid out. He is a perfect gentleman. I don't think anybody has opened a car door for me, ever.

We walked into the plush foyer and made for the reception desk. The hotel was full of people milling about. A young girl was standing behind the desk attending to people; she looked up and instantly seemed to acknowledge us. The girl left the two people standing there and popped her head round a door at the back. Almost immediately, a man in a black suit wearing an awful red paisley bow tie came out and walked towards us.

"Mr Varnicus," he said with a broad smile and arm outstretched to shake Richard's hand. "I am the manager. On behalf of the staff, we are very honoured to see you back at our hotel. Your table is ready; would you like to come through for a cocktail in the bar?"

We followed him through into an equally plush bar where he showed us to a table and seated us. He then clicked his fingers very professionally in the air. The barman, dressed in white jacket and black bow tie, came over to serve us.

"James will serve you this evening; I hope you enjoy your dinner." He then bowed and reversed away from the table as if we were royalty. What a performance, I thought; he was totally over the top.

We both ordered a gin and tonic and when the waiter had

gone Richard leaned over towards me.

"They're laying it on a bit thick," he said slyly out of the corner of his mouth.

"I know. Do they usually treat you like this?" I whispered back.

"No, mind you I haven't been here for about a year."

The waiter brought the drinks and we both took a sip.

"I've had a lot of media exposure since doing the London musical," Richard continued. "It was a mistake to do the television interviews."

"It would seem," I said, "that you are a celebrity."

"Oh God, don't say that. I've been happy doing all the stuff in the backroom; I don't want this kind of attention. In fact I had to install the security gate and CCTV camera at Cannock Brae. Press reporters recently invaded my house and, would you believe, local people wanted autographs. They just walked round the house as if it were a stately home. They even asked if I served teas on the lawn! I had to put a stop to that. I value my privacy," he said with a frown.

I could see that Richard was upset by the thought. Everybody these days wants to be a celebrity. I've even wondered what it would be like, but I can appreciate that it would be awful if you weren't up for it. I was just about to ask Richard how long it took to write a stage musical when, just to prove my previous statement, a middle-aged couple came up to our table.

"Mr Varnicus, I hope you don't mind us intruding," the well-dressed woman spoke. "But we so love your music. Our daughter would love to have your autograph. She is very shy. She has all your CDs."

Richard was very courteous, although I could feel him cringing; he duly asked what name to make it out to and filled out the back of a local postcard they had given him.

"I didn't know that you have made CDs as well," I said.

"I haven't actually made any CDs myself apart from the stage

22

musical," he replied. "But I have written lots of songs for other bands to make the recordings; some were hits too. Up until now, I was delightfully anonymous. That was until my business manager let the cat out of the bag. I'm going to have words with him."

I realised that I knew very little about Richard. I made a mental note that I must get out more. I was about to ask him what bands have recorded his music when two thirty-something women interrupted us again. One of them even had a photo of Richard, which he scribbled over.

"Shall we go into the dining room?" he said, lowering his dark eyebrows. "I'm really sorry about this. I didn't realise this would happen. Hopefully it will be quieter in there and we won't get bothered."

We decamped into the large dining room and were shown to a nice table by the windows. The room was practically a conservatory with floor to ceiling windows along the whole length. It was pleasantly cool with adequate air-conditioning. The view across the sea to the misty island beyond was stunning.

"I am going to sit with my back to the room," Richard said to the waiter and beckoned him to seat me in the corner. "Hopefully no one will recognise me."

"I shall see that you are not disturbed, sir," the waiter said and scurried off.

"I should have bought you a pair of dark glasses and a false beard," I chuckled.

We laughed and felt more relaxed. To our surprise, the waiter brought a huge magnum of champagne sitting nicely in an ice bucket, apparently compliments of the management. They were really pulling out the stops. We perused the menu and I ordered a tomato consommé and decided to have the steak. Richard had the same and wanted his steak well done with a large pot of horseradish. The waiter dutifully filled our glasses and Richard decided to make a toast.

"To the world and all that sail around her," he said as we

chinked our glasses.

"That's a strange toast."

"I'm a strange guy," he said chuckling.

By the time the steaks arrived, I had already drunk too much champagne and was really enjoying the moment.

"So tell me Richard, do you do many live gigs?"

"No," he said, "I couldn't do that sort of thing; far too many people. I would find it overwhelming although I do think live music is good. You can really feel the atmosphere when people are performing in front of you. In Victorian times, families would learn to play musical instruments and make their own entertainment. Then television and Hi-Fi music systems took over. I personally think it is sad that the human race has to herd together in huge crowds to listen to live music. I'm afraid I don't like crowds of people."

Richard frowned, put a huge dollop of horseradish on his steak and continued.

"About once a month I get the guys together. We test out some of my songs, smoke a little pot, and generally do a bit of jamming. It can be very creative."

"You smoke pot!" I said, trying not to slur my words and realising I had said it too loudly.

"It doesn't do any harm; moderation in all things. We have made some of our best recordings under the influence. What about you Lisa, what do you do to relax?"

"Well, I'm a bit boring really; I like to keep fit and do a bit of running and swimming. Incidentally, I used to play the drums when I was at university. Come to think of it, we did smoke a few dodgy cigarettes."

"I don't think you're the least bit boring. You must come and join us when the band gets together; you can try the drum kit at home. Good drummers are difficult to come by these days. It has to come from the soul. Nobody wants their kids to learn, far too noisy and these days everything is electronic."

"I'd love to," I said, "but I'm probably a bit rusty."

I looked into his smiling eyes and began to melt. I must go easy with the champagne.

For a sweet we both had the inevitable, a superb luxury chocolate mousse. We had also managed to finish the champagne or at least I did. The damn waiter kept filling my glass. I think I was well and truly plastered. Richard could see that I had a happy glazed expression and suggested that we leave and get a bit of fresh air. I was all for that. The restaurant was still very busy, so Richard settled up while I paid a visit to the loo. When I emerged from the ladies' room, Richard was in the foyer surrounded by people clamouring after autographs. I could sense his anger. He was relieved to see me. He made his apologies and whisked me out through the front door. To our surprise, there were at least four newspaper reporters outside waiting for us. They were flashing their cameras and firing questions at us. I was beginning to feel the annoyance that someone like Princess Diana would have experienced. Richard said we had to get out of here and, grabbing my hand, we made for the car. There was no time for seat belts. He started the engine and made his getaway, leaving the reporters running behind us in a cloud of dust.

We travelled up the coast for a while and Richard pulled into a small car park off the road. It was a lovely spot, with a view over the sea. The sun had disappeared over the horizon and the sky was glowing in a warm orange haze. The sea was completely calm and shrouded in mist. It was beautiful and Richard sighed. I could feel his relief. We got out of the car, or I should say I fell out. I kicked off my uncomfortable high heeled shoes and left them lying in the car park. We walked slowly down a grassy path towards the sea. I put my arm through his to steady myself.

"It is a lovely evening," he said and I felt his anger well up again. "I'm really sorry about the people at the hotel; I had no idea it would be like that. I'm going to have words with my manager in the morning. I can't afford to have that sort of media attention. This is entirely his fault. I've a good mind to sack him."

"Don't worry," I said, "I've had a lovely time and this view is perfect."

I clung onto his arm as the sea air made me feel dizzy, or was it the champagne? I had a sort of empathy with Richard, a mixture of sharing his annoyance and feelings. I could almost read his mind and it made me feel incredibly safe. I have never had that sort of experience before in the company of a man, except perhaps with my late father.

We stopped and Richard turned to me.

"Are you OK? You're looking a bit pale. There's a bench over there. Shall we sit and watch the sunset?"

He put his arm around my waist and I melted; all feelings of nausea disappeared. We sat on the bench. I put my arm inside his jacket and nestled against his chest. I could feel the warmth of his body and could sense his contentment. It was like being a teenager again and being in love for the first time. I haven't felt this happy in years.

CHAPTER 4

I woke up the next morning with a dreadful headache and found myself lying on top of the bed still wearing my black dress with my handbag and shoes strewn on the floor. I remembered the delight of being in Richard's arms and watching the sunset, but the rest was a blur. I can also remember being carried up my front path. Richard carried me in his arms and opened the door for me. Hell, I must have been out of it. What an arse! I should have been compos mentis for an experience like that. God, what must he think of me? I tried to subdue my anger and wished I could talk to him and apologise. I lay there for a while nursing my throbbing head and recalled the evening, which all seemed to go a bit wrong. But, on the other hand, it was absolutely wonderful. I don't suppose I will see him again.

I struggled to my feet and crept downstairs feeling positively miserable. I made some strong coffee and took two aspirins. Then I went through to the living room and flopped down at my little dining table. As I took a sip of coffee, I noticed a white envelope resting against the salt and pepper pots. It had 'Lisa' written on it in beautiful old English script. I tore it open. It was from Richard and was written using an ink pen. The handwriting was exquisite. It read:

'Dear Lisa,

I hope by the time you read this you are feeling better. I had a lovely time last night despite all that happened. I'm sorry the champagne did not agree with you. I know you are not used to it. I'd love to see you Sunday lunchtime if you are free. I'll ring you tonight (Saturday).

Love Richard.'

I immediately felt better. It was a lovely note signed with love and he does want to see me again. He must have left the note last night while I was out of it. He is right too; I haven't had champagne for as long as I can remember. It is very more-ish. I should have been more careful. I was due to visit my mother on Sunday; I must ring her and cancel. Slow down Lisa. I'll have a shower and go for a run, which will shake off this hangover. Hell, I was feeling better. How thoughtful of him to leave me a note.

At lunchtime I decided to ring my mother to cancel our Sunday lunch date. I told her I had a date with a man, but Mum was not in a good mood and obviously preoccupied. Apparently MI6 had been in contact again asking about my late father's line of work.

"Do you know," she said angrily, "they want to look through his personal things. He really didn't leave much behind. In fact all his personal things are in one suitcase, which I have put up in the loft. They will have to get it down themselves. I can't get into the loft now."

"Don't worry Mum; let them get on with it."

"They were asking about his family again," she continued, "and I have now realised that I don't know anything about his parents, or where he was born. All I could say was that he had Japanese origins and was supposedly orphaned during the war. I feel such a fool; I had been married to your father for nearly thirty years and I know diddly-squat about him. It's my fault;

he didn't have much time for me or for you for that matter. I've told them to contact the university to find out more. It is very annoying to drag all this up after his death. I would have thought MI6 would have files and resources to find out this sort of information. Do you know they even had the effrontery to ask me to confirm that you were his daughter? That was the last straw. I told them to sod off!"

Mum was beside herself and I tried to calm her down. I know their marriage was not a very happy one. After I was born they both led fairly separate lives.

"Please don't upset yourself Mum, it will blow over. I'm really sorry I can't come over tomorrow."

"What did you say you are doing, having lunch with a man? I hope he is worth it. Who is he?"

"He is lovely. I met him the other day and he has a big house up the coast. His name is Richard Varnicus."

"Richard Varnicus! I know him; he is famous. I saw him on television last week. In fact, I have his CD. His music is wonderful. You're going out with him?"

"Yes, he has invited me to lunch on Sunday," I lied. He probably will not ring me at all now.

"I think that is marvellous," Mum enthused. "You must ask him to come to tea here. I would love to meet him."

I think I managed to cheer Mum up with the news that I have a famous boyfriend. I was just glad to have a boyfriend, well maybe. I told her I would pop round to see her on Monday night and spent the rest of the afternoon giving the whole house a good clean in nervous anticipation of Richard's call.

Later that afternoon, I sat down and reflected about the secret service agents asking all these questions about my father. I must admit that I don't know much about him myself. I don't remember him when I was very young but I can remember my nanny, Miss Shepard. She was a nice woman and we had a lot of fun. Mum was always in the law courts and Dad was away most of the time. Then I was sent away to boarding school when I was ten, which was a horrendous experience. After that it was university. So that's my childhood in a nutshell.

My father was not particularly tall but well-built with a definite oriental appearance with dark brown eyes and thick dark hair. Where the name of Macdonald came from, I do not know. My mother was a Cameron before she married him. She has the Scots look with dark hair and deep-set blue eyes; in fact, she was a very attractive woman before she became ill and age got the better of her. I'm sure I have inherited a bit of both and I am certainly my father's daughter, without doubt. The short times that we did have together were extraordinary. We had a strange rapport. I can remember going for walks with him. I must have been only about eight years old, but we would have grown-up talks about all sorts of things, none of which I can remember now. The phone rang and broke the silence; I nearly jumped out of my skin. I answered it and to my delight, it was Richard.

"Lisa, how are you?" It was lovely to hear his voice again.

"Richard, I'm so sorry I drank too much. What must you think of me?"

"Don't worry Lisa; I know you're not a hopeless alcoholic. I didn't want to say anything at the time. Just blame it on the waiter for filling your glass."

"I am sorry. I'm not used to alcohol, but thank you for a lovely evening and thank you for getting me home."

"Did you find my note?"

"Yes I did, and I'd love to see you on Sunday."

"That's great; I'll pick you up about midday."

"You don't need to do that; I can drive out to your place."

"OK, if you are sure. I'll see you Sunday and by the way, if you want to swim bring your togs."

When I put the phone down, I shouted with joy and went straight upstairs to have a look at my swimming costumes.

CHAPTER 5

The next morning I was up bright and early. I went for a five-mile run. After my shower, I tried on my bikini. After a few adjustments, I was surprised to find it fitted very well. I wasn't sure if I dare wear it so I decided to take my all-in-one swimsuit in case I chickened out. I packed a small holdall with a towel, sun blocker and various other 'just in case' items. It was another glorious day so I thought I would wear something cool. After trying on numerous combinations, I finally decided to wear a pleated summer skirt with a lacy top. Time was marching on so in nervous anticipation I set off up the coast.

I approached the familiar gatehouse and pulled up, but before I could get out of the car the gates started opening so I just drove straight in. Once again, the lawns were immaculately mown and the gardens looked beautifully lush and green. As I pulled up outside the front portico, my heart was beating furiously as the adrenalin kicked in, but I didn't have time to think about the butterflies in my stomach. As I got out of the car, Bruce came tearing round the corner barking uncontrollably. The dog gave me an excited greeting as I bent down and offered my hand to him. No sooner than I had said hello he was off again at high-speed back round the corner with his little tail wagging furiously. While I stood there wondering whether I should follow the dog or go to the front door, Bruce frantically reappeared with Richard hot on his heels.

"Hello Lisa," he said, smiling broadly. "I hope you're feeling better after the other night; you're looking beautiful."

I blushed as he held my arm and kissed me on the cheek. I wanted to kiss him back but he whisked me round and with his hand on my bare shoulder, he walked me round the side of the house.

"I thought we could have a relaxing glass of wine or something in the garden. Jack and Mrs T are out for the day so we have the place to ourselves," he said while Bruce chased around us in circles. "I'm afraid I have to keep an eye on the mutt while they are away."

"That sounds lovely," I said, still in a daze. "But I'm not going to repeat the other night, just one glass for me."

"Don't worry, I want you to relax. After lunch we can take the mutt for a walk and see if we can tire him out."

Richard produced a tennis ball from his pocket; I wondered what the bulge was in his shorts. He threw it into the trees and Bruce tore off after it, disappearing into the bushes. Richard wore white shorts and a tee shirt. He looked ready for a game of tennis. He was quite muscular and had a bronzed tan and slightly hairy legs. I couldn't help thinking that he was very sexy. I managed to take my thoughts away from his legs as we rounded the back of the house. There was a large terrace with steps up to it. We stepped over the railway line that ran at the foot of the steps and disappeared across the lawn into the trees. To the right there was a large pond surrounded by reeds and flowering lilies. A wooden bridge for the railway line crossed a small stream. In the background there was a huge weeping willow tree; it was absolutely idyllic.

"It is a lovely garden," Richard said, stopping at the foot of the terrace. "Jack does most of the work keeping it in shape."

"I think it is stunning; you must show me round." I felt a bit awestruck and couldn't think of anything else to say. We went up onto the terrace. He sat me down on one of the comfortable padded garden chairs set around a white table. The table had a tray with an array of glasses and in the centre was a large parasol.

"What would you like to drink?" he said, standing over me

with his hand on my shoulder.

"Wine will be fine," I said, trying to pull myself together. He disappeared into the house and shortly came out carrying a bottle of white wine. The chilled bottle misted up in the warm summer air. He proceeded to open it with a corkscrew from the table.

"This is a Chardonnay," he said as he popped the cork. "Is that alright?"

"That's my favourite wine." *He seemed to know that already,* I thought and tried to relax.

"Tell me about yourself," he said as he poured the wine. "I know very little about you apart from the fact you're a very good vet and you have a doctorate."

I briefly outlined my life, my divorce, my late father, and mother recovering from breast cancer. Richard listened intently without taking his eyes off me. However, Bruce interrupted me. He was sitting at my feet wagging his tail furiously with the ball in his mouth. To his delight, I stood up and threw the ball as hard as I could. Of course, it went straight into the pond.

"Oh bugger," I said, "will he be alright fetching that?"

"He will love collecting that; he loves the water," Richard laughed, "but he won't let you alone now. He doesn't know when to stop."

"Spaniels are prone to getting a water infection in their ears," I said, as the veterinarian side of me surfaced.

"Don't worry, I know a very good vet who would sort that out." Richard laughed again and I laughed with him.

"Tell me about your late father," Richard asked. "What did he do and how did he die?"

The question surprised me. Many people have been asking about him. I explained that he disappeared in a plane crash and was a professor of geology at the university. Richard listened intently but thankfully did not pursue the subject.

"Bruce has found your ball," he said, pointing at the soaking spaniel.

He stood there on the lawn and shook the water off, ears flapping wildly. He seemed happy and flopped down in the shade of a nearby viburnum bush, keeping the ball close to his nose.

"Would you like to have a swim before lunch?" Richard asked. "Mrs T has prepared us a salad with cold meats and all sorts of tasty extras on the side. We can eat about half past one so we have plenty of time."

"That would be nice," I said, gulping my wine. "I love swimming and it will cool me down."

"I'll show you the shower room where you can change," Richard said as he got up from the table. I followed him into the pool room, which was magnificent with white marble, Roman style columns and exotic plants. It was lovely, cool and very inviting. I followed him through a door at the side into a large room with two shower cubicles, a washbasin and a loo. The whole room was white marble with gold fittings. The sheer opulence and effect was overwhelming and in a daze I suddenly realised that I didn't have my holdall with my costume inside.

"Richard, I'll have to get my things from the car; I'm not swimming naked." I suddenly felt embarrassed at what I had just said.

"That wouldn't worry me," he laughed, "you get your stuff and I'll see you in the pool when you're ready." He kissed me on the forehead. "You are priceless," he said and walked out of the room leaving me standing there with my mouth open.

I gathered myself together and went through into the garden. I found Bruce waiting for me. He followed me round to the front of the house proudly carrying his ball. When I returned with my bag, I threw the ball for him again, this time keeping it on the lawn. I took another large slurp of my wine before I went through to change. I could feel the alcohol kicking in. I must be careful. I do not want a repeat of the other night and I shouldn't even go swimming, but what the heck. Richard was already in the pool floating on his back, wearing a skimpy white costume. I told him I would be two seconds and changed in double quick time. There was no doubt in my mind, so I reappeared wearing my red bikini. I sank into the lovely warm water. I swam from one end to the other and finally ended up in the middle with Richard who was still floating about on his back.

"This pool is lovely," I said, "you are lucky to have such a beautiful house."

"I'm lucky to have such a beautiful girl swimming in my pool." *Damn, he says the nicest things.* I glared at him.

"Bet I can swim a length faster than you." He glared back.

"Bet you can't!"

We raced to the end, both doing the crawl and splashing wildly. When I was ready, he counted to three and we were off. At the other end, we both touched the side simultaneously and embraced each other in our excitement. It was lovely and he held me for an age. I didn't want to release him.

"Do you do a lot of swimming?" he said, finally letting me go. "You keep yourself very fit."

"The trouble is," I said, "public pools are not very hygienic places and there is always too much chlorine and too many people, so I'm not so keen these days. I would much rather go for a run in the countryside. I could swim for hours in your pool, though."

"Well, you take your time, we have all day." With that he swam off doing a very tasty backstroke. I followed him sedately with a breaststroke.

Richard eventually got out of the pool. He took a white robe from the back of a wicker chair. He certainly likes to wear white. I disappeared into the changing room and used the hair dryer that was in there. I had a silk kimono, another one of my mother's presents. It was brightly coloured with reds and black. In contrast to Richard's robe, I decided to wear it. I went out onto the terrace and into the warm sunshine. My wine glass had miraculously been topped up so I took a slurp and wandered glass-in-hand back into the pool room. I could see Richard through the open doors arranging plates on the dining room table so I went through to join him. The lovely big room was now familiar and had the same faint smell of lavender polish.

"Anything I can do to help?" I asked.

"It is all ready," he smiled. "Mrs T is a treasure. She left everything in the fridge all prepared. All I had to do was carry it through. I don't know what I would do without her."

There was a huge bowl of salad with rocket, radish, beetroot, peppers, you name it. There were all kinds of cold meats, mushroom vol-au-vents, prawns, smoked salmon and potato salad.

"Gosh that looks good," I said, feeling definitely peckish. "I don't think we will go hungry."

"OK, you sit down here," he said while pulling a chair out for me, "and help yourself." He sat down next to me at the end of the table and we both looked a bit lost in the huge dining room, which echoed with the chink of the plates.

"Would you like some background music?" Richard said. "It will make the room feel cosier." He seemed to read my mind, so I agreed.

"Computer," Richard spoke into the room and took me by surprise. I thought he was talking to me. "Play some Jack Johnson, level soft."

I wondered what he was doing and to my surprise, the music started playing.

"How on earth did you do that?" I said as he handed me the salad bowl.

"I'm sorry; I didn't mean to startle you; I'm afraid I take these things for granted. My father was a computer software engineer. A computer that he installed some years ago controls the whole house. It's all clever stuff and uses advanced voice recognition."

"I've heard of things like that. Did your father invent it?"

"Not exactly, but he used to develop systems for people before he retired." Richard had not talked freely about his father.

"You could make a fortune marketing a gismo like that,"

I said as I helped myself to a generous slice of ham.

"The system is more advanced than the sort of systems available today and would cause chaos if it were introduced on the market. It would be best if you didn't mention it to anyone." How extraordinary, I thought.

"Did your father make a living from computer software?" I asked, curiously.

"Yes, he did. He developed all sorts of systems that we still use today, faster computers, user-friendly software. He made a very good living as you can see. The house computer is a bit special and is for private use. He wasn't allowed to market it. Then he retired."

"And now they are in Australia?" I quizzed, but Richard ignored the comment.

"Would you like to try one of these vol-au-vents? They are very good," Richard said, avoiding the subject. I took two of them and he was right; they were superb.

There was definitely more to Richard than meets the eye, I thought to myself. *I am intrigued to find out more. I hope that I will have the chance to get to know him better.* Nevertheless, I wasn't going to pressure him. We chatted about various things for a good hour and I really enjoyed his company. The conversation was casual and I could weirdly sense his feelings. For some reason, I felt we had some sort of bond. I have never felt this relaxed in the company of a man, ever. We were so engrossed that we had forgotten that Jack Johnson was on his third time round and had exhausted his repertoire. So, Richard talked to the room and on came the Sugar Babies.

"You like the Sugar Babies?" I asked, surprised.

"I ought to," he said. "I wrote most of their songs." I was suitably impressed and smiled at him. He looked back into my eyes and I tingled all over.

Bruce was finally fed up with what it was he was doing in the garden. He skittered into the room and was now sitting up with his paws on Richard's knee. Richard gave him a slice of ham and he scampered off to devour it in the corner. *Another fat dog in the making*, I thought.

"Do you fancy a walk round the island? I promised Mrs T I would give Bruce some exercise today." Richard put his knife and fork neatly together.

"I would love to; you must show me round."

"Have you had enough to eat?" Richard asked. "Mrs T has left some chocolate cake in the fridge."

"I'm tempted, but I really have had enough thanks," I said and drained my wine glass. Richard offered me more but I declined. I definitely wanted to stay conscious this afternoon.

Richard cleared away the plates while I popped into the shower room. My bikini was completely dry but my kimono was damp so I put my skirt and top back on. I also realised that I was still in bare feet. I popped my sandals on and brushed my hair. When I came out, I caught Richard pulling on his shorts; he wasn't wearing any underpants. I must say he is a sexy man. He smiled at me and wasn't at all fazed by my uninvited view of his gorgeous bottom. He continued to put on his tee shirt and some cheap plastic flip-flops.

"OK, you ready?" he said as he picked up Bruce's lead.

"I'm ready!" I smiled.

We walked down a gravel road with beech trees on each side. Richard held my hand and I enjoyed his touch. Bruce had busily gone on ahead sniffing trees and cocking his leg. We went past the sweet little railway station complete with platform lights and signals. It was just like the real thing only in miniature. Richard couldn't resist showing me the engine shed. We peered round the door and saw two little steam engines with highly polished brass domes. I could see some brightly painted carriages that were just big enough to climb into. There were all sorts of bits of machinery. Richard said something about needing all day to play with those so we moved on, especially as Bruce was barking at our heels. We walked down a gentle incline. The sea was in sight with the trees and shrubs giving way to heather strewn moorland. The railway was still running alongside and then it wound round to the right and disappeared into the undergrowth. Further down we came to a small cove with a curving stony beach. The sea was calm and there were gentle waves just lapping the shore. It looked idyllic but we started talking about the dangers of swimming in the sea lochs and getting swept away with the tides; so we ended up moving on up a stony path flanked by rocky outcrops.

We continued upward through ancient oak woodland with the tree branches draped in moss and lichens and eventually out past the trees and onto a plateau with more rocky outcrops and lush green grass. At the top, there was a fantastic panoramic view. You could see for miles in a full 360-degree circle. Indeed, it was an island with the sea all around except for the narrow causeway and the access road. You could see the islands in the distance with their hazy mountains and small ships chugging up the Firth of Lorn.

I sat down cross-legged in the grass to take in the view and Richard lay down beside me looking a bit flushed after the climb up the hill. I lay back on one arm and smiled at him.

"You are lucky living in a place like this."

"I know. I'm very lucky in a lot of ways."

He put his arm on my shoulders, pulling me towards him, and gently kissed me on the lips. It was very nice and I kissed him back. We kissed again much more passionately and I really wanted him. We made love there and then, out in the open air, unashamedly. I don't think I have ever experienced sex like it before. He was inexplicably tender and aware of my needs, yet it was urgent and exciting. We climaxed gloriously together and I felt like a teenager without inhibitions. I was still fully clothed apart from losing my bikini bottoms. Amazingly, all I had to do was unbutton Richard's tennis shorts. We must have stayed there for over an hour, lying in each other's arms contentedly snoozing.

The sun was very strong. I could feel myself burning. Eventually we wandered back down the hill on a different path this time. Bruce had been very good during our romantic interlude on the hill; he was quite happy just lying in the grass with us. When we got back, Richard gave Bruce his supper and made us some coffee. We took the coffee upstairs and Richard showed me his bedroom. It was very tastefully decorated in light and dark browns; it was simple and masculine. The floor of the room was again polished wood. He had a huge bed that looked out on the back garden through French windows with a veranda beyond. I was now getting used to this style of living but the bathroom really took my breath away. It was all done in a sandy coloured marble and was a complete wet room. There was a large glass sided shower cubicle with multiple showerheads and a six-foot square sunken bath set beneath a window that overlooked the garden. The whole side of the room was mirrored with two modern vanity basins below.

"This is an amazing bathroom," I said for want of a better description.

"We can have a shower together if you like," Richard said with a glint in his eye. "Computer, turn on shower 2."

With that, the shower sprays all miraculously sprang into action. *Is there anything the computer doesn't control*, I wondered. I must admit I was feeling a bit grubby after rolling about in the grass so I agreed to a shower. Richard stripped off his tee shirt and shorts and stood in front of me naked. He didn't seem to have any inhibitions at all and curiously, I was not in the least bit embarrassed myself. He undid the buttons on my blouse and removed it and then my bikini top. He smiled at the sight of my naked breasts as he put the clothes on a chair. I quickly removed the rest of my clothes. We had a glorious shower together, taking turns to soap each other's backs. Afterwards we lay on the bed and made love again, this time slowly and tenderly.

When I awoke, I was curled up in the silk sheets. Richard

wasn't beside me. It was still light outside but I had a feeling it was getting late. I looked at the clock by the bed; it was half past nine and I must have been asleep for at least two hours. I lay back again feeling contented but exhausted and thought I must make a move and drive home. *Hell, I've got work tomorrow.* I lay there thinking about the afternoon. We seemed to have a sort of empathy, which I hadn't come across before in a man. The lovemaking felt so right, but then I started to wonder whether I had rushed into this too quickly. I still didn't really know Richard as a person and there was always a feeling that he was holding back in some way. *Doubts crept in; I hope he doesn't think I'm just an easy lay. Where the hell was he anyway?*

I dismissed my thoughts and agreed that I wouldn't have missed such great sex for the world so I decided I had better get dressed, go and find him, and make a move for home.

I crept down the stairs listening for any noise. All the wall lights were on and the house was brightly lit. I went through to the dining room but it was empty. The pool room was silent except for the hum of the air-conditioning. The water was mirror calm. I continued through another door and found myself in a large sitting room similar to the dining room but with an array of light tan leather easy chairs. There was a large fireplace laid with logs and the whole wall on one side was floor to ceiling with books. I tried to see what sort of books were there but I couldn't recognise anything. Also, the light was fading too much to be able to see. Then I remembered the music room and thought that must be where he was. I went through another door and was back in the hall. I stood there a minute trying to remember which door it was. I tried the most likely option and put my head round the door. He was sitting at his desk in front of a huge screen. I hadn't noticed it before. The screen was inclined at a slight angle like a school desk and had the texture of a plasma TV. I could just make out a sort of keyboard. He was furiously touching the icons projected on the screen. I had never seen anything like it before and I could only assume this was the famous house computer that his father had invented.

"Hello," I said, walking up to the desk. The screen went blank before I had a chance to see what he was doing.

"Lisa," he said as he stood up, "sorry to leave you on your own up there, but you were sleeping so soundly; I didn't want to wake you. Are you OK?" He put his arms around my waist and kissed me. I immediately warmed to his touch.

"I'm fine," I said, peering over his shoulder. "I must go home soon. You have an amazing machine there. What are you doing, composing music?"

"Not this time," he said, letting go of me. "I've other duties that I have to keep on top of and unfortunately things are a bit busy right now. I am sorry to have left you alone."

"I don't mind. I have had a wonderful afternoon, thank you. So what are these other duties?" I said, feeling inquisitive.

"I can't explain actually; it has to do with secret intelligence, something I do as well as the music. Music is really just a hobby." I sensed that Richard was starting to feel uneasy.

"James Bond, licensed to kill," I said flippantly.

"No, it is nothing like that. I'll explain one day. Would you like something to eat?" he said, changing the subject. "Mrs T is back and she can rustle up something."

"No, I'm not hungry thanks. I really must be going. I have to face the world and their pets tomorrow. I'll let you get on with your work."

I gathered up my things and he kissed me goodbye. He did say he would ring me, but as I got into the car, I suddenly felt insecure and had very mixed feelings about the day. I drove back thinking about the events and thought, *OK so if he didn't ring me I have still had an unforgettable experience. You are only on this planet once so make the best of it.* I do hope that I see him again. I gave myself to him willingly and uncontrollably and I don't regret it. But I don't know enough about him. Come to think of it, he doesn't know much about me, and he didn't seem to want to find out. Perhaps he has access to secret files and has been able to find out more about me than I'm aware of. The strange thing is there seemed to be some sort of connection between us that wasn't just sexual. I could somehow link to his thoughts, a sort of very strong empathy. I could sense a dark area that worried me and I felt compelled to find out about it. I wondered what sort of secret job he was involved in and suddenly realised that I had been confronted with a lot of secret intelligence people lately. Was there any connection with my mother's interview with MI6?

CHAPTER 6

The following day, the morning surgery went very quickly. I do not think I really had my mind on the job in hand. I seemed to be floating on air and couldn't keep my feet on the ground. I only hope I didn't wrongly diagnose the poor creatures presented to me. John was particularly concerned and when he brought in my late morning coffee, he could see I was away in the clouds. He suggested I should report sick and go home. He is a sweet lad. I told him not to worry. I only had a few calls to make in the afternoon so I decided to pop round to visit my mum early.

She was asleep in her chair when I let myself in and despite announcing "it's only me" she didn't wake up. I went into the kitchen and made a pot of tea.

"I didn't hear you come in," she said, as I brought the tray through.

"You were asleep Mum, I didn't want to wake you. How are you?"

"I'm not too bad," she said, propping herself up, "just a bit tired."

I put the tray down on the coffee table and sat opposite her.

"Good God Lisa," she said, "what have you been up to? You look as though you have been up all night. Are you well?"

"I'm fine Mum. I had an interesting weekend and I didn't sleep very well last night."

"I've just remembered, you had a lunch date with that man." Her eyes widened. "Obviously went well; what's he like?"

"He's very nice and has a beautiful house," I said in a matter of fact way.

"You must tell me all about him; he had better not be married. I'd love to meet him. Bring him round to tea." My mother was gathering enthusiasm.

"He isn't married and I have only seen him a few times. Things will take their course in due time. Who sent you the huge bouquet of flowers? Have you got an admirer?"

My eyes strayed to the sideboard, which hosted a huge arrangement of cut flowers in a cut glass vase. I am not a fan of cut flowers; it seems such a shame to cut the flowers down in their prime and shove them in water to die slowly. I was thankful to notice that the flowers in Richard's dining room were very good imitations.

"That's another thing," she said, crinkling up her nose in a frown, "the MI6 people came round on Saturday morning and took away your father's suitcase. Do you know, they brought it back an hour later and gave me this huge bouquet of flowers? Aren't they lovely? They were very pleased with their findings and said the flowers were by way of a thank you for my co-operation. They said they wouldn't be required to bother me again. All very strange, but I'm glad to be rid of them."

It was very odd; I didn't think that government organisations made gestures like that. Anyway, Mum was happy and we chatted for another hour.

I'm afraid I can only take Mum in small doses. Feeling very tired, I decided to go home and get an early night. I picked up a Chinese take-away on my way back, my favourite food. I settled down in front of the TV to devour it straight from the cartons. I had just picked up my fork when the phone rang. I thought it might be Richard so I answered it, but it turned out to be Maureen, an old college friend whom I have known for many years and with whom I have kept in contact. She is a good friend, if not a bit boring. We had a brief conversation and I got invited out for a drink in Oban on Thursday night with her. I thought it would be a good opportunity for a chinwag.

When I got back to my Chinese, it was nearly cold so I went into the kitchen and put it on a plate so I could heat it up in the microwave. I was just about to switch it on when the phone rang again.

"Hi Lisa." It was so nice to hear Richard's voice. "How has your day been? How is your mother now? Is she feeling better?" he asked.

"Yes, she's doing very well." I couldn't remember what I had said about my mother so I kept it brief.

"Can I see you tomorrow night?" he asked.

"Yes, I'm free tomorrow. Seeing as you fed me yesterday, why don't you come round here and I'll cook you a dinner."

"Thanks, that sounds great. Would seven o'clock be alright?"

"See you at seven," I said and he hung up.

Well, that was short and sweet but I will look forward to seeing him. It will be a good opportunity to roast the chicken that has been hanging around in my freezer for months. I finally got back to my takeaway meal and went to bed in a happy frame of mind.

The following evening I had everything ready in plenty of time. I was keeping it casual, dressed in tight jeans and tee shirt. The chicken was already in the oven and the vegetables were in their saucepans. I had put two bottles of Chardonnay in the fridge; I didn't have to drive anywhere so what the hell. It was another warm evening so I decided to get out of the hot kitchen and cool off in the garden. My house was an end of terrace with a small garden but I was lucky enough to have a view at the back over open tree lined fields. I was gazing out on the parched grass when a most extraordinary sight appeared before my eyes.

It must have been about 50 yards away when the figure of a man suddenly came into view. It seemed to grow out of the ground from the feet up and came from nowhere. Within seconds it was full height and started walking towards me. I blinked my eyes in disbelief and to my amazement I realised it was Richard!

Where the hell did he come from and what is he doing in the field?
In a daze I instinctively walked down to the bottom of the garden
and out through the back gate to greet him. We came face to face
in the field and he looked embarrassed.

"Where did you come from and what are you doing in my
field?" I said indignantly.

"I'm sorry, Lisa, I didn't mean to startle you."

"You seemed to pop out of the ground like a zombie; you
gave me an awful fright." I was trying to curb my anger.

"I'm really sorry. It is such a lovely evening, and I was just
having a bit of a walk." He turned on his helpless expression,
which calmed me down.

"How did you get here? Did you drive your car?"

"Horace gave me a lift; I didn't feel like driving."

"Who is Horace?" I asked, feeling mystified again.

"He is my part-time chauffeur; he dropped me off."

I felt he was telling the truth so I relaxed and smiled.

"Come on in and we can have a glass of wine. I think I need
it after that." I took his arm and we walked back.

"I still don't know how you popped out of the field," I said.

"It's a warm night; the hot air can create optical illusions."
He smiled at me and kissed my hand. I immediately forgot the
subject. We chinked our glasses and toasted the world again.

I finished cooking the vegetables. We decided to eat outside
on my little terrace. Richard wiped the bird poo off the table and
put some chairs outside while I took the chicken out of the oven.
We took everything outside, including the two bottles of wine.
We had a pleasant, leisurely dinner in the warm evening air. We
dined and chatted until it was dark. I gave Richard the full story
about my parents and my mother's condition. He seemed avidly
attentive. I explained that I was an only child and that the family
had dwindled to just myself. Neither of my parents had any living
relatives now.

He also talked some more about his family and mentioned

that he had a brother. But I couldn't get much information out of him. He was very vague about them. Maybe I might meet his family some day. Having drunk a whole bottle of wine I had an overwhelming desire to sit on his lap, so we went inside and cuddled on the sofa, listening to the CD of his musical. It was a lovely evening. We rounded it off by ending up in bed for a glorious night of sex.

When I woke up the next morning, Richard wasn't beside me yet again. He had left a note on the pillow apologising, with the excuse that he had an early meeting. I felt very irritated by it and longed to wake up with him beside me so that we could kiss and cuddle and greet the day together, but I suppose that is too much to ask. At least it was a nice note thanking me for a great dinner and promising to ring me tomorrow. I never heard him get up. I'm usually a light sleeper and all the bedroom windows were open. I wonder how he got home; I certainly didn't hear any car pick him up.

Later that afternoon I went to the hairdresser and had the works done. It was about time I had my split ends seen to and it always makes me feel better afterwards. Little did I know that my happiness was going to go down the toilet. While I was under the dryer, I glanced out of the window and by chance noticed Richard's green Jaguar parked in the street. What's more, he was sitting in it. My heart skipped a beat. I would have gone over the road to talk to him if it were not for being stuck under the dryer. I watched helplessly while he sat in the car and to my horror saw a good-looking, leggy blonde prinking up the road. She jumped in beside him. The hood was down and I saw them kiss each other on the cheek and then roar off down the road. I sat there dumb-founded and fuming. What was that all about? A sick feeling came over me. I couldn't help thinking the worst. Anger welled up at the thought that the bastard might be two-timing me; I so wanted him for myself.

While I drove home, I tried to calm down. The blonde could

be anyone and not necessarily a girl friend. I decided to play it cool. After all, if I hadn't been at the hairdressers I wouldn't have seen him and would have been none the wiser. At least I have some information regarding his activities.

I thought the best action would be to store it at the back of my mind until such time that it might become relevant. Despite the special nature of our relationship, I was determined not to be jealous or possessive.

After my night out with Maureen, my state of mind was not improving. Maureen is very nice, but to me she lives a very boring, prim and proper life. I suppose I am not much better so I shouldn't criticise. She is not particularly attractive. She has short mousy hair. She has been married for a staggering fifteen years to an equally boring husband who is a sales representative. He spends a lot of time away and she looks after two young children; I don't think she has ever worked in her life. However, she is a good listener and I monopolised the evening's conversation by talking about my relationship with Richard. She didn't help my current fears by telling me he had a reputation for being a womaniser and a playboy. I suppose she ought to know; she has read every magazine and newspaper article ever published about who is who. Maureen told me that she had recently read a newspaper article about Richard including a picture of him with a blonde female on his arm going into a celebrity dinner in London.

One consolation is you should never believe anything you read in a newspaper, although the photograph cannot lie. It doesn't sound like Richard; I was led to believe that he wasn't keen on being in the limelight and hated the thought of being a celebrity. Anyway, I was past caring and I think Maureen was a bit jealous. I went home that night feeling miserable.

The following night I got home fairly late after seeing my mother. She was not feeling too well and was due to go back into hospital for some tests. I was still in an unhappy frame of mind when I checked my answer machine. There was a message so

I pushed the button.

"Lisa, I haven't spoken to you for such a long time. Please ring me when you get in. If not I'll give you a call tomorrow morning, bye."

It was Richard and I longed to talk to him so I dialled his number straight away. Thelma answered the phone and she disappeared to fetch Richard.

"Hello Lisa." It was Richard's voice. "Thanks for ringing back; how are you?"

"I'm fine, how about you?"

"You sound really down, what's the matter?" Richard sounded worried.

"I'm OK, just a bit depressed; it's that time of the month," I lied.

"I'm sorry you are not feeling well. I must admit, I'm very tired. It has been very hectic lately. Hopefully after next week, business will calm down." *I'll bet it has been hectic,* I thought.

"Look," he continued, "I would dearly love to see you; can I come round to your place tomorrow night? I have a huge box of chocolates to cheer you up."

"Tomorrow night would be fine; I hope you're not so busy that you have to dash off early." I was feeling unnecessarily bitchy.

"I'm sorry if I upset you leaving early in the morning the other night. I have had so much to sort out lately. By the end of next week I can explain what has been going on; please be patient with me."

"I saw you in town the other day with a blonde woman." It just came out, I couldn't help myself and already I was regretting saying it.

"Oh dear Lisa, please don't think badly of me. That is my new commercial manager. She comes from London. She is going to manage all my affairs in the music business. The whole idea is to give me more time to concentrate on other things. Believe me, she is nothing more than that. I want to have more time to be with you; you are very special to me."

"I'm sorry I mentioned it," I said with tears welling up in my eyes. "I couldn't help it, I wasn't going to."

"We can talk about it tomorrow night. When I have got organised I can explain a lot of things to you and we can spend a lot more time together. That's what I want to happen; you have to trust me. Please don't be upset."

I composed myself and told him I would look forward to seeing him tomorrow night. After I put the phone down, I went upstairs and had a good cry and a hot bath. I slept much better that night.

The following evening my world fell apart. I was ready and waiting for Richard to ring my doorbell. When finally the doorbell did ring, I saw Jack standing there with a box of chocolates and an envelope.

"Evening Miss Macdonald," he said, "I'm sorry to inform you that Mr Varnicus won't be able to make it on account of this urgent meeting; he's very sorry."

I took the chocolates and card from Jack and threw them in the flowerbed. I just simply saw red.

"You can tell Mr Varnicus that he can sod off with his chocolates and I don't want to see him again."

I slammed the door in his face and ran upstairs crying.

CHAPTER 7

I was feeling very sad because the man in my life had let me down. While I lay on my bed sobbing, another man, worlds away from me, was busy at his desk. I would soon learn that his work was to affect my life significantly.

Philbin Dulus sat back in his chair smiling contentedly while viewing the huge monitor in front of him. It showed him two photographs side by side. The right hand picture was Nakito Nashira, a mysterious detainee who was found, without any identity chip, on the planet Honshu about a week ago. He had lost his memory but after corrective treatment, the detainee now claims to have been on Earth for the last forty years. He claims he must have been abducted and transported back to Honshu, but he doesn't remember anything until he found himself wandering the streets without a community address or any identity chip. Philbin had found a computer record naming him as a citizen of Honshu but there was no other information on record. His career was a blank; it looked as though the information had been erased somehow and there was no record of him emigrating to Earth.

Philbin had been investigating the disappearance of various people for many years now. It was a common occurrence on both the home planets and the distant colonies; the list of missing people was endless. The criminal fraternity have had access to the memory altering process for thousands of years; it has been impossible to completely stamp it out. Their main targets were scientists and children. The abductors would modify their memories and sell the people to a targeted buyer in the colonies. Philbin had a gut feeling that Nakito Nashira was one of their victims.

He had also been instructed by his superior to investigate a certain individual who had mysteriously disappeared from Earth around the same time. The images of the individual had come through to his station from his contact on Earth along with some sketchy information and a few Earth documents. The pictures were old-fashioned chemical photographs that had been scanned. So after he added the images to the database he asked the computer to check for any matches. Although the photographs were poor quality, there was no doubt in his mind that the two images on the screen were the same person. Now he could kill two birds with one stone; Nashira had been on Earth and was known as Professor Macdonald. It was the first bit of real evidence that confirmed Nashira's story.

He stood up and stretched; it had been a long day. He hadn't seen the light of day for hours so he asked the computer to open the blinds and send in a glass of beer.

The white glowing wall in front of him divided from floor to ceiling and gracefully glided apart, allowing the evening sun to stream in through the portal. It was a fine evening. Over the tops of the trees he could clearly see the distant planets of Terranus and Atlantis hanging serenely in the sky with a hazy deep blue glow. His aide brought in his beer and he sat down to enjoy the view. It had been an eventful day. Tomorrow he would contact Earth and see what further information they can give him. He can also now confirm that Professor Macdonald and Nashira are likely to be the same person and he would soon be able to confirm Macdonald's origin to his contact on Earth. At least that will get them off his back and he can concentrate on tracking down the abductors. Armed with this new information, tomorrow he will fly out to the terminals in space and further interrogate Nashira.

The next morning he was up early. After breakfast, he routinely checked his terminal. To his delight, a DNA analysis for Macdonald had arrived from Earth and he immediately checked it against Nashira's recent record. Lo and behold, it was a positive match and conclusive evidence. There was also more information on Macdonald's life and his family on Earth. It included a plane crash in which Macdonald had allegedly perished. Philbin was all too familiar with this same modus operandi. After uploading all the new information into Nashira's records, he took the stairs up to the roof and boarded his space shuttle.

The journey to the detention centre on Honshu would take about 30 minutes, giving him time to plan his strategy. He would have to keep the unfortunate man in custody until he had exhausted all possible leads.

CHAPTER 8

Nearly a week had passed since I had the outburst at Richard's chauffeur and I was still very miserable. I had spent my time slopping around in a dressing gown and slippers and was on my third box of chocolates. I have to confess to retrieving the box of chocolates from the flowerbed; after all, I didn't want to waste them. I carried on with my work as normal, but my mind would not rest. I really missed Richard and regretted my actions. I was sure our short relationship was special and he must have a good explanation for not turning up the other night. At least he did send his messenger and it was very rude of me to send him away with a flea in his ear. After all, it wasn't Jack's fault. Richard was like no other man and there were so many strange things about him. I knew instinctively that he was hiding some unimaginable truth or was involved in some sort of bizarre activities. I could only assume that, apart from his music, he was working for some top-secret government agency or he was involved in some sort of experiment. Despite all this I loved being in his company and I felt a special bond between us even though I didn't know him very well. The sex was fantastic and I was sure I was in love with him. All he could say was that I have to trust him and maybe soon he would be able to explain.

It was a Friday night and thankfully I didn't have to go into the surgery tomorrow. I couldn't contain myself any longer and had decided that afternoon to ring him and apologise. I just wanted to see him and I don't care about any explanations about how busy he is. I would just have to fit in with his plans. Perhaps he just didn't want me. Either way I had to find out. I was just about to pick up the phone when it rang. It made me jump and my voice was shaky as I answered. It was he.

"Lisa, I have to see you. Are you alright?" he said with an urgent tone in his voice.

"I'm fine," I said, trying to compose myself.

"I'm really sorry about the other night and I wanted to ring you earlier, but I had to go away again for a few days. I couldn't get a message to you."

I was so relieved to hear his voice but I decided I must play it cool.

"That's OK. I've been busy at work and the time has flown by."

"Look, I've had a meeting with my superiors and now have security clearance to explain what is going on. I really have to see you as soon as possible. I have really missed you these past few days; please don't be angry with me."

God, I have missed him too, I thought to myself. *If he really is working for MI6, I have to hear his explanation.*

"Are you doing anything now? Can I see you right away? I've got such a lot to tell you and it is really important," Richard continued excitedly.

"I can be ready in half an hour. Will you pick me up?" I realised that I was standing in my dressing gown with no make-up or knickers on.

"Actually I'm standing outside your house; I can wait in your sitting room if you like."

With that, the doorbell rang and I knew he was there. I rushed to the door, flung it open and wrapped my arms around his neck, phone still in my hand. It was lovely to smell his skin again and I felt a warm glow in my body.

"I'm so sorry I was angry with you." As I said it, he tightened his grip on my waist.

He gave me a lovely, long, film-star kiss and I felt the love inside me well up. I dragged him into the hall and slammed the front door. My dressing gown fell open and I remembered I was naked underneath, but I was past caring. He wrapped his arms around my naked waist and pulled me tightly against him. We kissed again passionately and I could feel his manhood against my body.

"Make love to me, Richard," I said breathlessly.

"I love you, Lisa," he whispered in my ear.

We went upstairs and lay down on my still unmade bed. I feverishly unbuttoned his shirt and then his trousers. We kissed hard and passionately as I fumbled with his trouser zipper. I managed to push his trousers off his hips; he was wearing silk underpants. I felt as though I was going to explode. I struggled out of my dressing gown while he pulled off his clothes. I felt his hands on my body gently running over my breast and tummy. He kissed me again and rolled onto me. Then I felt him penetrate me. We just held each other tightly with an enormous wave of pleasure and delight.

As we lay together in each other's arms, my mind was still troubled with the sudden change of events. Something was different. I was sensing his emotions and he was very excited yet relieved. He looked into my eyes and smiled. He was aware of my tension and it felt very peculiar.

"Darling Lisa, I do love you. I have so much to tell you, but you must be patient."

"It's OK, Richard," I said. "I have a feeling that something funny is going on; I'm just glad to have you with me."

We lay together for a while and relaxed. I felt so much better after our glorious moment of passion. However my mind was cluttered with thoughts and I decided to make us both a coffee. The excursion down to the kitchen would hopefully give me some release. Was I reading his mind? I got up and put my dressing gown back on. Glancing out of the window at the lovely sunshine, I noticed Richard's car was not outside and wondered how he got here. I then remembered the odd situation last week in the field at the back of my house when he seemed to appear out of nowhere.

"Richard, did you get a lift here again?" I asked inquisitively.

"Yes, I've got Horace for the afternoon," he said. "I want to introduce you to him."

"Why do you want me to meet your chauffeur?" I was beginning to suspect that something strange was going to happen. Although confusing, I was reading his thoughts.

"I am going to explain the whole thing to you," he said soothingly. "I have another mode of transport and it is difficult to explain it quickly. It uses a technology that is unknown to the general public and is very advanced. I have brought it so that I can show you. Please be patient. There is a lot you don't know about me. I don't want to sound mysterious and I don't want to scare you, but now I can explain the whole picture. It is going to take some time." He was urgent and sincere. I tried to relax, but his thoughts were probing my very soul.

"Horace isn't a chauffeur is he? He's a machine," I said in a self-satisfied way after strangely probing his mind.

"Well I can only explain it as a very advanced flying machine. You have to understand that it is top secret and no one else must know about it."

"This must be another of your father's inventions," I said while desperately trying to subdue a panic attack.

"No, it has nothing to do with my father; it is much more complicated than that."

"So what about all this shit with MI6?"

"Well, some people in MI6 know what I'm doing, but I don't work for them and it is far bigger than that."

"You have a bloody space ship, don't you?" I was beginning to get the picture while reading his thoughts. I felt as though I was going to blow a fuse.

"Yes, Horace is a space ship, developed by a race of people

from another solar system."

I knew he was telling the truth and I suddenly felt very ill; I couldn't tell him to stop talking crap because I knew he wasn't. I was probing his mind and it was overwhelming. The room just turned to grey and I must have passed out.

When I awoke, I was lying on the bed and Richard was leaning over me stroking my forehead.

"Are you feeling better?" he said. "You see why we have to take this slowly; this is only the tip of the iceberg."

I propped myself up, and he handed me a mug of strong tea. My hand was shaking but I managed to sip it without spilling it on the bed sheet. Richard continued to stroke my hair. He was much calmer and I felt much better with the touch of his hand. My mind wasn't so cluttered with his thoughts and I was able to think more clearly.

But what was he telling me? Space ships? Were there people from another solar system? I always liked to think that I had both feet on the ground. I lay back on the pillow and tried to think. I don't know what is was about Richard, but I had to believe him. If my mother had said there was a space ship in her back garden, I would have put her in a home and administered some horrendous medication. But Richard was telling the truth, so I decided to humour him and go with the flow.

"OK," I said slowly. "You are in contact with life from another planet and you borrow their space ship."

"That's all you need to know for now," he said, smiling as he kissed me on the forehead. "When you're ready we can go and meet Horace. Pack an overnight bag. I need you to stay with me tonight; we have a lot to talk about."

I just could not move for the moment. It was all so nonchalant. I had to believe him. Although it sounded weird, I instinctively knew everything was alright.

Richard went downstairs. I gathered myself together. I mechanically showered, changed and packed an overnight bag.

CHAPTER 9

My mind was reeling as we walked down the lane at the back of my house. I didn't know what to think; I just had a strange feeling of awe and wonder. He tightened his grip on my hand as a shiver came over me. I didn't know what to expect and I felt as though he was going to show me a fantastic new motorcar. But no, he definitely said it was a space ship.

"Don't worry," he said, "this is all going to be a bit weird to you but we will go through it slowly."

We turned into a field; the gate was already open. The field was quite empty except for a rusting old tractor in the corner. The grass was quite long and dotted with meadow flowers; trees surrounded the whole field. We walked to the centre of the field and stopped. I didn't know what to expect. Was this ship going to come out of the sky? He turned to me and smiled.

"Believe it or not we are standing right in front of the ship. The cloaking device is very efficient; it is very difficult to tell if it is there. If it were raining, you would be able to make out the outline. If you look very carefully you can see Horace shimmering in the heat of the sun."

"A cloaking device?" I said while staring into the empty field. "Do you mean the spaceship is already here and I can't see it?"

"Horace has a special skin that can imitate its surroundings, a bit like very clever camouflage."

He made a broad sweep of his arm. He was right. It was a very hot sunny day but I couldn't see anything. I squinted at the vista before me and as if by magic, an oval quivering outline became visible against the trees.

"Is that it?" I said. "It's as big as a house."

"It is about 100 feet top to ground and about 200 feet long, but we are looking at his front end at the moment," he said reassuringly. "I don't have clearance to remove the cloaking device. Security is very tight these days, but I may be able to show you what he looks like when we get back to the island."

I felt a wave of excitement come over me and could sense the object before me as if it were a living being. Although it was hot, my arms had goose bumps all over and my body tingled as if charged with electrical current.

"Are you going to take me for a ride in it?" I said nervously and instantly felt foolish.

"If you think you are ready we can go inside and I can show you around. I will have to introduce you to Horace first before we can take off."

"Who is Horace?" I said indignantly. "Does the ship have a captain?"

"I know it sounds like a silly name but Horace is the ship. He is a living being whose aim in life is to provide comfortable space travel. He is allowed to choose his own name. I can only describe him as a synthetic organic life form. OK, his brain is a computer, but it is so far advanced from anything we know. He has awareness, a sense of humour and I treat him as a person with a soul. He has access to an interstellar network and chose his own identity. I suppose it's a bit like a computer password. He has been alive for about 150 years now and is extremely knowledgeable."

"One hundred and fifty years?" I felt my voice rising in pitch. "Isn't that a bit old for a spaceship?"

Richard looked a bit embarrassed and I think he realised he shouldn't have given me that sort of information.

"Don't worry," he said, "he could well live for another hundred years. When you understand how he was created you won't worry about his age."

61

This information was flying over my head; he was talking about the ship as if it was a person and I felt intrigued with Horace. I tried to relax a little.

"I'm ready for anything you can throw at me," I said and managed a smile.

"Well we can take it one step at a time," he said. "The first thing is to get you on board before anybody sees us and wonders what the hell we are doing standing in a field."

I was starting to feel nervous again.

"What happens? Do you beam us aboard?" Richard laughed at me.

"No, unlike popular fiction, I'm afraid transferring living matter is a physiological impossibility. The ship has a lift that carries us upward into the cabin."

Richard gripped my hand and led me forwards. A few paces ahead I could see a flattened area of grass about the size of a car as if something heavy were lying on it. Suddenly I stopped in my tracks as a beam of green light, like a laser, framed the grass. The beam was a perfect rectangle and didn't seem to have any thickness; it seemed to shimmer in the sunlight.

"It's alright, we have to step onto the rectangle," Richard reassured me. "A wall of light will drop down around us and you will feel a rising sensation as if you were going up in a conventional lift."

We stepped into or rather onto the rectangle. I felt something hard under my foot but my feet seemed to be suspended off the ground. I wobbled around and thought I was going to fall over but Richard held me up with his strong arm around my waist.

"Don't worry," he said. "I've got you; you'll get used to it eventually."

I was suddenly surrounded by brilliant white walls and immediately felt a rising sensation as if I were going up in one of those American turbo-lifts. Before I could blink an eye, I was staring out into an amazing room. The air was suddenly cool and smelled like sea air. It was very pleasant especially after the heat outside, and I was only wearing a light summer dress. I shivered in awe at the sight before me. The room was egg-shaped as far as I could see and the floor was about half way up the egg, if you know what I mean. There was a lower area at the sharp end of the egg with a step down. I assumed this was the front end. The rear end of the egg had a partition across it. All the walls had panels with a rounded edge and glowed slightly with a pleasant light brown colour. The walls around the panels were what appeared to be a dark green fabric, the like of which I have never seen before. The floor had what appeared to be a tightly woven fitted carpet, which was a dark maroon colour. There were eight black leather easy chairs arranged tastefully around two round coffee tables. There was a faint sound of circulating air. It all reminded me of a Virgin Airways first class cabin. I must say it was all very pleasant and I started to feel a bit more at ease.

We were still standing in the lift cubicle looking out. I realised that Richard still had his arm around my waist. He turned to me and smiled.

"Are you OK so far? I hope you like the décor. Horace has over a thousand different interior themes; I chose this one myself."

"I think it's lovely," I said and wished it were a bit brighter.

I think Richard must have read my thoughts. As if talking to mid air he said, "Horace, can you open the viewing portals."

"Would you like it on your last setting, sir?" Horace's voice replied and seemed to come from nowhere. The sound seemed to be all around me, but it was a friendly male voice. I half expected to see someone standing in front of me.

"Yes, Horace," Richard replied.

The whole front section and side panels immediately started to glow brightly. I realised we were looking at the outside world. I could see the trees surrounding the field. Faint shafts of sunlight streamed in through the windows. I flinched at the sudden flush of light; it was an incredible space and looked like someone's futuristic living room. Richard guided me into the room, or I should say cabin. I didn't know what to call it. He still had his arm around my waist and I felt the warmth of his body. My mind was filling with questions; I wondered who or what had developed such an amazing craft. Richard once again seemed to sense my thoughts.

"All will be revealed in time," he said. "First I must introduce you to Horace; he runs the whole shooting match and I'm sure you will get to like him."

We faced the front window and I saw in the distance the trees waving gently in the breeze.

"Horace," he said, "I would like you to meet a very special friend of mine. This is Lisa Macdonald."

The kindly voice seemed to come from nowhere and once again I expected to see somebody standing in front of me.

"Lisa Macdonald, I am very pleased to make your acquaintance," the voice said and continued. "I am always pleased to meet new people from Earth. I will assist you in any way I can."

I didn't quite understand what he meant but it was like being introduced to the butler. Richard addressed the voice.

"Horace, Lisa has not been fully briefed yet; I have decided to show her the ship first, so I will require your co-operation. I presume you have received a communication from the council."

"I have sir and with your permission I will need to scan Lisa Macdonald for a security profile." Horace replied.

"Scan me?" I said and I gave Richard a worried look.

"Don't worry, you won't feel a thing. It's just for security purposes. Go ahead Horace."

I experienced a slight tingling sensation, which only lasted a fraction of a second.

"Lisa Macdonald has full clearance," the voice came back, "and we can take off at your command."

"Thank you, Horace," Richard replied courteously.

"How about I show you around?" Richard said, turning to

me. "And then we can have a coffee and a talk and then I'll show you what this ship can do."

I stood a moment trying to take it all in and realised that I had forgotten to go to the loo and had a full bladder.

"I hate to be a bore but I am dying for a pee," I said.

"No problem." Richard smiled. "I'll show you the ship's facilities."

I was impressed; it had a loo as well.

Richard finally released his grip on my waist and turned towards the back wall. A panel in the wall silently whizzed sideways and left a doorway. As we walked through, I quickly touched the wall; it definitely was some sort of fabric. Everything was so immaculately clean! We walked into a corridor, which was decorated in the same way. Richard touched a small red glowing panel on the wall. Instantly another door slid back exposing what was obviously some sort of bathroom. Richard told me to touch the red panel to close the door, so I eagerly entered. The whole room was ultra-modern and decorated with what seemed to be black tiling. As soon as I entered, the whole ceiling lit up. I recognised what was definitely a very modern loo with a somewhat conventional seat. I opened the lid and hurriedly sat down with blessed relief. I had forgotten to shut the door but I felt safer leaving it open. Richard had disappeared anyway. I looked around the room. There was what looked like a shower cubicle in the corner with a curved glass panel, but I couldn't see a showerhead or taps, just a red glowing panel in the corner. Adjacent to me I could recognise a basin with a broad spout, probably an automatic tap. Lo and behold, there was conventional toilet paper, poking out of a slot in the wall. The whole bathroom was decorated in black and was incredibly clean with not a seam or crack in sight as if it had been moulded out of one sheet of plastic. I finished up and yes the basin was automatic with warm running water. There was a built in paper towel dispenser. Typically, I couldn't get the loo to flush so I left it and hurried out to find Richard. He was in the next room that was obviously some kind of kitchen and was placing two mugs under some kind of coffee maker. I came up behind him and put my arms around his waist.

"Feeling better?" he said, turning round to face me.

"Yes thank you, but I can't make the loo flush."

"You have to close the lid and touch the red panel," he smiled.

I immediately went back to the bathroom and followed his instructions. It finally made a hissing sound so I assumed the job was done.

We sat down in the cabin on the plush leather chairs and sipped our coffee. I was feeling much more relaxed and started to collect my thoughts.

"So you work for an advanced secret agency that is in contact with extraterrestrial life?" I quizzed. "They are obviously far more advanced than we are and you have access to this amazing space craft."

"That's correct in essence. There's more to it than that and it is going to be difficult to explain it all to you," he said with a serious look on his face.

"I suppose I do sort of work for the government," he continued, "but although some government officials know what I'm doing, they are not in charge of my activities."

"Who is in charge?" I said feeling mystified.

"Well," he said, pausing, "you could say I inherited and accepted this responsibility from my father, who in turn took over from his father."

"So did your grandfather invent this ship?" I said, desperately trying to understand.

"You do believe in the possibility of extraterrestrial life, don't you?"

Richard had a very concerned look on his face. Now my thoughts were racing and my heart started thumping wildly.

"Yes I do. It would be very arrogant to assume we are the only living things in the universe," I said shakily. "Why do you ask?"

"Well, my grandfather is not from this world. He originated from a distant planet, not unlike this one."

CHAPTER 10

B efore I could fully take in what Richard had said, Horace interrupted my train of thought.

"Excuse me, sir," he said in a calm voice. In fact I thought I heard him cough before he spoke. "In order to comply with protocol we have to vacate our current position in precisely five minutes."

Richard turned to me. His face still looked worried. "We need to move from this place," he said with urgency in his voice. "I have to comply with the guidelines laid down for operating a space shuttle in this area. For security reasons we are not allowed to stay in one place for too long. There is still a huge amount you need to understand; are you going to be alright taking a short trip back home? We will have time to talk there."

My thoughts were still racing: *I must be mad. I'm sitting in a spaceship drinking coffee with a man with whom I think I'm in love and now he tells me his ancestors are from another planet.*

"I thought you said you were born in Scotland," I said, still harbouring a dislike for being lied to.

"It's true I was born in Scotland and I'm as human as you are," he said with the worried look turning into a plea.

"You have to understand. I'm in love with you. I haven't told you any lies and I'm greatly relieved to be able to tell you the whole story. Believe me there is a lot to tell. We need more time and you have to trust me. There is so much you don't know yet."

I could feel he was being sincere. I do believe he loves me! I suddenly felt a strong desire to throw caution to the wind and be adventurous. In any case, I had to see if this thing could fly.

"OK," I said, "take me for a ride then."

"Horace, set a flight for home as soon as possible," Richard said, turning to face the front end of the egg.

"Yes sir," Horace replied, "departure in one minute, please take your seats."

"Let's go and sit in the front," Richard said, picking up his coffee, "we will get a better view from there."

I was in a confused daze but excitedly followed Richard to the lower area at the front. I noticed a row of easy chairs similar to the ones we had been sitting on. We sat down together. I felt the warmth of Richard's hand on mine and happily grabbed hold of it. The front view window was fantastic with a panoramic 180-degree view. I could see the grassy meadow below and the scrappy line of trees and bushes surrounding the field. From where I was sitting, the window curved round and my feet were only a few feet from the edge.

The ground was at least twenty feet below and it started to make me feel a bit unsafe. Without warning, I felt a gentle sensation of movement in my stomach. Without a sound, the ground dropped away at alarming speed. The line of trees fell away and within seconds we were at least a thousand feet up with a view right across the valley with the mountains beyond. The ground just seemed to slide beneath us. Soon I could recognise the waters of Loch Etive. It was fantastic and mesmerising as if flying in a silent helicopter at great speed. The mountains below us looked beautiful in the sunlight. Soon I could see the rugged coastline and the sea lochs. Surely, no one on this planet could have developed such an amazing craft.

"What do think of your first flight in a spacecraft?" Richard said with his face beaming.

"It is absolutely incredible," I said without taking my eyes off the front window. I also realised that I was gripping his hand a bit tightly. "Is it safe travelling at this speed?"

"It's OK," he said reassuringly, "the ship is equipped with sensors that could detect a bird in its path from thousands of miles away, a bit like a super bat," he chuckled to himself. "You could try to fly this thing into a high rise building but Horace would be forced to take evasive action. He wouldn't want to damage himself so it is impossible to crash it."

Before I could realise it, we were approaching the peninsula. Horace piped up from nowhere and announced his landing in one minute.

We had already dropped in height; I could see the gatehouse below. We glided effortlessly over the trees and dropped down onto the lawn; the house came into view right in front of us. It was the smoothest flight I had ever taken.

"That was absolutely fantastic," I gushed, "can we do it again?"

"Unfortunately we will have to leave the ship," Richard said, prying his hand out of mine and flexing his fingers to get the circulation back. "Horace has another engagement elsewhere but I have got him back again tomorrow."

Richard took the cups back to the kitchen. I looked out on his lovely house and felt pleased to see it again. We walked into the lift cubicle; Richard put his arm around my shoulders. In his other hand he carried my overnight bag. I had completely forgotten about it. I was gratified to know he had been in charge of it throughout the whole experience. I felt like giving him a long kiss but my stomach jumped into my throat as the lift descended. The white walls retracted upwards and once again I was standing in the sunlight. I could now understand how he had materialised in the middle of a field from thin air the other week. The events of the past few weeks all seemed to make sense. I experienced an enormous feeling of relief and exhilaration. After such a roller-coaster ride, I think my endorphins must have kicked in.

We walked hand in hand back to the house. Behind me, I heard and felt a gush of wind. I looked behind me and saw nothing, but I instinctively knew it was Horace taking off again. What an amazing machine! We walked around the side of the house into the courtyard, past the row of garages. The beaten up old Land Rover was still parked in the middle. My mind was filling up with questions again. What fuel does the ship run on? How fast can it go? Where has it gone? Who is going to use it? I tried to blot them out for the moment. I still didn't know about Richard's parents and if I would ever meet them. If his grandfather is from another world why is Richard here with a living alien spacecraft?

We entered the back door; I hadn't been into this part of the house before; I was blissfully distracted. We went through a large storeroom, which was full of boxes with a row of Wellington boots lined up by the door. It was so comforting to see recognisable domestic clutter after the disinfected order of the spaceship. There were two washing machines and a dryer neatly fitted under an array of kitchen units with a sink above and a large basket of dirty washing. We went through a door into a huge kitchen. It was beautifully fitted out with light oak units. There was a large Aga cooker in a beamed recess with a gorgeous smell of something simmering on the hotplate. An enormous pine table in the centre dominated the room. Mrs Theaton was standing at the sinks. She turned round, wiping a dinner plate on a tea towel. She looked surprised to see me; the plate dropped onto the slate floor and shattered into tiny pieces.

"Struth," she said, "I didn't hear you come in."

"I have brought Lisa back with me, Mrs T. I hope you have something nice for supper," Richard said.

"Nice to see you again, Doctor," she said. Her Aussie accent was as strong as ever.

"How is Bruce?" I said. The Springer Spaniel was sitting wide-eyed in its basket beside her.

"Oh he's as right as rain now, thanks very much. I got Jack to take all the barbed wire to the dump so it won't happen again with any luck. Can I get you any refreshment?"

"I could murder a glass of wine," Richard said. "How about you Lisa?"

"I'd love some wine," I replied.

"Could you bring a bottle of the Sauvignon Blanc, Mrs T.?" Richard asked and promptly guided me out of the room and into the dining room. I always wondered where that swing door led. We went through the pool room and out onto the terrace. Richard seated me at the familiar table. I sat there in a daze for a while and stared vacantly at the garden. The sun was low in the sky and casting long shadows on the lawn. The air was cool and fragrant and I felt strangely happy. Mrs T broke my moment of tranquillity and came through with the wine and two glasses on a tray.

"I'm so pleased to see you here Dr. Macdonald. Mr Varnicus has been like a bear with a sore back these past few days. I hope things work out for you two; you're quite special to him," she said as she put the tray on the table.

"Thank you, Thelma," I said smiling, "and please call me Lisa."

Her round face beamed and with her hands clasped together, she bowed and walked away. I wondered what she meant by that and realised that Richard was missing so I decided to pour the wine. I was about to take a sip when Richard returned and sat down beside me. He picked up his glass and chinked mine.

"To us and the future," he said.

I could sense Richard's excitement; thoughts and emotions cluttered his mind. I wondered how I could be picking all this up; it was a strange sensation and very confusing. I tried to blot them out and collect my own thoughts.

"So," I said, "that picture in the dining room, I remember you said your grandfather painted it."

"Yes," he said plainly as he unnervingly looked into my eyes.

"So those planets are not a figment of his imagination?"

"Lisa," he said laughing, "you are a gem."

"You're laughing at me."

"I'm not laughing at you. I love you. Let me explain. The planet in the foreground is called Terranus. My grandfather and grandmother were born there and they came to Earth when they were only in their twenties as, let's say for simplicity, Council administrators. They were here on an official basis and were employed by the Planetary Council. They eventually had a daughter who is of course my mother."

"So," I said again, "your father is still alive and living in Australia with your mother and brother?"

"My older brother also works for the Council and is now stationed on Terranus. My father and mother have retired and live on Terranus to be near him. Terranus is now mostly a recreational planet and is a super place to be if you're retired."

"I thought Australia was a long way off," I said as I drank my wine. "I hate to think how far away Terranus is."

"Terranus is a beautiful planet about fourteen light years distant. It is very similar to Earth and has a sun approximately the same as ours. There are two other planets in the system supporting life. One is called Honshu, which has a much cooler climate, and the other is Atlantis, which is mostly ocean. In fact only one eighth is land consisting of small volcanic islands."

"Good grief," I said as I tried to take it on board, "are you serious? Planets called Honshu and Atlantis? Why do I get the feeling there is more to this than meets the eye?"

"Oh dear Lisa," he said as he picked up my hand, "I'm afraid there is a lot more to know; both our origins are not what we originally thought."

I stood up and walked along the terrace trying to clear my mind. I could think more clearly if I were not in close proximity to Richard. That is something else I must ask him. Why do I pick up his thoughts?

Thelma announced that dinner was served in the dining room. This interrupted my own train of thought. When she left

I whispered in Richard's ear.

"Do Thelma and Jack know all about this?"

"Yes they do. You don't have to be discreet; they have been in our employ for over twenty years. They too are immigrants; their ancestors arrived in Australia over 300 years ago."

We went through to the dining room. There was a very appetising aroma coming from the kitchen. I realised that I hadn't eaten much all day. We sat down to a beautifully laid table with full silver service and professionally folded napkins. I stared at the painting on the far wall. The last planet was a vivid blue; I wondered what Atlantis would be like. Thelma brought in a tureen of soup and served it to each of us with a silver ladle. It looked and smelled like Scotch broth and was steaming hot. She then hurried back with hot rolls and butter. I was in heaven. Richard smiled across the table at me and I passed the rolls to him. *I was sure he asked for them and realised that I had read his thoughts again. I have frequently heard of empathy between two people but this sensation was extraordinary.*

"How is your mother?" he asked.

"She had to go back into hospital to have some more tests. She has not been feeling well. I will have to go and see her on Monday."

"I'm sorry to hear that," Richard said. "With any luck we might be able to help her."

I wasn't sure what he meant by that and I didn't care. I was far too busy enjoying this fantastic soup.

"If you like," he continued, "I can go with you to the hospital. Hospitals are the worst places to be, especially if you're ill."

I knew he was actually being serious even though it sounded like a joke.

"I'd love you to come with me; in fact you must meet my mother. It would really cheer her up, and she is a great fan of yours."

"It's a date then," Richard said.

We finished our soup. Thelma brought in roast beef and Yorkshire puddings with a lovely selection of vegetables.

"Richard," I asked cautiously, "I've heard of empathy between two people who are close, but somehow I have this weird way of knowing what you're thinking."

"You are a darling, Lisa," he said as he helped himself to roast potatoes. "You're very astute."

"Well?" I said. "I assume it has something to do with your ancestry."

"You're absolutely right, but don't worry about it too much. It will all become clear to you. The fact is the existence of the human race in the Terranus system is about 20, 000 years older than that on Earth and a lot more evolution has taken place."

"There are a lot of people who claim to be telepathic here," I said and then wondered if I had said something silly.

"It is quite a complicated picture, best to take it one step at a time; it would be unfair to flood you with too much information," Richard said. "Tell you what, though, you would love it on Terranus. Since you are a qualified vet, I could show you some animals you have never seen before. Some of them have a high degree of intelligence. You would have a field day."

I felt a mixture of intrigue and apprehension. I tried to block out some of the questions that were backing up in my mind.

"So if your family are living on this distant planet, I don't suppose you get to see them very often."

"I get to see them about twice a year; in fact I was there only last week. That is why it was so difficult to contact you. They are very well and happy. I spent most of the time talking about you."

"How long does it take to get there?" I asked, while desperately trying to come to terms with my limited knowledge of astral physics. It was as though he was spinning some ridiculous yarn.

"It usually takes about forty-eight hours, depending on the interstellar transporter's schedule."

I didn't know what the hell he was talking about so I

concentrated on my delicious Yorkshire pudding.

"In the last 300 years interstellar space travel has advanced enormously," Richard continued. "We can travel vast distances in a short space of time, whereas before it took years to get anywhere."

I finished my plate and mopped up the last bit of gravy with my roll. It was lovely having a proper meal after my chocolate diet last week. At the same time, I was desperately trying to take in what he had said. I was feeling suspicious and confused, but at least the food had hit the spot.

"So your grandfather and grandmother came from this planet but your mother was born here," I said hesitantly.

"Yes, mother was born in this very house."

"What about your father, is he from this planet Terranus?"

"My father comes from Edinburgh but his family are from Terranus."

"Are your grandparents still alive?"

"Gosh yes," Richard said, "they are both the same age and celebrated their 120th birthday recently. It took a while for Granddad to get settled; he started a family quite late."

"One hundred and twenty!" I said in surprise.

"Life expectancy is about 150 Earth years on Terranus, even for Earth born people; it's all down to medical advancement," Richard said proudly.

"Good God," I said, trying to take this in. "So your grandparents are aliens." I realised what I had said came out wrong and hoped I hadn't offended Richard.

"That's one way of looking at it," Richard smiled. "It is best if you don't think of us as being alien at all. You must remember we are all the same species, Homo sapiens. My parents live on a planet that has a bit more evolution and technical advancement than Earth, to say the least. The human race has a lot more history behind it than you think. I will attempt to explain the full picture as best I can. There is a lot of stuff that I don't understand myself, bearing in mind that I received my education on Earth. My parents kept the secret about their origins from me until I was twenty years old. It blew my mind when they told me. Space is just an astrological soup of unimaginable proportions. So far the human race occupies a comparatively small area on just a handful of planets."

I sat back in my chair feeling full of food and too much information. Thelma came in and cleared everything away. I just sat watching her gratefully. Richard had excused himself and left the room so I had the chance to relax and think. I wondered what I was letting myself in for. I didn't know what to believe but I felt too tired to worry; it had been a long day.

"Is everything alright?" Thelma said as she came in carrying a crystal bowl full of fruit.

"Yes thank you, Thelma, it was a lovely dinner."

While I studied the bowl of fruit, Richard came back and sat down.

"Horace has returned," he said while he peeled a banana. "I can show you what he looks like without the security cloaking, if you like."

"Where has he been?" I asked in a total stupor.

"I share the use of the ship with several other people; he has been on another mission," Richard said. "Come on, I'll show you."

He popped the last piece of banana into his mouth and discarded the skin onto the table. I felt the need to tidy it up and put it somewhere but he got up from the table and I followed him into the hall, through the front door and out onto the lawn. It was now nearly dark and the sky was clear with a faint orange glow from the setting sun. In the half-light, I could see the whole expanse of lawn with the trees silhouetted beyond, but no Horace. I wasn't sure what to expect and looked around, but could not see anything like a spaceship out here. We stood for a moment. I was feeling scared not knowing what to expect. It was a bit like being invaded by beings from outer space. I thought I should lie down and forget the whole thing.

"I can't see anything," I said nervously.

"Hold on a minute," Richard said as he took my hand. "I have to communicate with him and he hasn't established clearance to turn off the cloaking."

"How do you communicate with him?"

"I have a device implanted in my brain," Richard said. "Horace has to check that there are no satellite scans, planes or people in the area."

"You have a device in your brain," I said pathetically. I wanted to sit down and felt my knees go weak. I was so tired and was sure I was having some sort of dream. Richard put his arm around my waist and held me close to him. I reacted by putting my arm around him. With my hand, I felt his naked muscular tummy under his tee shirt. I felt better just holding on to him.

I looked up and the whole vista was suddenly swamped with this huge egg-shaped thing. At first it looked quite transparent and ghostly but quickly took on a substantial form, blotting out the trees beyond. It had no undercarriage or wheels; it just hung in the evening air suspended on nothing. It was chocolate coloured and truly egg-shaped without any features or windows. Its underside glowed with a gentle white light, similar to moonlight, and lit up the whole lawn area. At the blunt end there was a black dish about the same diameter as the egg. It looked absolutely hideous and unlike anything I had ever seen before. It was definitely extraterrestrial and the sight made me feel faint; I could feel the blood drain from my head.

The next thing I knew I was in Richard's arms being carried up the wide staircase. I felt terribly pathetic and remembered this wasn't the first time I had been carried up the stairs. He laid me on his bed and loosened my clothing. I felt him kiss me on the lips and soon I fell into a deep sleep.

CHAPTER 11

The first thing I heard was the beautiful sound of a blackbird greeting the day. I had slept soundly and for the moment I just wanted to lie and listen to the dawn chorus. I opened my eyes and it was just getting light. The French doors were open and there was a gentle cool breeze moving the curtains. I turned over and, to my surprise; Richard was lying next to me. He was asleep and I could feel his breath on my arm. I delighted in seeing him like this; he looked so sweet and totally peaceful. I was so pleased having him next to me. I studied his features in detail. He was so handsome. His skin was Mediterranean, bronzed and free of any blemishes. His hair was dark and he had a black five o'clock shadow that stretched down his neck and over a pronounced Adam's apple. I can't for the life of me remember the colour of his eyes, but I am sure they were brown like the colour of my own. I gently kissed him on the lips and felt his sweet breath.

Eventually I had to get out of bed without waking him before my bladder burst. I went into his ultra-modern bathroom. I was still wearing my crumpled dress from the night before. Seeing myself in the mirrors, I decided I had better get my act together. I looked like a disaster victim. I used the loo, which had the same glowing flush panel as the spaceship. All the events from yesterday came flooding back. I realised I was on the verge of something remarkable. I resigned myself to take it one-step at a time. I went back into the bedroom to find my overnight bag. It was by the bedside. Not wanting to wake Richard, I quietly rummaged around for some clean clothes and my vanity bag.

I thought it would be nice to have a shower, but how the bloody hell do you make it work?

"Good morning, Lisa." Richard was awake. I turned around. He swung out of bed and stood up. He was completely naked and promptly put on a white towelling dressing gown. He came round the side of the bed and sat down beside me, putting his arm on my shoulder.

"Hello," I said sheepishly. "I'm sorry for last night; I was really tired."

"Darling Lisa, you don't have anything to be sorry about. You have been through a lot recently." He kissed me on the cheek. "I'll go and get us some coffee while you sort yourself out."

"Richard, how do I make the shower work?" I asked.

"Just press the red panel and it will come on at the right temperature. Mrs T has put lots of towels out."

Richard left the room and I had a glorious shower. By the time he returned I was dressed in clean underwear, jeans and tee shirt and was admiring the view of the garden from his balcony. I wondered if the spaceship was still lurking out there unseen. He pushed a trolley through the room and out onto the balcony. The trolley was laden with strawberries, boiled eggs, toast and freshly ground coffee. I suspect Mrs T had a hand in producing the breakfast. Richard had miraculously managed to shave and dress, no doubt from some secret wardrobe or bathroom somewhere in the large house. We sat on plastic chairs at a plastic table on the small balcony and had a lovely breakfast.

I avoided asking any questions for the moment so we just talked about normal everyday things. I say 'normal' except for one thing. He had some lovely tame birds that came and perched on the stone parapet. He put some toast crumbs on the wall. First a robin came and then a blackbird and then a whole host of house sparrows. The birds were totally at ease with Richard. He put his hand out and they just perched on his fingers and bobbed about, completely fearless. It was then I remembered that things were far from normal.

"You must have been doing this for a long time to get them so tame," I said.

"Birds are very ancient creatures; they love to be friendly given half a chance," he said while a robin took a morsel of toast from his fingers. "I don't normally feed them; if possible it's best not to interfere with the balance of nature. What people don't realise is that you can communicate with most animals on a subconscious level. Just project friendly thoughts and they will react accordingly. It is very handy sometimes and you should be able to do it. I can scare a cat away just by looking at it with hate in my mind. I hate cats; they are not indigenous to planet Earth. There are no feathered birds like this on Terranus. I despise the way cats stalk the birds for fun."

I shuddered and tried not to think about what he had said. The human race is not alone on this planet and I am sitting next to an extraterrestrial Dr Dolittle. Richard took hold of my hand; he was incredibly sensitive to my thoughts.

"Lisa, I'm sorry. I'm so happy being with you. I was forgetting myself. You really don't have to worry, and I still have a lot to explain." He pulled his plastic chair closer to mine and held my hand clasped tightly in both of his.

"We are very alike," he said. "Whereas my grandmother originally came from a distant planet, so did your father. In fact so did a hell of a lot of people. On Earth most people are not aware of what is going on. Earth has its own indigenous human life, but my original planet has been spreading itself around the universe for tens of thousands of years, which would include populating the Earth."

I looked into his deep brown eyes and time seemed to stand still. I could feel his thoughts and they were warm and loving. I could understand what he had said and despite a million questions filling my mind I felt an enormous sense of relief. I threw my arms around his neck and hugged him. A wave of emotion came over me and I sobbed relentlessly, tears wetting his shoulder. He talked quietly in my ear as I tried to control myself.

"What you won't remember is that I saw you about two months ago at the dog rescue centre. I was with Jack looking at some of the unfortunate creatures for Mrs T. That is where the spaniel came from. You were tending a sick animal and I accidentally bumped into you. It was just a fleeting encounter but I knew you were special. It took some time, but I organised some detective work to find out who you were. It is part of my job to find out who the most recent immigrants from the Terranus system are. There is always a strong empathy between recent immigrants. I dearly wanted to meet you."

Richard was also very emotional. I could sense loneliness from deep within him. Everything was very clear to me; I hugged him tighter.

"So you're responsible for the MI6 investigation?" I said.

"Yes, I'm sorry; I hope it didn't upset your mother too much."

"And meeting you was all a set-up. I didn't think you really needed me to come all this way to help the spaniel."

"Please don't be angry Lisa."

"I'm not angry. I love you. You bugger."

We embraced each other for a long time while I tried to gather myself together. Richard gently rubbed my back. I could smell his after-shave lotion. I was feeling much better.

"So let's get this right," I said, pulling away from him and looking him in the eye. "You're saying my father was also from outer space?"

"When I bumped into you at the rescue centre," he said, "I instinctively knew that you were a telepath, which usually means that you're either a recent immigrant or closely related to one. If you don't use the gift it eventually fades away."

"I see," I said cautiously. "I can sense your thoughts, or at least I have done it before. I'm not picking anything up right now."

"I'm trying not to project anything at the moment. If you're not used to it, it can be a bit overwhelming. The problem is you have to deal with the other person's emotions as well as your own."

"I see," I said again, "and if my father is from this solar system of yours, what about my mother?"

"I haven't traced her ancestry, but being dark-haired she is bound to be related somewhere along the line to an immigrant."

"I don't understand," I said, "is everybody on Earth from this system of yours?"

"Not everybody; colonisation has been going on for thousands of years. Anybody with fair hair and skin, dark hair with a Mediterranean complexion and especially oriental origin, will all have ancestry from the Terranus system."

"Good grief," I said, "my father has oriental blood and so do I."

He looked at me with his worried expression and I knew I was going to get landed with another bombshell.

"If you're feeling up to it, there is some more you should know."

"Go on," I said.

"We made the investigation on behalf of your father. That is usually the first step." He hesitated for a moment. "I had to do it; I really wanted us to get to know each other, but it is impossible if I can't tell you the whole story. We could never have a normal relationship. I had to get security clearance from the Council. That usually means tracing your ancestry. I knew you were recent; I just had to prove it to the Council." Richard paused.

"Go on," I said, bracing myself.

"It was easy tracing your father's origin and I learned about the plane crash. There was information about his arrival on Earth, but the database on Honshu had been tampered with; it was obvious that something wasn't right. I made a report and sent it back to Terranus. By an amazing quirk of fate it turns out that your father didn't die in the plane crash. He was in fact abducted from Earth. I have good reason to believe he is still alive on the planet Honshu."

I slumped forward and stared out at the garden. The birds were still landing on the parapet and jumping about expecting food. I felt as though I was having a dream and wished I would wake up. Richard's hand had found its way under my tee shirt; he was gently rubbing my back. It felt very calming. I could sense his thoughts; he was projecting an enormous feeling of relief and I was able to accept this information in total innocence. I had to face it. I am the daughter of an alien from another planet and my father could still be alive. I am also able to have this strange telepathic relationship with a man who is in contact with other planets, and to cap it the entire world has been populated by these aliens. It just goes to show that there is more to Heaven and Earth and I got the feeling that my life was just about to begin.

CHAPTER 12

Eventually we went downstairs. I greeted Mrs T. She was worried about me and said I looked a bit pale. *Not surprising,* I thought, *after all the mind-blowing revelations I had just received.* She disappeared to make me a pot of hot tea. Richard excused himself to attend to some matters on his fancy computer so I wandered around the garden with Bruce who, with a ball in his mouth, innocently tore about like a maniac.

It was a lovely summer's day and I took in deep breaths of fresh air to try and quell the feeling of butterflies in my stomach. I had time to think about the amazing facts presented to me without the odd sensation of having Richard's emotions cluttering up my mind. The more I thought about it, the more it seemed to slot into place. My perception of the world had dramatically changed. I still felt I was in some dream and I would wake up and come down to earth, literally. I resigned myself to be brave and ease myself gently into this new reality. Questions poured in. If my father is alive and from another planet, what on earth am I going to say to my mother, if anything? The shock would not do her any good in her present state of health, but on the other hand she might already know and it's just me who has been kept in the dark. Also, this empathy business was confusing. I could certainly sense Richard's emotions and sometimes I seem to know what he is thinking. I wondered how deeply he could sense my thoughts; the prospect was a bit unnerving. I remembered what Richard had said and resigned myself to take things one step at a time.

I went back to the terrace with Bruce hot on my heels to find Richard standing over the table pouring two mugs of tea.

"Are you OK?" he said as he kissed me on the lips.

I put my arms around his neck and he hugged me tightly. We sat for a while sipping our tea in the morning sun.

"What happens next?" I said. "Are there any more revelations I should know about?"

"One thing at a time," Richard said with a smile. "I think you have more than enough to think about. Let things sink in first and we can discuss the situation later." I was desperately trying to read his thoughts but he was blotting them out again.

"How do you feel about space travel?" he asked with a totally bland expression.

"What do you mean?" I asked. "Going up in your spaceship?"

"Well, if we are going to progress you will have to get used to it."

I suddenly felt excited. I loved the trip we had in Horace, but going into space, that was something else. How do I know it would be safe? I had read somewhere that weightlessness can cause awful nausea. Damn it Lisa, Richard supposedly does it all the time.

"What do you have in mind?" I asked cautiously.

"Well, how would you like to have lunch on the moon?" Richard grinned from ear to ear and I wasn't sure if he was joking.

"What do you mean?"

"We can go on a sightseeing tour of the lunar surface. It is truly spectacular. The moon has much higher mountains than Earth. Horace will provide the lunch, and it will be a good introduction to travelling in space. What do you say?"

Richard's enthusiasm was intoxicating and I realised he was serious.

"How long does it take to get to the moon?" I asked in panic. "It's a long way off. I'm not sure I can cope with the rigours of space travel. I could be very ill."

"At the moment it is approximately 238,000 miles," he said confidently. "Once we are out of Earth's atmosphere it would take about five minutes."

I sat for a moment in disbelief and did some math.

"That means we would have to travel at over 2,000,000 miles a second," I said eventually.

"More or less," Richard said, raising his eyebrows. "Given a clear trajectory Horace can travel at close to the speed of light."

"At the speed of light," I repeated stupidly. "What powers it?"

"Don't ask me that," Richard said. "I was educated on Earth and I'm no scientist. I think it's sort of nuclear powered, but it uses other sources, like gravity and solar winds. Apparently it projects a tubular force field into space and travels along it. To accelerate up to the speed of light requires an unbelievable amount of power. My father always said that Horace is like electricity travelling in a conductor. The technology is way beyond me. I'm a musician. You would be better off asking Horace, but I have tried that and he totally confused me."

"Do we have to wear space suits and magnetic boots?"

"Hell no," Richard laughed. "Horace provides an internal environment which is infinitely adjustable and he can mimic the environment of all the known planets in the universe. He compensates for inertia and most of the time you won't even realise that you are moving."

I wasn't completely convinced and sat quietly for a moment, thinking about it. Most people would give their right arm to travel into space. It would be an experience of a lifetime. I could sense Richard's relaxed, even nonchalant thoughts about the space flight. I was compelled to put my trust in him.

"Oh bugger," I said, "you have to fly me to the moon."

We got up from the table and I asked Richard if I needed to take anything. He told me that everything we need is on board but advised me not to take a camera. He said that it is a security risk and Horace would fry its circuits. I didn't have a camera anyway but I did go and get my handbag. When I returned, Richard was waiting on the lawn and I excitedly ran up to him. He was standing near the rectangle of light. I was completely unaware that Horace had even arrived. He was totally invisible. Richard took my hand and I confidently stepped onto the rectangle of light. After the stomach churning lift ride it was comforting to see the interior of the ship again. Nothing had changed; the windows were open and it smelled clean and sweet.

"Good morning Horace," Richard said to the ship.

"Welcome aboard sir and I am delighted to see Miss Lisa," Horace replied dutifully.

"Hello Horace," I said sheepishly.

Richard guided me down to the front of the ship and I sat down on the plush leather chair near the control desk that was quietly glowing to itself with the unfamiliar icons.

"Horace, I would like to have manual control please."

"Yes sir," he replied.

Immediately the chair beside me started to move. It made me jump and I slid away from it. It was literally growing a pair of armrests. They just seemed to grow upwards from nowhere and quickly matched the same black leather as the rest of the chair. At the end of each armrest, a black shiny appendage grew upwards as if someone was blowing it up like a balloon. I quickly recognised them as a pair of computer joysticks. It was like watching an animated movie. I sat and stared at Richard with wide eyes.

"Don't worry," Richard said, "this ship is full of tricks like that. The ship can rearrange its cells and grow into all sorts of things. I'm going to manually fly this bucket."

Richard sat down in the newly formed chair and I wondered whether Horace minded being referred to as a 'bucket'. The screen in front of Richard suddenly lit up with all sorts of dials and icons. I could recognise a conventional altimeter and a highly detailed GPS screen.

"Manual flight implemented at your command," Horace announced. I tried to relax but my excitement was overwhelming. Richard turned to me.

"Are you ready to go?"

"I'm at your mercy," I croaked.

Richard pulled back the right hand stick. The movement on the stick was almost imperceptible and I closely watched him in anticipation. I looked forward and without my realising it, we were lifting off the ground. We then started to slowly rotate and the roof of Richard's house slid into view. Richard tweaked his left hand joystick slightly forward and we gently started to move forward while slowly gaining height. I could see how the sticks controlled the ship; it was simplicity itself. I was pleasantly relieved that Richard wasn't showing off and scaring me more than I was already. In fact I definitely preferred him driving rather than have Horace control the ship. Richard broke into a snigger and I realised he had picked up my thoughts; I hoped Horace couldn't do the same.

We had now picked up speed and were gliding over the sea lochs and mountains. I could see from Richard's altimeter our height was now 2,000 feet and rising rapidly. The sky was dotted with fluffy clouds and the view was suddenly obliterated as we went through one. Before long, we were out of the clouds and skimming along the tops of them. We were travelling at an alarming speed as the clouds zoomed past us and dropped away. I felt as though I was in a supersonic fighter jet but there was no sensation of speed or any feelings of nausea. It seemed as though I was in the cinema watching a cinemascope movie. I could only just make out the mountains and valleys below now and I gripped my seat and tried to see from Richard's control panel at what speed we were travelling.

"We have gone past the speed of sound and are approaching Mach two," he said. "Don't worry; I'll get Horace to take over when we get into space."

The thought occurred to me that I was going to lose the power of speech if this telepathy thing got any worse.

"How fast is Mach two?" I asked.

"I think it's about 1,400 miles an hour." he said. "We must be about sixty miles up now."

I dismissed Richard's vagueness and stared out of the front window. All I could see was a blue and white haze. To my surprise the curvature of the Earth was clearly visible. I couldn't make out any land and assumed we must be over the sea. I started to panic and wanted to hold Richard's hand but thought better of it while he was engrossed with his joysticks. The view from the front window was now incredible. The horizon was a huge arc of blue and white and the sky was like a rainbow ranging from brilliant white through to dark iridescent blue. I certainly had never been this high up before. I'm sure jet planes can't fly at this altitude. It dawned on me that I really was going into space.

Our speed of ascent must have accelerated. It was quite possible to watch the arc of the Earth diminish; the top of the rainbow was now turning to black. Before long, I could see our band of atmosphere and the blackness of space, which was thick with stars. Below, the Earth was a beautiful blue and I could see individual weather systems masking the continents. It was far more spectacular than I could ever have imagined. I could appreciate why people would pay millions of pounds to see it. Richard was fiddling with the joysticks.

"Believe it or not, we have now come to a full stop and are stationary at exactly 124 miles above sea level," Richard announced proudly. "I shall let the computer take over now." Richard turned to me and all I could do was sit there with my mouth open.

"Are you OK?" he asked.

"Wow," I said, without taking my eyes off the vista below.

"It is beautiful, isn't it?"

"I've seen TV pictures like this from the Apollo missions,"

I said, "but to see it for real is indescribable. Shouldn't we be weightless or something?"

"As I said, the ship has its own artificial gravity; I can turn it off if you want to float around the cabin," he said. "In fact we can go swimming if you like."

"Go swimming! What are you talking about? We are in space, aren't we? For all I know this is just a very sophisticated computer game." I was feeling a bit frightened and didn't want to sound so harsh. I knew this was for real but it was a lot to accept. It was only yesterday that I got out of my warm bed in my little house somewhere back down on Earth. My normal life had been turned upside down and I was starting to panic.

I was desperately trying to ignore the revelations about my father. It all sounded so fantastic and I felt powerless to do anything about it. All I could do was burst into tears as panic took hold of me. I just couldn't help myself.

Richard put his arm around me and I buried my face in his chest. I don't often cry, or at least I didn't until all this started to happen. But it felt good and was acting like a safety valve. Richard said nothing and gently stroked my hair. I quickly felt better. Richard miraculously produced a clean handkerchief; the freshly laundered smell of it was very comforting. I blew my nose and put the handkerchief in my pocket.

"Would you like a hot drink?" Richard asked.

"Yes please," I said pathetically.

Richard got up and went into the kitchen. I looked out on the incredible vista below. I could make out the continent of America. We seemed to be hovering somewhere over New York. I shuddered at the sight and decided to go and find Richard. He was in the kitchen watching two mugs fill up from the drinks maker. The kitchen also had a small viewing window. I could see the curvature of the Earth with its mantle of atmosphere. It was an incredible arc of blue and white fading out to pitch black; the stars were thick and bright. Richard handed me a mug of tea.

I could sense he was worried about me.

"Sorry about that," I said. "I'm really alright now. In fact I'm on top of the world." I made a silly laugh and Richard smiled at me.

"It's my fault; I've loaded rather a lot on you. I should practise what I preach and take this much more slowly. Let's go and sit in a comfortable chair."

We sat down in the lounge area of the ship and put our mugs on the round table. The view from the window was different here; all I could see was space with clouds of stars. I wondered where I should be looking to see Richard's home planet and what sort of life forms were out there. I shuddered and sipped my tea. Richard was watching me; his face had a kindly, sympathetic expression. I tried to pick up his thoughts but he was blotting them out.

"Were you joking about the swimming?" I asked.

"No I wasn't joking," he said. "This ship was designed on Terranus and built on the sister planet Honshu. The culture on Terranus is very much geared to pleasure, health and exercise. In fact, there are very few lifts. People prefer to walk, climb stairs, and keep fit and active. Even the elderly go swimming and running. Medical science is so advanced; everybody is fit and healthy."

"It sounds like Utopia," I said.

"This ship has two recreational rooms, which you haven't seen yet," Richard continued. "They can be converted to suit all sorts of recreational activities, or if necessary act as sleeping quarters. The rooms can be converted into one large room that could be used as a gym or a theatre and even for swimming. Horace is programmed to provide all the equipment you need. I suppose it is a bit like the fictitious 'holodeck' on TV."

"Does that mean the room is filled with water?" I asked.

"No," Richard said, "for a ship this size it wouldn't be very practical. The ship has a clever effect that allows you to swim through the air as if in water. Don't ask me how it's done but Horace modifies the gravity and density so you have buoyancy as if in water. It is like swimming underwater but you can breathe. It is very good exercise and you don't even have to get wet."

"Wow," I said. "I'd love to try that. What is the plan? Are we going to fly to the moon?" I was feeling much better and curiosity was getting the better of me.

"I don't want to load you with too much stuff," Richard said. "It's entirely up to you; we will have to move soon though, for we are not allowed to stay in one place for too long when in close proximity to Earth."

"You said I have to get used to it. It is not often a girl gets the chance to fly to the moon." I was feeling very philosophical about all this and didn't want Richard to think I was a wimp.

We finished our tea and returned to the front seats. The chair Richard had been sitting in had quietly returned to its original shape. I was secretly pleased we were in Horace's capable hands, if he had any, that is.

"Horace, take us to the moon and set a slow lunar orbit about fifty miles above the surface so that we can see the Earthrise. Oh, and not too fast, we don't want to scare Lisa."

"Yes, sir," Horace replied. "I quite understand; departure in thirty seconds."

I was amazed at how casual it all was and felt as though I could fly this ship myself. Suddenly the view of the Earth slipped away and was gone. All I could see were the stars. I could feel the ship accelerate and the effect made me sit back in the soft seat. I grabbed Richard's arm for security. The moon swung into view. It was the largest I had ever seen it although half was in shadow. It was incredibly bright. I felt as though I should be wearing my sunglasses. As my eyes adjusted, it was visibly growing in size. I could clearly see features on the surface. I gripped Richard's arm tighter as the moon filled the front window. I felt as though we were going to crash into it. As we got nearer the pockmarked surface, it reminded me of a giant piece of pumice stone. It was littered with craters and cracks, some of which had been partially filled in as if with snow. Somehow Horace had managed to level off and slow down. I could see the lunar horizon as a gentle arc in the distance. We were now gliding over the surface at a comfortable speed. It all happened so fast, I didn't have time to be scared. I released my grip on Richard's arm and relaxed a little. I couldn't believe we got here so quickly; there had been no real sensation of acceleration or speed.

"In a few minutes we will be able to see the Earth rising," Richard said. "I'll never forget when my father showed me this spectacle. It made me feel very small and humble and taught me the true reality of space."

I could sense Richard's emotion; it brought a lump into my throat. I thought that I might burst into tears again. I snuggled up against him as tightly as I could and he put his arm around me. Before long, I could see a blue arc appearing on the horizon. It gradually rose from the lunar surface and was soon in full view. I was amazed at how far away it was. It wasn't much bigger than the moon as seen from Earth. Part of it was in shadow yet you could see the blue of the oceans and the patterns of clouds. It gave me a profound sense of isolation. Despite having the warmth of Richard's body next to me, I felt truly alone. We watched in silence as it rose in the sky. By the time it slipped from the viewing window most of it was in darkness. We were also soon in darkness and the glowing panels of the ship lit up the cabin. It now wasn't possible to make out any features on the lunar surface, just the milky stars of space. Richard stood up and stretched.

"Would you like anything to eat or drink?" Richard asked.

"I'm not really very hungry," I said, glancing at my watch. "It's not even midday yet. Something to drink would be nice."

"Let's be naughty and open a bottle of wine," Richard said with a grin on his face.

I agreed, and dismissing any thoughts of becoming alcoholic, I followed him into the kitchen. He opened a cupboard in the wall that was full of bottles with glasses neatly arranged on a shelf below. He took out two crystal glasses.

"Would you like red or white?" he asked. I told him I didn't mind so he opened a bottle of Claret. We took our glasses and the bottle through to the sitting area. I gulped my wine and the alcohol soon kicked in. It was very welcome after the visual excitement I had just experienced.

"It's amazing to have this sort of luxury while floating round the moon," I said, feeling quite relaxed and possibly capable of being a bit silly.

"This is the most unbelievable experience. If I told anybody about this they would think I've gone nuts, not that I'm going to, that is."

"You're coping with it very well," Richard said with a glint in his eye, "and today I don't think I have told you that I love you."

His words made me feel warm inside and I flashed a coy smile at him.

"Are you going to show me this recreational room?" I asked.

"Yes, would you like to try the swimming effect?"

"It sounds like fun," I replied.

"Horace," Richard said to the room, "prepare the cabin for swimming exercise, and use setting six with a temperature of about twenty degrees Celsius."

"Yes sir," Horace replied. "The room will be ready in sixty seconds."

I popped to the bathroom while Richard poured out some more wine. When I came out he was standing in the corridor holding the two glasses.

"Can we take glasses of wine into the room?" I asked.

"No problem, just be careful not to knock them over."

"Do we wear our clothes?" I asked.

"We can go skinny dipping if you like." I suddenly felt embarrassed and could sense some naughty thoughts going through Richard's mind.

"You would have more freedom of movement without wearing tight jeans," Richard said. "Let's see how we get on."

We went to the end of the corridor and a door whizzed open. The room was enormous and must have been as wide as the ship. The whole ceiling was curved. At each end there were viewing windows with the dark lunar landscape gliding past. The room was covered with turquoise blue panels that looked like they were made of foam rubber. The floor was also the same material. Behind the panels the walls and floor had a soft blue glowing light. It all looked very inviting and very alien. Richard handed me both the glasses of wine and then walked into the room. He launched himself into the air and just floated off. I stared in amazement; it was the strangest thing I had ever seen. I was standing there like a lemon holding two glasses and on the other side of the door he was floating in mid air on his back flapping his arms around.

"Come on in; the water's lovely!" he shouted.

I stood there for a while surveying the scene. He sort of backstroked to the end of the room and then somersaulted head over heels. He used the spongy walls to push himself forward with his legs and glided towards me. It was as if he was actually in water but yet flying through the air. He lost momentum by the time he reached the door and with a lot of arm flapping ended up standing before me.

"I know it looks weird," he said, "but you must try it. It can't do you any harm. In fact it's very healthy exercise; it is just like swimming under water with the bonus that you can breathe normally. The gravity is set so that if you stop moving you just slowly sink to the floor. If you're unhappy with the sensation or start to feel nauseous you can just walk out."

"OK, I'm game," I said as I put the wine glasses on the floor.

Richard got hold of me by the waist and gently pulled me into the room. Immediately it felt delightfully warm all over my body and I was suddenly weightless. The weight on my heels was gone and I instinctively pushed up with my toes. We both rose into the air and I grabbed hold of his arms. I looked down and I was floating two feet above the floor. I felt as though I should panic but the sensation was very pleasant. I let go of Richard. He gently pushed me upwards by the waist and let go of me; I rose into the air. It was a lovely sensation and I remained stationary above him with my arms outstretched. My long dark hair floated horizontally and then flapped the side of my cheeks as I gently floated back down to the floor.

"Good grief," I said, as we both stood there with our hair still flying about.

I stepped backwards out of the room and the sensation of weight returning to my body was immediate and unsettling. My feet hurt as the full weight of my body filled my trainers. I stepped backward and regained my balance while leaning against the wall.

Richard stepped out of the room and I was delighted to notice that he felt the physical change a bit disturbing also. He picked up the glasses of wine that I had set carefully on the floor and handed me my glass. My hand was shaking a bit but I gratefully accepted it. I felt alright and surprisingly refreshed. We finished our glasses and put them back on the floor. I picked up Richard's thoughts and knew what was going on in his mind; the notion was naughty and exciting.

"What do you think of that?" he said.

"I think we should try it again," I said.

"Do you think we should take our clothes and shoes off first?" he said.

"I would look pretty silly swimming in these clothes at the local pool," I said.

We instinctively stripped off our jeans and tee shirts in the corridor. This time, Richard was wearing black silk boxer shorts and as always looked very sexy. I was so glad to take off my trainers and socks; the floor felt warm and soft to my bare feet. I was also glad that I had put on my expensive red underwear. I always wanted to look my best for Richard under any circumstance, but hell, this was the strangest. I was going swimming in a weightless room while floating around the moon in a space ship.

CHAPTER 13

I watched Richard as he launched himself off into the room again. He did a rather ungainly breaststroke and quickly floated off to the other side of the room. While he wasn't looking I gingerly stepped into the room and instantly felt weightless in the warm air. I raised my arms above my head and gently lowered them again. The sensation wasn't the same as being submerged in water at all and I didn't feel the same sort of resistance you would normally get on your arms. In fact, I hadn't moved at all and was still just touching the soft floor with my toes. I made the same downward movement with my arms, this time with a lot more effort. I could now feel a resistance in the air and realised I had floated upwards. I gathered some courage and did a complete breaststroke, kicking with my legs also. I glided up at a slight angle and bumped my head on the ceiling. When I looked down, I could see I was at least ten feet off the ground. I started to panic and flapped my arms wildly. I somehow managed to end up on my back facing the ceiling. Suddenly I felt Richard's warm hands on my waist. He gently rotated me until I was on top of him, face to face.

We kissed and embraced while floating in mid air and the sensation was truly out of this world. I regained my composure and released him.

"Just swim as if you're in water," he said as he slowly drifted towards the floor.

I performed the breaststroke and found myself swimming through the air. It didn't take long to reach the end of the room.

I touched the soft curved wall and managed to turn back the other way. I continued to swim towards the other wall. Richard was floating on his back near the floor and I floated past him, gathering momentum.

"I think I'm getting the hang of this," I said as I bumped into the far wall.

I turned and swivelled, this time gently launching myself off facing the ceiling. It was less daunting not looking down. As I gently floated along the room, I felt Richard's warm body behind me. He put his arms around my waist and kissed the back of my neck. I thrilled to his touch and responded by putting my arms down, holding him on his buttocks. He undid my bra and took it off. He continued to kiss my back all over. The bra just gently floated off into the room. He slowly spun me round to face him and we kissed passionately. Before long we had floated back to the floor and regained our feet. We just looked at each other and removed the rest of our clothing. With underclothes floating in all directions, we embraced and spiralled up into the room. It was certainly the most passionate and erotic lovemaking I have ever encountered and needless to say we didn't get much swimming exercise.

Eventually we gathered our clothes and left the room. We had been in the weightless room for a few hours. Richard decided that we should return to Earth and let the patient Horace return to his duties. We sat in the front seats watching the Earth grow larger as we plummeted towards it.

"Where does Horace go when you're not using the ship?" I asked.

"If he hasn't got another mission, he will go and hide behind the moon," Richard said as he offered me a chocolate biscuit. "There are over 100 ships like him operating around the world and it is important that their presence not be detected, so when they are not in use they stay out of the way. You probably have heard all the stories about UFO sightings. Thankfully due to better security and a more advanced cloaking device, it is not as likely to happen now."

"When I was young I saw a strange orange glow in the sky; it was very weird and moved at enormous speed. Other people saw it too. Would that have been Horace?" I asked.

"Could well have been," Richard said. "Before I was born the cloaking device was quite crude. They had problems with it glowing when in contact with the Earth's atmosphere. You would have to ask my father about that."

I watched the blue planet fill the screen as we fell towards it at breakneck speed. This time I thought I would try and relax and behave like a seasoned astronaut, but it was not to be. We plummeted towards the Atlantic Ocean and I could recognise the Gulf of Mexico. Out at sea there was a huge tropical storm; I could clearly see the cloud mass swirling around the eye of the storm. We were getting closer and I was sure we were going to crash through it into the ocean.

I couldn't stand it any longer and Richard sensed my alarm. He embraced me and I buried my face in his chest. I clung on to him as tightly as I could. Richard whispered in my ear.

"Don't worry darling, Horace is making a standard manoeuvre; we will be home in a matter of minutes."

I felt better not seeing where we were going; the ship was completely smooth and there was no sensation of movement so I was happy staying where I was with my eyes tightly closed. It felt like an age but I had to look eventually. Richard was still holding me tightly and I looked out of the front window. We were skimming past storm clouds; they were bubbling up and were brilliant white in the sunshine. Below they were dark and heavy with rain.

"We are over the North Atlantic; the weather doesn't look too good, are you OK?" Richard asked.

We plunged into the clouds and suddenly there was lightning around us. All I could see was a dark mist highlighted by brilliant flashes of light. It soon passed and we were through the cloud and gliding at incredible speed across the ocean. We must have been just a few hundred feet above the waves. The sky above was dark and the lightning was still flashing all around us. In the distance, I could see the Scottish mountains rising out of the gloom. For me the view was more out of this world than gliding over the lunar surface. You could sense the full force of the storm around us.

"Won't Horace get fried in a storm like this?" I said, remembering my knowledge of computer systems and high voltage.

"It's alright Lisa, Mother Nature can do far worse than this out in space. This is a mere itch for the ship's systems; it's just a summer thunder storm." Richard was so happy and contented and I nestled against him. I really loved him; sensing his thoughts made me feel contented also.

Before long we were gliding over the familiar lochs. The ship did a fancy twirl over the island and gracefully came to rest in front of Richard's house. I was so relieved to see a familiar sight; it was like driving into your home street and feeling glad to be back. It looked dark and foreboding outside after the weeks of hot weather. We stood up and stretched. I felt as though I had flown to America and back in one day, but looking at my watch, it was only four in the afternoon and we had been away for just under six hours. When we left the ship the rain was coming down in stair rods so we ran back across the lawn to the front door. Needless to say, by the time we got there we were both wet through. As I hadn't put my bra back on, I was not looking very decent in my wet tee shirt. We both decided that the best move would be to have a bath and find some dry clothes.

We ended up sneaking upstairs and into Richard's bedroom suite. He ran the taps to fill the huge rectangular bath, using copious amounts of bubble bath in the process. We sat side by side in the lovely warm water. As we relaxed, my mind returned to the day's events and especially the revelations about my father.

It was very hard to believe and yet I was strangely compelled to accept the whole story. In fact, I was so sure of myself I decided there and then that I must confront my mother with the whole truth. For all I know she already knows more than I do. Either way the truth must come out.

Richard turned to me and smiled; he had been reading my thoughts and I could understand what he was thinking.

"Well, I really have to tell her; that's what I feel," I said.

"I think you're absolutely right and you have to tell her. In fact it wouldn't surprise me if she didn't already know something. What she won't know is that your father is still alive. The Terranus Council don't take these abduction cases lightly and they feel obliged to restore the status quo. One way or the other she will find out the truth."

"This is a nightmare," I said, screwing up my face.

"Do you want me to be with you when you talk to her?"

"I think I might need some back-up, especially if she doesn't know anything," I said.

"We will go together," Richard said assuredly. "Lisa, do you remember that I said we may be able to do something to help your mother's condition?"

"Yes, I do remember," I said cautiously. "What have you got in mind? I suppose you have an advanced potion to make it better."

"You are absolutely right," he said. "It so happens there is a Terranus Doctor on Earth at the moment, and I can get him to see your mother in a matter of hours. He can diagnose the problem there and then using a small mobile scanner. After analysis, he will prescribe a serum that is injected into the bloodstream. Within twenty-four hours the serum will have eradicated every cancerous cell and restored the immune system; she will feel like a new woman."

I lay back in the warm water and tried to absorb what Richard had said. Can some sort of alien technology cure my mother? That would be amazing. But there again, a lot of amazing things are happening at the moment. Do I have the right to accept this offer? I felt Richard's thoughts in my very soul and all I could think of was that I have to trust him.

"So you can completely cure her?"

"After what happened to your father, the Terranus Council would be only too happy to help your mother."

"How could it be arranged? I would have to talk to my mother first," I said, feeling confused.

"We have been in this sort of situation before. All that happens is Marcus will pose as a doctor. He has a small device that does the scan in seconds. Your mother won't even know that it has been done," Richard said, smiling. "He can just come in, take a scan and leave. Then he will get the serum ready and give her the shot. That's all there is to it, within twenty-four hours your mother will be cured and the hospital will have to discharge her."

"That's incredible," I said, feeling sceptical. "How does it work?"

"The technology is very advanced and difficult to explain. The serum, basically, contains an army of surgeons that are microscopic. They are organically based and programmed to destroy the cancerous cells without affecting the healthy body, a bit like using maggots to destroy dead tissue. They stay in the bloodstream for years boosting the immune system and destroying anything dodgy, but don't quote me on this explanation. I don't profess to be a doctor. I can assure you, your mother won't even know what is going on. Marcus is brilliant and uses a technology way beyond anything known on Earth. Two months ago, I broke my leg. It was a stupid thing to do. I fell off a ladder while repairing a gutter. Horace brought Marcus to the house. He fixed it, and within a week I was walking about as though nothing had happened."

Although as a vet I was familiar with broken bones, it would have been nice to have them set and healed within a week. I winced at the thought of having my mother eaten away from the inside out by microscopic programmed maggots. I was intrigued, but, considering all the past events, I just had to accept it.

"So you could do all this without her even knowing?" I said, while soaping his back.

"You could, but we must talk to her."

Although I cringed at the thought of talking to Mother, Richard was right; I would have to tell her what is going on. I put my arm around his neck and kissed him. I then suddenly picked up his thoughts.

"That's a brilliant idea!" I said excitedly. "When she is better we can talk to her then."

"I have a further idea," Richard said. "Before we tell her about your father and his origins, we should go and see him on Honshu and see what he wants to do about the situation. You are his daughter, and you must talk to him. By then your mother will be well enough to accept the situation."

CHAPTER 14

Philbin Dulus sat back and relaxed as his ship approached the terminal on Honshu. He wasn't interested in viewing the vast complex; to him this was just a routine visit. The terminal consisted of ten vast, saucer-shaped buildings each with hundreds of docking bays around the edge, all connected by a tubular system of roadways. The whole complex was twenty miles above the surface of the planet locked in equilibrium by massive anti-gravity devices. There were ten such terminals spread around the planet. All the ships entering and leaving the planet were programmed to dock at the terminal. If they did not pass security, the ship's drive would shut down and the occupants would be stranded in space until customs officials checked them out. Any offenders faced heavy penalties. The whole complex handled flight control, customs and excise, and illegal immigration. Luckily for Philbin, this complex also held Macdonald, formally known as Nakito Nashira. He would not need to go down to the planet's surface. After docking in one of the vast loading bays, he quickly passed through customs, using his security identity chip. The trip to the detention centre was about two miles away down a system of tunnels so he hailed a terminal taxi. He would be able to get there in minutes.

Professor Macdonald had now completed his memory correction treatment. He could remember everything apart from the last five years. His captors had done a very efficient job of permanently erasing the memory patterns for that time. He could remember his wife and daughter and his life at the university back on Earth. But he had no idea why he was lying on a hospital bed in the detention centre or how he even got there. He was confused and angry and was giving the nurses a hard time. Without doubt, Philbin's arrival was not a moment too soon.

Philbin entered the centre carrying his electronic notepad. His aide was following closely behind him. Philbin was a very short, stout man and not blessed with a good mix of genes. He didn't want to be married and have the responsibility of rearing a child so he enjoyed his work. His aide catered for his every need. He greeted the duty nurse and flashed his Security Council ID. The nurse sighed deeply and promptly led him to Macdonald's room.

"Good morning Professor Macdonald," Philbin said as cheerfully as possible. "I'm Philbin Dulus of the Security Council and I have been assigned to your case."

Professor Macdonald looked grey and gaunt and Philbin wondered what it was they had made him do for the last five years. He was sitting bolt upright and had grown a long beard.

"About time too!" he said angrily. "I can't get any sense out of these nurses. What the bloody hell is going on?"

Philbin ignored the professor's outburst and quietly pulled up a chair to sit beside him.

"Professor Macdonald, it is our intention to find out what has happened to you. Perhaps you would assist me by telling me everything that you know about yourself."

"I'm a geology professor; I was doing a lot of interesting research for the university on Earth. Damn it, I have a wife and daughter back on Earth and I have no idea why I am here. I have only just been told that I am back on my home planet. You people keep hooking me up to this blasted machine and messing with my brain. I don't know where the hell I'm supposed to be."

"Professor Macdonald," Philbin replied calmly, "you may remember that you were transferred to Earth at your own request nearly fifty years ago. You had the standard treatment to erase the memory of your origins and after what has happened to you, the treatment you have currently received to restore your full memory is bound to make you feel confused."

Philbin sat back in his chair and tapped his notepad.

"Can you tell me your wife and daughter's names, Professor Macdonald?"

"Of course I can," he angrily retorted. "The wife's name is Morag and I have a lovely daughter, Lisa. Now can you please tell me why I am here?"

"Unfortunately Professor, we think you have been a victim of abduction. We are unable to account for the last five years of your life."

"Five years!" the professor shouted, "What do you mean? Where have I been for five years? Have I been in a coma?"

"You have not been in a coma, sir. We know that the abductors have permanently erased your memory for the past five years."

The professor slumped down and both men sat quietly for a moment.

"Have you any idea where I have been for the last five years?" the professor said eventually.

"Because of your professional background you were most likely to have been taken by one of the illegal mining organisations on Honshu. They have access to our mind programming technology. You were probably brainwashed and forced to help them in locating new ore seams. It is a crime situation that has happened before."

"Bloody hell!" the professor said and promptly went very quiet for a while. Philbin just sat looking at his notes.

"You want to find these abductors, don't you?" the professor said quietly.

"Anything you can tell us would be helpful. We conducted a memory probe while giving you corrective treatment to restore your memory. You have been very lucky; they only permanently erased the time you spent working for them. Normally you would have been killed when they had no further use for your expertise.

This is unusual and we think they considered you to be a special case. We are hopeful that you may be able to give us a lead."

The professor winced and took a sip of water from the glass on his bedside cabinet.

"When you were kidnapped," Philbin continued, "we know you were returning from a field trip and the Cessna aircraft landed in the desert not far from Alice Springs in Australia."

"Yes, I do remember," the professor interrupted. "The damn pilot said he was having trouble with the engine. He set the plane down on a dirt airstrip. He got out to look at the engine. The next thing I knew was being attacked from behind. Something was put over my face and I blacked out."

"Can you remember the name of the pilot?" Philbin asked.

"No idea, but I do remember that he was an Aborigine and spoke perfect English; must have had a good education. Cranborne arranged the flight; he would know his name."

"What about the three men? Can you describe them?" Philbin continued while tapping the screen on his notepad.

"I didn't get the chance to see their faces properly, but I'm sure they were white. What about my colleague, Dr. Cranborne, what happened to him?"

"I'm afraid that Dr. Cranborne is still missing," Philbin replied. "What can you tell me about him?"

"He is Australian and came from the university, seemed a decent enough chap. He was assigned to me as my assistant and I had never met him before. I don't know much about him. I can't be bothered with small talk. We just talked about the job in hand."

Before Philbin could ask another question, his aide came in through the door. She was female, very beautiful with long blonde hair and was dressed in a petite blue uniform. She politely asked if either would require refreshments. Both requested coffee and she politely bowed, exposing a tight cleavage, and left the room with the door whizzing behind her.

"She is new," said the professor. "She could serve me anytime. If I'm not mistaken, she is an artificial life form."

"She is my personal aide," Philbin said possessively, "how did you know she is artificial?"

"Damn it, you can tell when someone is not at home."

"What do you mean, 'not at home'?"

"You know, the mind is blank; there are no thoughts or emotions, just a computer. Most of the nurses here are artificial. They do an excellent job of putting them together; they are far more sophisticated than when I was last living on Honshu."

"I am glad that you remember living on Honshu. Can you read my thoughts?" Philbin asked.

"I know you're not artificial, but you're not projecting much. I suppose you try not to; it wouldn't help in your profession."

"Could you read Dr. Cranborne's thoughts?" Philbin asked while keeping his demeanour as bland as possible.

"No, I can't say I ever tried. You don't think of it after the mind conditioning you receive for living with the Earth colony."

"In your opinion would you say Dr. Cranborne was an immigrant?"

"How should I know?" the professor answered, feeling irritated by the line of questioning. "He was an Australian white, you tell me. Damn it man, you must have records on him."

Philbin's aide came in through the door carrying a tray with two mugs of coffee and a plate of odd-looking green biscuits. She set the tray on the bedside table and smiled prettily before quietly leaving.

"You must try one of these biscuits. They are my favourite, and they are made from Andusian nuts," Philbin said as he offered the plate to Professor Macdonald. It was the first human gesture he had made since the interview, but the professor declined.

"Tell me," the professor asked, "what is going to happen to me? When will I be able to see my wife and daughter?" Philbin busily tapped his notepad while chewing on a biscuit.

"I see that you were orphaned at a very early age, Professor," Philbin said after a lot of chewing. "A most unfortunate and rare occurrence; your whole family were killed during a sudden tsunami tidal wave on Atlantis." The professor's eyes closed and he lowered his head.

"Good God," he said. "I had completely forgotten about that. My mother, father and grandparents went on a fishing trip. It was a silly idea. The planet has dangerous marine life. I was only fifteen and away at college at the time. If I had gone with them I wouldn't be here now. After their death, I got my qualifications. I decided to become an Earth immigrant and start a new life. I was an only child, I did not have any relatives on Honshu."

"I'm sorry you have to hear this news after such a long time." Philbin was warming to the professor. "I'm afraid you will not be able to return to Earth for a while until we are satisfied with the investigation. In the meantime, the Council will arrange a temporary apartment and provide for all your needs. It may take some time to arrange your return. You must understand the sensitive nature of the situation and as far as I know your family have not been informed yet. In the interest of security the matter will be dealt with by an agent on Earth and we will let you know as soon as possible what arrangements can be made."

The professor just sat thinking while sipping his coffee.

"I have just one more question, Professor," Philbin asked. "Can you remember anything at all, even the slightest thing during the last five years?" The professor remained motionless for a while.

"When I was attacked and before I passed out I think I heard one of the men use the name Jack, but I couldn't make out the conversation."

Philbin brought up a photograph on his notepad and showed it to the professor.

"Do you recognise this man?" Philbin asked.

"That's definitely Cranborne; he is a strange looking fellow, and I'd recognise him anywhere."

"Did you see Cranborne being drugged?" Philbin asked.

"Come to think of it," he replied, "I don't remember seeing him being attacked at all. He was sitting next to me when they drugged me. The next thing I remember is being arrested in the streets on this damn planet. There is absolutely nothing in between."

CHAPTER 15

I felt much better after our bath and was now beginning to grasp the situation put before me without going into mindless panic. We had another glorious dinner prepared by Mrs T. We ate in relative silence while the rain poured down outside. It was the first rain for weeks and it was torrential. The pool room doors were open and the noise of the rain on the roof was strangely comforting. I felt very much at home. After dinner, Richard poured us both a large brandy. We went into the sitting room and I sank into the plush leather sofa. Richard expertly lit the log fire; I think it must have been a very clever imitation fire powered by gas, but I didn't care. I thought it looked so homely and friendly. Richard sat down beside me, putting his arm around me, and I snuggled up to him.

"Well," he said, "I suppose we had better make some arrangements. When will you be seeing your mother?"

"Oh God," I said. "I feel really nervous about this. I went to see her on Friday afternoon; I had not been home long before you knocked on my door. She hasn't been feeling well and they wanted to do some tests to see if the cancer has spread. I told her I would visit her on Sunday afternoon."

"So she is in hospital now?" Richard said.

"Yes, she is in a private room in Edinburgh hospital."

"We will have to move fast; we don't want your mother to have unnecessary surgery."

"I don't suppose anything will happen before next week," I said excitedly.

"Computer!" Richard suddenly spoke to the room. "Locate Dr Marcus."

"Dr Marcus is currently at his apartment in London." The computer voice was female and very soothing; the sound was weird, a bit like Horace, and you felt as though the voice was in front of you. In fact, the thought crossed my mind that we should introduce her to Horace. I was being stupid and tried to calm down.

"How do you do that?" I asked.

"The house computer was manufactured on Honshu and my father installed it. It is very useful for keeping contact with agents. We all have implants that act like transmitters. Darius Marcus is a good friend of mine and luckily he is our own personal doctor on Earth."

I shuddered at the reality of the situation and realised that I still did not understand what was going on.

"How many 'agents' are there and are they all from Terranus?"

"I don't know off-hand. 'Agent' is just a term for people like me who haven't received corrective treatment to remove all memory of our original planet. Your father, for instance, did not know he was from Honshu when he arrived here and your mother probably doesn't know anything either. But the treatment is not one hundred percent successful. I really must do some research on behalf of your mother and see how far back her ancestors go."

I shivered at the thought and sipped my brandy for comfort. Richard excused himself and left the room, leaving me watching the dancing flames in the fireplace. I eventually lay back on the sofa and closed my eyes in an attempt to relax and clear my mind. The fire was very homely and I felt at ease. I think I may have nodded off, but not sure for how long. When I opened my eyes again, Richard was beside me. He was smiling and looking at me intently.

"Are you awake?" he said gently. "It is all arranged. Horace will pick up Darius and bring him here by 2pm tomorrow afternoon and we can all go to the hospital together. He has the serum with him. All things being equal he can administer the cure for your mother there and then. He tells me that he has looked at your mother's medical history and there are no problems with her treatment."

"Thank you," I said sleepily, but then sensed there were important plans on his mind. Suddenly I was wide-awake.

"Richard, what else have you arranged?"

"There is a scheduled flight to Terranus on Wednesday. I know it is short notice but my mother has informed me that I must be on it."

Richard was very agitated and I wasn't sure what to think. I really did not want him to disappear again, especially with all this stuff going on.

"It is important that I make the trip," he said. "I could arrange it so you could come with me. That is if you are up to it. You will have to take time off work. We would have to leave on Tuesday, returning hopefully on Friday."

My head suddenly went into a spin and I sat back thinking about it.

"You mean you want me to travel to this planet with you?" I said eventually.

"Yes, I know you can get the time off work." Richard said enthusiastically.

At the moment work was the least of my worries and I was due a lot of holiday time. He was very excited about the prospect. I sensed there was urgency for him to see his parents and I instinctively knew that he would want to introduce me to them. It was very flattering, and I wondered if he knew I was sensing his innermost thoughts.

His parents are very much an unknown factor as far as I am concerned. I wondered why he did not talk about his mother that much. Hell, this was weird; she is living on another planet. Considering unknown factors, my father is supposedly alive and

115

living in this fucking solar system somewhere in space? I took another sip of brandy and tried not to freak out. I wondered about my father who has been supposedly dead for the past five years? Jesus, this is all so overwhelming and it is happening too fast. I swore again under my breath and tried not to panic. I had to go with the flow.

"At the moment, going to work seems to be very insignificant. I have a holiday due," I said.

"Well, if you are sure," Richard said with worry on his face. "I don't want to freak you out. I'm sorry events are moving so fast."

"What is this transporter? Doesn't your ship take us there?" I asked.

"We would be going in Horace; the transporter is just like catching a ferry. Don't worry about it; I will explain it all en route."

"Will my father know we are coming?"

"I'll send a message to the agent on Honshu. He can meet us there and take us to your father."

"And we will also meet your family?"

"They would love to meet you and you must see Terranus; it is a beautiful world."

"This planet Honshu, is it far away?"

"No." Richard laughed. "You can see Honshu from Terranus; in fact you can't miss it. Honshu is three times bigger than the Earth's moon and about the same distance away, so you can imagine that it dominates the sky. Since you have already been to the Moon you know how long it takes."

I sat back in the comfortable sofa and tried to imagine the scene. It all seemed quite fantastic. I made a mental note to go and look at Richard's painting in the dining room. Richard turned to me, smiling, and kissed me on the forehead; he was reading my thoughts and was worried about me.

"I can show you some pictures," he said. "Computer, display the images on file of the Terranus system."

Immediately the huge TV screen on the far wall came to life.

We decamped off the sofa and sat in some easy chairs in front of the screen. He scrolled through the icons on the screen using a remote control and opened a picture. The image was almost identical to the dining room painting but with far more detail. It was very striking, showing the three planets and a distant sun. Remarkably, the picture seemed to be three-dimensional, giving the TV a sense of depth. He fiddled with the gismo and the picture zoomed in to the nearest planet and filled the screen; the detail was incredible and obviously not taken by your average digital camera. The planet was very similar to Earth but I could not recognise any of the landmasses. It was much greener than Earth; the oceans were a lot smaller with a greenish-blue colour and there were more clouds covering the land.

"This one is Terranus; it is much older than the Earth. About 30,000 years ago it was in a bad state with heavy pollution. Now it is lush, green, and covered in forests. There is very little industry now and the whole world is for recreation and leisure. There are no big cities, no roads or cars and compared to Earth the population is very small. People live in small communities and grow their own food. There are no shops. If you need something you can order, and they deliver to you in pollution-free shuttles. If you need to go somewhere, you use an animal very similar to the horse, or even better, you can walk. If it is long distance, a shuttle will get you there."

"Wow," I said. "It sounds like living in the Middle Ages but with the internet."

I was trying to understand this scenario, but Richard was in full flow. He zoomed in closer and plummeted toward a landmass covered with green forest. As if flying with Horace I felt a bit nauseous again, but then we were skimming across a beautiful forest of tall trees. Ahead was a clearing surrounded by lush green grass with luxurious flowering shrubbery. The colours were those of a rainbow. There was a huge rambling building with green curving roofs, too complex for me to comprehend. The walls were white and there were terraced areas. I could not see any windows. The whole structure was totally alien.

"This is where my parents live," Richard said.

"It seems to be a very large house for them."

"They are very wealthy and there is plenty of room on Terranus."

I sensed that Richard was feeling uncomfortable. Again he was hiding something from me. It was very weird, and I knew that I could get inside his mind and find out what was going on. However, I did not want to. I was in love with him, and he knew it. We were as one and I could trust him. I decided to leave it alone for now and changed the subject.

"Do they speak English on Terranus?" I asked.

"There are many languages that are not used any more. English has become the universal language throughout the system; it has been used for hundreds of years. In fact, people think and communicate telepathically in English. Most of the time it is possible to communicate without speaking. Language is used for group conversations, lectures, debates and so on. It also depends on your emotional involvement with the person with whom you want to communicate. You can't probe the thoughts of a stranger and it wouldn't be polite anyway."

Richard got up and walked over to the other side of the room. The room was huge compared to my little home. On the far side, sitting centrally in the wall space, was a large sideboard. There were cupboards below and more bookshelves above. He opened a cupboard and took out something. His feet were bare and he squeaked back across the polished oak floor. He sat down beside me and showed me an old-fashioned tin of Golden Virginia tobacco. He opened the lid. Inside was a neatly arranged set of white tubes. They looked a bit like cigarettes.

"What on earth are those?" I said.

"You want a smoke?" he said.

I laughed but then felt worried. Richard looked at me.

"Don't worry. It is a cannabis derivative. You don't even light it. It is not harmful or addictive in any way whatsoever. The plant grows wild in abundance on Terranus."

He handed me one of the tubes and put another one between his lips and sucked. I did the same. It tasted like mint chocolate and I instantly felt relaxed. It was nice, particularly after our stressful day. I was able to detach myself from Richard's thoughts. I realised that it would be possible to do this at any time I wanted. I just needed some practice. It was lovely just to be with him and I snuggled into his chest. He picked up the remote and presented some new and strange pictures.

"This planet is Honshu, where your father is at the moment," Richard said, as he zoomed out and flew back to the other planet. I felt dizzy again with the movement and unwisely sucked on my chocolate flavoured tube. The planet filled the screen. It was again similar to Earth but the polar ice caps were enormous and it was obvious that large areas were snow covered.

"What are the large structures floating above the planet?"

"That is for the security of the whole system," he continued. "Honshu is the industrial world. All flights, business or pleasure, are monitored from here. Most things are manufactured on this planet including Horace and other synthetic life forms. As you can see the climate is much colder than Terranus and not as pleasant."

"Synthetic life forms?" I queried in fascination. Richard looked embarrassed and I sensed he had given me too much information again. But I did have to know what I was letting myself in for before shooting off across the galaxy.

"Horace is classified as a synthetic life form. It is engineering on a sub atomic level," Richard continued. "The whole ship is a living thing; its cells are alive and can regenerate. Horace has been designed specifically for space travel. They manufacture synthetic people as well. For now, just think of them as very realistic robots."

"Good God, synthetic robotic people," I said.

I was happy to be in a subdued state while Richard flew from one planet to another.

"The third planet is Atlantis and as you can see it is almost entirely covered by ocean. The planet does not have many inhabitants. There are many small islands that are volcanically very active. The marine life is dangerous, so you can see why not many people live there."

"What are the other planets?" I asked in wonder.

"Terranus has two lifeless moons like Earth. Atlantis has none and Honshu has a large moon, but the atmosphere is toxic. It is however populated by synthetic life forms for the purposes of manufacture."

"Are you sure it would be alright for me to come with you? Would I need to have a passport or anything?" I asked in panic.

"I just need to book the transporter. Horace will arrange everything. He already has security clearance for you," Richard said with confidence.

"And I will be able to see my father?"

"If you're up to it."

"I don't want to be without you, not with all this going on. I have to come with you," I said eventually.

"That's great," he said. "I'll make the arrangements straight away. You really don't need to worry." *Easy for you to say.* I thought.

Richard showed me some more pictures of Terranus, mostly landscapes, but my eyes were starting to feel very heavy.

It had been a long and fantastic day and the brandy and chocolate sticks had kicked in. I was absolutely knackered. I told him I was going up to bed. I climbed the wide staircase, peeled of my clothes and got into Richard's huge comfortable bed. I was asleep in seconds. Later I felt Richard slide in beside me and kiss me on the nose. I smiled in my slumber and turned onto my side. I had no idea what time it was.

CHAPTER 16

The next morning the rain had cleared away. Richard had some business to attend to, so I decided to go for a run around the island. With Mrs T's permission, I took Bruce with me. He was delighted to go hunting with me. I jogged round slowly, following the little railway line. The island was absolutely beautiful with mature trees and open areas of unspoilt moorland. I passed the area at the top of the hill where Richard first made love to me. I stopped and savoured the moment while admiring the views over the sea lochs. I had a chance to gather my thoughts in private and decided to ring the hospital when I got back to find out how Mother was. I could not make up my mind whether I should tell her about father or wait until I had seen him with my own eyes. She probably would not believe any of it anyway. I had lost any sense of reality, so I decided it would be a good idea to get some evidence of some sort to back up my story. By the time I had returned, I had decided that meeting Richard and having a strange doctor examine her would be quite enough for one day. I would tell her I was going on a short holiday next week with Richard.

After my shower, I rang the hospital. They reported that she was not able to hold down any food and on a saline drip. I was relieved to hear that they had not done any tests yet, so at least the fancy treatment that Richard's doctor was going to administer would be timed well. I then tried her mobile number wondering whether she would answer. Luckily, my mother is a very spirited woman and she answered the phone immediately.

"Hello Mum, it's Lisa, I hear you're not feeling too good."

"Lisa darling, how was your weekend? Will you still be coming to see me today? Don't tell me you're busy."

"I shall see you this afternoon, Mum. Would you mind if I bring a friend?"

"What do you mean 'a friend' darling? I'm not feeling up to much socialising."

"You remember Richard; I met him a few weeks ago, and he would love to meet you."

"Darling, that's wonderful. I'm so pleased you are seeing him again. I know how smitten you were with him and by the sounds of it you were made for each other."

"I can't tell you, Mum, I had an indescribable day with him yesterday. He is out of this world. I would love you to meet him." I suddenly realised what an understatement I had just made.

"My friendly neighbour came to see me this morning. She brought some things from home and I have my expensive dressing gown and some make-up. I can be ready to meet Mr Varnicus by this afternoon so that would be lovely, darling. I shall look forward to it." Mum sounded delightfully cheerful, but I sensed that she was in pain.

"We will see you about three o'clock. By the way, the hospital tells me you have a specialist doctor coming to see you also, so it will be a busy afternoon. Do you need me to bring anything?" I said.

"I have everything I need, darling. I'll see you this afternoon with your gentleman friend."

I was glad that was all set up and I had primed her about Dr Marcus doing his thing, which was a white lie but it might allay her suspicions. I decided to put on a fancy summer dress with some make-up and smart shoes so that I would look nice for Richard and Dr Marcus. With careful packing, my voluminous overnight bag held my complete wardrobe.

I came out of Richard's bedroom and walked along the landing, my shoes clomping on the polished oak floor. As I descended the wide staircase, I could hear piano music coming from the dining room. It was Chopin performed exquisitely on the grand piano and I realised Richard was playing it. I had forgotten he was a musician, and for that matter, I had never heard him play before. I stopped on the staircase and sat on the step listening. I did not want to disturb him. He played the Nocturne in E flat and then the famous Valse in D flat. I was mesmerised by it. I loved classical music and Chopin was an absolute favourite of mine.

When he had finished, I wiped a tear from my eye. I stood up and continued down the stairs while he played something jazzy in complete contrast. I could not help thinking that it was staged for my benefit. He was so good at knowing what turns me on. Maybe that was conceited of me, but it made me realize that he was a gifted musician. When I entered the room, he looked up smiling. He had changed into a very smart dark suit with white shirt and red tie; he could have passed as a consultant doctor himself.

"That was really beautiful, darling," I said. "I didn't know you could play like that." He stopped playing, stood up and we embraced and kissed.

"You are more beautiful than any musical composition," he said in my ear. It was a very cheesy moment but I revelled in it and hugged him tightly.

We sat and had a light lunch of cold meats, hard-boiled eggs, new potatoes and salad, all professionally prepared and served by Mrs T. I felt as though I was staying in a five star hotel. We talked about my mother; I told Richard that she was expecting us and I was not going to say anything about Dad being alive.

"I have received a communication from Philbin on Terranus," Richard said. "Your father is well, and has completed his treatment. He has already mentioned you and expresses a wish to be reunited with you and your mother. He has his full memory back but is unable to remember what happened to him in the past five years. I told Philbin that we would be able to visit him next week. He is to tell your father that you know what has happened to him. Philbin will also tell him about your mother and while she is not well, she would not be informed yet. He will make all the arrangements and looks forward to meeting you."

Once again, my stomach turned over at the reality of the situation. Was I really going to see my supposedly dead father next week? I couldn't quite believe that I was going to fly off into the cosmos in a space ship. It felt like I was just going to take a boring thirteen-hour flight to Australia and I really wished that was the case. I was also just coming to terms with being with Richard. I loved his company and despite everything that had happened since meeting him, I would go to the end of the galaxy and back with him. Our relationship was special in so many ways.

"Don't worry Lisa," Richard said. "I so love having you with me; we will go through this together." He took hold of my hand and kissed it. "The trip to Honshu will be easy and comfortable; it is all a question of scale. I guarantee it will be a lot more pleasant than flying in the awful polluting jet planes on Earth where you are packed like sardines in a tin." Richard was picking up my thoughts and I wondered if I could learn to turn them off.

"So my father knows that I know," I said.

"Philbin will give him a full report."

"Who is Philbin?" I asked.

"Philbin is an agent for the Council; he lives on the planet Honshu. I know him quite well; he is a reliable man. He has been assigned to your father's case and we can trust him to be sympathetic. Your father has to stay in the detention centre for the time being while they investigate his case."

Mrs T brought in a pot of coffee and poured us both a cup. She smiled at me and left the room.

"Where do we stay when we get to this planet?" I asked.

"Well, I usually rent a holiday apartment," Richard said as he sipped his coffee, "but if you prefer we can stay with Horace."

I thought about it for a moment and decided that a holiday apartment had a better ring to it and Richard acknowledged my thought. He stood up and stretched.

"Darius will be here soon," he said. "I'll go and bring the car round; we will leave as soon as you're ready."

I finished my coffee and decided not to think and just go with the flow. I felt I could trust Richard implicitly and enjoyed him being in charge of the situation.

I was ready and wandered into the hall. The front door was open so I went through and stood under the front portico. The weather was turning bad after the morning sunshine and the rain was coming down in stair rods again. I had a light anorak in my Mary Poppins bag upstairs and decided to go fetch it. By the time I had returned Richard had parked this huge black BMW 4x4 with blacked out windows under the portico. He walked round the back of the car and took my anorak. He opened the back door and put it on the seat. He then took me by the waist and we stood under cover of the portico looking out onto the lawn.

"Horace is just coming in," he said. "Are you ready for this?" I put my arm around his waist in return and confidently gave him a squeeze. The rain was bucketing down but suddenly there was a warm breeze in my face, and the rain seemed to stop. Then I saw the shape of the egg lowering towards the ground. It was huge and you could easily see the rain running off an invisible imaginary surface. If I had not seen the ship the other night, I would have thought I was being confronted by a horrendous ghostly presence. The shape gently came to a stop about twenty feet above the lawn and hovered. It certainly wasn't so invisible with the rain pouring off it in rivulets down the sides.

Very quickly, a man appeared from the feet upwards at the base of the egg, a sight I was now familiar with, having seen Richard do the same in my back field at home. In an instant, the man was at full height, carrying a small black case in one hand and an umbrella in the other. He walked towards us and by the time he had reached the end of the lawn the dripping apparition known as Horace had slowly raised itself and was gone out of sight.

Dr Marcus was also wearing a dark suit but blue as opposed to Richard's grey suit. He was dark haired and tall like Richard but at least ten years older. He was very dapper and looked as though he had just come out of Harley Street. He walked up to Richard and shook him by the hand.

"Richard," he said smiling warmly, "good to see you. It has been quite a few months. Are you keeping well?" He had a slight Italian accent and sounded well educated. I thought he should impress my mother.

"Thanks for coming out at short notice, Darius," Richard said. "May I present you to my very dear friend, Lisa?" Dr Marcus turned to me and I immediately felt warmth emanating from him.

"Doctor Lisa Macdonald, I am very pleased to meet you. I have heard so much about you from Richard."

"Thank you Doctor Marcus," I said while I shook his strong hand. "It is very kind of you to treat my mother."

"Please call me Darius," he said, "and may I call you Lisa?" I nodded politely while Richard intervened.

"Let's get the show on the road and we can talk en route." He opened the front door of the car for me.

"Let Darius sit in the front," I said as I opened the back door. "I will be happier in the back and you and Darius can then talk."

We all climbed in and Richard roared off down the drive. En route, Richard and Darius chatted freely. I couldn't really make out what they were saying but I was content to sit and admire the beautiful Scottish scenery, which was all the more dramatic with the heavy rain blowing down the glens. I kept getting Richard's thoughts; they were vague but I knew he was thinking of me and it was extremely comforting. It didn't seem long before we were entering the beautiful city of Edinburgh with its wide streets and magnificent buildings. It was lovely to be driven so I could absorb the sights. But in no time at all we were entering the main entrance to the hospital.

A porter came up to the car as Richard pulled up and we all got out. Richard handed him the keys and he drove off leaving us right outside. A doctor in a white coat who seemed to know Darius soon came towards us with a greeting. Darius introduced us to the doctor. We were quickly ushered through the main entrance. I realized that there was something going on at a different level from what I was used to. We were being treated like VIPs and it was obvious that Darius had been to the hospital before, probably treating patients. I wondered whether the other doctor knew he was talking to an alien from outer space.

Darius told us he would be along to see Mrs Macdonald in about half an hour and we were to 'conduct our visit' normally. I got the impression that he had done this before. Reading his thoughts, I realised that he didn't want us to blow his cover.

I was getting used to my new telepathic qualities and consequently felt at ease with the situation, although I must admit he was the only other person besides Richard who knowingly understood the situation.

I suddenly realised that I had not brought anything for my mother, not even a bunch of flowers. Richard turned to me and took me by the arm.

"Tell you what, darling," he said, "you go on ahead and I'll pop to the garage down the road and get something for your mother. I'm meeting her for the first time and I should create a good impression."

Once again Richard was one step ahead of me and I thanked him for the kind thought. Darius and the other doctor in the white coat had disappeared and had been replaced by a nurse who was hovering by me. To my surprise she escorted me to my mother's room. I felt very important. It was a refreshing change when normally I would be fighting for a parking place and would have had to walk down miles of endless corridors. She had been moved to a different room; it was much larger with a lovely view of the city.

She had dolled herself up and was wearing her wig but although she looked good I could see she wasn't well; she had lost weight in her face.

"Darling," she said, "you look tired; are you alright? I hope that your gentleman friend is not tiring you out. By the way, where is he?"

"Hello Mum," I said as I kissed her on the cheek. She was wearing a lot of powder and I had to surreptitiously wipe my lips. "We haven't had much time and he has popped out to get you something nice; he will be along in a minute." I sat down in the plush chair by her bedside.

"Do you know, darling, I don't know what has happened. They have moved me into this room. I have been attended to hand and foot, and have had a lovely breakfast. The hospital service has really improved."

"I'm so glad Mum, how are you?"

"I'm fine. I have just had trouble holding food down, but it is better now. I should eat more sensibly. I'm not stupid though; there could be a strong possibility that the cancer is still there."

"Richard arranged for a top notch consultant to look at you; he has friends in high places," I said.

"I am looking forward to meeting Richard. He looks very handsome in the pictures I have seen. How did you meet him?"

"I had to treat his housekeeper's dog," I said. "But apparently he had met me before at the dog rescue centre. I don't actually remember the event but when his housekeeper had some trouble with her dog he asked for me by name."

"Darling, that is so romantic," she gushed. "So he made a point of meeting you again?"

"He is wonderful and he is going to change my life in a way I cannot explain, Mum." I suddenly felt very emotional and burst into tears.

Mum held my hand and I realised that I must pull myself together before I spilled the beans.

"Darling, what is the matter?" Mum stroked my hair and I desperately tried to control myself. "You must tell me if something is wrong darling. Are you pregnant?"

"No Mum, it is not that," I sobbed. "It is very complicated and I will tell you about it all soon. I'm sorry to be so silly; it is just that a lot has happened recently."

"Take your time darling. If you really love him it will sort itself out. I know you don't think my marriage with your father was particularly successful but I tried my best. He was very involved in his research but the times we had together were wonderful and I don't regret one minute of it. If Richard is difficult just give him some space and you will be fine."

I gathered myself together and decided that I would never wear mascara ever again. I used the hospital tissues and sorted myself out in the mirror on the wall. There was a knock on the door; it was Richard. I embraced him. I took him by surprise and he held me tightly.

"Lisa, are you alright?" he said, releasing me.

"I'm OK. I must be a bit tired and I was feeling very emotional."

He was holding a huge bunch of flowers. "Please come and meet my mother; everything is alright," I said shakily.

He walked over to my mother while I clung stupidly to his arm.

"You are obviously Mr Varnicus," Mum said. "I'm very pleased to meet you." She outstretched her hand and Richard graciously took it.

"I am very happy to meet you also," Richard said, "and please call me Richard. These are for you." He laid the flowers on the bed, drew up another chair and we sat down awkwardly while my mother eyed Richard up and down.

"The flowers are beautiful," my mother said after an age. "You shouldn't have bothered. It is a thrill to meet you. I have always admired your work. I don't suppose I could be very annoying and ask you for your autograph." I was surprised at my mother's request, but Richard miraculously produced a postcard out of his pocket with his picture on it and proceeded to write something on it in his lovely handwriting. I was quite taken aback; I didn't think my mother was in to that sort of thing and I didn't expect Richard to oblige either. As usual he was picking up my thoughts and looked at me with a whimsical expression.

"I know," he said, "my new manager makes me carry these cards around with me. I don't like them but it so happens I had one in my pocket."

"I hope I'm not being a bother," Mum said.

"Not at all Mrs Macdonald," Richard said, "and I don't know your Christian name."

Mum told him her name and Richard handed her the card. She was absolutely delighted and gave it pride of place, propping it up on her bedside cabinet. I surreptitiously looked at it; it read: 'To Morag, mother of the most beautiful daughter in the world'. They both started idly chatting and I felt a little out of it so I went into a daydream. I didn't pay attention until I heard my name mentioned.

"Lisa is looking very tired. I think she overdoes it at work. You will make sure she is alright while I am stuck in this hospital, won't you Richard?"

"Mum! You don't need to say that. I'm fine," I said indignantly.

"I'm afraid that it's my fault," Richard said. "We have had a very busy weekend and Lisa does work too hard. I have persuaded her to take some time off work next week and we will have a short holiday together. I do hope you are in agreement."

"I think it is a wonderful idea," Mum said. "She hasn't had a holiday for as long as I can remember. I hope you take her somewhere nice." *Clever Richard*, I thought, *he managed to get that sorted out very quickly.* I really thought Mum would be upset if I went away while she was in here.

"We are just going to take a three-day visit to the Mediterranean; I thought Corsica would be nice," Richard lied. "Lisa can ring you to see how you are getting on and when you are better you should have a similar break."

Mum opened her mouth to answer when there was another knock at the door. A nurse entered, carrying a tray with a blue cloth covering it. Following closely behind her was Doctor Marcus who swept into the room with an air of authority.

"Good afternoon Mrs Macdonald; I am Doctor Marcus. How are you today?"

"Good afternoon," she said, "are you the consultant?"

"I am indeed, Mrs Macdonald; I will only take up a few minutes of your time."

I noticed he was already holding a small handheld device that looked like a mobile phone but he held it at waist level with the screen pointing at my mother. Mum didn't see it at all.

"Would you like my visitors to leave while you examine me Doctor?" Mum asked with a worried look on her face.

"That will not be necessary, Mrs Macdonald. I am fully aware of your case. All I would like to do is give you a small injection. The injection is necessary so that we can carry out a test tomorrow morning; there is nothing to worry about. The injection will make you feel more comfortable. Excuse me for a moment."

He turned to the nurse and placed the device on the tray. I couldn't see what they were doing but within seconds he turned back to my mother and took hold of her hand. He stroked the veins on the back of her hand a few times and pointed a cylindrical object no bigger than a fountain pen as if he were going to write a note onto her hand. It was all over in seconds. The fountain pen went back onto the tray and the nurse covered it all up with the blue cloth.

"Thank you, Mrs Macdonald. That will be all for now. You will be feeling better very shortly." They both smiled and left the room. My mother lay there with her mouth open.

"What on earth was all that about?" she exclaimed. "The hospital staff are all going quite mad."

"The hospital has got some new procedures," Richard said. "I know Doctor Marcus personally and he is the best in his field."

My mother soon dismissed the incident and Richard chatted freely to her. Mum asked about his family and she got the story I had received about his parents retiring and going to live in Australia. He was a very convincing liar but it didn't worry me any more. I instinctively knew better now. Mum also talked about Dad. It was a bit unnerving. She never usually liked to talk about him, but Richard was very interested and Mum was in her element. She could really open up to him. It made me wonder if she had any idea what was really going on but I dismissed the paranoid thought. I actually learned a few things about my father that I had not realised before. Apparently Mum was bowled over by my father when they were courting. She said that she had never known a man so sensitive and caring about her own feelings. It occurred to me that this was a result of his planetary origins.

I was feeling very tired. Richard decided that we had better get back home; he could see that I was beginning to glaze over. We left Mum in good spirits and I felt so relieved that the visit was over.

It was just the two of us driving back. We made plans en route or at least Richard did. I was having trouble just staying awake. Richard told me that Doctor Marcus was staying on at the hospital and had other patients to see. Horace was going to pick him up and take him back to his apartment in Hampstead Heath when he had finished. Richard also told me that he had to go to London on Monday to do a recording session with a newly established pop group. I was worried that he would be overdoing it, but Horace was going to take him there and the session was all planned and should be routine. I shouldn't worry about Richard; he is a very good organiser and I was too tired to concern myself. Apparently, Doctor Marcus had a docking station for Horace at his apartment enabling Richard to make the trip from Scotland to London and be in the centre of the city by taxi in an amazing twenty minutes.

I had not been home since Friday, so we picked up my stuff and Richard thankfully took me home. He told me that I was to go in to work on Monday morning as normal, although I wasn't sure what was normal, and then book a holiday for the rest of the week. If Hamish got snotty about it, I was instructed to ring Richard so that he could pull a few strings. What strings he could pull were beyond me but I now knew he had friends in high places and anything could be possible. Richard said he would call in at my house on Monday night to see that all was well. He also gave me his mobile phone number so that was that.

We finally got back to my place in his comfortable BMW. My head was reeling, but I had the plan in place and was secretly happy to see my little house. It was a warm evening. The sun was low and red in the sky after the rain. We embraced in the car and kissed sensitively. I knew I loved him and despite my tiredness I felt very happy and at ease with the situation. Watching him drive away made me feel suddenly alone, but it was lovely to get in through my front door into familiar surroundings. I got very busy and sorted myself out doing some laundry and a bit of house cleaning. I put a frozen ready-meal in the oven and had a hot bath. By the time I had finished my domestic chores and had a meal it was nearly midnight. I must have got a second wind to revitalise myself, but after the meal I crawled into bed for a welcome sleep.

The next day all was quiet at work and Hamish granted me my holiday leave for the rest of the week without any fuss. In fact he insisted upon it. I told him my mother was ill and I had a lot of things to sort out, which was all very true. I was able to leave work early. After doing a bit of shopping, I got home and cooked up a Bolognese. I made some extra just in case Richard wanted a meal, if and when he called round.

It was about six when the phone rang. It was Richard saying that he was just about to arrive and Horace was landing in the field at the back of my house. I ran out into the garden and saw Richard materialise in the field just as he had done before. Suddenly, I felt concerned that none of the neighbours were watching, but it only took a few seconds. He walked towards me looking fresh and well dressed in a brightly coloured summer shirt and white trousers. I had forgotten that Horace had bathroom facilities on board. He had showered and changed en route from London. How civilised, I thought.

After opening a bottle of wine we sat down in my living room, glasses in hand. The air outside was damp and humid.

"How was London?" I asked.

"Hot and busy. I had three songs to rehearse with the group. They got it together really well. I am very pleased. Janet said the group were very pleased as well."

"Who's Janet?"

"She's the blonde bombshell who sorts out my musical stuff."

"Oh yes, I remember her. Who's the group?"

"I can't tell that. I'll let you know if they are successful."

"It's a boy band isn't it?" I said reading his mind.

"How do you feel about the trip tomorrow?" he said changing the subject.

"Bugger, I'm trying not to think about it too much," I said, putting my head in my hands. "At least I have had a normal day today."

"You don't have to go if you are not sure. You can always take some time to think about it. It can be arranged at a later date." I suddenly wondered if Richard was trying to put me off. But then I read his mind again.

"Have you got something arranged with your parents?"

"No. But my mother has arranged something for me. I can't really get out of it. It won't affect your reunion with your father."

"Do you want me to come with you?" I said, looking into his

eyes.

"Darling Lisa, I don't want to be without you. I want you to see for yourself what this is all about. It is just amazing that this business with your father has complicated the situation. You will see another world and some strange things. I just want to know that you are up to facing it." It didn't matter what he said. I could sense that it was alright.

"Fuck it. I wouldn't miss this for the world."

We embraced and kissed. I could sense love and passion. We didn't have to say anything. We went upstairs to my bedroom and made love. As always, it was glorious and we were in bed until the sun had set and my Bolognese was cold and forgotten.

CHAPTER 17

The next morning Richard woke me quite early. He said he had some preparations to make. I watched in the garden as he vanished feet upwards in the field at the back and was whisked away in the invisible Horace. The dawn chorus was in full swing, ignoring the event.

I was revitalised and ready for a weird and exciting day. I packed my case with enough clothes for a week, although Richard said we would only be away for four days. It is not often you get to travel to another solar system fourteen light years away to see your father who was supposedly dead. I was very nervous so I made sure I was well prepared.

Richard picked me up at noon right on time; this time he was driving the Jag. I rushed out to greet him. We embraced and kissed. I sensed that he was happy and excited about the trip. I was beside myself with apprehension at the thought of the adventure that lay before us. At least he would be with me and I soaked up his Aura, which was full of assurance.

He put my heavy case in the back seat and we drove to the island without speaking while Richard played some 1940s' jazz music on the car stereo; it was very soothing and I closed my eyes, ignoring his speedy driving. It wasn't long before we pulled up outside the front entrance. Jack was waiting at the front door; I hadn't seen him since he called at my house with the box of chocolates. He managed a creaky smile and pulled my case out of the back of the car. Richard handed him the keys and he drove off, presumably to park it in the garage.

"We are going to board Horace from my bedroom balcony," Richard said, as he ushered me through the huge oak front door. "I had this new access route installed weeks ago and I haven't used it yet. It is very similar to the one Marcus uses in London. It is better for security and convenience as it doesn't require the use of the ship's lift, which, as we know, can be very confusing to an innocent bystander."

I didn't question the statement as we climbed the stairs; I was ready for anything and felt completely at ease as we went into his bedroom and through the French doors onto the balcony. There was a cluster of house sparrows on the balustrade. They were chattering amongst themselves and pooping on the stonework. They ignored us completely.

I didn't have time to think about them. Suddenly the balustrade opened, creating a wide gap. The birds fluttered off. Then a vertical black line seven feet tall appeared in the air and a dark porthole opened up. I took a step back in utter amazement. I could see inside the porthole and recognised the interior of the ship. The windows were open and you could just see the trees beyond. It was quite weird as if looking at a room suspended in mid air and, to the uninitiated, you would not have known that a huge spaceship was lurking outside the window. I shivered at the sight. Richard put his arm around me.

"Don't worry," he said. "I know it looks strange. When we get to Terranus we won't have any of this security business. The ships that move around on the planet surface are all brightly coloured and you can actually see them." I tried to create a mental picture of lots of brightly coloured Horace shaped ships. Richard disappeared into the bathroom. He quickly returned carrying his own suitcase, which was a fraction of the size of mine. I was thinking that I must go and fetch my own.

"Jack should be bringing your case up shortly," Richard said with his normal anticipation. Jack soon appeared struggling in through the door with the case; he was puffing and wheezing alarmingly.

"Jack, can you put it into the ship."

"Right you are," he muttered, limping through into the void and disappearing.

Richard looked at me; we didn't need to say anything to each other. We stepped off the balcony onto a familiar, but suspended maroon carpet and into the body of the ship. Once inside all was well. I got my bearings. The front view window was open and I could see the trees and a glimpse of the sea beyond. It was certainly a far better way of entering the ship without the stomach-churning ride in the lift from the ground. Jack appeared from the corridor and wished us a good trip; he shook hands with Richard and with a broad grin on his face he went out of the porthole and through Richard's bedroom. I wondered what was going through his mind but realised it was a blank to me and I could not read it. Perhaps he didn't want me to.

"OK, Horace, what is the status?" Richard said, snapping me out of my mind wanderings.

"We are clear to go at any time up to one hour. Passage on the transporter has been allocated." Horace replied dutifully. "May I say how pleased I am seeing Dr Macdonald on board again."

"Thank you Horace," I said. "But please refer to me as Lisa."

"My apologies," Horace replied. "You shall now be referred to as 'Lisa' until I am advised otherwise."

I was sure I could sense sarcasm in his otherwise bland voice.

"OK," Richard said, "let's get the show on the road. We have to spend a night in this bucket so let's get the bedroom sorted out."

I followed him into the rear corridor and we entered the now familiar 'let's get weightless room'. The room was not as I knew it with the padded walls and floor. It had a thick white carpet and there was a double bed with white silky sheets. There was a built-in cupboard for hanging clothes and a built-in table with a mirror behind it. I say 'built-in' but in actual fact, the whole arrangement had a seamless appearance similar to the bathroom as if moulded from black shiny plastic.

"Is this the same room we were in before?" I asked.

"Yes, the ship has only one recreational room. Depending on what you want, it can be set to any program. Don't you like the décor? I can change it if you like."

"It is the same as the bathroom and it looks a bit stark for a bedroom," I said. "Perhaps it could be a different colour, say maroon and soft velvet."

"Horace, did you hear what Lisa said? She wants maroon and soft velvet."

"Perhaps Lisa would prefer this program," Horace replied. The sarcasm was there again. I wondered whether Richard and Horace were ganging up on me. The room miraculously changed before our eyes. The black shine went matt and grew a textured finish. Then it went a lovely rich dark red colour. I ran my hand over the walls in disbelief. All the black plastic looked and felt like soft velvet.

"Would Lisa like some matching drapes over the porthole walls?" Horace said. I suddenly thought he might be gay, but dismissed the idea as ridiculous.

"OK Horace," I said, but I didn't understand the question.

There were no open windows, or I should say portholes. But there were plasma screens at each end of the bedroom, measuring about four feet long by three feet high. They were raised from the walls and had rounded edges. They had a soft amber glow and illuminated the room similar to candlelight. I hardly noticed it, but above the porthole a black rail was growing out of the curved wall along the length of the room. Then at each end a curtain dropped out of nowhere. I touched one as it lightly rested on the carpeted floor. It was cream coloured with a gentle pattern of what seemed to be wild red roses. It was absolutely beautiful.

"Thank you Horace, it looks lovely."

"You are welcome, Miss Lisa."

"You get yourself sorted out and join me up front when you're ready," Richard said with a bemused smile. I don't think he was concerned with the décor.

He kissed me on the cheek and left the room. I started to unpack a few things and hang them up in the cupboard. The room was very claustrophobic. I wasn't sure if the portholes would give a view of the outside world. I decided to be brave and ask Horace.

"Horace, can you hear me?" I said doubtingly.

"Yes Lisa," he replied instantly, "how can I help?"

"Oh, er … thank you for answering," I said, somehow surprised he would answer me. "Is it possible to have the windows that look outside open?" I realised that the question did not quite come out right.

"There are two windows that can be activated to give an external view; it is not possible to open a porthole to the exterior atmosphere. If you are not happy with the temperature or quality of air, just let me know and I will try to make it comfortable for you. Would you like me to activate the window to give an external view?"

"Yes please, Horace."

The panels on each side glowed with light and lit up the room with sunlight. I could see the garden with the pond outside. I was feeling much happier, and secretly pleased to have communicated with Horace without Richard being there. When I had finished sorting out my things I was tempted to unpack Richard's small bag, which was set down by the bed, but thought better of it. I went through to the front cabin and found Richard sitting at the console tapping something on the screen. I could see the words 'Terranus Security Clearance' with some strange symbols below that I did not understand.

"Tell me darling," I asked, "when you talk to Horace can you hear him all over the ship?"

"If you're in another room he will only answer you in that

room. You'll find that he is very discreet and a mine of information. Feel free to ask him anything; he can be a real friend. If you need to get his attention, just call 'Horace' or 'computer'. He doesn't normally listen to conversations unless he detects a security risk."

"I can do that," I said sitting down beside him. "I have a thousand questions to ask him."

"Are you ready to go?" he said. "I'll explain what happens when we are underway; it will take about nine hours to get into deep space and join the interstellar transporter. The transporter will only take about half an hour and then we just decelerate on our approach to Terranus, which takes about thirty minutes." I didn't really understand what Richard had said but nodded and smiled confidently.

"Horace, you can get under way," Richard said.

"Take off will be immediate," Horace replied.

The shaft of light created by the doorway to Richard's bedroom balcony rapidly closed up and within seconds the ship gracefully and silently lifted. The ground dropped away at alarming speed; we seemed to be rising vertically with the sea and mountains soon becoming misty and losing definition. I felt as though I should feel a rising sensation but if I closed my eyes there was no sense of movement at all. Before long we were way above the clouds, which looked angry and explosive with more impending thunderstorms.

Soon I could clearly see the curvature of the Earth and the haze of atmosphere surrounding it. We now seemed to be accelerating forwards as the blue planet dropped away; it was a sight I would never tire of, but this time it disappeared in the blink of an eye. Now the blackness of space and the bright stars lay before us; it all happened so quickly.

"Beginning light speed acceleration in one minute," Horace said, "please remain in your seats."

Richard was still touching icons on the console in front of

him and had not taken his eyes off the screen during the whole take-off.

"I suppose you have done this many times," I said.

"Done what?" he said finally looking up from his unintelligible hieroglyphics.

"Travelled into space," I said, feeling irritated.

"I'm sorry darling; I didn't mean to ignore you. I only do this sort of interstellar trip once or twice a year. I must admit it is always a good time to do a bit of work, but I can do this later."

I suddenly felt a surge of power, a bit like taking off in a jet plane; Horace was always so smooth with his manoeuvres but this time I felt as though I had suddenly gained a hundred pounds in weight. I gripped Richard's arm in panic.

"What on earth is happening now?"

"Don't worry, the sensation will only last a minute or two. We are starting the acceleration to light speed. It will pass when we are free of Earth's gravity. It will take about nine hours before we reach the transporter. It is usually much faster."

"Why do we have to go to this transporter? Can't Horace fly us all the way there?" I realised the question sounded puerile but I thought it was about time I understood what was going on.

"OK," Richard said, taking my hand. "Horace is quite capable of taking us to Terranus. The only thing is he can only travel at the speed of light. He is not equipped to open time and space gateways like the transporter. Without that ability it would take us a long time to get there. One day it may be possible for Horace to do it."

"Fourteen years to fly to Terranus," I said intelligently.

"That's right. The transporters have the technology to move us through the time and space continuum so we can travel the distance in a matter of milliseconds. All we have to do is accelerate up to their speed, which takes a lot of power and a bit of time. When we are travelling fast enough we can rendezvous with the transporter and hitch a ride."

"So this transporter is already travelling at the speed of light."

"Yes, I think about 190,000 miles a second. Once in commission the transporters never stop. They just do a huge figure of eight in space collecting passengers en route and when they have a full load they do the space time warp thing and you end up somewhere else. They work on a schedule and Horace ties up with them so that we don't have to wait for the next time warp."

"So we have to meet up with this transporter while travelling at a mind-blowing speed?" I was desperately trying to get my head round this. "It all sounds incredibly dangerous. What if we hit an asteroid or a planet or something?"

"Don't worry," Richard said, "they have been doing this for 300 years. The space that we travel in is all mapped and recorded. Any obstacles are dealt with by a course correction or destruction. Space is a vast area, which is an understatement, and the ship's path is monitored. Horace projects a tubular force field ahead of him. That is the purpose of the large disc at the rear of the ship. Horace travels down the tube like a bullet in a rifle. The computer's sensors can make minute course corrections if necessary. This sort of flight pattern is never done in uncharted space. There is nothing to worry about."

I sat back and tried to relax while thinking about time warping and travelling great distances in seconds. I dismissed my concerns while I felt a wave of confidence emanating from Richard. It made me feel more comfortable. I knew I could completely trust him. I looked outside the window and was mesmerised.

We were now moving past the stars and you could get a sensation of speed. I could recognise a planet; I watched as it grew larger and we flashed past it in seconds. It was a vivid bright orange colour and I wondered what it was.

"That was Pluto; we are leaving our solar system," Richard said, obviously tuning into my thoughts again.

"Light speed acceleration has now been implemented," Horace announced. "You may leave your seats."

Without realising it, the heavy sensation I felt earlier had passed. Apart from the slight hissing sound the ship was perfectly quiet. My mouth was dry and, feeling confident, I wondered whether I could get a drink. I stood up and stretched. My rather short black skirt had ridden up. I adjusted the hem.

"You have the sexiest legs," Richard said, looking up from his colourful screen.

"Don't be saucy," I replied, smiling down at him. "Can you show me how to work the gismo in the kitchen? I want to see if it is possible to make some tea."

"Tell you what," he replied. "I'm a bit busy here, and it's very easy. Ask Horace to tell you what to do."

I went into the kitchen and stared at the machine. It looked a bit like the machines you would find in a motorway café, with a place for putting a cup underneath and four spouts so you can watch it spill everywhere.

"Horace," I said, "can you show me how to make a cup of tea?"

"I certainly can, Lisa. I'm assuming you mean using the drink maker; if not I have some interesting video footage of Delia Smith making tea."

"Horace, you are a wag."

"Please explain 'a wag'."

"Oh dear," I said, "don't worry Horace. I thought you were making a joke."

"I shall remember that 'a wag' is a joking person," Horace said. "I have a huge repertoire of jokes; would you like to hear one, Lisa?"

"Not now, Horace, I want some tea. Where are the cups kept?"

"They are in the cupboard above. Place the cups on the circles below the dispenser and tell me which beverages you require."

I followed Horace's instructions; there were four circles so I placed two clear glass mugs each on a circle.

"I would like two cups of tea with milk and one with sugar."
I waited in anticipation to see what sort of mess the machine
would make and wondered if I had placed the cups on the correct
circles. Nothing happened. Then I remembered what Richard
had said.

"I'm sorry Horace, did you hear."

"Yes, Lisa," came the reply, "I heard your last statement. I
don't know whether the Master has explained. I can only respond
to a command by name. Although I can use my discretion, I
prefer this arrangement to avoid confusion. Please specify your
preference regarding the type of tea."

"Oh dear," I said to myself, feeling a bit irritated. "Just ordinary tea, Horace."

"Ordinary tea with milk," said Horace, "the right hand cup
will have two units of sugar; please confirm."

"Thank you Horace. That's fine." The cups filled and the
machine behaved itself. Feeling relieved, I took them through to
the front cabin.

Richard was now sitting at the table staring out of the window.
The stars were flashing past like streaks of light. Richard was
looking at a beautiful orange and red glow in the distance that
reminded me of a distant thundercloud. I sat down on the plush
chair next to him and put the cups on the table.

"What is that you're looking at?" I asked.

"It's a small nebula, a cloud of dust and gas."

"Tell me Richard," I asked, "are there any intelligent beings
on Terranus that don't look like us?"

"You mean little green men with poppy-out eyes?" Richard
laughed.

"You know what I mean; surely there is intelligent life not of
our own species."

"Curiously enough, that is a difficult question to answer,"
Richard said with a bemused expression. "We only know of the
three planets in the Terranus system. Then there is our own

Earth and one other, which is twenty-five light years away. These planets are the only ones we know of that have the right conditions for supporting life as we know it. A truly alien life form, in other words, a life form that doesn't share our DNA, has not been discovered yet. There are plenty of planets that have weird and hostile environments but our scientists haven't come across any recognisable life forms. Space is a huge place and anything is possible. Our scientists have only scratched the surface. So far, the farthest any explorers have been is 150 light years away. However, there are a wide variety of mammals that have advanced intelligence," Richard continued with gathering enthusiasm. "In fact, there are many species of primates living on Terranus who have developed language, albeit rather crudely. They have a simple way of life and live in harmony with humans. There are also several tribes of bipedal people who survived the past wars. They are the products of evolution. One particular tribe is very similar to our chimpanzee. They are only about three feet tall. They have a language and their own culture. They are brilliant at growing their own food and carving wood. They make souvenirs for the tourists. The craftsmanship is outstanding."

"How fascinating," I said. "I would love to meet them. What other animals are there?"

"There is an animal similar to the horse. They also have intelligence and language. They are very common on Terranus. In exchange for food, they provide us with transport. They have telepathic abilities and have their own network. If you asked one to take you on a 1,000-mile journey, they would organise it for you. The amazing thing is, they don't use any blasted mobile phones." Richard sat back and sighed.

"You have only mentioned mammals so far," I said, intrigued. "What about other species?"

Richard sighed again. "One thing I can tell you is that there are no reptiles. There are no birds or feathered creatures. No snakes or lizards and certainly no dinosaurs."

"Why is that?" I said, now totally out of control.

Richard sipped his tea. He looked tired. "Terranus was a cold planet thousands of years ago. It was colder than the sister planet Honshu. Maybe that could be the reason. Horace can show you a vast amount of information on the planet's history. As a biologist I am sure you will find it very interesting."

Richard got up and left the room. I knew he was tired but I had to know what to expect while we hurtled past the stars. I had thousands of questions. I would much rather ask him than talk to Horace. It felt very strange talking to a spaceship.

When he came back, he carried two glassed of wine and his box of Golden Virginia. He handed me a glass and a chocolate tube, took one himself and sat back looking contented.

"This space transporter. How does it work.?" I asked.

"Well, the concepts of travelling through time only work if you know where you want to be and at what time you want to be there. You cannot just materialise anywhere at random in the future. It just doesn't work like that. In fact, you could quite easily arrive in the centre of a sun and get fried if you don't know where you want to be. On the other hand, if you don't know the time period you could materialise near a sun that was about to explode. They are building new transporters all the time and gradually opening up new gateways. We at least stand a chance of spreading our net a bit further now, but you can only do it in stages. It is not safe to travel through the time continuum at random. Before you ask, you also can't change the future."

"OK," I said.

I took a sip of wine, sucked on my chocolate straw, and contemplated the subject. I didn't want to flood Richard with questions but I couldn't quell my apprehension.

"So, Earth is just another planet that has been populated by the people from Terranus," I continued. "Did we evolve from the apes or come from outer space?"

Richard turned to me with a concerned look on his face.

"Don't dismiss evolution. When planet Earth had been discovered some 10,000 years ago, it had undergone its own cycle of life and evolution. Darwin had the right idea. You can't stop animal life from evolving to combat the fight for survival. The same thing is happening on Terranus and it is an unchangeable fact of nature. There were primitive people already inhabiting the planet Earth. We tried not to interfere with their way of life and let them evolve naturally. However, although the new immigrants were conditioned and had the memory of their origin removed, the treatment was not successful. Their own evolution was in advance of the indigenous life. Their brains were much larger. They were able to create powerful civilisations. They prospered, they fought, and in ignorance, they died. They were confused and worshipped many gods. You know I am referring to Inca, Aztec, Egyptian, even Roman civilisations. There are many. The only good thing is that the ancestors have survived. Most of planet Earth's ancient history comes from outer space. It is a sad story of life and death. Give the Earth another 10,000 years and the other primates will be using a more sophisticated form of language. I'm afraid all we did was add to the population, both human and animal. The Terranus system was overcrowded, polluted and war torn. Ever since man first learned how to overcome gravity and fly to other planets, a terrible war broke out between Terranus and Honshu. People left the system in search of a better place. Thankfully, now we are wiser and the balance of life is controlled. Although we are carefully monitoring the situation on Earth, the same will happen there. Homo sapiens are an incredibly successful species. We feed off the planets like bacteria; you have to believe the concept that planets are living things. Compared to the life span of a planet, we can overpower it in a very short space of time."

I sat back and drank my wine. I wasn't sure what Richard was saying and needed to think about it. The concept was overwhelming. One thing was for sure, as a biologist I certainly believe in evolution. Darwin was ahead of his time and even in his day; he managed to hit the nail on the head. In fact, he is the reason why I am an atheist.

"Richard," I said tentatively. "Do you believe in a God? In fact what religions are there on other planets? Is the story of Jesus from Terranus?" I felt Richard cringe and thought maybe this was a subject for a later date. He looked embarrassed, but smiled at me.

"Lisa, I am so sorry. You are quite right to question me. We still haven't got to know each other yet. I am being very selfish dragging you off into the unknown. I wish we had more time."

"We have plenty of time," I said sternly. "Answer the question." I now felt embarrassed, and hoped I hadn't overstepped the mark.

"Well, I know you are not religious, I can see inside your mind." Now I was really embarrassed and started to feel hot. I turned my gaze to the fireworks outside the window. I could at least sense his emotion, which was kindly, but I was unable to read his thoughts.

"It is very difficult to answer your questions," he said diplomatically. He touched my arm and made me look at him. "I believe in natural forces in the universe that are way beyond our lowly status. There are forces that still require understanding and scientific exploration. I don't believe in Christ. He is an Earth bound fictional character who has absolutely no origins from the Terranus system. Politics and religion, in their corrupt form, do not exist on Terranus. There is a strong sense of community, exploration and scientific discovery. We worship a communal understanding. There are many cultural events that encompass council decisions, entertainment and topical debates. Given time you will feel more at ease with the situation. I do love you and admire your spirit."

I kissed him. But I was still in full flow.

"So where did we come from? Is Terranus the origin of our species?" I asked.

"There is no absolute evidence that Terranus was populated by other planets. Also, there is no positive evidence that our species evolved on Terranus, bearing in mind that people have been on the planet a lot longer than Earth. Archaeological evidence is inconclusive but suggests that life evolved as it did on Earth. Until proven otherwise we believe that our species may well have originated on Terranus. Space is a bit like the ocean with life floating at random in it. It is a matter of scale; space is so vast. To us the soup is watered down."

Again, I looked outside the window and watched the stars streak by like fast moving bolts of lightning. Some were just like straight beams of light stretching as far as the eye could see, and then they would suddenly disappear in a flash of bright light. I didn't want to think about the fact that I may have come from outer space. Thankfully, Richard intervened.

"We have another eight hours before we join the transporter; shall we have something to eat and then get some sleep? We have a long day tomorrow."

"I should have made some sandwiches," I said and Richard laughed.

"Horace carries a stock of food. They are a bit like airline meals but very nice." Richard addressed the room, "Horace, what is there on the dinner menu?"

"I have Topian stew, Braised Pyland Fish Steaks, Atlantis Sea Salad and Bangers and Mash, sir," Horace replied. I could not believe my ears.

"Did he say 'bangers and mash'?" I asked.

"Yes he did," Richard laughed again. "Marcus has that put on board; it is his favourite. He has a top restaurant in London prepare it and they put it in the special trays that Horace uses to store it. You can't get bangers and mash on Terranus."

"How resourceful," I said. "I don't recognise anything else so that sounds like my favourite also."

"I'm going to have the Topian stew," Richard said. "It is very good; you should try it."

"I'll see what yours looks like first. Do we have to cook it?" I asked, feeling out of my depth with the strange names.

"Don't worry, Horace has an automated machine. He will unfreeze the meals and heat them up. Horace, can you prepare a Topian stew and bangers and mash?"

"Yes sir, it will be ready in fifteen minutes."

"Do you have the chocolate cake and strawberries?"

"Yes sir, I will prepare that also."

Richard was wonderful; he always knew what I liked the best and went out of his way to provide it. He got up and went into the kitchen to open a bottle of wine and get some cutlery. I sat back looking out of the window, wondering what sort of bizarre situation I was in. The cosmos outside was behaving in a very strange way, not that I would know what is normal. It was like a fireworks display outside, with streaks and balls of light flashing past. Occasionally there would be a flash of lightning, very bright like a camera flash bulb going off. Curiously, the light didn't penetrate the cabin; there was no noise at all. When Richard came back, he laid the table complete with serviettes and condiment set; he poured the wine into two exquisite crystal glasses.

"What the hell is happening outside?" I asked as the cosmos streaked and flashed.

"It is alright. We are accelerating up to light speed, and by the morning all will be quiet." He looked at me, smiling warmly.

"You have no idea how pleased I am that you are with me, Lisa," he said. "I do love you so very much. You have no idea how wonderful it is to be able to have you with me on this trip back to my home planet."

He handed me a glass of wine. I could see tears in his eyes and sense his emotion.

"Richard," I said, "I love you too. I don't understand anything at the moment but I feel safe with you even though my life has been turned upside down." We stretched across the table and kissed.

"Sir, your meals are ready," Horace exclaimed, interrupting the tender moment.

Richard disappeared into the kitchen again and soon came back carrying huge trays of food. He placed them on the table. The trays seemed to be made of white china, or was it plastic, I'm not sure. Mine was recognisable with a mound of mashed potato with three sausages poking out of it surrounded by asparagus tips and topped in rich gravy. It looked wonderful and I felt very hungry. I looked at his tray. There was a mound of unrecognisable vegetables and what looked like feta cheese. On the side, there was a baked potato cut open, the inside of which was bright orange. We ate heartily, having missed my Bolognese the other night. Richard made me try his Topian stew. I had to admit it was very tasty if not a bit too spicy. The potato tasted like the sweet potato we have on Earth. *Good grief, I'm talking like an alien!* If not reminiscent of airline quality, the food was very good and the strawberries we had for the sweet tasted very fresh. You would never have thought that the food was prepared from frozen. After our meal, we decided to turn in and get some sleep before boarding this transporter. The bed was lovely and comfortable and heated to just the right temperature. We snuggled up together under a fluffy blanket.

"Horace," Richard said quietly, "wake us when we near the transporter and reduce gravity to the Terranus setting."

I wondered what Terranus gravity meant, but suddenly felt my body feel lighter. The sensation was blissful while lying in the bed and felt very comfortable despite the fact that we were hurtling through space at heaven knows what speed.

CHAPTER 18

Horace woke me with a start.

"Wake up call. Rendezvous with the transporter will be in thirty minutes' time." Horace kept repeating it until Richard told him to shut up.

I had a quick shower in the strange but efficient shower room. We got dressed in double quick time. By the time we sat down in the front cabin with a coffee in our hands, we could already see the transporter in the distance. It was a shiny cylindrical object that seemed to glow in the gloom. There was very little light and no stars at all. It grew in size rapidly as we approached and I realised that it was absolutely huge. We seemed to be coming down on top of it. I could see that a whole section inside the craft was hollow. It was a huge void with vertical sides running the whole length of the ship as far as the eye could see. As Horace skilfully manoeuvred us into the void, you could see hundreds of doorways and thousands of windows. It was all brightly lit. Beyond the windows you could see people milling about just like at an airport terminal. Horace parked himself against the wall in an available space. It was a bit like parking in a weird, multi-storey car park. There were ships of all shapes and sizes around us.

"Docking procedure is complete," Horace piped up. "You may leave the ship. Customs officials are waiting at the gate to inspect the ship. Departure will be in thirty-five minutes."

"Thank you Horace," Richard said, turning towards me. "We have just enough time to get a coffee and a bite to eat. It will be a chance for you to see what the transporter is like. Do you fancy having some extraterrestrial food?" I nodded stupidly in agreement while gazing through the window. It did look like an airport terminal but on a massive scale.

The porthole flashed open. Richard got up and walked towards it. I grabbed my handbag, although I wasn't sure why, and followed him to the doorway. Richard met two official-looking people dressed in what I could only describe as smart boiler suits. They were waiting outside the doorway. Richard greeted them, saying something unintelligible. They bowed courteously and pointed an electrical device at him. He then took me by the arm and guided me through the porthole. The doorway opened straight onto the terminal floor, which was highly polished with the finish of pine but without the knots. The two officials bowed and looked me up and down.

"Welcome to the Terranus system space transporter," one said with a smile while the other pointed his device at me. "We are always pleased to see visitors from Earth and hope your stay will be enjoyable." They seemed happy with us and stepped aside to let us pass.

We walked into the terminal. I was astounded by the sheer size of the place. There were people dressed in unfamiliar clothes carrying luggage and walking back and forth. Richard took hold of my hand and with a reassuring smile guided me across what seemed to be a roadway that had an occasional vehicle skimming along it. They moved silently and looked a bit like a car but without any wheels. On the other side of the road there was a recognisable shopping precinct with shops and restaurants lining the road as far as the eye could see. The atmosphere was relaxed and gentle with the sound of people talking and music playing in the distance. We walked down the road for a while. I felt very self-conscious dressed in my black short skirt with black tights. People were looking at me in a funny way. A lot of the men were wearing what looked like a smock or nightshirt, which was full length and pleated. The women were wearing something similar but at least cut in such a way to show the figure. I certainly couldn't see anybody showing his or her legs and I very much felt like a foreigner. Then, in complete contrast, some young people walked past in tight revealing clothes. They were wearing what I could only describe as hot pants from the seventies. I felt better and not so exposed. Perhaps anything goes in this strange world. I made a mental note to change into some trousers when we got back to the ship.

Richard guided me into a restaurant and we sat down at a very plush table with comfortable, soft fabric covered seats. Within seconds, a beautiful young woman dressed in a figure hugging all-in-one suit was hovering over us. She had a pleasant but false smile and looked absolutely fabulous. She had no make-up, but her skin was tanned and she had immaculate long blonde hair.

"Welcome to the Bonfiglio Refreshment Lounge," she said in a false but cheerful way while handing us what looked like thin plastic calculators. The waitress smiled and walked off with a slightly overdone wobble in her bottom. I stared at the plastic sheet that was the size of an A4 envelope and realised it was an electronic menu. It had a screen with pictures of unrecognisable food scrolling down it. I promptly put it on the table as if it were going to give me an electric shock.

"Don't worry about the menu," Richard said. "You can have anything you like."

"I can't think," I said. "You choose."

"I'm not sure what some of this stuff is myself so I'm going to have a bacon sandwich and a coffee."

The thought of being able to have anything made my mind go completely blank so I said I would have the same. Richard then fiddled about with the plastic card and placed it down on the table.

"The waitress seems a bit odd," I said. "Is she from Terranus?"

"You have just met your first synthetic human," Richard said. "She was manufactured on Honshu."

"You mean she is not a real person, but a robot."

"She is a real person," Richard said. "She is made from synthetic living tissue and has a highly intelligent brain. She will have her own individual personality but has certain programming so that she is happy doing jobs like being a waitress."

"Wow," I said, "does she eat?"

"Yes, she will behave just like a normal warm-blooded person, although I think they have a special diet."

The synthetic waitress soon returned carrying a tray with our food and I realised that Richard had ordered it using the plastic menu. She placed it all neatly on the table complete with cutlery. I had a chance to study her at close range. She looked amazingly realistic although her skin was a little too perfect and she was wearing perfume, which I thought was strange for a robot. She graciously hoped that we enjoy our meal and wiggled away.

What lay before us was not bacon sandwiches. I was wondering if Richard had pressed the wrong buttons on his electronic menu. We had both been given a plate with triangular shaped pieces of fried bread, or at least I think it was bread. Poured over it was a yellow sauce which looked like custard. In the centre of the plate, there was a mound of ham that had been lightly fried and was almost recognisable. We also had several jugs placed in the centre of the table with two clear glass mugs. Richard smiled at me and proceeded to pour the contents of the jugs into the mugs and we ended up with what looked like two glasses of chocolate milk shake. I stared at the alien presentation.

"Try it," Richard said. "I have had this before; it may not look like a bacon sandwich, but you will find it tastes like one."

Richard dug in while I studied the food. I must admit it smelled absolutely gorgeous. I plucked up courage and grabbed the knife and fork. It was lovely. The bread was soft inside but crisp outside and the ham tasted smoked and melted in the mouth. The sauce was like creamy butter. The coffee did in fact taste like coffee flavoured chocolate and was heavenly. We both ate heartily and

I completely forgot where I was.

"Have we got time to look at the shops?" I asked as the last morsel of food disappeared. I felt as though I was going on holiday abroad and then realised I was in a strange alien environment and wouldn't know how to pay for anything anyway.

"I'm afraid we will have to get back to Horace very soon," Richard smiled. "We have now been transported and soon we will be approaching the Terranus system."

"You mean we have done the time warp thing? I didn't feel a thing."

"Basically we ceased to exist for a fraction of a second and then regained our existence elsewhere in space," Richard said. "It is a painless process. The fascinating thing is that if we were back on Earth it would be yesterday."

"Yesterday!" I frowned. I looked at my watch and the date was correct.

"Don't worry about changing your watch; it won't be right when we return and Earth time is useless on Terranus. The good thing is we have gained an extra day in our lives in relation to Earth time. Always useful so you can do the things you should have done yesterday," Richard chuckled.

I sat back in the soft seat and tried to get my head round it, but Richard thankfully interrupted my train of thought.

"Horace is calling us back," he said, "we will have to return. You can do some shopping on our return journey; we will have more time then."

My head was reeling as we got up from the table. I remembered that Richard had a communication device in his brain. He took me by the hand and I felt comforted by his touch.

"Should we have paid for the meal?" I suddenly realised as we walked down the wide street.

"Don't worry," he said, "it's all taken care of automatically."

I tightened my grip on his hand as we quickened our pace. I was completely lost and had no idea where we were going.

There were hundreds of doorways with strange writing above them. I would have absolutely no idea which one would be ours.

There were only a few people walking around now in their brightly coloured nightshirts so I assumed that they too had to return to their ships. Before long Richard walked towards a doorway that slid open on its own and as we walked through I thought I recognised the ship. But, as we entered, it all looked slightly different and I wondered if we had gone into the wrong ship. All the windows were closed and just glowed with a gentle magnolia coloured light. It felt very claustrophobic and to my surprise the tables with their neatly arranged seats were missing and instead there were two large black leather sofas.

"We've gone into the wrong ship!" I said in a panic.

"It's all right," Richard said as he put his arms around me. "Horace, what is our status?"

"Welcome back, Lisa, all is as it should be. Please do not be concerned," Horace said. I was relieved to hear his voice. I was about to thank him, but he interjected. "Master, we shall be leaving the transporter in five minutes. Deceleration will take thirty minutes and we shall dock at the Terranus terminal in forty-five minutes. You are advised to remain in your seat during deceleration for your own comfort."

"Thank you Horace," Richard said as he turned to me. He kissed me on the lips. I was feeling hot and perspiration trickled down my neck. I immediately responded to his touch.

"Shall we sit on the sofa?" Richard said.

"Where on earth did they come from?" I said in dismay and wished that the windows were activated so I could see what was going on.

"The viewing windows are best turned off while we decelerate; it gets very wild outside until we get down to sub-light speed."

Richard had read my thoughts before answering my question and I tried to calm down.

"Don't worry about the sofas. Horace made them. I activated

one of his programs. I thought we might be more comfortable while this bucket dropped out of light speed. It can be a bit bumpy."

Bumpy! I was still trying to get used to Horace's ability to change the environment. Did he grow the sofas in some sort of weird metamorphosis, or were they carried in from outside from the space station? I remembered the way he changed the bedroom in front of my eyes. Then there was the weird computer chair at the front end, when Richard revelled in flying this strange craft manually. I was not in charge. I had to accept the new pieces of furniture.

We sat in the strange creation and I snuggled against Richard's chest. I do not know what came over me but I felt very randy. I started to stroke his thigh. He responded and we kissed passionately. Unashamedly I removed his beautifully pressed trousers and took off my tights and knickers. I sat astride him, urgent with the moment and we made love there and then. The strange motion of the ship heightened the experience as Horace decelerated, or was he just vibrating his newly created sofas? The delight was so intense, we became as one mind, experiencing a mutual ecstasy that bonded us. I was too absorbed to worry about Horace and what was going on out in space. I did feel safe.

CHAPTER 19

I must have dozed off. When I opened my eyes the windows were open and I could see a profusion of stars. I was lying on the sofa in a dishevelled state so I gathered my things and stood up, pulling my ridiculously short skirt down to cover my bare legs. Richard was sitting at the front doing something on the computer screen. I padded over to him in my bare feet carrying shoes and underwear. The view from the front window was spectacular, thick with stars and a bright distant sun. I squinted at it in wonder and kissed the top of his head.

"Are you alright darling?" he said, without looking up. "We shall be at the terminal in about ten minutes."

"The view is amazing," I said. "Is that Terranus?"

"Yes, the sun is ours and the planets will be in view shortly. I am just arranging for some transport so we can get to the planets."

"I'm going to change into something sensible; I'll just be a few minutes."

I shuffled off into the bedroom and tidied myself up. When I returned to the front seat, I was wearing a formal long length skirt with a shirt and jacket and I felt dressed well enough to meet a queen. I could see four planets in the distance; they appeared to be clustered together with a distant sun beyond. As usual we seemed to approach them at a frightening speed and before long this beautiful green and white orb dominated the screen. It certainly wasn't planet Earth even with my limited knowledge of its appearance from outer space.

As I sat mesmerised, this huge space station loomed up before us out of nowhere. It consisted of several enormous flying saucers that were all connected by a complicated tubular framework. We headed towards one of the saucers and I could see openings all around the extremity. We plunged towards one of the openings at incredible speed and I clutched hold of Richard's arm in fright. There were other ships flying around and zooming past us. They were all shapes and sizes; some were plain silver in appearance, others were brightly coloured in green and red. Thankfully, we seemed to slow down as we approached one of the huge openings and gently drifted through it. Once inside all I could see was a brilliant white wall. Horace just kept going towards it. I tightened my grip on Richard's arm.

"Don't worry darling," he said, "it is a kind of force field that acts as an air lock, and we will just pass through it."

He was right. Within seconds the wall disappeared and we were floating in an enormous hall. It was all brightly lit and surrounded on three sides by several landings, which were edged with hand railings. Like in the transporter, people wearing smocks were walking about on the wide landing. Beyond I could see what looked like shops and restaurants. It all looked modern but reminded me of the Art Deco style in Britain during the 1920s with curves and rounded edges. I was relieved that it all looked so colourful and inviting. There were ships docked against the landings. Some looked identical to Horace as I remember him back at Richard's house on Earth. Some were cigar shaped, others looked like a teardrop and they were all different colours. Horace gently manoeuvred us against the railings that looked as though they were beautifully crafted from polished wood. It all had a five star appearance with a spotless dark green carpet that must have been at least 100 feet wide.

"Docking procedure is complete," Horace announced. "Prepare to be boarded by customs officials."

"Thank you Horace for a good flight; you can open up now."

"Thank you sir; have an enjoyable visit."

The door whizzed open and we both stood up. A man and a woman were standing at the entrance. They greeted us. They were dressed in smart all-in-one suits with a fancy badge on the front. They both bowed courteously and entered the ship. The official looking man shook hands with Richard heartily.

"Welcome back to Terranus, Lord Varnicus. We are honoured to have you visiting us again and hope your stay will be enjoyable. I have made all the arrangements at your request."

"Thank you Master," Richard said, "may I present Doctor Lisa Macdonald." The official turned to me with a smile on his immaculately shaven face, which was very Japanese looking. He bowed as we shook hands.

"May I wish you a pleasant stay, Doctor Macdonald."

"Thank you," I said and bowed back awkwardly. I noticed the woman pointing a gismo around the cabin. She looked satisfied and handed the thing to Richard. He punched something onto the screen and gave it back to the official. He smiled and bowed again. "Thank you, Lord Varnicus, you are most gracious. My assistant will help you with your luggage and show you to your transportation."

The Master then bowed again and left the cabin. *Bloody hell, what is the matter with these people?* I thought.

The Master's assistant was also oriental and very beautiful with jet-black hair tied at the back in a bun. I turned my attention towards her. She was waiting by the door with her eyes lowered. I thought I should say something to her but felt dumbstruck. Richard disappeared into the back of the ship and I followed him. We collected our things from the bedroom.

"Why did he call you Lord Varnicus?" I asked while I stuffed my cosmetic bag into my suitcase.

"He is the director of the terminal; he runs the whole shooting match. He is known as the Master, and out of courtesy he is compelled to call me Lord. Don't worry about it for the moment. I will explain later."

I decided to let it lie for the moment and put on a long black coat that I hadn't worn since my father's memorial service; it felt very strange, especially as I would supposedly be meeting him soon. The whole situation was bizarre, but I was glad to be formally dressed. Richard was also wearing a dark suit with an unusual pleated round-necked shirt that I had not seen before. He did look very smart. I wish I knew what the hell was going on?

Somehow the bed had miraculously made itself. Everything looked immaculate so I was happy leaving Horace in a tidy state even though I didn't have to do anything. We left the ship. Richard told Horace we would see him later and he sweetly replied, "Have a nice holiday." We stepped out onto the landing through a gap in the fancy handrails and followed the Japanese official across the green carpet. She had put our suitcases on a trolley thing, which weirdly followed her, hovering just above the carpet. We walked down a short corridor and through a sliding door into a large room with desks and computer screens. There sitting at a desk was a rather seedy looking man with a beautiful blonde woman wearing a figure hugging blue all-in-one suit. He was about fifty and slightly overweight. When he stood up, he was only about five feet tall. It took me by surprise as most of the people I had seen so far were six feet plus. He shook hands with Richard and bowed. I was surprised that people were so courteous and respectful, a quality that was sadly lacking back on Earth.

"Philbin," Richard said, "it is good to see you again. How have you been?"

"I've been very busy," he said, "too much work and not enough play."

Philbin turned to me and smiled in a nasty smarmy way that reminded me of Hamish at the practice back home.

"You must be Doctor Macdonald," he said. "I can see the likeness in your father."

He gave me a limp, sticky handshake and turned back towards

Richard. The blonde woman just stood there smiling prettily and batting her eyelids. She reminded me of the waitress on the transporter and I realised she was one of those manufactured people.

"Professor Macdonald has been discharged from the detention centre. We have provided him with an apartment on the Pompeii's Province not far from your holiday apartment," he continued and handed Richard another of those electronic gismos.

"All the information you require is recorded on this notepad. If you learn anything that might be useful to me, please record it and inform me immediately. I have a lot of information that has to be followed up. I have to make a trip to Earth this afternoon and I'm not looking forward to it."

He frowned unpleasantly and turned back to me.

"Doctor Macdonald, I am sorry that you have to endure this situation and I will do everything possible to rectify it. Your father is free to decide what he would like to do next. He is a very difficult man. Good luck."

I stood there feeling very uncomfortable and sensed a lot of agitation coming from either Richard or the funny little man, whom I did not like at all. Richard and Philbin went off together through the door, talking. The blonde woman just stood there looking coyly with her eyes lowered while the Japanese official stood at attention by our suitcases, which were still hovering behind her on the oversized skateboard. I didn't know what to say to anybody so, to avoid an awkward silence, I wandered off towards a line of windows on the other side of the room. I looked through and gazed upon an open highway. There was a sort of car park with several vehicles that looked like cars but had no wheels. The roadway was a tunnel with wheel-less cars flashing past at ridiculous speed. It all looked very alien and I had to turn away. Happily, Richard had returned and the funny little man and his blonde left the room. He came up to me and put his arm around my shoulders.

"I'm sorry about all this," he said. "Philbin can be a surly bastard sometimes, but he is under a lot of pressure. Your father is not alone. There have been a lot of abductions over the decades, some unfortunately involving children, and it is a sort of black market. The council have made it a priority to stamp it out. I always said that having the ability to mess with peoples' minds would lead to no good."

"What happens now?" I said, feeling very lost.

"Well, it's up to you really," Richard said, while he fiddled with the screen on his gismo. "We have a rented house set in the forest by a lake, sole use of a shuttle to get us around and fortunately Philbin had the sense to move your father to an apartment that is very near so we won't have to make the trip to Honshu. I hope you will like the arrangements. We should have more time for you to get used to your surroundings and have a sort of holiday."

"We must also go and see your mum and dad," I said. Richard smiled at me and kissed me on the forehead. I could feel warmth and love emanating from him and I knew he wanted to see his family; it was very important to him. However, I could still sense that he was uncomfortable about them and it worried me.

"We have to take a trip in the shuttle to get down to the planet surface," Richard said. "It can be a bit of a roller-coaster ride if you are not used to it but I can assure you it is quite safe. There is still more that I need to tell you and I think we need some time together before you meet your father." I was not sure what he meant by that, but I had the feeling I was going to find out soon.

"I'm in your hands darling, lead on," I said.

Richard spoke to the Japanese woman who was still relentlessly guarding our baggage. I felt that she too must be a robot but much better than the blonde bimbo whom Philbin had in tow. She ushered us out of the door and onto the street. We walked up to this green vehicle that looked a bit like my Volvo at home but was twice the size and much sleeker. It had blacked out windows so you could not see the interior; and it had absolutely no wheels at all. A door in the side slid back in an instant and revealed the inside, which on first sight looked like a minibus. The rear of the vehicle had a sloping back that had now miraculously opened. Our suitcases were deposited into an enormous boot area. I stared in amazement as the boot just covered itself over and devoured our luggage. She then came up to me and directed me into the vehicle. I suddenly realised that she wasn't a robot at all and sensed her thoughts. She was full of honour and admiration and I weirdly felt that I was being treated like royalty. In fact, I am sure it has something to do with Richard's parents. However, I didn't have time to dwell on the thought and was directed into the interior of the vehicle. There were eight seats inside in pairs of two with a wide central aisle. You could stand up straight once inside and it all looked very comfortable and strangely like a miniature version of Horace.

"Please enjoy your stay Madam," she said as she directed me towards the front of the vehicle. I thanked her; she bowed and left the bus. I was relieved to be able to see out of the windows so I sat down in one of the front seats. There was no steering wheel or controls, just a central console with a computer screen that glowed quietly to itself. On either side there was storage space and several glove boxes so I put my handbag on one of the shelves and settled down in anticipation.

Richard soon joined me and I moved up a seat so he could sit beside me.

"Well that's all out of the way, we can have some time to ourselves," he said, feeling relieved. He looked at me with apprehension in his eyes. "Are you feeling OK for a ride down to the planet surface?"

"I'm ready when you are; I hope you know how to drive this thing."

"The ride could be a bit alarming; we are still in space about twenty miles above the planet surface. The shuttle will take us to our destination. I don't have to drive it, but maybe it would be better if you didn't see where we are going. I can turn off the viewing windows."

"I wouldn't miss this for the world," I said and he looked at me doubtingly.

Richard looked at the notepad given to him by the little man and then touched the screen in the central console. He did it so quickly as if playing the piano and the screen flashed at him in recognition.

The vehicle suddenly pulled out and accelerated down the cream coloured tunnel. Once again, there was no feeling of inertia and no noise. I felt as though I was watching a computer game but the sensation was real. We zoomed down the cream tunnel, which was lit at regular intervals, only adding to the visual impact of speed. We flashed down a left turn in the tunnel system and I was aware of a steep downhill sensation. Suddenly we were in space as if spat out of some orifice. The sky above was dark and the glorious white and green glow of the planet surface was below us. This time Richard took my hand and I felt his apprehension. For the first time I think he was more worried about the flight than I was and in a way, it was comforting to know he could feel vulnerable too.

The ship plunged towards the planet surface and before long we were skimming along the tops of clouds at tremendous speed. It was a wee bit bumpy on the way down but luckily it was all over very quickly and I didn't feel any uncomfortable sensations. Richard on the other hand was looking a bit white.

"Are we nearly there?" I said childishly. "How long does it take?" Richard did not answer while he tapped something into the screen in the central console. The ship immediately slowed right down and dropped through the cloud layer. Suddenly, I could see the green mountain tops for as far as the eye could see. The ship was gently moving above them and as we descended in height I could make out thousands of huge trees. The ship was moving at a sensible speed. The mountains were not particularly high. It reminded me of the Scottish Highlands but with heavily

167

wooded valleys that looked like they were straight out of the Jurassic period.

"I've set the ship to run in sightseer mode," Richard said with a relieved sigh. "We are travelling at a comfortable 100 knots and according to the GPS we only have about twenty miles to go."

I looked at him and smiled, and I was glad to see that the colour had returned to his cheeks.

"It is absolutely beautiful," I said, returning to the front screen and ignoring the flashing computer. "What region is this, it looks very wild and uninhabited?"

"This is part of the Pompeii's Province," Richard said proudly. "Believe it or not, quite a lot of people live here including my family and, at the moment, your father."

"Wow, I haven't seen one single house or a road," I said while straining to see out of the window.

"There are lots of single dirt tracks, but you don't need roads when you fly around in one of these."

"Are there any cities?" I asked stupidly. "I still haven't seen any sign of habitation."

We flew low across a huge lake and suddenly I noticed a building by the water's edge. It was unlike anything I had ever seen. The house was perfectly spherical and sat on top of a tall column. There were no windows and it was painted in such a clever way that it seemed to mimic the backdrop of trees. If I had not been looking I would have easily missed it.

"You will be able to see what a town looks like; there are no more big cities. Most of them were destroyed in the wars," Richard eventually said. "Believe it or not, according to ancient historical records, one of the cities was known as Rome."

We crossed a narrow piece of land with a lake on the other side. It was all still densely wooded with the trees right up to the edge of the lake. We slowed down and approached a small clearing by the water's edge and I could see a very cleverly camouflaged log cabin. It was built like a Swedish house with a low overhanging roof and several large balconies; thankfully it also had recognisable windows and a front door. The sight of it made me think of home.

The house was built of wood and was weathered with streaks of grey. It all looked beautifully hand crafted. We drifted over the roof and swung round to the side. To my amazement I could see that the roof was made of fine grass, giving the house a fairytale appearance.

The spacecraft came to rest in the corner of what was a massive balcony. The screen flashed and blinked while Richard tapped it again. The side door whizzed open and immediately a lovely scented warm breeze entered the cabin. I leapt out of my seat and made for the door. The air smelt of pine and grass and was sweet and warm. I stumbled as I stepped out of the cabin. The boarding of the deck was a bit slippery and at first I couldn't find my feet. Getting a sense of balance was somehow different. I stood for a moment and then gingerly walked across the balcony and reached the beautifully carved balustrade. When I looked up the view was astounding.

I gazed across the greenish blue lake that was mirror calm. There were huge trees on the other side. Beyond, misty blue mountains rose from the canopy. It all looked very beautiful and different from anything I had ever seen on Earth. In the distance there were two egg shaped spaceships silently streaking across a blue and green sky. It dawned on me that I really was standing on another planet.

CHAPTER 20

I was standing in a mesmerized state for an eternity until Richard came up behind me and put his arms around my waist. He instantly brought me back to reality.

"This is just amazing," I said dumbly, "what time of day is it?"

"Do you know," he said while he kissed my neck, "I have absolutely no idea but I think it must be some time towards the middle of the day. We have to adjust to the fact that the days are a bit longer here."

"What do you mean, a bit longer?" I asked while grimacing at Richard's amazing ability for accuracy. "When will we know when to go to bed?"

"I think we will know."

"Is this summertime?" I asked again.

"I have no idea I'm afraid, but this region is subtropical and I don't think the temperature varies much. But it does get a lot of rain."

"I think it is absolutely stunning. Are there any wild animals to worry about?"

"Well, as I said before there are no reptiles and unfortunately, no feathered birds. The mammals rule on Terranus but they will not harm us. It is best to keep away from mountain lions and bears, but you will rarely see them. We can go for a walk later and I'll show you."

"I'd rather you didn't show me any lions."

"Shall we go in and sort the house out?" Richard asked.

I followed him back to the spacecraft, which was still silently hovering a few inches above the decking. The rear compartment slid back and revealed our heavy luggage. To my surprise, I was able to lift my case out with ease. It seemed a lot lighter and I wondered if someone had been tampering with it. Richard read my thoughts.

"Don't worry, he said, "you will get used to it. Gravity is a bit less here compared to Earth."

He was right, I hadn't realised that I was a lot lighter on my feet. I managed to carry the case to the front door without any trouble. Richard had brought his electronic gismo that somehow opened the ornately carved front door. We went into a large sitting room; it was simply furnished and instantly reminded me of any modern home on Earth. There was a stone fireplace that was already loaded with logs. All the walls were made of rustic wood planks. It made me think of a Swedish log cabin. I thought of home and wondered how my mother was getting on after her strange treatment with the doctor. Richard was standing beside me.

"Unfortunately we are too far away to pick up the telephone," he said after annoyingly reading my mind again. "I can send an email to the hospital and get a report if you like."

He was immediately embarrassed. Without speaking I told him not to worry and I will control this mind thing eventually.

"So you can send emails from here?" I said.

Richard fiddled with his gismo that never seemed to leave his side. *Typical man*, I thought.

"There you are," he said, "it's done; we should get a reply in a few minutes, and if you don't want me to read your mind, don't open up so much. I'm sure you will get used to it. To be as one, both sides have to be in control. I am sorry, I will give you some space. I don't want to make you feel uncomfortable."

"It's OK, darling." I said, although I had no idea yet how to control it, but at this precise moment I didn't give a fig.

I walked across the room and into what looked like a

conventional kitchen. Still in a dream, I tried the water tap in the sink to see if it worked and noticed a lovely view across the lake from the window.

"Where is the bedroom?" I asked.

"It's upstairs," he said. "There is a sauna up there as well."

I climbed the wooden staircase and found the bedroom across an open landing. The room was lovely. The wide bed was already made up and there was a balcony with views over the lake and a lovely bathroom with a sauna all en-suite. I unpacked my things and put them away in a built-in wardrobe with ornate carved doors. I tried to calm down and decided to change into jeans and tee shirt.

When I came downstairs I found Richard rummaging around in the kitchen. He had found some mugs and put one under a drink machine similar to the one in Horace's kitchen.

"Computer, tea white, no sugar please," he said in a matter of fact way. He asked me what I would like and quickly organised it. We sat at the kitchen table and Richard produced the gismo again.

"I have had a message from Darius about your mother. Do you want to read it?" he said while handing me the plastic card.

It read:-

> *'Mrs Macdonald is already showing signs of recovery and is doing very well. The hospital will monitor her condition for the next few days and then reassess the situation. Hope you are having a nice time back home, you lucky devil.*
>
> *Regards Marcus.'*

I smiled with relief to hear that Mum was OK and mused at the second comment. It was odd to think that Darius would be envious of our epic journey to another world but I had to remember that he is from this world. I put the plastic thing down on the table before it did something horrible.

"Are you all right, darling?" Richard said, snapping me out of my thoughts. "That is good news. With any luck your mother will be out of hospital by the time we get back."

"Yes, it is wonderful news," I said. "I am just feeling a bit overwhelmed by everything."

I sipped my tea and started to feel refreshed. The kitchen was lovely with a view over the lake from the sink and another window looking onto a jungle of ferns and broad leafed bushes. We sat at a small wooden table and the edges were expertly carved with a leaf pattern. Even the four chairs had a similar pattern on the backrests. Richard just looked at me sympathetically and I realised he had something on his mind.

"Well," I said doubtfully, "I know there is something else you are going to tell me."

"The problem is," he said with worry lines appearing on his forehead, "we can't really visit your father yet until I have told you something. If I don't tell you now, your father will and I don't want to upset you."

Realising that I wasn't in possession of all the facts, I started to get a sick feeling in my stomach again, so I braced myself.

"I hope this is the last of your revelations," I said with a frown.

"The thing is I haven't exactly told you the whole story about my family either."

"Oh dear," I said. "I had a feeling about that also."

"Well, you know my father is an engineer and my brother is now working for the Council." I nodded with wide eyes.

"What I didn't mention is that my mother is a bit special. She is the descendant of a long line of political leaders and is now the First Lady. In fact she has been for some years now since her aunt died unexpectedly." I sat back and thought a moment, still with a frown.

"What do you mean? Does she have something to do with the president?"

"What I mean is she is the president if you like. Terranus has always had a figurehead and the bloodline goes back for centuries. Being the First Lady is a bit like being the Queen of England except that my mother's kingdom is the entire planet." I sat back and tried to absorb what he had said.

"So your family is royal," I said in a high voice. "Does this mean you are a prince?"

"Absolutely not. It cannot be described like that. I shouldn't have used the Queen of England as an example. I'm sorry if I have misled you. The politics are completely different here. There is no bureaucracy. My family is wealthy and they have been patrons of the council for centuries."

"But you could become the planet's ruler," I said with my voice rising in pitch.

"Traditionally I would have to take on the job if my older brother didn't survive me. At this moment in time I am not involved too much with Terranus politics. My brother has an ancestral interest in it. I only get involved when the issues are directed at Planet Earth. I suppose I am being selfish, but I would much rather pursue my musical career on Earth. My mother is now enjoying her position and she is very good at it. I have my obligations but I will not be her slave unless I think it is absolutely necessary." I felt Richard cringe at the thought and I cringed with him.

For the moment I couldn't look at him so I focused on my cup of tea. I was confused and angry. What the hell was he telling me now? I felt as though I was living in some sort of fairytale and none of this was real. Richard was upset and his thoughts were cluttering up my head so I stood up and walked out onto the veranda to breathe the fresh air. I tried to feel calmer and stared out onto the landscape. It was all very alien and different. I hadn't noticed before, but the forest was alive with weird cries and whistles. The sounds were unusual and not what I would expect of a typical rainforest back on Earth. I stood and listened for a long time and allowed my heart rate to slow down.

I had sensed that Richard was holding back on something and in a way, I felt strangely relieved. I knew Richard had been dreading telling me this and I could feel his apprehension. The whole situation was so bizarre that I was beyond caring. Only recently had I learned that the world has already been taken over by aliens. My father, who isn't dead at all, happens to be one of them. My mother is recovering from a terminal illness after being injected by an army of organic robotic antibodies and now I was standing on this strange planet with a planetary ruler.

I really missed my mother and wished I could sit with her and tell her the whole story but hell, that would be a delight yet to come. I started to feel oddly confident. I know I am in love with Richard and I don't care that he has some sort of important ancestry. I felt that there weren't any more secrets between us and all the past events seemed to make sense. It explained the VIP treatment that we always seemed to be confronted with.

Suddenly, I felt Richard's hand on my shoulder. I didn't hear him come up behind me. I should have sensed it.

"Are you alright, darling?" he said gently in my ear.

"I'm just thinking about all this, I'm OK." I turned round and embraced him. Yet again, tears started streaming down my face.

He took me upstairs and we lay down on the bed. We kissed, cuddled, and spent the rest of the long Terranus day talking freely about our families and Terranus culture. Then we sat on the veranda drinking coffee while the planet Honshu slowly set behind the mountains.

CHAPTER 21

When I awoke, it was fairly dark outside. I lay back feeling happy and contented. There was no dawn chorus. I wasn't even sure if it was dawn and had absolutely no idea what time of day it was, or for that matter, was this even a day? I really did not care. I turned to see that Richard was not beside me, but it didn't worry me. He always got up early anyway. I could see out onto the veranda and noticed it was pouring with rain and there were distant rumbles of thunder. The air was still warm and fragrant. I got out of bed and walked onto the veranda. It also did not worry me that I was stark naked as I looked out at the dark sky. The rain was torrential and pouring off the grass roof in rivulets. I felt strangely intoxicated by the experience and walked into the rain and let it wash over my body. It was incredibly refreshing.

I was still on this strange planet, but I felt good. Without drying myself off, I just grabbed my black and red dressing gown and decided to go and find Richard. He was downstairs, sitting at the kitchen table playing with the gismo.

"Good morning, darling," he said looking up from the computer. "You are looking radiant this morning, if not a bit wet."

"Thank you darling," I said nonchalantly, and kissed him on the forehead. "What are you doing?"

"Not anything important; I'm ordering breakfast and checking the weather."

"Ordering breakfast?" I asked. I already knew what the weather was doing, while I dripped on the wooden floor.

"Yes," he said, "you send in your order and the ship goes off to collect it. When it comes back it will have a hamper in the back."

I looked out of the window. The rain was still thrashing the huge veranda and the ship was missing. I sat down at the table where a coffee was waiting for me.

"That's damn convenient," I slurred, "room service with a difference, the spaceship fetches your breakfast." I realised that I was feeling very woozy although we didn't have any alcohol last night and I don't think I smoked any chocolate tubes.

"Are you all right, darling?" Richard said as he reached across and held my hand.

"I'm fine and dandy," I said without a care in the world. He smiled at me sympathetically.

"You do realise that we didn't have any proper food last night. You do need to eat something. There is proper sugar in your coffee, and you will feel better if you drink it. Also the air is very different here; it takes a while to get used to it and it will make you feel a bit light-headed for a while."

"OK darling," I said while sipping my coffee. "By the way, when was last night?" Richard gave me a funny look.

The sugar was good and I was grateful for the fix. I was beginning to realise that everything about this planet was totally different and much unknown. Perhaps the air was full of Nitrous Oxide or whatever. I seemed to be on some sort of high, but I didn't care. I felt good.

I sat in silence and wondered what I was going to say to my father or for that matter what would he be thinking. As far as he is concerned, he cannot remember five years of his life and wakes up wandering around an alien planet. The aliens give him his memory back except for the past five years and then tell him he has been returned back to his original forgotten planet. He then finds out that his daughter has been brought back to meet him (after five years), accompanied by the planetary ruler's son.

I was amazed at how I could recall this whilst in a strange

inebriated state, but my mind was clear and sharp. It was all so bizarre. I decided my father would have to do all the talking. I will listen and assess the situation. After all, this is his world, not mine.

I still have to deal with my mother. I hoped that she was all right. I have no idea what to say to her. I have to bide my time and go with the flow.

Richard smiled at me and snapped me out of my thoughts. He reached across and held my hand.

"Sorry darling," I said. "I was a million miles away."

"Well, you're a good deal further away than that." I ignored his quip and took a second large gulp of my coffee.

"When do you want to meet your father?" Richard asked tentatively.

I shuddered and drew a breath, but I knew it had to be done.

"Will you be with me when I meet him?" I said in desperation.

"Of course, darling, if that is what you want."

"I am not sure what to say to him; the circumstances are weird."

"If you want, I can arrange for the ship to bring him here for lunch. We can just see how it goes." Richard held my hand tightly and I felt his power. I willingly succumbed to his dominance and agreed. I was feeling much better and had a huge amount of curiosity at being able to see my father again after five years. I had been transported to this amazing world and he is the link. This system of planets was where he was born and it would be reassuring to talk over the recent events with my own flesh and blood. Richard's gismo suddenly beeped and I flinched.

"Food has arrived," he said gleefully and jumped up to fetch it. I looked out of the window. It had stopped raining and the sun was shining strongly with shafts of bright light penetrating the mist. Sure enough, the ship had returned and parked itself in the usual place on the now steaming deck. Richard lifted out a large white box and put it down on the deck. Bizarrely the box followed him into the house. By the time he had reached the kitchen, it had parked itself neatly behind him. He opened the box and lifted out several dishes, placing them on the table. When he had got the plates and cutlery, he lifted the lids. It was a fully recognisable English breakfast with fried eggs, fried bread, bacon and sausages all piping hot. It was heart-warming to see recognisable food and I wondered where it came from. We ate heartily; both of us were absolutely starving.

The morning seemed to fly by and I decided to go and change into something nice. My father was going to arrive in about half an hour. I started to go into hyperactive mode in order to quell my panic. After I had tried on my entire wardrobe, I finally settled on a plain white summer dress. I also decided to only use a little make-up after my previous disasters, and having washed my hair earlier, I brushed it straight so it hung long over my shoulders. Surprisingly, my hair was much darker and shinier than usual and it made me look more oriental. I suddenly felt very much at home and with confidence, I finally braced myself to go down the stairs. I saw Richard standing in the doorway with a man.

The man bowed and shook hands with Richard. When he looked my way I realised it was my father. We stared at each other for an eternity. He looked younger than I remembered him. His hair was streaked with grey and he had a very tidy goatee-style beard that had obviously been trimmed by a professional. The only familiar thing was his light brown khaki style jacket that he so often wore on his field trips. I was overcome with emotion and went up to embrace him. He reciprocated and we hugged for the first time for as long as I could remember. We finally stood apart.

"Lisa, you look as beautiful as ever," he said with a broad smile on his face.

"I just can't believe this," I stammered, with my face flushing.

"You must be going out of your mind with all that's been happening," he said sympathetically. "Why don't we sit down and talk things over?"

"Would you like a glass of wine, Professor Macdonald?" Richard asked.

"That would be a good idea," the professor replied, "but please call me Jim." Richard went into the kitchen to open a bottle while we sat down on the sofa.

"We are both a bit in the same boat," Dad said awkwardly. "We have both had a huge shock." It was lovely to think of him as Dad and I felt that we immediately had a father-daughter bond. In my youth, my father wasn't always there for me; he was totally absorbed by his research work. But now things felt very different.

"You look so young Dad," I said in a girlish way.

"Well I have had a lot of clever medical treatment; apparently I was in a mess when they found me. I have never been on this planet before and I must say it is very agreeable here." I could sense that Dad was feeling very emotional; he continued with watery eyes. "Thank you for calling me Dad; I don't remember the last time you called me that. It is wonderful to see you; to me it is only yesterday and you are exactly as I remember you. I have no idea what I have been doing for the past five years but I do know I was kidnapped when we were returning from my Australian expedition."

"It must have been awful for you Dad," I said sympathetically, "and this is your first time on this planet?"

"Yes, the truth is I was born on Honshu. My family were killed on Atlantis in a boating accident and I don't have any relatives. I moved to Earth over fifty years ago to start a new life and all memory of my home planet had been erased, a bit like the last five years. This brain programming technology has caused a lot of trouble."

"Why have your memory altered?" I asked.

"It was just so that our presence on planet Earth would have a minimal effect on the natural environment. A fat lot of good it has done," Dad grunted. "Tell me, Lisa, how is your mother? Does she know anything about all of this?"

"I haven't said anything to her; as far as she is concerned we are on holiday somewhere in the Mediterranean."

"How is she? I heard she has cancer."

"When I met Richard and found out about him, he arranged to have some special treatment for her. She seems to be recovering well."

"If she has been treated by a Terranus doctor, she will be fine. They have amazing technology here and I'm living proof," Dad said with confidence.

Richard brought in the glasses of wine and placed two of them on the table. He was just about to slope off, which was very diplomatic of him, but I called him back and made him sit down beside me. I grabbed his hand and held it tightly.

"So how long have you two known each other?" Dad asked, directly to Richard.

"Well," Richard hesitated, "a lot has happened and I feel that I have known Lisa for ever, but I suppose it can't be much more than a month." Dad turned towards me.

"You do realise who this man is, Lisa?"

"Of course I do!" I retorted. "Although I only found out yesterday and I still haven't had time to appreciate the situation. One thing that I do know is I love him and I don't care who he is." Richard kissed me on the cheek and I tightened my grip on his hand until my knuckles went white.

"I am so pleased you are happy together," Dad said, and I was so pleased to feel the warmth in his smile.

"We all have so much to think about and discuss," Richard said as he turned to Dad. "Lisa and I are scheduled to return to Earth tomorrow afternoon, so there isn't much time. I have to go to see my parents; I will be gone for about three hours Earth time. It will give you a chance to talk and decide your future; this is the main reason we are here." Richard then turned to me and looked me in the eyes. His expression was urgent and I immediately knew that he had important matters to sort out, although I did think that he wanted me to meet his parents, so I felt a little bit put out.

"Can't I come with you to meet your parents?" I pleaded.

"Darling Lisa, I would love you to meet my mother and father and they also want to meet you. Unfortunately, they are busy people and you will meet them sooner than you think. I actually have to attend a Council meeting. One day you must come with me, but I won't have much opportunity to talk to my parents myself and I would rather you saw them on a more casual level."

"It is OK darling, I understand, and you're right. Dad and I have a lot to sort out."

"A ship will be collecting me soon," Richard continued, "and I have ordered a cold buffet for your lunch. If you need to go anywhere, the shuttle is at your disposal. Your father will know how to operate it. Will you be alright, darling?"

"I'm going to be fine," I said, picking up my glass of wine for a little alcoholic support. "By the time you return, Dad and I will have sorted ourselves out." I looked at Dad and he just sat there beaming. I could sense that he knew something but I could not quite make it out.

Richard went upstairs to change and I sat back in the comfortable sofa for a moment wondering what to do next. I finally looked up at Dad and he was still looking at me with that unfamiliar smile.

"What are we going to do about all this?" I asked, feeling irritated by his stare.

"Don't worry, Lisa, it will all sort itself out. One thing is for sure, we owe it to your mother to tell her the truth about me. And you need to explain to her what has happened to you. I would very much like to see her again, but at this moment I really think she should make up her own mind about the situation we are in."

Dad was right. If I did not tell her, I would be harbouring the fact that my mother married an alien and I am an alien daughter.

I do not think I could cope with that and I am certainly not having my own memory erased.

We are both in a situation and I reflected a moment about my own problems. The fact that Richard was the son of a planetary ruler in an alien world was a daunting thought. I had no idea how it was going to affect us. One thing I do know is I want to be with him. All I can do is wait and see what happens. My mother is an intelligent woman and I decided that I must tell her about the whole situation; it would be a relief to hear what she has to say.

Richard clomped down the wooden staircase. He was wearing a suit that I had never seen before. It was dark blue and double-breasted with cheesy military style gold buttons. On the breast, it had a gold embroidered emblem that was totally unrecognisable. As he hurried towards me he had a very important air about him.

"There has been a slight change in plan," he said with a worried look. "Mother has hitched a ride with the escort ship and she will be here any minute." I was surprised at Richard's agitation and grabbed his arm.

"That's all right darling. I can meet your mother," I said calmly while trying to hide my excitement.

"Thank you for being so patient with me," Richard said with a look that would melt butter. "I didn't know there was going to be a council meeting; if I had, I would have rescheduled this trip. My mother deliberately told me at the last minute so that she knew I wouldn't get out of it and now she is making sure I get there. Ironically, Earth is the subject of the meeting and it has a high priority label. Although I hate these things, it would damage the status quo if I didn't make an appearance. Mother knows this so she has got me against the wall."

I listened to Richard's statement with amusement; I know that Richard finds having an important position in this world very irritating, but I think he had an idea what was going to happen. I suspect he has carefully orchestrated the course of events. I smiled at him and he sensed that I understood. I could feel him starting to relax.

Suddenly, the room went dark and through the window I could see this enormous black cigar-shaped vehicle slide up alongside the veranda. A door opened and the balustrade slipped back to reveal a wide dark opening. Two suited men spilled out. Richard looked at me, pulled a silly face and walked towards the door. Dad was now standing up with a more serious expression on his face so I went over to him, took his hand and we followed Richard to the front door.

A tall elegant woman stepped out of the ship. She immediately reminded me of Elizabeth Taylor. She was wearing a deep blue full-length gown with a matching button-less coat that was edged in gold braiding.

She smiled warmly at Richard and they embraced. Despite the alien environment, it somehow seemed quite natural and heart-warming. The two suited bodyguards had spread out and were standing like sentries on either side of the ship's wide opening.

Richard and his mother were chatting and laughing in a relaxed way. I only wished that I could hear what they were saying and I wondered if we should go out to meet her. She took Richard's arm and walked towards us. I tightened my grip on Dad's hand.

"You must be Lisa," she said warmly with her hand outstretched. I suddenly realised that I had no idea what sort of protocol should be adopted, so I took her hand and did a silly curtsy.

"Yes, yes I am," I stammered.

"You are absolutely lovely," she said. "I am so happy to finally meet you." She took me by the elbows and kissed me on the cheek. I nearly lost my balance, but I instantly felt at ease with her.

"I am so sorry to drag Richard away from you, Lisa, especially while you are going through so much." She turned to Dad, who bowed again in a strange courteous way.

"Professor Macdonald," she said while shaking Dad's hand,

"we deeply regret the crime that has been committed against you and we can assure you that the offenders will be caught."

"Thank you, your Ladyship," he said with his head lowered. I realised that I knew very little about my father and started to feel lost in a different reality. I had never witnessed him behaving like that to anyone. Richard's mother turned back to me and took my hand. The sensation made me tingle all over.

"I shouldn't tell you this Lisa," she said surreptitiously. "My husband and I will be making a trip to Earth very soon for a short holiday; we are both looking forward to it. We would love to get to know you then, when we have more time to talk. I am so sorry that our meeting has been so short."

I smiled at her and before I could think of anything to say she had ushered Richard towards the door. Richard pulled that face again and, over his shoulder, he looked at me. I immediately read his thoughts. *He said, 'three hours tops'.* They disappeared into the dark interior of the ship and the doorway closed up in the blink of an eye. Within seconds, daylight returned to the room and silently the ship was gone.

I stood there feeling very alone and wondered when I would see him again.

CHAPTER 22

I tried to quell the butterflies in my stomach and hoped that Richard would be alright at this 'official meeting'. Dad came and stood beside me. I looked at him and he smiled at me. He was looking much more relaxed. He had lost that strange false smile and had a more serious expression. His dark eyebrows were now lowered and his appearance was as I remembered him five years ago.

"I think it would be a good idea to get a bit of fresh air," he said wisely. "We can go for a short expedition in the forest. We can then talk and I can show you some amazing things about this planet."

"OK Dad, give me ten minutes to gather myself together."

I went into the living room and found my wine glass. I drank the contents and took it into the kitchen. I climbed the stairs and changed into some jeans and put some strong shoes on. I sat on the bed in a daze. I had to talk to Dad. Eventually I went downstairs. Dad was on the balcony looking at the view. He had a glass of wine in his hand.

"Well, that was quite exciting, meeting the First Lady," he said without moving his head. "They are a very powerful and wealthy family and are more highly credited than even the Honshuian Emperor. It is so strange to think that you are involved with them and it is also an amazing coincidence that I get my life back at the same time." I put my arm around him and gave him a squeeze. I was totally confused and said nothing. We stood looking at the mountains and watching the occasional ship streak across the sky.

I could sense that Dad was as confused as I was. Eventually he led me down another wooden staircase that led to the forest.

There was no garden around the house; the natural vegetation grew against the walls of the house with broad leafed bushes and tall ferns of all kinds. The weather was now warm and sunny and we followed a path leading into the cool of the forest. The trees reminded me of some kind of beech. They were extremely tall with huge trunks at least ten feet in diameter with grey smooth bark. They were well spaced apart and the forest floor was covered with a carpet of fine moss. Where shafts of sunlight shone through, grasses and ferns grew. There were no paths but the going was easy and we strolled side by side. Dad was fascinated by occasional exotic plants. He kept stopping to examine them enthusiastically. There were no birds chattering, but you could tell there were animals not far away. I kept hearing rustling sounds, odd cries and eerie whistling noises in the distance.

"I have never seen anything like this before," Dad said as he pointed at a large succulent plant with round dark green leaves the size of dinner plates. It had pretty red flowers. While Dad was fingering the hapless plant, I noticed another array of succulent leaves. They were light green in colour and quite profuse. I grabbed Dad's arm. To my horror the whole thing started to move away form me.

"Dad! That green thing is moving." He looked at me and then turned his attention in the direction of my pointing, trembling finger. He turned towards me and smiled.

"Well done, Lisa, for spotting that," he said with excitement. "These animals are difficult to find."

"Animals?" I said indignantly. He stepped over toward it. It was wobbling along like a Tortoise. He stood in front of it and it stopped and crouched down. I got behind him and looked at the thing. It was just a blob of glistening green diamond shaped leaves. It was quite still but you could just see it breathing.

"What is it?" I said, looking over his shoulder.

"It is an invertebrate, like a slug or snail. Somehow during the process of evolution it now behaves like a plant. It will move into the sunlight and photosynthesize like a plant absorbing carbon dioxide. At the same time it has legs like a frog or newt and with a voracious appetite will eat any agreeable green foliage from the forest floor. The best of both worlds, I would say! They are common but difficult to spot. There are many species and some just sit and grow false appendages to simulate a flower, usually to attract a mate. Be careful what flowers you pick; the difference between animal and vegetable is hard to distinguish on this planet. The plants are not poisonous but can be dangerous. You must know about the flycatcher plants on Earth. The plants here will eat animals the size of dogs and won't think twice about entrapping your whole arm."

"That is amazing, Dad, but I am not going to stick my arm into a plant until I have studied it first." He was not going to scare me. His explanation was actually making me feel more at ease. I knew about flycatchers. I am sure I read about photosynthesizing animal life in the National Geographic.

"What other animals roam these forests?" I asked, trying to keep an open mind.

"Mammals, not unlike Earth but very diverse," he said vaguely.

"Richard tells me there are bears and lions."

"There are a lot of carnivorous hunters and many species of cats. You will rarely see them and the Hooches will keep them away from us. For some reason, reptiles and birds never evolved on this planet, or for that matter on Honshu. There are insects, but not as diverse as those on Earth. Thankfully there are no flies or mosquitoes. Only those that eat vegetation. The diverse mammal population removes the debris and clears the forest animal effluvia. Tiny bats no bigger than a bee pollinate the plants. They live inside the bamboo canes and crevices of tree bark. There are a lot of flying mammals. Some of them are very strange. If you are not used to very large bats, the flying mammals can be a bit intimidating." I absorbed the information and tried to focus.

"Hooches?" I said, querying, while dismissing the large bats.

"Yes, Hooches are very common in these forests. They are stout, strong creatures, about the size of a small horse. They act as guardians of the forest and are extremely intelligent. They are very protective towards us and we repay them with fruit. They have a highly sophisticated language and communicate over large distances by whistling. I am sure they are watching us right now.

"That strange whistling sound, it comes from the Hooches?" I said feeling uneasy.

"Don't worry Lisa, they are very gentle creatures."

We continued wandering for some time and reminisced in between the occasional botanical lecture. I could hear sounds behind me as if we were being followed. I was intrigued but did not dare look. Eventually, we came to a lush, green clearing where one of the enormous trees had fallen. We sat and rested in the warm sunshine by sitting on one of the large branches that had embedded itself conveniently into the forest floor. I tried to relax. When I looked around I suddenly noticed a group of strange looking animals standing between the huge tree trunks. There were four of them and they were watching us. They reminded me of a cross between a pony and a camel. Dad noticed them and stood up. He amazed me by giving them an oriental bow. He then sat down again and waved them towards us. All I could do was sit in fear.

The animals strolled into the clearing and started grazing on the lush grass. They looked at us while still munching with bits of green leaf and grass hanging from their wide mouths. Before long they were only a few feet away from us.

"It's OK," Dad said, sensing my tension. "These animals are very friendly and highly intelligent. If we had some fruit they would be your friends for life."

The Hooches seemed to be listening to us. They swung their

heads round to each other, making strange whistling sounds. In fact, they seemed to be talking among themselves. I pulled a large tuft of grass from the ground. I held it out and whistled as if beckoning a dog. I quickly had their full attention as eight large brown eyes looked intently in my direction. They seemed to have a quizzical expression on their faces as they looked at one another. To my horror, the larger one of the group walked slowly towards me. It had its head lowered and did not seem threatening. I stayed motionless. Eventually it stood inches away from my face and I could smell its vegetable breath as it gently sniffed me. At this range, it had large eyes with enormous eyelashes. The mouth was wide with fat fleshy lips, not unlike a camel. Its teeth were similar to those of a cow and were surprisingly clean and white. The body was of a small fat horse with fine chestnut coloured fur and large wide horse-like hooves. It had a friendly countenance and gently took the grass, bowed its head and noisily chewed it. I reached out and stroked its face like you would a horse and to my amazement it creased up its eyes and smiled in a very human way, exposing a row of white cow teeth. I smiled back and the Hooch emitted a low-pitched whistle. The others then strolled over and surrounded us. Dad was also petting them and making friends; they seemed to enjoy our company.

"I think they like us," Dad said while one of the Hooches nibbled his ear with its big rubber lips.

"Just as well," he continued. "I have just realised that I have no idea how to get back to the house."

"Dad, what do you mean?" I exclaimed. "Are we lost?" My Hooch stepped back, bowing its head.

"Don't worry Lisa, we can either get the ship to pick us up or we can get a ride back on a Hooch." I was preoccupied while tickling mine under its chin. He loved it; at least I think it was a he. I could almost hear him giggling.

"I haven't ridden a horse in years," I said.

"I have ridden one of these. You don't have to do anything,

just sit on it." Dad spoke to his animal as if it were a helicopter pilot. "Would you mind taking us back to the house; I think we are lost?"

The Hooches conferred with each other with their eerie whistles. How did they understand what Dad was saying? I decided to test them and told my friend that there were some apples back at the house. It was extraordinary; he immediately looked me straight in the eyes, nodded his head and knelt on his knees. He was not that big so without hesitation I easily climbed onto his back. I sensed that we had made a deal, although I did not understand how. I really hoped that there were some apples back at the house.

"I think you have impressed them. We have a lift," Dad said as he clumsily got on the back of the other one.

"He seems to understand what I have said. How do they know where to take us?"

"It is alright, Lisa. They understand our language, especially if there is a reward. They have been watching us since we left the house so they know where to go. Did you know their language is complicated and very sophisticated? They communicate over vast distances by whistling to each other. The sound carries through the forest and is passed on from one animal to another without error. It is a vast network."

The Hooches gave us a surprisingly comfortable ride, gently walking side-by-side back through the forest with the other two following on behind in procession. We got back to the house very quickly and I realised that we had probably been walking in circles. I was relieved and then wondered how we could repay them. Dad read my thoughts. He told me that it was always good to have a supply of fresh fruit in the house, if just for this occasion. I don't remember seeing any fruit, but he told me it was in a bowl in the kitchen. I ran upstairs and looked around. I had completely missed a large bowl of apples standing on a side cabinet. The apples were huge but I took the whole bowl and carried them downstairs. Dad was standing with the animals and I just put the bowl on the ground. I think there must have been half a dozen large bright green apples. My Hooch friend came forward. His smile was alarming and very weird. He took an apple and moved away. He whistled through his nose and the others followed suit. I watched them as they emptied the bowl of apples in turn. The two Hooches that walked behind us only had one apple each but they were quite content. The Hooches that gave us the ride had two each. There was no squabbling. They seemed to have an organised society. I talked to them and told them my name. They listened intently and whistled to each other. I felt they were my friends. I would have loved to spend more time with them to study their behaviour and understand their language. They truly had awareness and intelligence that I had never seen before in a similar animal.

After lunch we finalized our plans. Mum was to know everything and I had to formulate a plan to break it to her gently. Depending on how she reacted, I had to tell her that Dad wants to see her again. He even gave me an email address so that I could communicate with him direct using my home computer. He did say that the message could take up to a day to arrive but I was to stay in contact. He also emphasised the fact that Richard would help all he could as far as arranging transport for a possible meeting. Dad also confided in me and told me that he did not want to leave Terranus. I could understand why. It is a truly beautiful and fascinating place and I had only scratched the surface. He said that I must persuade Mum to make the trip to Terranus. I completely understood what his intentions were.

I had no idea of the time but my instinct told me that three hours had passed. I started to wonder what had happened to Richard. Dad said that he had to get back to his apartment. I could see that he was feeling very tired so I strode into the kitchen to see if I could make the coffee machine work. It was similar to the one on board Horace, so after placing the cups I gave it similar instructions. The outcome was successful with no spills. It made me wonder where Horace was. Strangely, I missed him.

I took the cups through and handed Dad his coffee. He looked absolutely drained.

"Are you OK Dad? Why don't you take the shuttle thingy and go back to your apartment? In fact take me too; I want to see where you live."

"Lisa, you are such a good girl. You have a lively spirit, just like your mother. I am very proud to be your father." He kissed me on the cheek. "I have a lovely house on the beach, albeit temporarily, and I am being looked after very well while I sort myself out. In any case, Richard will be returning soon so we must say goodbye for now."

I gave Dad a cuddle and before the impending tears had a chance to well up, the front door flew open with a sudden gust of wind. The sky went dark and I recognised the egg shape of Horace drawing up against the balcony. Why it was always windy when he made an entrance, I do not know, but this time he seemed astronomically huge and completely blotted out the view. He was chocolate coloured and reminded me of an enormous Easter egg. I was so pleased to see him. He gently parked his bulk against the railings. The railings opened and the his door split apart.

I ran outside towards the doorway. I embraced Richard lovingly before he had a chance to walk through the door. He smelled of the forest. I sensed he was upset, but he held me tight.

"Darling Lisa," he said in my ear. "I love you."

"I love you too," I said and kissed him.

"Welcome back to the ship Lisa," Horace said with an unusually loud friendly tone. There was no doubt in my mind that they had been plotting something together. With unnerving insight, I could sense that Richard knew something that had something to do with me.

"Horace, it is so nice to hear your voice," I said over Richard's shoulder.

Richard took me by the waist before I could get an answer from Horace. I knew something was going on. He guided me towards the house. He told me we were to leave right away in order to catch an earlier transporter. He was totally wound up and I could not read his thoughts. He went upstairs so I left him alone.

Dad was intrigued with Horace. He walked towards the doorway.

"Amazing," Dad said while he looked inside. "I have never seen a ship of this class before; the whole thing is living tissue with the ability to regenerate at an incredible rate."

Having spent days living with Horace I took Dad's hand and we walked inside. The air once again was sweet and cool.

"Horace, I have my father with me," I said.

"Lisa, I have missed you; have you enjoyed your experience on the planet? I have security clearance for Professor Macdonald. I am very pleased to meet your father and it is good that you have been reunited."

"Thank you Horace. I have missed you also." I felt strangely emotional. "Would it be OK for Dad to look around?"

"I am sorry, Lisa, please confirm that your reference to 'Dad' means Professor Macdonald." I stood for a moment and looked at Dad. He wasn't paying attention.

"Horace, 'Dad' and Father mean the same thing."

"I am sorry Lisa, just checking the application. I do have the term in my database. Your 'Dad' is quite free to look around. Let me know if you and your 'Dad' require any information." He accentuated the word and I could sense sarcasm in his voice.

"Lisa, do you realise that this ship is a living thing? It is incredible technology. I would like to show you something." He took out a penknife from his jacket pocket.

"Horace, do you mind if I show Lisa how you can regenerate your cells?"

"What do you have in mind, Professor Macdonald?" Horace said.

"Well Horace, let's say this knife accidentally slipped and damaged your upholstery."

"I am aware of the sharp implement you have in your hand, Professor Macdonald," Horace said. "Normally you would not be allowed on the ship with it."

"Horace, I just want to demonstrate to Lisa your amazing abilities," Dad said enthusiastically.

"I would rather you didn't. But as it is for Lisa's benefit I will allow it."

I stood there wondering what Dad was up to. He took the knife and made a two inch long cut in the back of the chair.

"Dad! For heaven's sake stop," I exclaimed.

"It's OK. Just watch."

Before my very eyes the cut instantly healed over and within seconds had disappeared.

"There you are, it is impossible to permanently damage this craft," Dad said with satisfaction.

I decided I had better go and pack my things and left Dad tinkering with the control panel. I hoped he wouldn't do anything silly. I went into the house and up to the bedroom. Richard had already changed and looked calmer. We were soon ready. I leaned over the balcony to say goodbye to the Hooches who were still lazily standing around. They nodded their heads in recognition and whistled. Feeling satisfied I had not forgotten anything, we all went on board.

Dad was still scrutinising the control panel so I put our bags in the bedroom. Everything was exactly as it was before and I felt very relieved. When I returned, Dad and Richard were huddled over the desk. They were in their element planning something and I assumed it was a flight plan back to Dad's apartment but I did not interrupt.

I nonchalantly sat down beside them in the now familiar leather seats and admired the view from the front window. I ignored them like a seasoned traveller. Eventually Dad seemed satisfied and patted Richard on the back.

"Horace, we have to return Professor Macdonald back to his apartment; leave as soon as you can," Richard said urgently.

"I shall be honoured to assist," Horace replied. "Departure will be in thirty seconds."

The door silently slid shut. We gently lifted off, swung to the right and accelerated over the tops of the trees. Soon we were travelling at an incredible speed. I tried to look calm as the mountains and trees flashed below us. We zoomed across a huge grassy plain and I could see a turquoise green sea in the distance. We slowed and dropped in height. Before me, I could see a lovely sandy beach stretching for miles with acres of sand dunes thick with Marram grass. The sea was gentle with small fluorescent green waves breaking onto the sand. We glided down to a settlement of white bungalows at the seashore and Horace came down to rest on the wide beach. From here it looked wonderful. There were children playing on the beach and groups of people in swimsuits taking in the sun. They completely ignored the arrival of the space ship as if it was an everyday occurrence. I wondered which house Dad was living in.

Richard urgently wanted to get going so that we could catch the transporter so there was no time to linger. We said our goodbyes and Dad disappeared down the lift. As we took off I saw him waving on the beach. I instinctively waved back but realised he could not see me. I felt confused and a little sad and wished I had more time to talk to him.

The journey back to Earth was quick and smooth. We didn't go to the terminal as before but accelerated out into space at breakneck speed, leaving the planets behind us in order to rendezvous directly with the transporter. We had a bit more time to shop on the return trip. I bought my mother a charming ornament depicting a Hooch grazing in long grass. The model was incredibly detailed and lifelike and obviously not terrestrial. For its size, it was very lightweight and Richard assured me it was completely unbreakable. He said that the so-called Indians had made it on Terranus. The workmanship was quite exquisite and I wished that I could have met them. I thought it would be interesting to tell Mum that I had ridden on one of these in an alien world and hoped that it might make her believe me. I did not know how to pay, so Richard took care of it. He wouldn't tell me what the actual cost was.

He then surprised me. I found myself browsing in a jewellery store and was admiring the most exquisite diamond necklace. It was unlike anything I had seen before and Richard bought it for me there and then; in fact, he must have done it electronically without me realising. He clipped it around my neck. It looked fantastic even though I was still wearing jeans and a tee shirt. When we got back to Horace, I changed into a black evening gown to show it off. Richard was very impressed but had more serious thoughts on his mind. He had set the ship to normal Earth gravity. Although the sensation was gradual it was a bit of a shock but he said we have to get used to it before getting back to Earth. I was also instructed to keep the necklace and ornament in a discreet place for the moment, something to do with customs regulations. I could certainly understand why. It must have cost a fortune.

We were, however, both very tired and needed to catch up on sleep so we put our trust in Horace to get us home safely. We spent the rest of the journey in bed, fast asleep while the cosmos streaked past our window at the speed of light.

CHAPTER 23

Richard lightly kissed me on the lips as I opened my eyes. He put a mug of coffee on the bedside cabinet and knelt by the bed. For a moment, I thought I had been having an amazing dream until I saw the lifelike model of the Hooch standing beside the coffee on the strange velvet bedside table. The reality of the past events came flooding back into my mind.

"Where are we?" I said sleepily. "I think I have been asleep for a thousand years." He was dressed in a suit and tie and smelled of his familiar aftershave. I pulled myself up and sat in the bed tucking the fluffy blanket around my chest.

"We have landed in the field at the back of your house. The weather is warm but cloudy. It is 9.00am and only Thursday."

"It's Thursday?" I said, feeling relieved to know what day it is and thinking that I don't have to go to work until Monday.

"We have gained an extra day," Richard said with a whimsical smile. I put my arms around his neck and kissed him, letting the blanket drop.

"I have some stuff to sort out for my mother and I have to go to a blasted meeting tonight in London. I shall be back Friday lunchtime. I don't want to leave you, but I have no choice. You must ring me on my mobile if you need to talk and I will ring you this evening. I'm really sorry that I am going to disappear again. I shall miss you."

"Don't worry darling. I have got to see my mother; we have a hell of a lot to talk about." Richard then handed me a large plastic envelope.

"Your father asked me to give you this," he said. "It is for your mother just in case she thinks you have gone completely off your tree when you tell her what has been going on."

I realised that Richard had things to do so I got dressed quickly. With my packed bag in hand complete with gift-wrapped Hooch, we shot down the lift and Richard accompanied me back to my house. We kissed and he hurried back to the ship. I watched as he disappeared from the feet upwards and vanished into thin air.

It was nice to get back into the familiar surroundings and smell of my house. As soon as I had unpacked and sorted myself out I phoned Mum. She picked up immediately.

"Mum, it's only me, I'm back."

"Lisa, you're not supposed to be back until tomorrow; is everything alright?"

"Everything is fine Mum; Richard had some business to attend to so we came home a day early. How are you feeling?"

"I'm feeling really well. The doctors have been doing all sorts of tests and think I am well enough to go back home so I'm going to arrange for a taxi to pick me up this afternoon. I think they have done a wonderful job of sorting me out."

"No need to arrange a taxi, Mum. I shall pick you up this morning. Can you be ready by midday? We have to talk. I have such a lot to tell you," I said excitedly.

"What on earth has happened Lisa, you sound as though you are going to explode?"

"I have bought you a present; I can't wait to tell you where it came from."

"It sounds intriguing darling. You must have had a good time. You should have a holiday more often."

"Now that you are feeling better Mum, I think you must have a holiday. In fact, I know just the place."

"I don't know what you're talking about darling but I am glad you can come and fetch me. Tell me all about it when I see you."

I managed to get to the hospital at the agreed time. She was ready and waiting at the main entrance. A nurse was with her with her bags at her feet. She was pleased to see me. I was amazed at how good she looked. She had dolled herself up with her best wig and her face had filled out, making her look ten years younger. Considering that I had only seen her a few days ago, the change was remarkable. The nurse shook my hand.

"Thank you for collecting your mother," she said. "She has made a remarkable recovery. Doctor Marcus has given your mother a clean bill of health. He is a wonderful doctor."

She handed me a large brown envelope and told me that Doctor Marcus would contact her shortly. She walked away with a tear in her eye and I sensed her emotion.

I wasn't surprised at the hospital reception. I knew that there were other forces at work. I ushered my Mother into the car and said nothing.

On the way home she questioned me about the holiday. I desperately tried to contain myself and keep the conversation on a mundane level. I know my mother was suspicious and I was glad to get back to the house. Once home, I flung all the windows open and made a pot of tea. She retreated to the sitting room and sat on the sofa. Eventually I brought in the tea together with the gift-wrapped ornament of the Hooch and set it on the coffee table.

"It is unusual paper," she said as she carefully removed the wrapping. "How does the paper stick without Sellotape?"

She took out the model from its wrapping and put it on the table along with the envelope from Dad.

"Good God," she said. "What is it? Is it alive? Where did you get it?"

"I bought it from a shop somewhere out in space," I said and she gave me an old-fashioned look. She gingerly stroked its back.

"Is it some sort of stuffed animal?"

"It's called a Hooch," I said.

"It is very unusual. Where did you say you got it?" Mum

looked very confused and sipped her tea.

"It came from outer space," I said confidently.

"Lisa, are you losing your marbles? What do you mean 'outer space'? Is that a new trendy shop?"

"I have got a lot of explaining to do and you're not going to believe any of it." I started to panic and realised that I had no idea where to start.

"What is in the fancy envelope?" she asked while eyeing up the item on the table.

"Oh dear," I said with a worried look.

"Lisa, what is the matter? You are acting very strangely. Please tell me you are not in trouble. This must have something to do with Richard."

"Oh dear," I said again. "Mum, I hope you are feeling strong; what I am going to say is going to seem very weird and you must believe me." I sat back in the chair.

"Come on, spit it out child," she said crossly. "I know you are holding back from me."

"Mum, Dad didn't die in that air crash. He is very much alive and I have spoken to him." She went very white and didn't say anything for a while so I waited for a reaction.

"Do you mean he faked his own death?" she said eventually.

"No, Mum, he didn't die, he was kidnapped and has been held prisoner for the last five years."

"Kidnapped," she exclaimed, "by whom?"

"By aliens."

"Aliens!"

"Yes, extraterrestrial beings, and he is living on another planet."

"Another planet?" she said, as she got even whiter.

"Yes, he was taken by a mining company for his geological expertise."

"His geological expertise? Lisa, have you completely lost your mind?"

"It is true; the letter is from him and he told me to give it to you so you would understand what has happened. There is so much more I have to tell you." Mum sipped her tea. I could see her hand shaking. She seemed to be taking it very well. Maybe she does know something. I couldn't read her thoughts but I was sure there was something in the past that had finally reared its ugly head. She was keeping a secret from me.

"You mean to tell me that your father was taken by little green men from another planet?"

"Don't be ridiculous," I said. "There are no little green men. These people are just like you and me."

"I know your father is a little eccentric, but this story beats everything. Are you sure you actually spoke to him?"

"What you don't know is that our world has already been invaded by extraterrestrial people."

"Invaded!" she said. "I need something stronger than tea." She got up, wobbled a bit, but energetically left the room, leaving me wondering what to say next. She took a long time but eventually returned with two crystal glasses and a bottle of brandy. While she poured the drinks all I could do was blurt out the whole story.

"You see, Mum, Richard's parents are from another planet in some other solar system. They are very important people and their civilisation is far more advanced than ours. They can travel huge distances across space." I took a deep breath and just let it all flood out. "I haven't been on holiday. Richard flew me in an incredible spacecraft called Horace, and we travelled at the speed of light. We spent a few days on this beautiful planet called Terranus and Richard's mother is a very important person. Dad was taken to another planet called Honshu; it is where he originally came from. It is an amazing coincidence that he was found at the same time that I met Richard. You see, Richard had our family investigated because he knew that I was related to someone from this solar system. Remember the MI6 people. He couldn't tell me the truth until he had security clearance and this is how they found Dad. Dad was actually born on another planet. That model on the table – Dad and I have actually ridden on those animals. Richard bought it because I didn't know how to pay for it. He also bought me a beautiful diamond necklace but he said we have to keep quiet about it because of security."

I took another deep breath and a sip of brandy; Mum just sat there with wide eyes and a confused look, clutching her now empty glass. After another period of silence she slowly leaned forward.

"Well," she said as if I were a child, "you certainly couldn't have made any of that up."

"There is a lot more that I need to explain."

"Let us take this slowly," she said. "I am not at all sure what you are talking about. I also know that a lot of things regarding your father don't add up."

"Dad has written you a letter explaining everything," I said excitedly.

Mum picked up the strange white envelope and took out what seemed to be a stiff black card and several sheets of paper. I could see the letter was handwritten and I let Mum read it in silence. I finished my brandy glass and put it on the table. The brandy had gone to my head so I decided to go into the kitchen and make some strong coffee. With any luck there might be some biscuits in the tin. When I returned, Mum was sitting there with tears streaming down her face.

"Are you alright Mum?" I asked. "What does the letter say?" She produced a handkerchief and dabbed her eyes.

"Well this is certainly your father's handwriting. He has explained the whole story, it is quite incredible, and I would never have believed it. He was born on this planet Honshu. I don't know what any of this means."

"I don't know either Mum. I don't understand the full picture myself. May I read the letter?"

"I'd rather you didn't; there are some personal things in it which only your father and I know about." She folded up the letter and picked up the black card.

"Your father said the black card has some pictures on it and I have to press a corner." She squeezed the corner and I could see the card light up; the glow reflected in her face. She sat there mesmerised for an age.

"Good God," she said eventually.

"Can I see it Mum?" I said impatiently and she handed the card to me with a stunned expression on her face. It was about A5 size and seemed to be made of thin plastic similar to Richard's gismos. I squeezed the corner and the whole card lit up. I was astounded at what I saw. It played a video clip of us all at the holiday house. One scene even showed me being kissed by Richard's mother and another was of my father giving a Hooch an apple. The pictures were very detailed and you could clearly see the huge black spaceship that Richard's mother had arrived in and the fantastic scenery beyond. The moving pictures were also holographic, giving the impression that the card was thicker than it was. It was a good example of advanced technology and I wondered how Dad had got them; I didn't notice anybody filming us.

Mum undid the top button on her blouse; she had been looking pale but was now red faced with a wild look in her eyes. She took the card from me and studied it again closely while I sat there in stunned silence. Eventually I gathered myself together.

"Mum, you must remember the doctor who came to see you in hospital. He comes from this planet. They have advanced medical technology and Richard arranged for him to see you. He gave you an injection that contained advanced micro-organisms that seek out and destroy the cancer cells. They boost the immune system and it has cured you of the disease. Richard said you could well live to over a hundred. In fact he probably saved your life." After a long pause, Mum finally spoke.

"This does explain a few things," Mum said. I don't think she was listening to me. "Your father didn't have any family and I always suspected something a bit strange about him. He said he was orphaned during the war when he was a baby and wasn't able to trace any of his family. He did not have any records of his childhood, no photographs or letters. When I first met him I felt sorry for him; he was a lonely intelligent man with no past. This story of coming from outer space is quite incredible. I have always believed in extraterrestrial life but this is insane. I have only just got used to him being dead. He says in the letter that I must come to this place, what is it called, Terranus?"

"You must, Mum," I said. "We can all go together."

"Hold on a minute," Mum said. She jumped out of her chair and went over to her bureau in the corner of the room. She quickly returned with a silver necklace that she handed to me.

"Your father gave this to me when we were married."

The silver chain had a black pendant about the size of a penny and it looked like black onyx. At first, it looked plain but when you looked into it, there was an exquisite iridescent picture of the planetary system, not unlike the picture above Richard's piano.

"That's it," I said excitedly. "Dad and Richard's parents come from this part of space." The pendant linked the whole scenario together and we smiled at each other in agreement.

"Your father says that Richard's parents are important people," Mum said after another long pause. "He says that they are visiting Earth next week and if I am in agreement your Father could come with them to see me. He also wants me to see this planet. Good grief, this is a lot to take in and I just don't know what to do."

"Take your time, Mum, you think about it. I'm going to pop down the road and get some food from the local shop."

By the time I had returned, Mum was already in the kitchen making scrambled eggs so I popped some bread into the toaster to go with it. It seemed like days since I had some food so we sat at the kitchen table and tucked in. Mum was very quiet. I could see that she was deep in thought but I was so pleased to see how well she looked. I can't remember the last time she had actually wanted to cook something. She looked strangely younger even after a few days. After the meal, she sat back and looked at me sternly.

"What do you make of all this?" she said. "It must have been a shock for you."

"It was," I said. "Richard has been wonderful and I am having the time of my life. I have been flown to the moon and back and halfway across the galaxy in a very comfortable spaceship that has everything you would possibly need. It has been amazing to see Dad again. You really must see this planet; it is beautiful."

"I don't know about flying in any space ships," Mum said after another pause. "I have to think about this. If your father is alive I will have to see him. I shall have nightmares until I do."

"That's settled then. I'll get Richard to organise it when he rings tonight."

CHAPTER 24

I spent the rest of the afternoon describing in detail my extraterrestrial experiences and Mum listened in disbelief and fascination. However, I was glad to get back to my little house and happy to know that Mum had accepted the whole scenario so well. I had a hot bath and sat down in my living room with a cup of coffee. I actually had a chance to relax and think about the recent events. It all seemed like a dream now that I was back in my own personal space. I chuckled at the pun and wondered how it was all going to turn out. I decided to turn the television on and see the news. For all I knew the Prime Minister might have died, but I fell asleep and did not see the program at all. The telephone woke me with a start and I answered it with a croaky voice.

"Sorry darling, did I wake you?" Richard said.

"No, I just dozed off for a minute."

"Did you talk to your mother? How is she?"

"She is extremely well and I explained the whole picture."

"How did she take it?" Richard said with a worried tone.

"Surprisingly well," I said cheerfully. "It all seemed to make sense to her."

"It was a good idea for your father to write her a letter," he said.

"Yes, but that picture card thingy was brilliant. How did he get those movie pictures?" I quizzed.

"I'm afraid that was my idea. I borrowed a robotic camera from Horace. You wouldn't have noticed; it is no bigger than a fly on the wall." Richard sounded agitated.

"Is everything all right Richard? I do miss you."

"I miss you too, darling. I'm just a bit worried about meeting the Prime Minister tonight."

"The Prime Minister!" I said excitedly. "Why do you have to see the Prime Minister?"

"I just have to make arrangements for my mother's visit this week."

"Does your mother know the Prime Minister?" I said, feeling shocked, especially as I was only just thinking about him. "Does he know who she is?"

"Don't worry Lisa, the PM is from Terranus and is fully aware of the situation." Suddenly I felt overwhelmed and did not know what to say.

"Lisa, I'm sorry to put pressure on you and your mother," Richard continued. "I'm staying at Darius's house tonight in London and I would love to see you tomorrow. Also, Darius would like to check over your mother; just routine to make sure she is OK. We both have a lot on our plates now. Would it be possible to get your mother to come here tomorrow morning in Horace? Then I can come back with you. I will be finished here by ten." I sat for a moment with my head reeling.

"Lisa, are you there?" Richard said.

"I'm here," I said. "But I don't know how to drive Horace. I'm not sure if I can get Mum to come with me."

"Don't worry if you can't. The problem is Darius is going back to Terranus at the weekend and he won't have time to see her now for a few weeks." Richard sounded very agitated and I felt sorry for him. "Try your best," he pleaded. "All you have to do is get her into the field at the back of your house by 9.30, take your mobile phone and punch in my home number. That will connect you directly to Horace and he will tell you what to do. He knows all about it and will take you to Darius's house. All you have to do is board the ship."

I felt strangely excited about whizzing my mother off to

London in Horace without Richard and felt I had to support him as much as I could. After all, Darius did save her life.

"I shall get her there," I said with confidence.

"I shall look forward to seeing you tomorrow. I have to go now; I love you."

"I love you too. Bye."

I sat in the chair next to the telephone for a long while thinking about our conversation and decided to dismiss any thoughts about having an alien Prime Minister for the moment. I also decided that Mum must come with me after considering the circumstances. I concocted a plan to get her to my house. I completely trusted Horace. I picked up the phone and dialled her number.

"Mum, it's only me."

"Lisa darling, what's up?"

"I have just been talking to Richard. Dr Marcus would like to see you tomorrow for a routine check-up."

"A routine check-up. That is short notice; I am visiting some friends tomorrow afternoon."

"Dr Marcus is very busy at the moment. It is a very early appointment; you should be back home by midday."

"Ok darling, do I have to drive to the hospital?" I was surprised to hear her say that. She had not driven her car for over a year and it threw me.

"Are you OK driving your car all the way to Edinburgh?" I asked in panic.

"Of course darling. I used to do the trip all the time." I thought quickly and decided my plan would still work.

"Richard has already arranged for a private helicopter to take us both there," I said boldly.

"How exciting!" she said. "I have never been in a helicopter. Will Richard be with us?"

"Yes, you will see Richard." It was a white lie, but I didn't want her driving to the hospital in Edinburgh to find that Dr Marcus wasn't there.

"I shall look forward to it. Where do we board the helicopter? I could get used to this VIP treatment. I must thank Richard." Mum was genuinely excited and I was surprised at how game she was.

"If you really want to drive? Can you be at my house by 9.30 in the morning."

"No problem, I shall see you tomorrow morning."

Once again, I was amazed at my mother's reaction and decided that perhaps I should have some of the same treatment that Dr Marcus had administered to her. Needless to say I didn't get much sleep that night.

It was a bright sunny morning and I was feeling excited about our impending trip and looking forward to seeing Richard. I was wearing my white summer dress with my hair long and straight with absolutely no make-up on at all. I had just finished my toast and coffee when I heard the toot of my mother's little car in the road. She strode into the house looking very smart in an expensive green skirt and floral blouse. She too was wearing very little make-up and looked absolutely fabulous. She went into the living room, looking in every corner.

"Lisa darling, you really must tidy this place up," she said scornfully.

"I haven't had much time Mum," I said irritably.

"Where do we meet the helicopter?" Mum asked. She was obviously a bit wound up.

"In the field at the back."

"How decadent," she said with a smile. "Won't the neighbours complain?" I ignored her question.

"We have to go; are you ready?"

"Ready and waiting," she said.

I grabbed my mobile and handbag and we went out of the back door. It was good that neither of us liked to wear high heels for the field at the back was damp and the ground soft.

"Where is the helicopter?" Mum asked impatiently. "Surely we would have heard it arrive. I don't want my hair blown around by the thing."

I ignored her again and got out my mobile. I dialled Richard's number and it answered immediately.

"Hello Lisa, I have been expecting you." It was Horace's voice and I felt so relieved. "I have you in my sights," he continued. "Turn to your left and walk about twenty paces. You will see the boarding platform." I grabbed Mum's arm, guided her to the left and counted the paces.

"What are you doing?" Mum protested.

"It's OK, I'm just finding out what has happened to the helicopter. My phone reception is not very good." Mum walked with me and soon I saw the familiar green frame of the lift platform. I held Mum's arm tightly and stepped onto it, literally dragging her with me. She stumbled onto it but I held her up. My heart was beating wildly.

"Lisa, what in hell are you doing …Oh my God …" The white walls immediately surrounded us and to my surprise the rising sensation was much more pleasant than before. Within seconds, we were looking out into the ship's cabin. I turned to Mum and she was a bit white and shaken.

"Oh my God," she said, with her jaw open.

"Welcome aboard, Lisa and Mrs Macdonald," Horace said.

"Oh my God," Mum said again.

I guided my speechless mother into the cabin and sat her at the round table in one of the plush black leather chairs. The viewing windows were all activated and Mum stared outside. You could see my little terraced house at the end of the field.

"Horace," I said, "the ride in the lift was much nicer. Thank you."

"I was instructed to alter the dynamics to make the experience more pleasant for you."

"Well thank you anyway. What happens next?" I asked.

"When you and your mother are ready we can set off by your

command."

"Thank you Horace."

I looked at my mother; she was looking around with her mouth open and her eyes wide.

"Are you all right Mum? Would you like something to drink? You look a bit pale."

"I suppose it is too early for a brandy," she stammered.

"Horace," I said. "Do we have any brandy?"

"Dr Marcus keeps a bottle in the wine cupboard," Horace said. I left my mother rigidly sitting there bolt upright and went into the kitchen. When I returned she was standing looking out of the front viewing window. I handed her the crystal brandy glass and she took a sip.

"You have got me into this space ship," she said eventually.

"I'm sorry to deceive you. I had to. Dr Marcus is in London and it was the only way to get to see him before he goes back to his home planet."

"His home planet?" Mother said dumbly. I sat her down again in the front seats and she clutched her brandy glass with both hands.

"This is all very real," she said.

"This is the ship that took me to see Dad. The ride is very comfortable and Horace is wonderful."

"Thank you Lisa," Horace said.

"Where is that voice coming from?" Mum said.

"Don't worry, it is Horace. He is in charge and totally reliable. Horace, I would like to introduce my mother."

"Welcome, Mrs Macdonald."

"Thank you but I don't understand how we got here. I was in an empty field only a moment ago."

"We went up in a lift." I tried to reassure Mum. "Just relax, it will all become clear."

"Clear!" she said. "You have beamed us into this spaceship thing of yours that wasn't there in the first place."

"Don't worry Mum; it will be alright. We have to set off. There's not much time and Horace can't stay too long in one place in case somebody sees him. Will you be alright? We have to take off."

"Sees him? Sees what? I haven't seen anything yet. Lisa, this is a strange experience and I seem to be at your mercy. I hope you know what you're doing." She sipped her brandy and sat back staring out of the front window.

"Horace," I said while secretly feeling happy being in charge of a star ship. "Engage!"

"Lisa," Horace said, "I have not heard that command before but I know what you mean and I like it. Departure will be immediate, please keep your seats."

The ship moved vertically upwards and we were soon beyond the fluffy white clouds and above the atmospheric haze with the deep blue sky above. We seemed to be moving forwards but there was no sensation of speed. The ship appeared to move in an arc at an incredible rate and within minutes we were descending and skimming the tops of the clouds again. We went through the white of the cloud and suddenly the huge metropolis of London was below us. Mother was transfixed by the vista spread before her through the panoramic window.

"This is London," Mum said. "I can see the Houses of Parliament, and that is Big Ben."

The Thames snaked below us as we glided over the city. Soon we turned north over the concrete jungle of London and I recognised the green of Hampstead Heath with the park lakes below us. We suddenly descended onto a huge lawn area and a large Victorian house came into view. The ship docked expertly against the upstairs balcony and came to rest. Mum swallowed the rest of her brandy.

"Good God," she said. "We are in London within the blink of an eye. I would never have believed it."

CHAPTER 25

The door at the side of the cabin slid open and sunlight poured in. Richard was waiting there and I jumped up and went to greet him. He was wearing a smart grey suit. I flung my arms around his neck and kissed him and he squeezed my waist in return.

"You made the trip OK," he said.

"No problem," I said.

"I was hoodwinked into this," my mother said from behind me. "But it was very enjoyable and quite incredible." I released Richard. He walked into the ship and shook my mother's hand.

"I'm glad that you didn't find it too uncomfortable, Mrs Macdonald," he said. "I'm sorry to arrange this trip at short notice and I'm sure you found the experience very strange but Dr Marcus needs to check your progress."

"I'm a little confused," Mum said. "Was Dr Marcus the physician who saw me when I met you in hospital?"

"Yes, he is our personal family doctor; he has to return to Terranus shortly. I'm so sorry to rush you but we only have limited time before we have to leave so that he can board another ship." Mum was looking spaced out but she retained her dignity.

"I cannot begin to understand what is going on, Mr Varnicus. I only saw Dr Marcus very briefly. I think he gave me an injection. Other doctors have been examining me. I didn't realise I would be meeting him again in London. Where did you say he was from?"

My mother seemed to go weak at the knees. Richard helped

her through the porthole and onto a large balcony. There were wicker chairs placed around a glass-topped table with stainless steel legs. He sat my mother down in one of the chairs and asked if she would like something to drink. I couldn't hear what she had said but within seconds a beautiful woman with blonde hair dressed in a nurse's uniform came onto the balcony carrying a small tray with a single brandy. My mother took a sip with a shaking hand.

"I am very pleased that it has gone well for you," Richard said. "It is important that you are well. Now that Lisa has explained the situation to you, I can understand that it must be very confusing. I love your daughter and I have subjected her and now yourself to a truth that is only known, at the moment, to a select few. It must have been a shock to learn about your husband. I do hope it will all work out well for the future."

I don't think Mother was paying attention. She was staring at Horace's open porthole, which she had passed through earlier.

"I just don't understand," she said. "Is the spaceship invisible?"

"We can't have visible spaceships flying around London," Richard said as he sat down, "it would cause panic." With that, the porthole whizzed shut leaving no trace of Horace at all.

"How did your meeting with the PM go?" I asked Richard. I could sense that he was worried about something.

"It went fine, just routine; my mother will have a lot to sort out next week." The nurse returned and addressed my mother.

"Dr Marcus will see you now, Mrs Macdonald," she said in a rather bland way. I was sure she was one of those synthetic people. She had perfect skin.

When we were alone, I asked Richard what the problem was.

"I spoke to Philbin last night," he said. "He is now in Australia and is going to arrest some people in connection with your father's abduction."

"That is good news, isn't it?"

"Well, yes it is, but he told me he went to Cannock Brae to

interview Mr and Mrs T. Apparently he found the house deserted with the front door left wide open. They seem to have disappeared without a trace and taken all their things. Philbin got some special police officers to check the place over and luckily nothing has been taken. He thinks that they could be implicated in some way."

"That's awful," I said.

"The awful thing is that I myself could have been a security breach. It is possible that Jack could have accessed classified information from the house computer and sold the information to interested parties. The computer has a direct link to the Terranus Council record systems. I should have been more careful and I stupidly trusted them. After all they did have security clearance from the Council."

"It is not your fault Richard," I said. "As you said, they have security clearance."

My mother returned with her arm linked to Dr Marcus; she was beaming and I hoped she had not been flirting with him. Dad would be mortified.

"I have a clean bill of health," she said, "thanks to this wonderful man." She sat down looking very pleased with herself and sipped her brandy. Dr Marcus shook my hand and bowed courteously.

"It is very nice to see you again Lisa," he said in his posh Italian accent. "I have some time to spare. Would you mind if I checked you over before I go?"

"Why not, you have done wonders for my mother and thank you for your help," I said and followed him into the huge consulting room. The room was Victorian and heavily ornate. He sat me in a plush red leather wing chair and pointed an electronic gismo at me.

"Do you have any health problems, Lisa?"

"No," I said. "I'm as fit as a fiddle." He looked at his hand held computer for a while.

"Have your periods been regular?"

"I haven't had one for a while," I said, "why do you ask?"

"Well, you certainly have remarkably good health and you keep yourself very fit. I don't see any problems at all."

"That's good news, Dr Marcus."

"Please call me Darius," he said. "There is one thing you do need to be aware about though."

"OK Darius," I said cautiously.

"You are with child; you were fertilised about one month ago."

I felt very stunned. Fertilised? It seemed like a strange word to use. There again, Darius was a strange doctor. After all the past events, this was the last thing that would have crossed my mind. I think I had remembered to take the pill but I might have forgotten. I had missed my periods before. The thought that Richard would have to be the father gave me a warm feeling inside and I think my face must have flushed. *Good grief, now I'm bloody well pregnant.*

"I'm sorry if this news has shocked you Lisa," Dr Marcus said with a concerned look. "I can see it has taken you by surprise. You shouldn't worry; it is in the early days and if I can be of assistance in any way just ask me. Perhaps you need to talk things over with the father of the child."

"Richard is the father and I have no idea what he is going to say," I said excitedly. Dr Marcus broke into a broad smile. I could sense that he has already spoken to Richard. He seemed to be very pleased. He stood up and I reciprocated.

"Congratulations Lisa, I think it is wonderful news," he said as he warmly shook my hand. "You take care of the baby and I will see you soon."

I went back out onto the veranda feeling stunned; Richard was sitting next to my mother huddled in deep conversation. He looked up at me and immediately I knew that he knew I was pregnant. I realised that I could never keep a secret from him.

Thankfully, he did not say anything. I think the shock might have been too much for my mother.

"I can see that everything is alright with you darling," he said with a wink and an apologetic smile. He stood up and kissed me. "Now we have to board the bucket and get out of here."

"I have to use the wee little room," my mother said with her Scots accent breaking through. I think she was a little tipsy.

"There is a bathroom on board Horace," I said. "You can use that."

The porthole whizzed open again and Richard disappeared into the house to say goodbye to Darius. I guided mother to the suspended doorway and she teetered on the edge frightened to step into the abyss so I went first and helped her across. Once inside she was fine so I showed her how to use the loo and then went to make some coffees. I thought it would be best to get her home as soon as possible so that hopefully I could get Richard alone for a much needed chat.

By the time Mum had finished in the 'wee room' Richard had returned and we got underway. The flight back to Scotland took no time at all. Richard got Horace to circle around the Highlands on a sight-seeing tour. Mum was now used to flying and loved every minute of it as we skimmed across the tops of the mountains that she knew so well. Eventually we landed in the field at the back of my house. I escorted Mother back to her car and told her I shall be in touch regarding the reunion next week.

I quickly sorted out my overnight bag so I could stay with Richard over the weekend and then rejoined him in the ship. We flew to Cannock Brae at a leisurely pace at low altitude.

"How do you feel about the news?" he asked.

"I must admit it was the last thing I expected to hear. How do you feel about it?"

"I have known about it for some time. That's why I wanted you to see Darius just to make sure everything was in order and in any case it is better to hear it from your doctor."

"How on earth did you know about it?" I asked although I was not surprised.

"Horace discreetly tipped me off."

"How on earth did Horace know about it?" I exclaimed with my voice rising in pitch.

"Don't worry," Richard said. "Horace scans all life forms that enter the ship for security reasons. He just noticed that there was an additional life form inside you and felt that I should know about it."

"Horace could have told me," I said indignantly, although I had suspected something was in the air because of Horace's strange behaviour.

"I'm sorry Lisa, but it is not my place to advise you of such things," Horace said.

"It's OK Horace, I don't mind really," I said.

"Well, how do you feel about it?" Richard repeated.

"I think it is wonderful," I said. "After all I'm not getting any younger and it's kind of nice to think I'm going to be a mother. Speaking of mothers, I suppose your mother knows about it already."

"No, I haven't told her yet. I needed to know how you feel first especially as the child will be my heir."

"Hell, I hadn't thought of that," I said. "You mean it would be next in line to represent Terranus."

"Yes," Richard said with a proud smile. I could sense his delight.

"What will your mother think? After all I'm not of royal blood and I wasn't even born on Terranus. Would your mother prefer a boy or girl?"

"Don't forget I wasn't born on Terranus and it doesn't matter what sex it is. Mother will be absolutely delighted. She thinks you are wonderful and so do I."

I gave Richard a big hug and a long kiss. I noticed that Horace was descending onto Richard's lovely house. He parked expertly against the bedroom balcony and I noticed how neglected the lawns looked.

"You don't have anybody to cook and clean for you," I said.

"That's alright, I can cook," he said with a false smile. I did not believe him. "Anyway my mother is going to bring a chef, housekeeper and gardener from Terranus on Monday. They will be artificial so I know I can rely on them." Damn, I thought, more people with perfect skin.

"I can cook for you this weekend," I said, "and I'll give the house a good clean as well."

"Thank you darling," he said. "In that case I will give the garden a tidy up if I can remember where the lawn mower is."

We had an idyllic weekend, just the two of us doing domestic chores. We made love in various locations inside and out and had candle lit dinners, which I prepared on the wonderful Aga stove. I was surprised at the size and opulence of Richard's house. There were ten plush bedrooms and Mrs T had left them immaculate with all the beds beautifully made. I lost count of the bathrooms but once again I didn't need to do anything and it gave me a chance to get to know the whole of the house. By the side of the kitchen there was a whole wing devoted to servants' accommodations with three bedrooms and two more bathrooms. It was obvious that Jack and Thelma must have left in a hurry but at least these were the only rooms that needed sorting out. Mrs T was certainly a very thorough housekeeper. It put me to shame with the state of my own little house.

Richard had all sorts of clever gadgets for cleaning the house, including a robotic floor polisher that would walk up and down the stairs all by itself, apparently one of his father's creations. Richard made a superb job of cutting the grass. We were all ready for the arrival of his parents and my own father by Sunday night.

As we were both feeling exhausted, I made a pot of freshly

ground coffee and we flopped onto the sofa in the sitting room with a feeling of self-satisfaction. I silently contemplated my cup and my mind kicked into gear.

"Darling," I said tentatively, "how come your mother knows the Prime Minister? Why is she meeting him next week? I know it is probably none of my business but there is an awful lot I don't understand. How many people from your planets live here on Earth?"

"Don't forget that your father comes from Honshu," Richard said, smiling at me. "The problem is that a huge majority don't know that they have originated from outer space. Erasing the memory of the people was not a good idea and it doesn't always work. The mind-altering process is going to be banned completely and will only be used for correcting mental health problems. The history of mankind on Earth has been sporadic and out of control and has not had the chance to take a natural course. For instance, take a look at the Roman civilisation and the Victorian industrial revolution. More recently, the digital age would never have started without the technology from the Terranus system. These historical events should never have taken place. It is the fault of intervention from our home planets."

"I certainly didn't know I was from outer space," I said, "so how many other people are there who don't know about their origins?"

"I have no idea darling. People have been arriving here for thousands of years. We are all just one small part of the huge soup we call the universe. Plants, animals, everything, it is all part of the universe. Life either evolved or was brought here by some means or other. For example, mushrooms arrived on Earth on an asteroid being part of a planet that exploded light years away. I like to think of the universe as an ocean teeming with life but on an unimaginable scale."

"So why is your mother meeting with the Prime Minister?" I asked again in confusion. I could immediately sense Richard's concern. "After all he is just the British Prime Minister and we are talking about whole worlds and the universe." Richard sat back uncomfortably and took a gulp of his coffee.

"I am not really supposed to talk about it," Richard said with a frown. "But you are family now, so what the hell." I looked him in the eyes and sensed his love. I suddenly felt that I had joined some sort of cosmic Mafia.

"Mother will in fact be meeting with a large majority of world leaders with the help of a team of Council Leaders," he continued. "One of the problems is the fact that our species is unique and highly successful. Consequently, planet Earth is over-populated and heading for disaster. Depleted resources, famine, deforestation, rampant disease, wars and global warming, these are all issues that we have encountered in the Terranus system. Population control and advanced technology saved the planets from total destruction."

"It would seem that your mother has a lot to talk about," I said stupidly while trying to understand the extent of the situation. I was amazed to learn that world leaders already know that an unknown quantity of people originally came from outer space. It seemed like an invasion on an insidious level.

"You will have to talk to my mother. She will explain the situation and I think you should take next week off work," Richard said, changing the subject rapidly.

"Oh God, I have completely forgotten about work," I said. "I don't think Hamish is going to like it at such short notice."

"Don't worry; we have a lot on our plate. I'll sort it with Hamish," Richard said as he kissed me on the cheek. I had the feeling that a little bribery was going to be used but I was grateful not to have to worry about my stupid job.

I got up and went into the kitchen to check on the lamb stew that had been cooking gently in the slow oven. I was glad to have a break from cosmic issues. The food was ready so I laid the table and we had a relaxed dinner talking about life on

Terranus. I desisted from asking questions about the fate of our own planet.

After dinner, Richard surprised me yet again. He got down on one knee and proposed to me. I accepted without hesitation. He presented me with the most enormous diamond ring I had ever seen.

CHAPTER 26

I spent the whole of Monday morning cleaning my house and clearing out the fridge, which was full of mouldy food and smelt like a sewer. Richard wanted me to move in with him so I jumped at the chance. I had borrowed the Jaguar, which was worrying at first but fabulous to drive once you got used to it. I packed all my clothes and some personal belongings. I filled the boot of the car with them. I was going to leave the Volvo in the drive for the time being. I had arranged to pick up my mother at 2pm and take her to Cannock Brae. Dad and Richard's parents were arriving at six so now the stage was set. It was all very exciting. I locked up the house and climbed into the Jag. It was a fine warm day so I decided to put the roof down once I had found the right knob to press.

I swung into my mother's driveway and pulled up outside her front door. I was a bit early so I got the keys out to let myself in but she beat me to it and flung the door open before I had the chance to insert the key in the lock. When I saw her, I had the shock of my life.

"Mum! What have you done to your hair?" I exclaimed. Her hair was cut in a boy's urchin style and was jet black. I had to admit that it had been cut very well and looked very stylish. She looked twenty years younger.

"Don't you like it darling?" she said. "I used to have my hair like this when I was a teenager. This is so much better than that itchy wig." She did a twirl and pulled me into the house by my arm.

"Is that your own hair?" I asked. "What happened to your wig?"

"That lovely doctor told me it would grow back quickly after I had that injection and he was right. Isn't it super? He gave me a tablet to slow the growth when it got long enough. My hairdresser nearly had a heart attack when he saw me. He thought I was my daughter, isn't that so bizarre?"

"I can't believe how young you look," I said. "It makes me feel old."

"Don't be silly darling, you look beautiful. I wish I had your looks. Come and sit down. I'm sure you have something to tell me."

"What do you mean, something to tell you?" I said while we flopped on the sofa. I started to wonder if she knew about my baby.

"Come on darling, don't keep me in suspense. Did he propose?"

"Why is it that everybody knows everything before I do?" I said feeling annoyed. I thrust out my hand and displayed the huge diamond engagement ring.

"Darling it is beautiful!" she said grabbing my hand and scrutinising the ring at close quarters.

"Richard is such a gentleman," she continued, "he asked me permission for your hand in marriage. Isn't that so delightfully old-fashioned? You did accept, didn't you?"

"Of course I did," I said. "In any case, I'm going to have his baby."

"What?" Mother's eyes went wild. "You're going to have a baby? My only child is going to have a baby! I'm going to be a grandmother!" Her eyes welled up and she pulled out a lace handkerchief from her top jacket pocket.

I left her sitting on the sofa blowing her nose. She was over-reacting so I left her to it and took her heavy case out to the car. I lifted it in and put it on the back seat. By the time I had closed the door she had followed me out.

"You shouldn't be lifting heavy things in your condition," she said.

"Don't fuss Mum; I'm perfectly alright. Are you ready? We should go."

Mum was talking almost constantly all the way to Cannock Brae and I have to admit I was only half listening; there was so much happening in my own life. I think she was pretty wound up about becoming a grandmother and the thought of meeting Dad after five years. In addition, she has to meet her future in-laws who happen to have come from another solar system. By the time we had reached the gates she had calmed down and was hopefully coming to terms with the situation. The gates were open so I sedately drove up the long driveway and pulled up outside the front portico.

She got out of the car. I left her making comments about the splendour of everything while I went inside to find Richard. I could not find him but bumped into a maid who was wearing a tasty black uniform with a white apron. She had blonde hair and perfect skin so I instantly realised she was an artificial life form from Terranus.

"You must be Miss Lisa," she said whilst making a curtsy.

"Yes, I am," I replied. "Where is everybody?"

"The master of the house is showing the rest of the staff their living quarters. May I assist you in anyway?"

"Yes er ... do you have a name?" I asked.

"I am the house maid. I am called Prudence."

"Well Prudence, nice to meet you. Would you help me with the suitcases?"

"Yes madam." She followed me out to the Jaguar. Mum was standing on the lawn surveying the house with her head back and her mouth open. Prudence quickly lifted Mum's case out of the car as if it were made of polystyrene.

"Prudence, do you know which bedroom my mother is staying in?"

"Yes madam, would you like me to show Mrs Macdonald to her room?"

"Yes Prudence, if you would," I said in a haughty manner.

I gathered up my mother and got her to follow Prudence while I went to find Richard. As I went into the dining room, he crashed through the swing doors.

"Darling, I thought you were back. Is your mother OK?" He kissed me on the nose.

"Prudence is showing her to her bedroom," I said.

"Oh, you have met Prudence," he said. "I'm sorry about the staff. Mother sent them on ahead. She thought I might need some help. We now have a cordon bleu chef, three housemaids, a gardener and a chauffeur-cum-butler. I think she has gone a little over the top but I have organised their accommodations. The chauffeur has taken the chef to the supermarket to stock up on food; the gardener has already started on the flower beds so we just have house maids at our disposal."

"Well, I suppose we will have a houseful of people," I said with a sigh.

"Don't worry darling, it is a big house. Let me introduce you to the other two and we can get your stuff into our bedroom."

He disappeared into the kitchen and returned almost immediately with two other people. They were both dark haired and oriental, which was a change to the blonde bimbo known as Prudence. They were both perfect in appearance and one of them, to my surprise, was male and wearing a smart black tunic.

"This is Mini and Max," Richard said with a slight smirk on his face. They bowed quickly.

"How do you do Miss Lisa," they said, almost in unison. I put my hand up to my mouth to hide a laugh.

"I'm sorry about the names," Richard said. "It is their own choice; Mini and Max are married and will be sharing a bedroom in the servants' wing."

I immediately decided that my favourite would have to be

227

Prudence and wondered how my mother was getting on with her.

We all trooped out to the car and I opened the boot. I handed Max and Mini various cases and boxes and a few plastic bags full of Heaven knows what. Richard instructed them to put it all on our bed in his room. They walked off heavily laden. When they had gone, Richard put his arms around me. We had a sneaky cuddle and walked round the garden holding hands.

"How are you feeling?" Richard asked. "Have you had morning sickness yet?"

"Oh don't," I said, "so far I'm absolutely fine."

"If you have any problems Darius has a cure for anything."

I left Richard giving the gardener instructions and decided I had better go and see what my mother was up to. I knocked on her door and went in. She was sitting on a chair talking to Prudence.

"Lisa, do you realise that Prudence isn't a real person. She says that she is only one-year-old and manufactured on this planet Honshu where your father comes from. Isn't that amazing? She has been telling me all about it. Look, feel her hand. You wouldn't know the difference. It's warm."

"Mum! You're embarrassing her; leave her alone."

"Oh, it's alright, we have had a lovely conversation. She has been telling me all about these planets. It is all quite incredible."

"If you will not be requiring anything else I shall return to my duties," Prudence said.

"Prudence, would you be able to rustle up a pot of tea and some cakes?" I asked.

"Certainly madam; shall I serve it in the dining room?"

"Yes, thank you Prudence." She hurriedly left and I am sure she was relieved to be excused.

I took Mum on a guided tour of the house. She was suitably impressed and wanted to try out the swimming pool but luckily did not possess a swimming costume. I eventually got her to calm down and sit on the terrace. I diverted Prudence to serve her tea. Once she was settled, I decided to go for a run around the island. We were all very stressed and I thought it would do me good. I quickly sorted out my stuff and threw it in one of the empty wardrobes. I found some running shorts and a tee shirt and set off down the stairs. Richard met me halfway down.

"I know what you're doing," he said. "May I come with you? I could do with a break from all this."

"I would love you to come, but you won't be able to keep up." He smiled at me and disappeared upstairs to get changed. I went out on the terrace to wait for Richard and Mum was sitting there in her element. Not only did she have her tea and cakes but somehow she had got hold of a bottle of sherry and a crystal schooner. She was obviously taking advantage of Prudence. I told her I was going for a run and I would be annoyed if she overdid the sherry. After all there was less than an hour to go before Dad arrived.

I jogged gently up the track towards the trees. I suddenly realised that Bruce wasn't with me and wondered how and where he was. I got to the bottom of the hill in the cool of the trees and then heard Richard crunching up the gravel track behind me. We jogged side by side until we got up to the viewpoint. At the top we sat on a rock and admired the view. Richard had survived the climb very well and seemed quite fresh.

"Do you realise," he said, "this is the place where our child was conceived"

"You don't know that," I said while catching my breath.

"It was when we made love for the first time on this very spot. Marcus knows the exact date of conception."

The sexy interlude was indelibly imprinted in my memory and I wondered why we didn't think of using a condom, which was very careless of us. I must admit that in the heat of the moment the thought had never entered my head. Richard put his arms around me and I clung to his warm body. If it were not for the fact that we had to get back, I would have been quite prepared to repeat the incident there and then but we had to jog back down the hill. I had to be content with just the memory.

When we got back to the house, we only had a matter of minutes to get showered and changed. I decided to wear the black dress to show off the diamond necklace that Richard had bought for me on our trip to Terranus. When I finally got downstairs, I found Richard sitting on the terrace with my mother. He looked very smart dressed in a light brown sports jacket with a white shirt and white trousers.

I smiled at Prudence who was standing primly by the door. Richard got out of his chair and kissed me on the cheek. I sat down and Richard poured me a glass of white wine. Mum still had her schooner of sherry. She leant forward and examined the necklace.

"Darling, your necklace is absolutely stunning," she said while delicately fingering it.

"I know," I said and exposed my engagement ring by placing my hand on my bosom. "I'm positively dripping in diamonds." I sat back in my chair and sipped my wine, feeling like a million dollars. Richard was looking a bit tense. I could not sense his thoughts and I was sure he was nervously awaiting the arrival of his parents.

"Their ship is just coming in to land," he said, clutching my hand.

We all went out onto the lawn and walked round the side of the house. I was not prepared for the sight that lay before us. There was a huge black space ship hanging just above the trees. It wasn't discreetly cloaked but in full view. It looked like a nuclear submarine suspended in the air. It shimmered in the afternoon sun like black velvet and there were no recognisable features or windows apart from a large black disc at one end. I felt a wave of fear and glared at Richard. He was still holding my hand and he tightened his grip.

"Trust Mother to make an ostentatious entrance," he said while shaking his head.

Mum just stood transfixed to the spot with a look of awe and wonder as three people materialised from the feet upwards beneath the monstrous ship. The figures walked towards us with an array of suitcases following bizarrely behind them on a hovering trolley. My mother remained motionless and wide-eyed while Richard and I walked towards them. The spectacular space ship slowly and silently started rising into the air and gradually faded until it was completely invisible.

I could see Dad with a smile on his face wearing his usual khaki safari jacket. It was wonderful seeing him again. It was confirmation that I had not been dreaming all the recent events. I gave him a big hug. I momentarily forgot about Richard's mother and father and eventually released Dad to see my future mother-in-law. She had a warm smile on her face. She was casually dressed with a wide collared white shirt and black slacks but she still looked amazingly glamorous.

"Lisa darling, it is lovely to see you again," she said as we kissed on both cheeks. She always had an incredible feeling of warmth and again I felt completely at ease.

"Lisa," she continued, "you must meet my long suffering husband, William."

William was a tall thin man with striking blue eyes and short black hair. He had a broad smile showing a full set of gleaming white teeth. He took me by the hand and kissed me on the cheek. I could detect the slight smell of carbolic soap and engine oil.

"Wonderful to finally meet you Lisa," he said while shaking my hand vigorously. "I have heard so much about you."

"Thank you," I said while noticing his dirty fingernails, "you must both meet my mother." I turned to find that Dad had already walked on ahead towards Mum, who was standing to attention with her hands firmly clasped in front of her. Richard's mother turned to me and put her arm through mine. She guided me in the opposite direction. We left Richard talking to his father. The telepathy thing was very strong and although I could not hear what they were saying, I instinctively knew they were talking about the railway line.

"We will give your mother and father a moment to talk," she said in my ear. "I'm sure the situation must be very difficult for them. I am dying to get to know you Lisa; we have a lot to talk about. You have no idea how thrilled I am about the baby; it is about time Richard took on some responsibility."

I had no doubts in my own mind. I thought Richard was very responsible and I knew he was delighted with the pregnancy.

"Don't worry Lisa, I'm not going to be the overpowering mother-in-law," she said reassuringly and reading my thoughts. "I am so pleased that you are both in love." She squeezed my arm and I tingled all over.

"I don't know what to call you," I said awkwardly.

"My name is Mary, second daughter of Lord Vinci. You must call me Mary."

We strolled up to Mini and Max who were standing quietly on the edge of the lawn. The suitcases had somehow joined them and were hovering behind.

"Max, would you hand me my bag and then take the luggage up to the rooms and unpack," she said authoritatively.

"Yes, your Ladyship," Max said with a bow. He picked up a small plain black evening bag. He handed it to her with another bow and they scurried off towards the front door with the cases following in hot pursuit. She opened the bag and pulled out another little black velvet bag with a drawstring. She produced a beautiful eternity ring in deep yellow gold that was studded all round with huge diamonds the size of garden peas.

"I want you to have this," she said. "It has been handed down in the family for centuries. Wear it as often as you can." She placed it on my right hand finger and it fitted perfectly.

"There," she said, "that will balance you up while you wear

your engagement ring."

I looked at my hands and felt very ostentatious, secretly pleased that I had the time to paint my nails.

"I can't accept this," I said as tears welled up. "It must be worth a fortune."

"Don't be silly Lisa. Diamonds are much more abundant on my home world. In any case this is a family ring that is centuries old. You must keep it and hand it on to your own family. Just be discreet when you wear it on Earth." I embraced her. I could feel an unexplainable bond reciprocating between us. It was a strange sensation that I had only experienced with Richard. When I finally let go of her we both had tears in our eyes.

"Come on," she said with a smile, "let's go and break up the men. We have to meet your mother and I could murder a gin and tonic."

CHAPTER 27

Richard and his father were still talking nineteen to the dozen while standing on the lawn. Mum and Dad were nowhere in sight. It felt quite strange to refer to them like that after so many years but I was happy with the situation. I just hoped that their reconciliation would be successful despite the weird circumstances. Mum has gained a new lease of life. She is coping with it all very well. Dad seems to be fine, but I do need to talk to him. I was not sure of his objectives.

We approached the men. As soon as we were within earshot, they were quiet. Richard sensed that I was feeling emotional. He came up to me to give me a hug, kissing me on the forehead, and I instantly felt stronger. We strolled round to the terrace arm in arm, with Richard's parents following. We found Mum and Dad sitting at the table both with large glasses of wine in their hands. Prudence was standing dutifully by the door. To my relief they both looked happy and relaxed. They rose from their chairs and I introduced Mum to Richard's parents.

"Mum, this is Lady Mary Vinci and William Varnicus. Please meet my mother, Mrs Morag Macdonald." They shook hands and I felt proud to get all the names right. Mum behaved impeccably and it felt very strange to introduce her to my future in-laws. It seemed as though I had transported back in time and were living my life all over again.

We all sat down and ordered drinks. Mary ordered a large gin and tonic. I felt like having one as well but decided I had better not considering my condition so I told Prudence to get me an orange juice.

"Don't be silly, darling," Mary exclaimed, putting her hand on my arm. "Prudence, get Lisa the same as me." I sat there thinking that Richard's mother had a strong character and strongly tuned to my thoughts.

"If you think it's alright," I said.

"Moderation in all things does you no harm," she said and I immediately felt my mother's eyes on me. I hoped there would not be any friction between the two of them.

"Did you have a good trip, your Ladyship?" Mother asked. "My husband tells me it takes about twelve hours."

"When I'm not on duty you must call me Mary," she said with a disarming smile. "The journey time varies according to the position of the transporter in actual fact. Doesn't it, William?"

"Absolutely," William said with wide eyes. "I think the shortest trip we have made was six hours in the ship each way. Of course you always gain an extra Earth day."

"So that means Morag and I could go to Terranus and back and not know that we've been," Dad said.

We all laughed and the atmosphere became more relaxed. The conversation seemed to flow freely. I was enjoying my G&T but when Mary ordered her second glass, I resisted having another one. Richard was holding my hand under the table. I think he was nervous about the situation but our minds were in tune and I got him to relax especially when he had downed his third glass of wine. We were passing rude comments to each other telepathically. It was comforting and I tried not to snigger, but nobody seemed to notice. I only hoped that Richard's mother was not able to pick up the secret transmissions. It would seem that everybody was getting plastered except me but I did not mind. It was interesting to watch the proceedings with a fairly clear head. Eventually, Max came out onto the terrace and announced that dinner 'is served'. We all weaved our way into the dining room and sat round the table. Lady Mary insisted that I sit between her and Richard's father. Mum and Dad were on the opposite side with Richard at the head of the table. I felt a bit lost. The table was very large. Mum and Dad were locked in conversation and I couldn't hear what they were talking about, but at least they were smiling. Richard and Lady Mary were discussing something weird. I have no idea what it was about. I sat back and tried to relax. I studied the table. It had been laid beautifully with full silver service. I then realised that Prudence was standing beside me with a bottle in her hand.

"Would you like some champagne, Miss Lisa?"

"Yes please," I said in a trance. She filled the champagne glass and went round the table in a clockwise direction. I felt like picking up the glass and downing the contents. I thought better of it. It was comforting that Prudence had served me first.

When Prudence had finished I felt a warm hand on my shoulder.

"With your permission, I am going to propose a toast," William said flashing his dazzling array of teeth. I nodded stupidly and he stood up, tapping his wine glass with a silver spoon.

"I would like to welcome Lisa to this family occasion," he said simply. "Especially as Lisa is now with child. We welcome the thought of becoming grandparents."

"Lisa is pregnant! I didn't know about this," Dad said with surprise in his eyes. Mum then burst into tears. There was an awkward silence while she pulled out her handkerchief again.

"I'm sorry, Dad. I should have told you. I thought you already knew. I have not had time to think about this myself. I have not turned on my laptop in weeks. I should have sent you a message," I said with embarrassment.

"Please don't upset yourself Lisa; I have a lot of catching up to do. I am delighted to hear this news."

"I am most terribly sorry, Jim." William said. "I fear I may have put my foot in it. Events have been happening so fast. I didn't realise."

"Think nothing of it William, I couldn't be happier," Dad said while smiling at me. Mum had managed to compose herself and Lady Mary sat quietly with her head lowered. I had the feeling that she was going to bend her husband's ear later on. It was my fault and I tried to project the thought to Mary. I was not sure if I was doing it correctly but she turned to me and smiled.

"This occasion can only be described as both a family gathering and a reunion," William continued. "I would like to propose a toast wishing all parties health and happiness."

After the toast, everybody settled down while the first course was served. We had Aberdeen Angus beef for the main course with chilled champagne flowing freely. I did allow myself one or two glasses. William was telling me all about Terranus. He missed not being able to play with his steam engines. Apparently there is nothing like that on Terranus. Hundreds of years ago, metallic elements and mining were banned. He spends his time lecturing students about planet Earth's history. He was particularly focused on the Victorian industrial revolution, the use of steam power and the internal combustion engine. Dad was very interested in the conversation and I again felt a bit lost while they discussed the depletion of Earth's mineral resources. The two mothers were monopolising Richard, much to his annoyance, but it was all very pleasant. They all seemed to have something in common. By eleven o'clock, they all staggered off to bed leaving Richard and myself supervising the staff with their clean-up operation.

A knock at the door woke me the next morning. Richard was fast asleep beside me so I got up and put my dressing gown on to open the door. It was Prudence carrying a silver tray with toast and coffee.

"Good morning, Miss Lisa," she whispered. "The master instructed me to bring coffee at eight o'clock."

"Thank you Prudence," I whispered back. "Set it on the table." She carried it over and put the tray down. On her way out she looked at me with a knowing smile.

"I know it's not my place Miss Lisa," she said, still in a whisper, "but I think you might like to know that your father stayed in your mother's room last night." With that, she quietly closed the door behind her. It was amazing to think she had been manufactured on an alien planet only a year ago. In a peculiar way I felt quite fond of her despite her perfect skin.

I poured the coffee and put a cup on Richard's bedside table. He looked so peaceful but he soon stirred.

"Good morning darling. I see Prudence has been in," he said blearily. I sat on the bed beside him.

"How's your head?" I asked.

"A bit woolly but I'm fine. I'm glad last night is over." He put his arm around my waist, pulling me onto the bed, and after opening my dressing gown he began kissing my neck. I thrilled to his touch.

"Did you know, my father stayed in Mother's room last night?" I said shakily while he kissed my breasts.

"How do you know?"

"Prudence told me."

"That's good, isn't it?"

"It's bloody brilliant," I said. He then gently peeled off my dressing gown and began caressing my body all over. After a while, I couldn't stand it any longer so I climbed in next to his naked body and we made love.

By the time we finally got up it was nearly ten and the coffee was stone cold so we went downstairs to find some breakfast. Mum and Dad were in the dining room having breakfast together and they greeted us cheerfully. Prudence was standing in attendance by the kitchen door and she winked at me as I sat down.

"So what are you two up to today?" I asked.

"Well," Dad said, "I feel as though I haven't been home for a hundred years so we are going to get a taxi, go home and then we will go for a drive in your mother's car and see the mountains."

"Sounds good," I said.

"Max can drive you out in the BMW," Richard said. "No need for a taxi."

"If you're sure that's alright," Mum said. She was looking positively radiant and almost unrecognisable.

"I know what you're up to today," I said to Richard while lavishly buttering a piece of toast.

"Are you sure you don't mind?" Richard said pleadingly. "Father wants to get steam up and we have some track repairs to do. I'm afraid I have neglected the railway line lately. In any case Mother wants to get to know you one to one and she only has today before she goes to London."

"It's fine by me; I look forward to seeing the little steam engine. By the way, where are your mother and father?"

"Father will be in the engine shed lighting up the boiler," Richard said while downing a huge plate of porridge. "I expect Mother is still in bed with a hangover."

Richard soon excused himself and I knew he was off to join his father to play with the trains. I also waved goodbye to Mum and Dad while Max drove off down the drive. I was so happy that they were getting on so well.

It was time for a run around the island so I followed the railway track to the north past the picturesque station. As I went past the engine shed neither Richard nor his father could be seen but the shed doors were open and grey smoke was billowing out through the doors and through the roof vents. It smelled like bad eggs and I dreaded to think what Richard would smell like tonight after getting kippered in the shed. By the time I had returned for a shower, I personally felt rejuvenated by the fresh Scottish air. I came downstairs boldly, wearing jeans, perfume and just a camisole without a bra. I found Richard's mother sitting on the terrace in the sunshine. She was dressed exquisitely and nursing a cup of coffee.

"Good morning Lisa darling," she said, getting up and kissing me on the cheek.

"How are you this morning?" I asked tentatively.

"I am feeling very relaxed. I really enjoy coming back home. At the moment it is like having a holiday in a familiar environment. I know that William is in his element and I am glad that he is happy." I could sense her contentment and she was not hung over at all.

"How are your mother and father?" she continued. "I do hope they are coping with their situation."

"Very well," I said. "They have gone out together for the day."

"I'm glad. I must confess that Prudence has kept me up to date; she is a very good spy. I hope you don't mind. I asked her to keep an eye on things."

"I like Prudence," I said. "It is hard to think she is not a real person."

"She is very real and has feelings like you and me. In fact she is very fond of you. You must keep her on here when we return to Terranus. You will need some help during your pregnancy." *Moreover, a spy in the camp,* I thought.

"Everything has happened so fast, I haven't thought about the future yet," I said with a worried look.

"We have all day to chat," she said putting her hand on mine in a comforting way. "I want to get to know you first and if you feel like it we can discuss the future."

She beckoned Prudence over, who seemed to spend all her time standing by doors. She ordered another pot of coffee and a cup for me.

"Tell me Lisa, do you enjoy your job as a veterinarian?" I could already sense where she was going with this question. The telepathy thing was very strong.

"I hate it," I said with venom. "I enjoy natural history and studying animal behaviour but I certainly do not like experimenting on animals in the interest of science."

"That's interesting," she said, "you used to work for the

government in that line." *She is certainly well informed,* I thought. "You won't mind giving up your job to have the baby."

"Not at all," I said. "I don't know what Richard's plans are but I would give up my job tomorrow if he so wished."

Mary sat back in her chair with a satisfied smile. I could tell that I had given the right answer. I could sense that there was something in the back of her mind that involved me but I couldn't quite make it out.

"I am so pleased that you and Richard get on so well," she said. "He absolutely adores you. Have you discussed your wedding day with him yet?" Once again I knew what she was thinking and I already had the answers.

"We haven't talked about it yet, but I know he would want to get married soon. I'm sure that, considering his position, it would have to be a special wedding."

"Lisa darling, you and I are going to get on just fine."

Prudence brought in the coffee and placed it on the table and with a demure smile retreated to her position by the door. I poured us both a cup and we sat looking out on the garden. It was a lovely day with a gentle breeze swinging in the trees and we chatted idly about family and general things in a relaxed way. However, the conversation came round to politics and government and took on a much more serious tone. I was brought back to reality and started to wonder what Lady Mary's meeting with the PM was all about.

"Not that I understand anything about this planet any more," I said, "but what on earth is going on?"

"I know I can trust you Lisa," she said. "I'm sure Richard has explained a few things to you and I don't know how much you know already but I will try to explain the picture."

"I am only just getting used to the idea that the human race also lives on other planets and our trip to Terranus seems like a dream," I said.

"I'm sure it all must have been a shock, especially finding out

241

about your father. Mind you, I am glad you are closely related to a person from our system. It means you have compatible genes."

I sipped my coffee and wondered what she meant by that, but she read my thoughts.

"Having children on Terranus is strictly controlled," she continued. "After all, in nature, natural selection ensures that the strongest genes are passed down the line. Obviously you are aware of the telepathic qualities we have that are due to natural evolution."

"Yes, it is very strong with you and Richard but I don't control it very well."

"You will in time."

"So is it all right for me to have Richard's baby?" I asked.

"We are all delighted, Lisa darling. I have to confess that when Darius saw you last, his scan checked that everything was alright and you passed with flying colours."

I poured myself another coffee and sat back in the chair feeling relieved.

"I'm sure you know that people from the Terranus system have been populating this planet for thousands of years," she continued. "In the early days it took years for them to travel the distance. One thousand people at a time travelled in huge ships that were totally self-contained, complete with livestock and crop growing facilities. Everything was recycled and they lived full lives in space. When Earth was discovered they started whole new races of people and tried their best to blend in with the indigenous life. Unfortunately, it was not always successful. In the last 300 years, it has been very different. With the invention of travelling through the time space continuum, people were able to come and go more freely but we didn't want to upset the balance of life on Earth. Any ships visiting Earth were cloaked and new people had parts of their memory removed so that they were not aware of their origin. In recent times your father was one of those people."

"So when your parents came here they had their memories erased?" I asked with fascination.

"No, Lisa," she said, holding my hand, "by birth my mother is a Council leader and was a vital link between the two civilisations and still is back on Terranus. Since my mother's sister died I have inherited the responsibility and the family tradition."

"So what about your husband?" I asked.

"William is Scottish and has relatives from the Terranus system living in Edinburgh. We met in Edinburgh and had our wedding in a little kirk not far from here. It is similar to your relationship with Richard. When you encounter a person from the Terranus system, you instinctively know it without even any communication. In time you will grow more sensitive to it."

CHAPTER 28

Lady Mary excused herself to go and powder her nose. I sat there thinking about the conversation and realised I was just part of a circle of life that was on a scale I could not have even imagined. I sat deep in thought until I became aware of Prudence, who was now standing beside me.

"Can I get you anything, Miss Lisa?" she asked.

"Thank you Prudence. I am fine. Sit with me for a minute." I do not know why I said that but I felt a need for her company. She sat next to me with her perfect hands on her perfect lap. I looked her straight in the eyes, something I could not do before. She had a warm friendly countenance with a pretty face, bright blue eyes and long blonde hair tied neatly in a bun.

"Are you alright Miss Lisa?" she asked.

"I'm fine Prudence," I said, and realised I was talking to a neutral person with no telepathic interference; it was quite refreshing and allowed me to think clearly. I was starting to become used to these so-called artificial life forms and realised that they were real people and not just mechanical robots. There was something about her nature that was unusually pleasing.

"What do you think about all of this? I am feeling a bit over-whelmed," I said.

"I can sympathise with you regarding your position but it is not my place to give you my opinion," she said, "but I don't think you need to worry. If I can help in any way, please ask. I possess a vast amount of knowledge regarding the Terranus culture."

"Lady Mary says you will be staying on here to help me. Are you happy with that?"

"If you are happy with it I will be highly honoured to work for such an important family. I do think this country is beautiful. I have never seen the ocean before," she said with a smile.

"Do we pay you?" I asked stupidly, ignoring her strange comment about the ocean.

"That is all taken care of by the Council," she said. "They provide enough currency for my needs. I also have training in many fields, including nursing and childcare. I can also speak over 100 different languages."

"That's settled then," I said, feeling suitably impressed. "By the way, do you know why Lady Mary is visiting the Prime Minister?"

"I cannot comment," she said. "I think you will have to ask her Ladyship yourself."

"Ask me what?" Lady Mary said as she glided onto the terrace.

"I was just being nosey about your meeting with the PM," I said apologetically.

"I'm going to talk to you about that Lisa. You may go Prudence." Prudence got up, did a little curtsy and went into the house. "How about we go for a little stroll around the garden and see what the boys are up to?"

I stood up and followed her onto the lawn. She linked her arm through mine. She had a serious air about her and I chose to remain silent.

"There are going to be some major changes for planet Earth," she said. "As you know, this business with your father is totally unacceptable. The mind corrective procedure is going to be totally banned except for extreme medical cases. In addition, there will be no more immigration from the Terranus system except for administrative personnel. Having learned from our own past mistakes, we consider that Earth is now overpopulated, which from experience will have disastrous consequences on the planet itself. The planet's resources are depleting rapidly and pollution is at a dangerous level. The Council have formulated a plan to introduce our advanced technology, starting with the clean and efficient use of nuclear energy. Eventually fossil fuels will be outdated. The plan also includes more efficient food production and a program to restore the world's forests. We are also going to introduce the technology to make space travel a reality for ordinary Earth people."

She paused after hearing a shrill whistle in the distance. I was glad of the break while my brain went into overload. We got as far as the little level crossing. Someone had already closed the gates across the driveway. I was looking forward to seeing Richard drive the little train. However, I was still full of curiosity.

"Won't all this cause mayhem in the world?" I said.

"Technical advances in the past have been sporadic," she continued. "The last major changes were during the Industrial Revolution in Victorian times and recently the electronic age. Nobody noticed where the technology came from so we can do it again gradually without upsetting the balance too much. If it is for the good of the people of Earth, they will accept it without question. Eventually space travel will become second nature and the whole world will understand the true nature of their existence. There will be a sense of unity, a quality that is sadly lacking at the moment."

"Isn't this a bit like an invasion?" I said in confusion.

"No Lisa," she said, holding my arm tightly. "You have to think on a much larger scale. The human race has been invading each other's territory for thousands of years; it is a fact of nature. We are a very successful species of animal and when it gets a bit overcrowded we find somewhere else. You only have to look at Earth history to see that. We have the technology to stop the dreadful things that have happened in the past both on this planet and on our own. You have to remember that you are a descendant from another world and your father comes from the planet Honshu. America, for instance, has a population made up of descendants from all over this world and from space. The Cosmos is one big melting pot of humanity."

The sound of the whistle made me jump while my brain was absorbing this information. I could see a plume of smoke and steam rising from the terrace area. The train wound its way through the bushes and over the bridge. It appeared in full view, clattering across the lawn on its little railway lines towards the road crossing. It was painted green with a polished brass dome and pulled two flat trucks. Richard was kneeling precariously on one of the trucks, surrounded by tools. The second truck had been filled to the brim with stone chippings. The whistle sounded again as they trundled across the driveway with the engine making impressive chuffing sounds. Richard waved frantically as they disappeared into the trees with a cloud of foul smelling smoke and steam. I was missing him and wished he were with me now.

"We won't see them for a while," Lady Mary said. "The sun is over the yardarm. Let's go and get a glass of cold wine."

We sat on the terrace again and Prudence brought a bottle of Chardonnay and a large bottle of soda water with a silver bowl containing marble-sized ice balls.

"There is something important I need to tell you that has been a major influence in the Council's decision to intervene in the affairs on Earth," Lady Mary said with a serious air. "This information is highly classified and must not be repeated. We have discovered a new solar system similar to this one. Our scientists tell us that the system has planets capable of sustaining life as we know it. It so happens that planet Earth is approximately halfway between the Terranus system and the new system. Already we are setting up a transporter link to the new system so we can come and go easily and gather scientific information. We are committed to exploring the universe for new worlds capable of sustaining human life. It is like trying to find a needle in the Sahara Desert. We have made this decision because it means the solar system is going to become busy. We also need manufacturing facilities on Earth and possibly the Moon or Mars. It is a huge project and over time will create prosperity for Earth."

"And you will be discussing all this with the PM?" I said in awe.

"The meeting is in Washington," she said as she filled her glass with chinking ice cubes. "My ship will take us there after picking up the PM."

"Washington!" I said, desperately trying to get my head round the scale of it.

"It is a summit meeting that has been, so to speak, in the pipeline for quite some time now and involves all the major world leaders. Global coordination is most important for a change of this magnitude. It is very important now for world leaders to unite into one central global government. It is a very detailed plan outlining future development for humanity over the next 100 years. The aim is to save this planet from destruction and improve the lives of everybody who chooses to live here. The Council has 1,000 years of experience; planet Honshu is a shining example of what can be done."

Lady Mary sat back in her chair and sipped her wine spritzer. She actually looked a bit exhausted. I felt completely stunned by the information. I do not think she was being despotic in any way despite the scale of the plan, but I needed to think on my own without her influence. Lady Mary had a strong link to my own thoughts.

"I am going to do some work in Richard's room and then have a little nap," she said. "It will give you some time with your own thoughts. In the meantime, would you organise a picnic lunch for the boys? I am sure they will be hungry. I think they are down by the tunnel that goes underneath the road."

I excused myself and went into the dining room secretly relieved to be on my own. I was longing to go and see Richard and see what they were up to, so I decided to take Lady Mary's advice and get a packed lunch together. I found Prudence in the kitchen.

"Prudence, I'm glad to find you," I said. "I'm going to take some packed lunches for the men. Could you rustle up something?"

"Of course, Miss Lisa," she said. "I have already packed a hamper with warm pasties, cheese sandwiches and fresh fruit. There are also some cans of beer. Lady Mary said that the men would need something to eat." She pointed to a wicker hamper and a large tartan picnic rug.

"May I come with you, Miss Lisa?" she said. "The hamper is very heavy and I can carry it for you. I would love to look at the ocean."

I was surprised at her request but grateful for her neutral company. I agreed and ran upstairs to put my trainers on. By the time I got down to the front door she was waiting there wearing shorts and a tee shirt with the hamper strapped to her back; she looked like a tourist. We set off walking briskly down the drive and turned right to follow the railway line. It curved through the trees and bushes. We passed the gardener, who was clearing the track where the undergrowth had encroached on it. I was wondering about Prudence who was quietly following on behind.

"So you are only a year old, Prudence?" I asked awkwardly. The comment seemed ridiculous considering she was a grown woman.

"Yes Miss," she said. "My ascension was approximately one Earth year ago."

"And you have never seen the ocean?"

"I spent the last year receiving my education on the planet Honshu," she said. "I have seen many images of the oceans but when I left the factory I was brought straight here. So I have not seen it for real."

"We call the ocean around here a sea loch."

"I have not heard that term," she said. "I shall call it 'sea loch' from now on."

We came out of the trees. The railway followed a gravel roadway across open heath land. The sea was not far away. Beyond you could see hazy mountains in the distance. When we reached the shoreline, the railway swung round to the left and we stopped to admire the view. A stiff breeze was whipping up the loch and waves were breaking noisily on the stony beach. The sight mesmerized Prudence.

"The sea loch is truly beautiful," she said with a smile. "May I go down and touch the water?"

I found her request quite amusing and decided to humour her.

"Of course you can Prudence," I said. "But be careful, the beach is very rocky."

She sprang down off the cliff like a gazelle and leapt from boulder to boulder. She still had the heavy hamper strapped to her back. I quickly realised that she had superhuman strength and agility. She quickly reached the water's edge and splashed the water with her hands with childlike enthusiasm.

"Come on, we must deliver lunch," I shouted above the noise of the waves. She turned and waved at me. With the same agility, she leapt back across the boulders jumping high into the air. It was a strange alien sight and made me realise just how different she was to a normal person.

"Do you swim in the sea loch, Miss Lisa? I have never tried swimming. I would like to learn," she said excitedly.

"Swimming in the loch is dangerous, Prudence. There are strong tides." I had the feeling she could probably swim like a torpedo. "I can teach you how to swim in the pool back home if you like."

"That would be wonderful, Miss Lisa, thank you." She smiled.

We followed the railway line as it wound its way around the edge of the island and eventually ended up at the causeway where the railway disappeared through a small stone built tunnel. I clambered up onto the driveway and down the other side. Prudence was already there standing by the little train. She was studying the engine with cautious curiosity. Richard was shovelling stones onto the track from the railway truck. I called to him. He waved at me, threw his shovel down and jumped off the truck. I flung my arms around his neck as if I had not seen him for months.

"Are you alright darling?" he said. "You look a bit stressed. I hope Mother has not been upsetting you."

"No Richard, your mother is lovely, but she has been explaining the situation and I find it all quite mind boggling," I said, while flicking some soot off his shoulder. He gave me an oily kiss on the cheek.

"Don't worry; it will all work out for the best. There are going to be some good changes on this planet. We have to talk about our own future. We have time to decide how it is going to affect us."

"Where's your dad?" I asked.

"He is in the tunnel repairing the walls with some cement. I see you have brought Prudence. I'll get her to give him a shout."

Prudence had already laid out the blanket on some grass by the water's edge and was taking out some goodies from the hamper. Richard went down to the shoreline and washed his hands in the salt water while I gave Prudence instructions to tell Lord William that lunch was ready. She walked up the line, giving the hissing steam engine a wide berth, and disappeared into the tunnel. We sat on the rug and ate our delicious homemade pasties.

"I won't be able to work on my music so much," Richard said with his mouth full. "I have been roped into getting more involved with planning and administration."

Richard picked up a can of beer and cracked it open.

"I was wondering," he continued, "if you would be prepared to give up your job and help me. There will be a mountain of so-called paperwork and you won't be able to continue now that you are pregnant." He gave me his adorable pleading look and took a huge swig of beer. I did not have to think about it.

"Of course I will give up my stupid job," I said, taking his beer can from him and taking a gulp. "I feel privileged to learn about all this stuff first-hand. This is such an amazing situation. Your mother has told me about new worlds and I have witnessed fantastic new technology! I just hope I am not dreaming all of this. One thing for sure is I love you. I miss you when you are not with me. In between cosmic administration, I will be having your baby!"

Richard was positively jubilant and we hugged. At the same time, the little engine's safety valve lifted and let off a huge plume of steam into the air; it made a deafening noise and I nearly wet my pants with surprise. We fell about laughing. Richard got up to tend the engine.

While he was tinkering with the engine, Prudence appeared. She was absolutely filthy with black marks down her tee shirt. Her hair was undone and trailing on her shoulders. Her hands were completely black. For the first time, she did not look so immaculate but she had a wonderful smile on her face.

"I'm sorry Miss Lisa," she said, "I have been helping Lord William repair the tunnel and it is dark and dirty in there. He says the cement will go off. I do not understand where he thinks the cement will go to so I have helped him lift some large stones in place. He asked me to take him a can of beer and some food. He asked me if you wouldn't mind if I continued to help him."

"Dear Prudence," I said, "if you are happy with that, carry on." She collected some sandwiches, a can of beer and the remaining pasty and disappeared past the noisy engine into the tunnel. I had a sneaky feeling that she was actually enjoying herself.

I joined Richard at the engine that had now settled down. He was sitting in the cab. I could see the fire door open while he placed a neat shovel of coal to one side of the furnace. The cab was full of fascinating dials, gauges and levers all brightly polished in copper and brass.

"Let's leave them to it," Richard said with a naughty smile as he hopped out of the cab. "Dad will be fine with Prudence helping him. She is far stronger than I am."

We walked off hand in hand down the track discussing Prudence. She certainly was very strong, but I did not know that she would be interested in engineering. Maybe Lord William had some input with her programming.

We rounded a small headland and the line disappeared inland into the woods. I was glad to be with Richard alone. We found a small cove. It was protected from the wind so we lay down on the grass. The cove was completely private with the sea gently lapping the shore. We stripped off to our pants and soaked up the sun. Richard turned to me. The look on his face was priceless and he looked painfully sexy in his black boxer shorts.

"You seem to be coping with all this very well," he said with a gentle smile. "You look so lovely lying there. I do so love you." I could sense and see what was going on in his mind.

"I love you too Richard. We have so much to sort out. We must talk."

"There is plenty of time to make plans," he said as he kissed my bare breast. "Let's wait till my parents go back to Terranus and then we will have the place to ourselves."

The sunshine was warm as he stroked my thighs. All I could do was surrender to his loving advances.

CHAPTER 29

The next morning I awoke to find Prudence placing a breakfast tray on the table. She looked clean and tidy after her experience as a builder's mate. She turned towards me and did a curtsy. I must say I could get used to being waited on hand and foot.

"Good morning Miss, I hope you slept well," she said prettily. I noticed Richard was missing and must have got up early, probably to play with the train set.

"Good morning Prudence, do you know where Richard is?" I asked sleepily.

"The master is in his study Miss; I believe he has had a communication from Mr Dulus. Lady Mary has already left for London. She will be back in a few Earth days. Lord William is in the engine shed. If you agree, he would like me to help him today. I find this historic pastime most illuminating."

As usual, Prudence was a mine of information and I told her she was free to help Lord William for as long as she wanted. I lay back in bed and wondered who Mr Dulus was so I decided I had better have a shower and show my face downstairs. By the time I had descended the wide staircase and crossed the hall I met Prudence coming out of the study. She was dressed in a blue boiler suit. With a smile she scurried off towards the kitchen.

Seeing her dressed like that prodded my memory and I immediately thought of the blonde bimbo that accompanied that horrid little man when we arrived at the Terranus space station. The penny dropped and I remembered Philbin Dulus, the agent who was investigating my father's abduction and Jack, Richard's former chauffeur. I hurried into the study and found Richard sitting in front of the computer with a cup of coffee in his hand. I kissed him on top of the head.

"Did you sleep well darling?" he said without looking up.

"What's up?" I said. "Have they found Jack?"

"Yes," he said. "We have a bit of a situation here. Jack, Dr Cranborne, Mrs T and two other people are holed up in a shack somewhere in the Australian desert. Philbin has the place surrounded by armed police but the gang are also armed and threaten to shoot Mrs T if they don't get a helicopter. I just wouldn't have thought that Jack would be capable of such a thing."

Richard was very upset. On the computer screen, I could see video pictures of the police cars with their headlamps trained on a ramshackle building. Police were everywhere, holding rifles. Philbin was clearly visible in the gloom crouching behind one of the cars.

"The problem is," Richard continued, "Philbin doesn't have a ship at his disposal so I have summoned Horace here so I can get onto the scene. He is on his way now. I'm really sorry about all this Lisa, but I have to sort it out."

"I'm worried Richard. Is it safe to go out there? You must not put your life at risk. Anyway, how can Horace help?" I asked with my heart beating wildly.

"Don't worry darling, it is completely safe on board Horace. He has a weapon that can quickly put an end to this situation. In any case his presence should be enough to make them give themselves up, that is if Jack has got any sense at all."

"Please let me come with you. I couldn't bear it if you left me on my own," I pleaded.

Richard looked deep into my eyes and I could feel him probing my thoughts. He smiled at me and took my hand.

"You had better get ready. We leave in three minutes."

I tore upstairs, put some trainers on and grabbed my handbag. Richard was close behind me and went through the bedroom onto the balcony. Already the porthole had opened and I could see the green carpet of the ship. I quickly followed Richard. As soon as I entered, the porthole slid shut behind me so I quickly sat next to Richard at the computer console.

"Good morning, sir and Lisa," Horace said. "I assume we have an emergency situation."

"Yes Horace," Richard said. "Do you have Philbin's signal?"

"Yes sir."

"Get us there as soon as you can; you have permission to break all protocol code 10."

"Yes sir," Horace said with enthusiasm as if addressing a general.

The ship immediately shot vertically upwards. I was pushed into the seat as we gained height at an incredible speed. I gripped the edge of the seat in terror. Within seconds, the Earth's mantle was visible and the blue planet below started to spin. I started to feel giddy while looking at the unnatural vista. Within minutes, we were plunged in darkness and it was impossible to see where we were going. Then my body weight changed and it felt as though I was going to float off the seat. I started to feel nauseous and stared at Richard. He also was looking very white and he took hold of my hand.

"I'm sorry about this darling," he said through clenched teeth. "It can be a bit rough when Horace travels at this sort of speed. We should be at our destination soon."

Soon I could make out scrubland and desert as we zoomed across the gloomy surface of what could only be the Australian desert.

"Horace, remove the cloaking device, code 5," Richard ordered.

"Yes sir," Horace snapped back. I got the impression that he was enjoying himself.

The shack was now visible with a ring of police cars surrounding it. Somehow, we managed to slow down and come to rest right over the spot where Philbin was crouching. We were literally only twenty feet above his head and he waved his short little arms. The whole area was floodlit. I realized the lights were coming from the ship. I could not believe how quickly we got there. The police officers lowered their rifles and stared up at us with confused expressions on their faces. I realized that they probably hadn't seen a spaceship before.

"Philbin, what is the situation?" Richard said.

"No change sir." Philbin's voice came from nowhere; I could see his lips move from where I sat. "No shots have been fired and they are still demanding a helicopter. Mrs Theaton is being held against her will and I am confident that her husband will shoot her if his demands are not met."

"I am going to talk to him on the hailer; stand by," Richard said with authority.

"That bastard," I said.

Richard touched some icons on the control console. "Jack, this is Richard Varnicus; if you look outside you will see that I have the ship. I am sure you realise that your demands are useless. You have one minute for you and your friends to surrender and come out with your hands above your heads."

All went quiet while Richard touched some more icons.

"Horace, can you identify the life forms in the building?"

"Yes sir, there are four men and one woman. One of the men is Jack Theaton and the woman is Thelma Theaton; the other three are unknown."

"Can you stun the men without affecting Mrs Theaton, Horace?"

"Yes sir, Mrs Theaton is tied up and on the other side of the room."

"Good, stand by Horace." Richard looked at me with an evil smile. I was wondering how Horace could stun the men inside the building.

"No problem," he said, "Horace has a sonic device that he can target at an individual. The device will knock them out instantly and painlessly; they won't know what hit them. I am hoping that Jack knows this."

Sure enough as he spoke the men started to come out of the building with their hands on their heads. They were all looking up at us as they stumbled out one by one towards the waiting police. The police quickly moved in and searched them spread-eagle against the cars. When they were handcuffed, some of the officers stormed the building with their rifles ready. It was not long before one of them brought Mrs T out. She was huddled over and covered with a blanket.

"The area is secure sir, shall I stand down?" Horace piped up.

"Yes Horace, thank you," Richard replied. He turned to me. "I'm going down to have a word with Philbin and see how Mrs T is."

"I'm coming with you. I'm sure Thelma will be in need of some comfort," I said.

We jumped up and went into the lift. When we stepped out at the bottom the evening air was chilly. I took deep breaths of air to calm my nerves as we walked towards Philbin, who was talking to a police officer. The men stared at us as if we were beings from another planet, which I suppose wasn't far from the truth. Philbin gave me a nasty smile and shook hands with Richard. I decided to leave them to it and went to find Mrs T. She was sitting in the back of a police car with the door open. There was a police officer standing over her, she had an incredulous expression on her face.

"Struth," she said, "that's some vehicle you have there. I thought Thunderbirds weren't real."

I dismissed her comment and knelt down beside Mrs T. Her face was dusty and tear-stained; her eyes lit up when she saw me.

"Miss Lisa," she cried, "what are you doing here?" She started sobbing. "I'm sorry about all this. I swear I had no idea what Jack was up to. I was happy working for Master Richard." I put my hand on her shoulder.

"Don't worry. When we sort things out you can come back and continue with your work." I couldn't think of anything else to say to console her. I quickly examined her and felt her pulse. She obviously was not very well at all.

"What happened to Bruce?" I said foolishly and she burst into tears again.

"That bastard shot him," she sobbed, "and threw him into the ditch." I cringed at the thought.

"Don't worry, there are lots of rescue dogs desperately needing a home. We can get another one."

I decided to leave her alone for the moment before I made things worse. I went to join Richard. He was talking to the officer in charge.

"Can I rely on you to keep a lid on this incident?" I heard Richard saying.

"Agent Dulus has explained the situation sir," he said. "We don't often deal with the Secret Service but you can be assured that there won't be any publicity that will undermine your position. My officers will be sworn to secrecy."

"What will happen to Mrs Theaton? I understand that she is not implicated in any way," Richard said.

"She is free to go sir," the officer replied.

"Richard, she is not well and very upset. She should go into hospital," I said.

"We will take her back with us and I will arrange something on the flight back," Richard said with a comforting smile. "Get her into the ship and I'll wrap things up with Philbin. We need to get out of here before anybody spots us."

"No worries," the officer said, "you'd have to camp 'ere for days before anybody came past."

I shook his hand and hurried off to collect Mrs T. She was still in the back of the police car. She was slumped over with her head in her hands. I put my arm around her and told her not to worry and that she was to come back to Cannock Brae with us. She looked up at me.

"How did you get here Miss Lisa?" she spluttered. "Did the Master bring you?"

I realised that she must be very confused and needed medical attention.

"Richard and I are going to take you back to Cannock Brae," I said soothingly. "Do you feel well enough to walk?"

She gathered herself together and got out of the car. I held her by the arm as she stood up. She looked up at me and said, "I wanna get out of here."

We staggered back to the ship. It was now surrounded by police officers. They were staring at Horace and wandering around under his huge belly. It was like a vast neon light. His chocolate coloured velvet skin seemed to glow in the dark. He looked truly awesome in the desert twilight.

Thelma was a large woman. I was struggling to keep her on her feet. Luckily, a curious policeman offered to help and between us we managed to coax her onto the lift platform by propping her up on either side. She looked up at me in wonder. I felt her thoughts and realised she had not seen Horace before. She stared at him with a glazed expression and open dribbling mouth. We thankfully rose up into the cabin and I was relieved to feel the warmer air of Horace's body.

"Bloody hell!" the police officer exclaimed.

"Lisa, can you vouch for the police officer?" Horace said calmly. "He does not have security clearance."

"Yes Horace, it's alright. Richard will be along shortly. We have an emergency."

"Let me know if you need any help," Horace replied. "For your information, Mrs Theaton is dehydrated and requires water administered in small quantities."

"Thank you Horace," I said as nicely as possible. "I'm a doctor, I will attend to her."

"Struth and strike a light," the police officer said.

We sat Mrs T down on one of the leather chairs. She slumped forward with her arms on the table. I touched the red panel in the corridor and the kitchen door slipped sideways. I took a glass out of the cupboard and filled it with water from the automatic tap. I took it through to Mrs T and lifted her head. She looked at me.

"Bless you Miss Lisa," she said and took the glass and drank.

"Take it slowly Thelma," I said.

"Bloody hell," the officer said again. "I've never seen anything like this before."

"Thank you for your help officer, but I'm afraid you must leave now," I said with authority.

"Sure thing Miss," he said looking round in wonder. "I don't know how I got here, and sure as hell I don't know where the door is."

I guided the confused policeman to the lift and stood him inside. After giving him instructions to wait until he was on the ground, he disappeared downwards. I wondered how Horace knew when to operate the lift and decided he must listen in and use his initiative. While I was making a mug of tea for Thelma, Richard returned to the ship. I put the mug in front of her and she clasped it in both hands.

"Where am I?" she said. "What is this place?"

"Don't worry Thelma, you're in a special ambulance and we are taking you home," Richard said reassuringly.

"Thank you sir," she said and took a sip of her tea.

"Horace," Richard said, "stand down code 10, engage the cloaking and get us home."

"Yes sir," Horace replied, still in military mode.

We slowly started to lift away from the ground, sending the

police running in all directions. Soon we were back in space, this time travelling at a reasonable speed. Richard said we would be back home in thirty minutes so I made us both a coffee and we joined Thelma at the table. Thankfully, she was looking a little better; the colour was returning to her cheeks.

"Well," Richard said, "that is quite enough excitement for one day."

"I can't believe it is all over so quickly," I said. "Especially as we have flown halfway round the world."

"You handled it all very well darling," Richard said proudly.

"What about security? Those people didn't know what hit them seeing Horace like that."

"Hopefully Philbin can sort that out," he said. "I gave him instructions to call in Darius to administer some mind correction treatment even though we are not supposed to use it any more. At least they won't remember what happened. Nevertheless, I have a sneaky feeling there are going to be some repercussions. The speeds that Horace used to get us to the scene made him visible because of the heat generated by friction on the atmosphere." Richard put his head in his hands and rubbed his eyes. "It is a pity it was dark. He will have looked like a fiery asteroid streaking across the sky."

"What will happen to Jack?" I asked. Thelma started sobbing so I bit my lip.

"Cranborne and Jack will probably go to the detention centre on Honshu," he said with a frown. "It is ironic to think that the mind correction procedure that got us into trouble will also help us out."

"Richard, I really think that Thelma should be admitted to hospital for a check over. She is not well." Richard looked at me and somehow gave me reassurance.

"Horace, can you locate Dr Marcus?"

"Dr Marcus is not on this planet. My records indicate he is currently on Honshu."

"Damn," Richard said. "Horace, can you connect me with his PA?"

"Yes Sir. Please wait."

"It would be best if she was in the Marcus Clinic," Richard said. "They will look after her well and it would minimise security. When my mother and father return to Terranus tomorrow, we can get her home and I will be off the hook with this whole affair. It would be nice to get back to some sort of normality."

Normality, I thought, what is that? Suddenly, the window panel above the table lit up. It had a strange, official looking logo. The windows, of course, were video screens. I stared at it and then looked at Thelma. Luckily, she seemed to be asleep with her head in her hands. The screen came to life and an oriental woman in a white coat appeared. She was sitting at a desk.

"Richard, good to see you, how can I help?" the screen said.

"Hello Kao, nice to see you too," Richard said without looking up. "I have had a security breach and Jack Theaton has been arrested. I would be grateful if you could admit his wife Thelma. She has had a bit of an ordeal and may need medical attention."

"I have heard of this incident Richard. I am glad it has been resolved. We can take Mrs Theaton into the hospital straight away. I am honoured to be of assistance."

"Thank you Kao, we should be with you in about half an hour." Richard sat back in his seat. "Horace, take us to the Marcus Clinic and end the transmission."

"Right away sir," Horace replied.

The screen reverted to a deep blue with a warm morning sun glowing on the curved horizon. I sat back feeling relieved and impressed that the situation had been sorted out so efficiently. Soon we were back skimming over the city of London. Horace docked at the usual balcony and we stepped out into a warm summer's day. A nurse took Thelma into the hospital in a wheelchair. She was given a nice private room and after a warm bath, put to bed. We had not picked up any of her belongings so Richard had thoughtfully arranged for some new clothes. She was fast asleep by the time I saw her to say goodbye. All we could do was go back to Horace and head for home.

CHAPTER 30

Nobody was around when we got back, apart from Lord William and the staff. Prudence told me that my parents had gone back home to be on their own. Lord William was waiting for us when we landed on the lawn. He greeted us and Richard gave him an update regarding Jack and Thelma. Apparently Lady Mary was going to spend another night in Washington. He boarded Horace straight away so that he could meet up with her. Horace disappeared into the Cosmos leaving us on our own.

It was just as well. I was feeling unwell. Prudence gave us something to eat and I took to my bed. I awoke in the night feeling hot and feverish. I could not go back to sleep. All I could think about was Thelma and the Australian desert. I do not know what time Richard had gone to bed but he turned over and looked at me.

"Are you alright darling?" he said as he turned on the bedside light.

"I don't feel very well and I can't get to sleep."

"You have a high temperature," he said, as he kissed my sweaty forehead. "I will get Prudence to come and check you over."

"I don't need Prudence," I croaked. "What time is it? We do not need to wake her up. I just need a couple of aspirin." I then started to feel sick.

"It is only midnight," Richard said as he got out of bed. "Prudence is a fully qualified medical practitioner and she does not sleep anyway." He put on a dressing gown. Within minutes, Prudence knocked at the door.

She came into the room and scanned me with one of those strange gismos that looked like a mobile phone.

"I'm sorry you are not feeling well Miss Lisa," she said calmly. She was wearing an old-fashioned Victorian lace nightdress that looked very becoming. Was Richard sure that she did not go to sleep at night?

"It would seem that Miss Lisa has not been inoculated yet," she said, turning to Richard.

"It is my fault, I just didn't think of it before we left for Terranus."

"Miss Lisa has been infected by a virus from Terranus," Prudence said. "Don't worry, we have caught it in time and the baby is quite healthy. Doctor Marcus has scheduled an injection, but I think Miss Lisa should have it administered now. The virus is only a few days old. Lady Mary or Lord William or more likely Miss Lisa's father may have carried the virus. I will have to examine them in the morning. I will go and fetch the appropriate medication." Prudence immediately left the room.

I lay there feeling nauseous. Now I have a bug from another planet.

Richard stroked my hair. I could sense he was feeling uneasy.

"How did Prudence get here so quickly?" I asked.

"Don't worry," Richard said. "I have a communication link with Prudence. I'm so sorry. You really should have had an inoculation. Although Mother and Father are immune, they can still carry the virus. I just didn't think about it. The injection will make you feel much better and it will boost your immune system."

Prudence came back into the bedroom. She was carrying one of the pencil things. My mother had been injected with a similar one. She placed it on the back of my hand. I felt nothing, not even a pinprick.

"There you are Miss Lisa. Give it a few minutes and you will feel better than ever," she said, beaming with satisfaction.

She left the room. Richard continued to stroke my hair. It was very soothing and already the nausea had disappeared.

I woke in the morning feeling a lot better. I think I must have fallen asleep very quickly. I sat up in bed wide-eyed. I could hear the birds singing outside even though the French doors were closed. I got out of bed and opened the doors. Some of the birds were again sitting on the parapet expecting food. There were several house sparrows and a blackbird. They sat there cocking their heads from side to side and peering at me. I ignored them and sat on a plastic chair. It was still very early and I did not have any food for them. I had no idea what time it was. It was just getting light and there was a morning mist in the trees. I sat back and collected my thoughts. Last night I felt very ill. It came on very suddenly and felt like a bad attack of flu. Did Prudence inject me with something or was it a dream? I did not know she was a doctor as well as housemaid and engineer. Anyway, whatever it was she injected me with, it had certainly done the trick. I was feeling brilliant and full of energy. I think Prudence must have given me a dose of those nano thingies. The injection my mother had received had transformed her. I wondered if I might start to look younger too.

I was only wearing a flimsy nightdress and there was a chill in the morning air. I decided to go back to bed. I spooned next to Richard and felt his warmth. He pretended not to wake up but I knew differently. He was content and I dozed until Prudence brought in the coffee tray.

"Good morning Miss Lisa, I hope you are feeling better," she whispered as she put a cup of coffee on my bedside table.

"Thank you, Prudence. I need to ask you what happened last night. What did you give me? It has worked wonders. I feel great this morning."

"I will check you over later," she whispered. "Just to see if there are not too many side effects." She took another cup around the huge bed and put it onto Richard's table. She then left the room without a sound.

After a hearty breakfast of scrambled eggs and bacon, I remembered that Prudence wanted me to teach her how to swim. I felt sure that she would be very capable and decided to test my theory later this morning. I told Prudence to meet me in the pool at 10am. Richard looked at me quizzically.

"What are you up to?" he said.

"I am going to teach Prudence how to swim," I said.

"That is unusual," Richard said as he picked up his electric notepad thingy. "I will just check that it is alright. As far as I know some synthetics are not suitable for an underwater environment. I don't want to make any more mistakes."

"You haven't made any mistakes," I protested while he fiddled with the gismo. "Surely Prudence must take a bath. She got filthy while helping your father. She herself must know if it is bad for her."

"I just want to make sure. I forgot to get you inoculated before we went to Terranus. This business with Mrs T was my fault. I should have been more aware of Jack. Now you are pregnant, I have to be more responsible instead of messing about with steam engines and music. Everything has happened too quickly."

Richard looked stressed. I got up and kissed him.

"None of this is your fault. We will sort this out together," I said in his ear. The notepad was showing some colourful text boxes. At the top, I could see the name 'Prudence' with a huge serial number underneath. Richard scrolled the screen down and I began to lose interest. I sat down and sipped my coffee.

"Prudence is an advanced model," he said proudly. "She can dive to a depth of ten metres without breathing equipment and stay submerged for six hours without requiring oxygen. Mother has bought a Rolls Royce with no expense spared. She will be able to swim expertly."

"Do you mean that she doesn't breathe like us?"

"All her bodily functions will be similar to ours. She is just physically enhanced." I had a flashback of Prudence leaping from rock to rock on the beach.

"I knew she could swim like a torpedo," I said. Richard smiled at me.

"It would be good to be friendly with her. She will be a huge asset."

Richard went into his study to arrange for the return of Mrs T. I went to the pool room and sank into the warm water. I was feeling good and swam four lengths without even getting out of breath. I then did a whole length underwater without coming up for air. When I resurfaced at the other end, Prudence was waiting with an enthusiastic look on her face.

"Miss Lisa, that looks like fun," she said with a smile.

"Hello Prudence," I said while wiping the water out of my eyes. She was still wearing the maid's black uniform. "Do you have a swimming costume and towel with you?"

"No Miss Lisa, I do not possess such things."

I got out of the pool. She was about the same height as me although a bit fuller in the figure.

"Wait here Prudence. I have a spare costume that should fit you."

"Please do not trouble yourself Miss. I can remove my uniform so that I don't get it wet." I thought about it for a moment, but decided to maintain a high level of decorum.

"You really must have the right costume Prudence. You cannot go skinny dipping whenever you want, it would not be polite." Prudence looked away with a curiously human expression. She seemed to be biting her lip and frowning. She turned back to me with a smile.

"What is 'skinny dipping' Miss?" she said. I cringed.

"It is exactly what we are talking about Prudence," I said tartly. "You cannot swim without any clothes on."

"I quite understand Miss Lisa. I know where your other costume is. It was freshly laundered only last week. May I go and fetch it while you continue your swimming exercise?"

"Yes Prudence," I said with relief. I had in fact left my wardrobe in an awfully untidy mess when I had quickly moved in with Richard. The other day, I noticed how everything had been miraculously laundered, hung on hangers and sorted into drawers and cubbyholes in military fashion. I could not find a thing, but it was lovely to see it so neat and tidy for a while. I continued swimming five more lengths.

Prudence arrived back in double quick time. She had a large bath towel tastefully wrapped around her. I got out of the pool.

"I am ready Miss Lisa," she said. "I am really excited about swimming. I have not been immersed in water before."

"Do you not take a bath?" I asked.

"I wash in the shower Miss. I have not considered using a bath. The shower is much quicker."

She took her towel off and put it in on a wicker chair. She was wearing my black all-in-one suit. It fitted very well. She had a perfect form with perfect skin. It was very annoying.

"You look very beautiful in the suit Prudence. I am very jealous of your perfect skin," I said with a frown.

"Thank you for allowing me to wear your suit," she said coyly.

"You are welcome Prudence. In fact I think you should have the suit and swim as often as you like."

"I am very honoured by your generosity," she said with her eyes lowered. She looked up at me with an innocent smile. "Please tell me what you mean by 'jealous of my skin'."

"I am sorry Prudence. It is just that your skin doesn't have any blemishes like moles, cysts or birthmarks." I felt a bit embarrassed. "They are skin marks and defects that I have inherited from my parents."

"I understand Miss Lisa. You have a genetic origin that is organic and natural. You are very different from me. Unlike you, I am synthetic. I realise that it must be difficult for you to understand my own existence. I can have modifications to produce skin defects if you wish. If it helps you, I think your skin is also perfect."

I was standing face to face with Prudence in the pool room. She was in my swimsuit and I was wearing my red bikini. I made a mental note to buy a new swimsuit. I felt embarrassed and overwhelmed by what she said.

"I have a couple of moles in this area," I said shakily. I pointed to my lower stomach just above the bikini line, which has two annoying moles. When I looked for them, they were not there. I searched my stomach but there was not a mole in sight.

"I don't understand," I said. "They were there the other day."

"Please do not worry Miss Lisa," Prudence said soothingly. "It would be a result of the injection I gave you. The serum will repair any damaged tissue it can find, including moles and cysts."

I stood there for a second feeling a bit shocked. I then ran into the changing room and looked at myself in the mirror. I could not believe what I saw. The mole on the side of my neck was missing. My skin felt tighter, any wrinkles and skin blemishes had disappeared. It must have happened overnight. Why did I not notice it this morning? I suddenly looked ten years younger. My hair even looked shinier. I always wondered how Richard's skin always looked so good.

I ran out of the bathroom in excitement. Prudence was still waiting for me to take her swimming.

"Prudence!" I shouted. "I look ten years younger." I grabbed her by the shoulders. She looked at me with a calm, coy expression.

"You do look so much better now Miss Lisa," she said. "The treatment has been very successful. It is a good sign."

Her presence calmed me down and I tried to focus on the task in hand.

"We must give you your swimming lesson," I said brightly. "Then I have to talk to Richard. Are you ready?"

"Yes Miss."

"Just follow what I do," I said.

I stepped onto the ladder and lowered myself into the lovely warm water. This was the shallow end, but the water was four feet deep. This pool would certainly not do for young children. I stood there hopping about while Prudence gently lowered herself into the water. She held her arms above her head and grimaced like a little girl.

"This is a very strange sensation," she said with an uncomfortable expression. "Not unlike the anti-gravity rooms at the Honshu Education Centre. However, it is very pleasant."

I told Prudence to put her arms down and relax. It felt a bit like the blind leading the blind, but we both calmed down and faced each other.

"Just lower your whole body into the water," I said, while slowly sinking down until the water was just over my chin. Prudence dutifully followed suit. She kept her eyes closed. The water had gone past her nose and she continued to disappear under the water until her blonde hair floated. I felt a bit worried about her but she suddenly popped up and looked up at me.

"Archimedes Principle," she said. "I understand!"

I ignored her comment and swam a whole length using the breaststroke. I could see her watching me intently. When I returned, she launched herself into the water and copied my movements exactly. She quickly did a perfect length and returned. She stood opposite me with a bright smile.

"I followed what you were doing Miss. It was lovely."

"That was very impressive Prudence," I said with a giggle. "That is called the breaststroke." *This is going to be easy,* I thought to myself.

I set off using the crawl. I tried to swim the length as quickly as I could. By the time I was on my return length, I noticed Prudence swimming along by my side. She was mimicking the movements perfectly. When I reached the other end, Prudence had beaten me to it.

"That was called the crawl," I said while catching my breath.

"I am going to leave you so that you can practise the swimming strokes on your own."

"Thank you Miss Lisa," she said while jumping up and down like a schoolgirl. "I shall swim some lengths using the strokes."

I left her thrashing up and down the pool like a crazed teenager. Perhaps I should say 'like a torpedo'. In either case, it was a relief to get out of the room. I made a beeline for the bedroom and had a quick shower. I studied myself in the mirror. I seemed to have lost some body fat. I was sure I looked slimmer. I had not weighed myself in years so there was no way of checking. I was not sure what to wear but eventually settled on jeans and tee shirt. There was no doubt about it. I had lost weight. The jeans slipped on like a glove.

I went downstairs excitedly. Prudence was still in the pool. I found Richard in the study in front of the computer. I walked over to him. He seemed to be talking to himself, but I realised he was addressing the computer. I kissed him on the head and sat in the chair next to him. He looked up with a smile.

"How did the swimming lesson go?" he said, while the screen flashed at him.

"You were right. Prudence can swim like a bloody fish."

"I thought so." He laughed.

"Richard. Have you noticed anything different about me?" I said excitedly.

"I noticed a change this morning. I am pleased that the treatment has made such a difference. It proves that you have a strong family bloodline. I must admit, I was concerned how you would react to it. It was encouraging that your mother and father have benefited so well." He cupped my face in his hand and studied me closely. "You certainly look good. I hope you have no side effects. How do you feel about it?"

"It is fucking fantastic!" I was beside myself. "My moles have vanished. My skin is clear. I look and feel so much younger. I have even lost some weight. You could make a fortune selling that vaccine on the beauty market."

"Darling, calm down. It is not about beauty. It is about feeling well. You must remember that this treatment is not for commercial use. The origin is extraterrestrial. You must be discreet. It is for your eyes only and security is important. Technology of this sort will eventually be introduced into Earth society, but only at the right time. It is not about making money."

"Don't worry. I understand. I just have to get used to it." I could sense troubled thoughts. He was thinking about Thelma.

"How is Thelma?" I asked.

"She is fine. When Horace returns this afternoon, I shall go and collect her. If she still wants to, she can carry on as housekeeper."

"Are your parents coming back with Horace?" I said while scratching my invisible mole.

"They should be back about lunchtime. They won't be staying. They are going to board their own ship straight away." Richard smiled. He had a lot on his mind and I could sense relief that his parents were leaving.

"What about all the staff now that Thelma is coming back?" I asked.

"They will take them back except Prudence and the gardener. I don't know the gardener's name yet. Mother wants you to have Prudence. She is highly trained for child care."

I was secretly pleased to have Prudence stay with us. There was something comforting about her. I had not seen hide or hair of the gardener. The gardens were looking very tidy. If the gardener were synthetic, he would be able to do the work a lot faster than Jack could ever manage.

"I must go and find the gardener and see what he is up to." Richard was reading my mind.

"I must go and see my parents and see what they are up to," I said.

"That reminds me," Richard said. "I have been meaning to talk to you. Your father has asked if I can check Earth records so that he can stay with your mother. As they never found a body, I assume he would have been reported as missing, presumed dead. I will arrange for our family solicitor to sort it out. It could be difficult to arrange. People will start asking questions if he suddenly turns up after five years' absence. We have to dream up a plausible story. They will certainly have to move house and re-locate. It may be necessary to give them both a completely new identity. We have to be careful that the newspapers don't find out."

"Dad is going to stay here," I said excitedly. My mind was racing.

"It is not certain yet. As I said, it might not be possible. I am very sorry that this business is causing so much upheaval." Richard looked troubled.

"Don't worry," I said. "I will go and see them. Maybe we can come up with some ideas."

Prudence came into the room with a tray of coffee and biscuits. Thankfully, she was now properly dressed in her uniform. It was a welcome break while my mind went into overdrive.

After Prudence had left, Richard turned to me and held my hand.

"There is something else we need to talk about," Richard said seriously.

"The wedding," I said, reading his mind. I was very tuned into him this morning. I could sense panic.

"I'm not sure how to explain this," Richard continued. "Mother is putting on the pressure again. So far, there have been no news releases regarding the wedding or the pregnancy."

"News releases?" I said.

"Because of Mother's position on Terranus there would have to be a press release. A short film would be made of the wedding for distribution on the planetary news network. I know that sounds daunting but she is quite insistent."

I sat and thought about it for a second. This complication had not entered my head.

"The ceremony would be on the planet Terranus?" I said calmly.

"Yes, it would have to be."

"Are we talking about processions and a long church service?"

"No," Richard said. "Unlike Earth culture, there is no pomp and circumstance. There are no churches. Nobody wants to create an impression. The ceremony will be in my mother's house. She will conduct the vows and then there will be a big party. We will use tiny robotic cameras for the news report. You won't even know they are there."

"That's OK," I said. "I can handle that." Richard felt relieved, but I could sense that there was more to come.

"The only other thing," Richard continued, "the wedding will have to be very soon."

"I know what you're going to say," I interrupted. "Your mother doesn't want to make an announcement about the baby until after we are married."

"You are being very understanding," Richard smiled. "The thing is having children on Terranus is strictly controlled. Couples have to be married and are usually only allowed one child. People are screened for compatibility. They also have a choice of the child's gender, but sometimes even that is overruled. So you see it is our duty to set the example."

I thought about it for a moment. It seemed a bit harsh, but I could understand why. We have already ruined this planet with a worldwide population explosion.

"Does this mean I have to be screened? What about the child's gender?" I asked.

"You have already been screened when you saw Darius," Richard said. "There are no problems and we are genetically compatible. Would you prefer a boy or girl?"

"I would prefer a boy."

"I would too," Richard said with satisfaction.

"So, if we both want a boy, what happens to ensure that is the case?" I asked.

"We can arrange for Darius to check you over in about four months' time. He will give you some treatment to ensure it is a boy, if that is what you want."

I was quite happy with the situation and he sensed it. After putting my arms around him and kissing him, I went off to phone my parents.

Lady Mary looked completely washed out after Horace had dropped them on the lawn. The staff were waiting on the lawn with all their luggage. We just had time to say our goodbyes. The whole party, including the luggage, boarded the platform and disappeared into the bowels of their own invisible ship, which was hovering silently above our heads.

After lunch Richard went to London with Horace to collect Thelma. I had an appointment to see my parents.

I drove round to their house in the Jaguar. By the time I had pulled up outside the front door, Dad came out to greet me. We embraced emotionally.

"You are looking very well Lisa," he said. "I think this new reality is suiting you."

I looked at Dad. He had shaved his beard off and was wearing a shirt and tie. He looked very smart.

"I might say the same about you," I said.

Dad took me through to the front room. Mum was waiting there and I kissed her on the cheek. They sat on the sofa together and I sat opposite. I felt dumbstruck while I looked at them. They had taken on a new lease of life. Were these people my parents?

Emotion welled up in my throat. I burst into tears. I just could not control it. So many bizarre fairytale events had happened in such a short time. I think it had finally caught up with me. It was a different reality. Dad came over and sat beside me. He put his arm around me and I buried my face in his chest. There was silence while I sobbed.

Mum went off to make some tea. She soon returned with mugs of hot tea and a box of tissues. I blew my nose loudly and tried to gather myself together.

"I'm so sorry," I croaked. "I am happy really. I am getting married and having a baby. You two are back together. Thelma is coming home and we have all been given a new lease of life by some alien medicine." Dad took my hand.

"Don't worry Lisa," he said. "An awful lot of strange things have been happening. You will also have to adjust to the effects of the serum. I heard about your flying visit to Australia. I don't think Richard should have taken you with him."

"I didn't want him to leave me behind. I was worried about his safety," I protested.

"At least it has all worked out well," Mum said.

"Richard said you might not be able to live together on Earth," I sobbed. "Couldn't you live on this other planet?"

"Darling," Mum said, "we want to be with you. I want to see our grandson and watch him grow up."

"You already know it is going to be a boy?" I said with suspicion.

"Your father has a communication device," Mum said with a smile. "I'm sorry but we have to be in contact with Richard until our situation has been sorted out. He is concerned that there will be a security breach. We don't want the newspaper reporters finding out. The nosey neighbours have already been looking at me with suspicion. Your father cannot go into town just in case he is recognised. That is why he has shaved the beard off. I think he looks really good without it."

"I think he looks good too," I said, "but what the hell are we going to do?"

"We have a few options," Dad said calmly. "As I see it, the best thing is for me to take on a new identity. Richard can arrange it. I will continue to be missing, presumed dead, and your mother will become a widow." Dad chuckled. "With a new identity, I will become your mother's new boyfriend. I could actually use my original Honshu name."

I sighed loudly at the thought and sat back to think about it. I suppose it was a reasonable idea, but I could see some problems.

"You can't continue to live here together," I said eventually. "It will arouse suspicion."

"I realise that," Dad said. "Your mother will sell up and we will buy a cottage in the highlands. In the meantime we can rent something and put the furniture in storage." I had a flash of inspiration.

"Why don't you use my little house in the meantime?" I said. "I never see my neighbour and they certainly don't know Dad. Horace is quite used to landing in the fields at the back. You could even put your own furniture in. That would save on storage costs."

"That would make sense," Mother said as her eyes lit up with the thought of saving money. As far as I was concerned, it was a great idea.

"What about your furniture?" she asked.

"I haven't got much furniture," I replied. "I can store it in Richard's barn and sell it. You can even use the Volvo as well. Richard prefers me to use the Jaguar. I must admit I prefer it as well."

"Hold on a second," Dad interrupted. "I will see what Richard thinks about it."

Dad went quiet for a few minutes. I glared at him with nervous impatience.

"Richard thinks it would be a good idea," Dad said with a smile. "In fact he thinks we should move in right away."

"How did you do that?" I asked indignantly.

"Don't worry about it Lisa. It is a miniature device implanted in my brain. It is a bit like having an automatic built-in mobile phone."

"I could do with one of those," I said.

"You would have to talk to Richard about that," Dad said. "It takes a bit of getting used to. You can't have too many people connected, it would be very annoying."

I went back home feeling much happier. It would seem that things are falling into place.

CHAPTER 31

The journey to Terranus was very fast. As soon as we docked with the transporter, it did its space warp thing. We did not even have time to do any shopping. Horace took us down to the planet surface straight away. I sat at the front of the ship and watched the green planet grow larger. Soon we were gliding over the lush forested mountains. Prudence was sitting quietly beside me. I had decided that she was to be my maid of honour and it was comforting to have her with me. Richard, as usual, was engrossed with the ship's computer.

The past two months had flown by. We had got married in a registry office. It was a small affair. We did not have many friends and my own relatives were few, but it was a nice occasion. I was very proud to be legally married to Richard, if only by Earth standards.

Mum and Dad were happily using my house. They had gone to Terranus two weeks before me for a holiday. Dad wanted to show Mum the planets. I hope she is coping well with the experience of a lifetime. Now I was to be married again on this alien world.

In the distance, I could see a large clearing in the trees. As we got closer, I could see a large building with a green roof. I recognised it from the pictures Richard had shown me and realised we had arrived. Horace dropped in height and slowed down. The building was huge and shaped like a wagon wheel with eight spokes. There was a large central hub with a green domed roof. The external circle had no visible windows. Horace gently lowered himself towards one of the eight triangular courtyard gardens. The gardens were filled with brightly coloured flowering shrubs. There were other ships docked in the courtyards. Horace came to rest against the wide covered veranda that had ornately carved wooden balustrades.

Richard stood up and came over to me. I could feel a panic attack coming on. He took me by the hand.

"Well, we have arrived. Are you alright darling?" he said.

"I'm feeling a bit nervous." I smiled.

"Don't worry. Mother and Father are away. They send their apologies for not being here to greet us but at least it gives me a chance to show you around." Richard turned to Prudence. She was sitting as if in a trance.

"Prudence, would you be so kind and bring our luggage. Horace has to leave soon."

"Yes Master," she replied. She stood up and did a curtsy.

"Thank you for a lovely trip Horace," I said.

"You are welcome Lisa. I am proud to witness this historic event. I shall view the occasion with great interest."

I was not sure how he would be able to witness the event and ignored the comment. Perhaps he could view the network film recording. The door whizzed open and we stepped onto the veranda. It was a pleasant feeling being light on my feet in the Terranus gravity. The air was warm after the cold of the impending Scottish winter. I stood for a while looking around while Prudence produced a mountain of luggage on a floating trolley. The wide veranda stretched 100 feet in either direction. I followed Richard as we walked towards the outer rim. At various intervals there were stairs built from carved wood that led to the floral garden below. Along the entire length there were carved wooden doors and conventional wooden framed windows. It reminded me of a holiday apartment block.

"I am told this whole wing is empty," Richard said. "I think it would be best to take rooms near the outer rim. We don't want to be anywhere near the central conference centre."

"Conference centre?" I repeated.

"Yes. It is where the marriage ceremony will take place. I'll show it to you later."

I looked down the veranda. There was a door at the end. It seemed to be miles away, but I could see the circular building with the green domed roof. I noticed that Horace had quietly disappeared.

Richard went through one of the doors. Prudence and I followed. The room was huge with a polished wooden floor and white walls. The walls had an array of ornately carved wooden panels that gave it a warm appearance. The furniture was simple and could have come from a Holiday Inn. At least somebody had made up the large bed. The bathroom was nice. It was floor to ceiling white marble with a large shower cubicle. It was very similar to Richard's bathroom back home without the bath.

"This is your room Prudence," Richard said. "We will take the room next door."

"Thank you sir, I shall be very comfortable here."

She proceeded to lift one of the cases off the trolley that had followed her into the room. Then we all went into the room next door. It was identical. There was a number on the door and I made a mental note of it, otherwise I could get seriously lost. I wondered how many rooms this hotel had.

"There are seventy guests' rooms," Richard said after reading my mind. "Very rarely do they all get used. Mother and Father have a whole wing to themselves. My brother occupies part of the adjacent wing. It is all a bit over the top."

"Will I get to meet your brother?" I asked. "I don't even know his name."

"His name is Peter. They all get back tomorrow in time for the dress rehearsal. You will meet him then."

Prudence wanted to do the unpacking in her own regimented style and Richard was keen to show me around, so we left her to it. We went through another carved door into the outer rim. I was astounded at what I saw.

The curved corridor was at least thirty feet wide. The outer wall was floor to ceiling windows continuously extending in either direction. I do not remember seeing any external windows when we came in to land. The view over the gardens and trees was spectacular. In the far distance, I could see a green sea or lake. I had not realised how high up we were. The screens must have been the same as those on board Horace. They were allowing shafts of sunlight to pour in.

"This building used to be a leisure hotel. My parents bought it. Mother thought it would be ideal to use it as a home as well as managing Terranus Council business. She hit the nail on the head," Richard said proudly.

I looked about me. There was a fifteen-foot wide expanse of blue water at the foot of the viewing windows. The water was gently flowing in a clockwise direction. It followed the curvature of the corridor in either direction. Along the side there was a walkway covered with green carpet. It looked like fine grass.

"This goes all the way round," Richard said. "You can either swim or run until you get dizzy."

"I will have to try the water," I said while we started to walk upstream. "We will not be able to keep Prudence out of it."

"Prudence is probably the only person who could swim all the way round upstream," Richard laughed.

Eventually we came to some steps. The river continued in a steep sided ravine. It was lined with attractive natural stone. The room widened out into a large area with a domed ceiling. The ceiling seemed to emit sunlight, making it bright and warm. I felt as though I had stepped outdoors into a courtyard. There was an attractive carved wooden bridge over the river. The bridge led to heavy wooden double doors. To one side, the river widened out into a large circular pool with natural stone steps leading to the water. There were various potted plants placed around the area. They looked like large ferns and colourful orchids. It was extremely attractive.

Richard had walked over to a reception desk and was talking to a woman behind the desk. I wandered over to him.

"Lisa, I would like you to meet Jane," Richard said. "She is our PA."

"I am pleased to meet you Jane," I said while I shook her hand.

"I am showing Lisa around so she can get her bearings," Richard continued. "I will catch up with you later to discuss the wedding arrangements."

Jane did a little bow, but Richard whisked me off down a wide corridor before I could say anything else. Paintings lined the walls. They were mostly portraits. I started to panic again.

"Richard, when are you going to tell me how this ceremony works?" I said impatiently. Richard stopped and put his arms around my waist.

"Don't worry Lisa," he said reassuringly. "I do not know how it works. As soon as I find out, I will tell you." I did not feel reassured and he sensed it.

"You will have to be fitted out with the traditional ceremonial dress first. Then there will be a dress rehearsal. In time we will know what to do," he said.

"We only have two days before the ceremony," I said, still in panic mode. "I don't even know how long a Terranus day is and I still haven't even been measured for the dress."

"As far as I know, the gown has already been made."

"How can that be?"

"Mother has the measurements from your scans. I am sure it has all been arranged." I put my arms around his neck. He tightened his grip and I calmed down. I had already realised that I would not have the chance to choose my own wedding dress.

We continued down the hall. I made a mental note to look at the strange portraits on my own when my mind was clear. We came to a set of carved double doors. Richard threw them open.

"This is the council chamber where the marriage will take place."

The chamber was circular with a high domed ceiling. There was a complex array of carved ceiling beams. It immediately reminded me of the Scottish Parliament building. There were steps down to a circular arena below. A large ornate table dominated the area. There were wooden seats and desks arranged in tiers around the whole arena. Every desk had a computer screen. We walked round the room at the top level. There were doors all the way round.

"There is a quick way back to the room through these doors," Richard said.

"What are the doors marked 'service'?" I asked.

"Ignore those. They lead downstairs to the kitchens and staff accommodation. I think we are in wing eight. Just look for a door with an eight on it."

"We are in room eighty-six. I took a mental note of it in case I got lost," I said.

"That was a good idea." Richard smiled. "I can still get lost in this place."

We eventually found a door with an eight on it. I opened it and walked straight out onto a veranda. I could see Prudence in the distance. She was gazing down towards the gardens below. She was watching a gardener tending the colourful shrubs.

"This is definitely it," I said.

"Lisa, do you mind if I leave you for a while. I have to talk to the PA and find out what is going on. If you need anything just press the service button on the video screen in the room. You can also contact me if you need to. By the way, my mother has some strange pets wandering around the complex. If you meet any, I think you will find them quite interesting." I was becoming used to strange things and decided not to worry about any pets.

"I shall be fine. I am going to try this amazing ring of water.

I need to get some exercise."

I kissed him and strode down the veranda. I wanted to explore this complex on my own. I met up with Prudence. At least she did not clutter my mind.

"Madam," she said, "I have coffee and biscuits in your room in case you required them."

"Thank you Prudence. Please remember to call me 'Lisa'."

"I am sorry madam," she said, "but it is the correct way to address you now that you are married to the Master."

"Perhaps you could just refer to me as 'madam' when we are in company," I said. "I like to think of you as my friend."

"I can do that madam, I mean Lisa. I have never had a friend before." She had an emotional look in her eyes.

I sighed and walked into my room. Prudence followed. We sat at the table and consumed the coffee and biscuits.

"Would you like to go swimming with me Prudence?" I asked.

"I am familiar with the layout of this building. I would love to try the ring of water. I have the swimming costume."

We met in the outer ring. Prudence was still using my old costume. I had bought a new one in Oban. It was very expensive, but although I was not working for Hamish any more, my parents had insisted on paying me rent while they sold their house. Thankfully, I did not have a mortgage, so I enjoyed a bit of disposable spending money.

I could see some steps down into the water. Prudence led the way with her usual enthusiasm.

"I will swim against the water flow," Prudence said, as she lowered herself into the water.

I followed suit. The water was not deep and the flow was gentle. I decided to float downstream with a backstroke, enjoying the view through the windows. I could make out the crescent shape of Honshu hanging low in the sky. It looked like a large moon in the daytime sky. With the help of the current, I was making good progress. Before long, I shot out into the pool by the main entrance. I decided to take a rest and swam towards the steps. I sat on the steps and admired the area. I could not see Richard or the PA. Where was Prudence?

"Hello," a voice came from behind me. I turned round in surprise. I saw two furry animals. They were standing upright side by side. I looked around me. There was no one else in sight. They were looking at me intently.

"Hello," I said stupidly. "Who are you?"

"I Winnie. This, brother Pooh," one said while pointing at its companion with a black five-fingered hand.

I stared in amazement. They were both about five feet tall. They had thick black fur on their shoulders, arms and back. The fur was white on the chest and tummy. At first I thought they were monkeys but then realised they looked more like lemurs. They had long furry tails. Either way, they were primates. The large brown eyes continued to stare. Their snouts were short, exposing a row of teeth. I think they were smiling at me.

"You are bride?" Winnie said, pointing her finger at me. Her voice was childlike. I felt as though I was in a fairytale land again. These animals were the product of evolution. I had to embrace it.

"I am pleased to meet you. I am the bride, my name is Lisa," I said, as if talking to a four-year-old child.

"We look after you. Lady Mary look after us. She give food."

"You have interesting names," I said.

"Father gave us names," Winnie said. "He read from books. He teach us also. Lady Mary happy with names."

I was amazed. I looked at the male. He was obviously male. The primates were not wearing clothes.

"What about you Pooh?" I said, while poking a finger at him.

"I can read. I learn quickly," he said rather shyly.

"Where is everybody?" I asked. Pooh opened his mouth to answer but Winnie butted in.

"Lord and Lady not here. Master in office room."

"Have you seen Prudence?" I asked Winnie.

"Not know Prudence. Woman come past. She swim quick."

I could not believe I was having a conversation with a furry primate. They were endearing and if I have time, I would like to talk to them again. Perhaps I should help them with their grammar. I told them I would see them later and they seemed excited about the idea.

CHAPTER 32

I was feeling peckish so I set off down the river to find my room. By the time I got back, Prudence had already showered and changed. I quickly did the same. By the time I had dressed Richard had returned.

"I don't know what time of day it is," I said, "but I could definitely do with something to eat."

"What would you like, darling?" Richard said. "I'll order it."

"How about some hot soup, bread rolls, cheese and pickled onions."

"OK, if that is what you want," Richard said with an odd look in his eyes.

The food arrived very quickly. Mini brought the food on a hovering trolley. It was lovely to see her and she greeted me warmly. For a change, the food was totally normal. Apparently Lord William has food shipped in from Earth. Prudence joined us and I ate heartily. I was eating for two.

"So, did you find out anything?" I said with my mouth full of pickled onions.

"Yes," Richard said. "The dressmaker will be arriving in about one Earth hour for a fitting. They will also bring a selection of dresses for Prudence. You and Prudence at least get the chance to choose the bridesmaid's dress. The dresses are all standard size to fit her."

"That is wonderful," I said.

"I have a bridesmaid's dress?" Prudence said enthusiastically.

She did not eat anything, but continued to sip a cup of some horrible looking liquid that reminded me of 'Bovril'. I continued with the bread and cheese. It was fabulous Stilton.

"I have an Earth time conversion table just in case we get disorientated," Richard said. "It is about three o'clock in the afternoon. We must remember that the Terranus days are longer, so we will have to go to bed using Earth time. It will still be daylight."

I looked through the window. It was gloomy and pouring with rain. I didn't care.

"Also," Richard said, "your parents will be arriving in about three Earth hours' time. They will take the apartment next to Prudence."

"I shall look forward to seeing how they got on," I said. However, my mind was preoccupied.

"Richard, I met Winnie and Pooh. It was incredible to be with intelligent primates. I had a conversation with them. I must talk to them again."

"You can see them tomorrow. Get them to show you the gardens. They know the forest like the back of their hands. I can see you inviting them to the wedding ceremony," Richard laughed. I was not put off.

"That would be a wonderful idea," I said. "They should take part in the procession."

"We will see. I will have to get Mother's permission." I could feel Richard's thoughts. *He was not sure about it and didn't expect me to take him up on the suggestion. But he did think it would be a good diversion. It would be my own personal touch.* I kissed him on the lips with pickled onion breath.

"I do love you," I said. Prudence looked away in embarrassment.

We all went to the reception area just before the dressmakers arrived. There were two of them. He had a smart suit and his female colleague wore an all-in-one green tunic. She had blonde hair, but her features were different to Prudence. There were no thoughts so she was definitely synthetic. They had a huge floating white cabinet following behind them. The large outer doors closed behind them automatically. It was still raining outside but the reception area was still bright with subdued sunlight emanating from above.

The cabinet came to rest on the marble floor. Richard greeted the man and he bowed respectfully. He was in his forties, as far as I could tell, with fair hair and bright blue eyes. He stepped over to me and bowed again.

"You are without doubt the bride-to-be," he said with confidence, "you are very beautiful." I felt shy at his forward approach.

"Please call me Lisa," I said, looking him directly in the eyes.

"I have your ceremonial dress Lisa. I have also been instructed to show a large selection of dresses to fit your personal maid. With your permission, I would be proud to show you." I could sense his thoughts. They were honourable and sincere.

"Please proceed," I said in an authoritative manner.

As if by magic, the doors to the cabinet folded out to create a small room. The doors had hanging bars that folded out on their own. He proceeded to bring out a fabulous array of colourful full-length dresses. He carefully placed the dresses on the bars. Richard had stepped back and was talking to Jane.

When the dressmaker had finished, I had to walk forward into the instant boutique to have a closer look. Prudence was right behind me. The dresses had been arranged by colour and there were many different styles. I could not take it all in. Until I had seen what I was supposed to be wearing, I thought it best to leave her to it.

"OK Prudence," I said. "Knock yourself out."

"I do not understand what you mean madam, but may I have a look at the clothing?" I sighed and smiled at her.

The dressmaker brought my dress from deep within the cabinet. It followed him on a hovering manikin. I wondered how they managed to do that. It had a fitted strapless bodice and a full pleated skirt. It was made from a sort of velvet material. It was royal blue with gold trim on each pleat. I remember when Richard wore a similar pleated suit the last time we visited this planet. I think he had to go to some sort of council occasion.

The dressmaker then brought out a screen. He placed it on the floor near the circular swimming pool. He opened it out to form a three-sided cubicle. I could read his mind and knew what was going to happen next. As usual, I was dressed like a slob with tracksuit bottoms, tee shirt and no bra. At least I was wearing knickers.

"Madam," the dressmaker said. "If you would step behind the screen my assistant will fit you with the dress."

I obeyed and the dress followed me as if on wheels with the assistant close behind. I stripped off down to my knickers. I was not embarrassed about undressing in this strange environment until I noticed Winnie and Pooh sitting on a rock near the pool. They were watching me with their wide eyes. I stared at them with a frown on my face. They looked away and lowered their heads. They are so sweet. I didn't have to say anything. The assistant lowered the dress onto me. It looked heavy, but once in place it was unusually light and cool. It had a lovely soft lining. The bodice fitted like a glove without revealing too much. She then produced a cape made from similar material. It had a band around the neck, which was studded with diamonds, and an internal tie, also studded with diamonds. It was then attached around my waist. She then produced some shoes, thankfully with flat heels. They were also studded with diamonds with a matching material. After my past experiences, it was obvious that diamonds were in abundance on this planet but I was still determined to wear the necklace that Richard had given me. The assistant had not spoken to me until now.

"The fitting is complete madam. Please feel free to walk around."

"Thank you," I said in surprise.

I stepped out from behind the screen. On the other side the

whole screen was a mirror. I looked at myself. I was very pleased with the dress. I looked unreal. The cape trailed behind me, but the dress was comfortable and luxurious. Richard had disappeared, but Jane was standing in front of the reception desk. She was smiling at me. I decided to find Prudence. The cape was very long and trailed on the floor behind me. I had to gather it up in order to walk sensibly. It was then I had a moment of inspiration. I had the perfect job for Winnie and Pooh.

Prudence was standing in the boutique. She had completely rearranged the dresses.

"I have selected my favourites," she said, "but I will require you to make the final choice."

I looked at the dresses. They were all lovely, but I immediately decided on a cream satin dress. It had a full skirt and fitted bodice similar to my own.

"Why don't you try this one on?" I said.

"Thank you madam that would be my first choice." She beamed.

While Prudence disappeared behind the screen with the assistant, I gathered up my cape and walked round to find the primates. They were still sitting on a rock. I waved them over to me. They stood up and walked over to me. They were holding hands as if to give each other encouragement. Apart from their long arms they had a very human gait. They stood in front of me.

"I wonder if you would help me out," I said awkwardly. "I have this long cape. I would like you each to hold a corner so that it doesn't trail on the floor. I cannot walk properly."

"We help," said Pooh.

"Yes, we help," said Winnie. "We make you walk properly."

"Shall we try it out?" I said.

They bounded behind me and unfolded the cape, each holding a corner. Clever primates, they already had got the idea. We paraded up and down. It worked very well. If I was going to act out this fairytale, I might as well go the whole hog and include these delightful creatures. Jane, who was standing by the desk, had her hand in front of her face. I was not sure if she was laughing or crying. I made a turn. Winnie and Pooh gracefully followed suit. Suddenly Richard was standing in front of me. He was wearing his dress suit. Uncannily, it matched my own dress.

"So this is what you had in mind," he laughed.

"Well, I can't walk with this thing trailing about behind me," I said.

"It is a brilliant idea." Richard smiled. "I think Mother will love it. To include our fellow animals is a good political statement. We won't say anything until the dress rehearsal. I look forward to seeing her reaction. She has not allowed the lemurs into the conference centre before."

Prudence appeared from behind the screen. She looked surprised at the sight and raised her arms in a human gesture as if greeting young children. Prudence took up her position behind Winnie and Pooh. Her dress was perfect. She always looked very beautiful.

I took Richard's arm and we paraded up and down one more time. Jane was taking pictures with a little gismo. I hope she doesn't show them to Lady Mary before the rehearsal. She seemed to be very excited.

"Well," Richard said, "I think we are all set. Let's rap this up before your parents arrive."

We changed back into our clothes. After saying goodbye to the dressmaker and his assistant, we went back to our rooms. The dresses followed eerily on their floating manikins like headless ghosts. Thankfully, Prudence took them into her room. Winnie and Pooh also followed us back. While Richard was changing, I had a little word with them. The rain had stopped and it was warm and humid.

"Would you both help me out again for the dress rehearsal?" I said. "I have no idea when it is."

"We know," Winnie said. "We tell you."

"Do you live in this house?" I asked. I was intrigued with the scenario.

"Mother and Father have big room downstairs. They help in kitchen. Lady Mary give books and food. We help. We collect food and wash dishes," Winnie said.

I suddenly realised that I should give them something. They were dropping hints and I was too engrossed to notice. I remembered there was a huge bowl of fruit in the room. It was a necessity in this strange world. I remembered the Hooches and their love of fruit.

"Wait there," I said. I left them sitting on the veranda with anticipation in their eyes. I went into our room. Richard was singing loudly in the shower. It sounded good but I could not stop to listen. I managed to find the fruit bowl. Apart from some apples, there was nothing I could recognise. In haste, I decided to bring out the whole bowl. It was a mistake. They deftly took as much as they could carry and laid the fruits on the veranda. I sat with them cross-legged and decided to try an apple before everything disappeared. With smiley faces, they tucked into the green looking plums.

"Would you show me the gardens and forest tomorrow?" I asked.

"We know the forest well," Pooh said. He was eating daintily. He peeled off the skins and dropped them over the veranda. "We have friends in forest. I find most fruit."

The sky went dark and a warm breeze ruffled my hair. It had to be Horace. This time he was velvet green. He dominated the garden below as his egg shaped bulk lowered towards the balcony. I stood up and watched him. Winnie and Pooh collected their fruit and scuttled down the staircase to the garden below. I shouted to them.

"Don't go I want you to meet my mother and father."

It was too late. They had disappeared. I was determined to find them tomorrow but I was not sure when tomorrow was.

I walked towards Horace. The door slid open along with a section of the balustrade. My parents appeared. They were each wearing brightly coloured full-length pleated smocks. Dad was in bottle green and my mother in bright yellow. Despite my initial surprise I kissed them both.

"While in Rome," Dad said as he hunched his shoulders.

"You both look great," I said. "I will have to buy some for Richard and myself."

I peered through Horace's door to see where their luggage was. There was a blond haired man standing in the cabin. He was wearing a green velvet tunic and was obviously synthetic. He had a big smile on his immaculate face.

"Hello Lisa," it said. "I am Horace."

I stepped back in surprise when I recognised Horace's voice. Dad took hold of my arm.

"Don't worry Lisa," he said. "Horace has had an update on Honshu. When the ship is not in use he can now transfer his being to a human life form and leave the ship. He is only just getting used to it."

I looked back at him. He was still smiling. I walked toward him and embraced him. I am not sure why. He was warm to the touch and very handsome. I was shocked and stepped back. I then felt Richard's presence. He was standing behind me. I glared at him.

"You could have told me about this," I said angrily.

"I didn't know he was having the modifications so soon," he said apologetically. "Nobody tells me anything around here."

Richard greeted my strange looking parents and then shook Horace's hand. I went onto the balcony and tried to calm down while he showed Mum and Dad to their room. Horace joined me on the balcony.

"I am sorry to have given you a surprise, Miss Lisa. I have a new format. I am not familiar with it yet."

"You and me both," I said while trying to clear my mind.

"Have you met Prudence?"

"I know of Prudence," he said. "I have not experienced her in my current form."

"Then you should meet her," I said. I strode to her room and knocked on the door. She opened it immediately.

"Come and meet Horace," I said, while pulling her out of the room by her arm.

"Who is Horace?" she said.

"He is in charge of the space ship," I said. "You have to look after him. He is unfamiliar with his surroundings. You must show him around."

I threw them together and in a frenzy I went into my own room. I sat on the loo and took some deep breaths. There was too much going on. I needed to calm down. What was Horace doing walking around in human form? At least he could talk to Prudence. I had to go and see my parents. It was warm so I changed into a light dress and made my way to my parents' room. Horace and Prudence were nowhere to be seen. I hoped I had done the right thing. Horace would have to meet Prudence eventually anyway.

Mum and Dad were sitting down drinking a strange blue coloured wine. Richard gave me a glass and gave me one of his 'it is not my fault' looks. The drink was nice and very alcoholic. I listened to Mum and Dad's adventures while getting sozzled. They had visited many museums on the planet Honshu. They had even gone to Atlantis but were not allowed to land because of excessive volcanic activity. I had the feeling that Dad did not want to go there considering his own family tragedy.

Mum handed me a gift-wrapped present.

"This is our wedding present to you."

I opened it. It was a gold watch with a large dial. The face of the watch was unrecognisable but it had more diamonds surrounding it.

"It is beautiful." I studied the confusing dial.

"This watch will tell you the time of day and night on Terranus," Dad said enthusiastically.

"I would give my back teeth to understand that," I said. Dad knelt down beside me.

"It is easy to understand. There are still twenty-four hours in a Terranus cycle. The hours are longer than those on Earth. A full cycle is twenty-nine Earth hours. The dial also tells you when night time falls and dawn begins on Terranus. The inner dial tells you the equivalent in Earth hours."

I was now incapable of understanding anything and felt sleepy. I looked at the watch and decided it was half past my bedtime. Richard, as usual, was sensitive to my thoughts.

"I think we need to turn in," he yawned, "it has been a long day."

After Richard's understated comment we returned to our room. Horace's spaceship was still there with the door open but there was no sign of him or Prudence. I looked at my new watch. I think it was two in the morning Earth time.

CHAPTER 33

We all slept well. After breakfast I prepared myself for a brisk walk around the gardens and forest. Richard told me that the dress rehearsal was at two in the afternoon, Terranus time. His parents were arriving at twelve. I was so pleased to have the watch. I had an itinerary and the means to tell the time. I was feeling confident, but Richard insisted that Prudence went with me just in case I got lost or was molested by a wild animal. I was not concerned, but I agreed. It was nice that he was thinking about my welfare.

I went out to knock on her door. Again the door opened immediately. I think she must stand behind it and listen.

"Good morning Prudence," I said.

"I am ready for a walk in the forest," she said. "Would you mind if Horace walked with us as well? I have had interesting conversations with him. He would like to see the plants and flowers. He has not touched them before. He is very knowledgeable."

I was getting used to this scenario. I turned toward the green velvet ship and Horace was standing by the door in matching tunic. We all went to the front desk. The front doors were wide open and sunlight streamed in across the wooden bridge. I wondered where my two primate friends were. Jane was in attendance behind the desk.

"Good morning Madam," she said. "I hope you had a restful night."

"Yes, thank you Jane," I smiled. "Have you seen Winnie and Pooh?"

"They are in the garden waiting for you madam."

There was obviously a communication link going on, but it did not bother me. I went over the bridge and out through the doors. There was another balcony and some wide stairs down to a huge expanse of green grass. I went down the stairs and walked towards an area of small trees to my left. Winnie and Pooh bounded towards me. They each grabbed my hands and led me toward an orchard of knurled ancient trees. The trees were unusual and seemed to have both flowers and fruits growing together. There were many different varieties giving a dazzling display of colour.

Beyond the orchard we came to a large area of cultivated vegetables. I walked towards it but Pooh held me back.

"Can't go there," Pooh squealed. "Animal fence will shock."

I stood and looked. I could recognise rows of onions, cabbage and carrots. There were many other unrecognisable plants. I could not see any fence. Pooh picked up a handful of grass and threw it. It highlighted a wall of red light.

"There is a force field around it," I said.

"Yes. Force field not nice." He looked relieved.

"Who tends this garden?" I asked. Pooh looked at me quizzically with his large brown eyes. Winnie intervened.

"'Codi' do garden," she said. "They know how to go into field. They shy. Work at night. They carve wood and make things. Winnie wants to carve wood and garden." I took Winnie's hand and wondered whom the 'Codi' were.

"In time I will show you both what they do. I want to teach you. I need to know also. We learn together." We had a group hug. I nearly burst into tears again. I must not talk in their stilted way.

Prudence and Horace finally caught up with us. They were talking nineteen to the dozen and were not even slightly interested in their surroundings or us for that matter. I continued down towards the forest with Winnie and Pooh holding my hands. As soon as we entered the trees they let go and were off. The forest was very dense and I followed a path that had been cleared of undergrowth. I could hear Winnie and Pooh swinging around in the trees and chattering loudly. They certainly had not lost their climbing abilities. I continued at a brisk pace. Apart from some odd rustling sounds, the forest was very quiet. Winnie and Pooh had disappeared and I had left Horace and Prudence lagging behind me. Suddenly there were loud squealing sounds coming towards me in the undergrowth. I stopped dead in fear of being attacked by a wild animal. I turned around ready to run for it back down the path, but I was too late. The undergrowth shook as a large herd of pink animals dashed across my path. I realised that they were nothing more than domestic pigs. They were large and fat. Thankfully they ignored me as they bounded across the path and into the trees. Winnie and Pooh appeared behind the pigs, carrying sticks.

"These our pigs," Winnie said proudly.

"We look after them for Lady Mary," Pooh said.

"That gave me a fright," I said. "I thought it was a wild animal."

"Many animal in forest," Winnie said. "They not hurt. We keep for Lady Mary."

Prudence and Horace finally caught us up.

"Are you all right Lisa?" she said. "You look pale."

"I have been surprised by a lot of pigs, but it is not a problem." Prudence looked at me strangely and I don't think she understood.

"Pigs," Horace said. "Animals of the **genus Sus**, within the Suidae family of even-toed ungulates." I looked at Horace incredulously. He was spot on.

"Horace, you are so clever," Prudence said while hooking her arm through his. I sighed and walked on. My party of clever primates and synthetic intelligence followed me. It would have been interesting to have Darwin with me to discuss the scenario.

Eventually we came out of the forest onto an expanse of lawn. The hotel complex was in sight through a grove of palm trees. I walked towards it. By the time I had gone through the trees, a black torpedo shaped ship was lowering down towards the hotel. It was the submarine that Lady Mary uses. She must be returning home. I turned to my entourage.

"I need to get back to my room," I said in panic. Winnie stepped forward.

"I have quick way," she said. "Follow."

We ran towards the hotel while the black ship disappeared behind the green curved roof. I followed Winnie through some broad leafed shrubbery and she opened a little carved wooden door. I had to crouch down to enter. It led to a storeroom full of old-fashioned earthenware jars. I realised that they were cider jars. Glowing panels gave dim light to the room. We went through another door and found ourselves in a garden courtyard. Horace's velvet egg was there. We then ran up some stairs and ended up on a veranda. The numbers on the doors started with an eight. This was home. I kissed Winnie on her furry cheek and Pooh wrapped his huge arms around me. I was happy to get back to the room. Richard was missing, but he had left a note on the table. It said that when I was ready, I was to go to the reception area and Jane would show me to his mother's rooms. I dutifully obeyed and put on a posh frock.

Lady Mary and Lord William looked well and relaxed. Apparently they had been on holiday. I also met Peter. He was very nice. Apart from the age difference, he and Richard could have been twins. We sat on large leather sofas while Mini served coffee.

Lady Mary was sitting beside me. I was feeling nervous about the dress rehearsal.

"I understand that you are organised for the dress rehearsal this afternoon," she said while putting her hand on mine in a comforting way.

"My dress is lovely," I said. "I hope you like the dress that Prudence has chosen."

"The ceremony is for you as well as the people of Terranus. I can sense what you have in mind and I can assure you I will be delighted with any choices you have."

I was not sure what she meant by that. I wondered if she knew about my idea to get Winnie and Pooh to help me with the cape. Then I realised she had been probing my thoughts. The empathy was strong and I knew that she knew.

"Do you mind if Winnie and Pooh help me with the cape? They are such darling people," I said boldly. I had to come clean.

"Dear Lisa," she said with a smile. "I don't mind at all. We will see how the rehearsal goes. I have sensed that Richard considers it to be a beneficial statement to include them and I agree. Our animal friends have to be treated with due respect."

Richard looked at me with one of his innocent expressions. I was living in a society where secrets and surprises were difficult to sustain. It was very refreshing.

After lunch we trooped off to change into our finery. We went to the reception area where the procession was to begin. Prudence was enjoying the experience of wearing her fancy new dress. I was wearing my diamond necklace and rings. Prudence had worked a miracle on my hair. Somehow she had fluffed it up into large curls. I wondered where Winnie and Pooh were.

"We have about five minutes before we start," Richard said while he dusted off his pleated jacket. "Filming will begin as soon as we go down the corridor and the music will start."

He looked nervous and I was worried that my pageboy and girl would not turn up. I would have to get Prudence to help me with this damn cape. There was no way I could walk sensibly otherwise.

"One minute to go," Richard said. He was looking pale. I kissed him on the cheek. He smiled at me wistfully. I had the annoying feeling that once again he had not told me the whole picture.

There was a commotion behind me. It was Winnie and Pooh. They had obviously been washed and brushed. They were wearing sweet little matching waistcoats with gold trim. It was the same material as my dress. We were a set. They looked very smart.

"Where have you been?" I said.

"We sorry," Winnie said. "Mother made coat for us. She fuss too much. Made us late."

"You both look lovely," I said as the music started.

They took up their positions and held up the cape. I took Richard's arm and held on to it tightly. We then proceeded down the wide corridor. The music surprised me. It was 'The Arrival of the Queen of Sheba' played on an exquisite pipe organ.

"I didn't expect such conventional music," I whispered.

"It is traditional," Richard said through his teeth. "Handel has strong family links to Terranus."

The doors to the conference centre were wide open and we proceeded in stately fashion down the stairs. Mother, Father and Horace were sitting on a lower tier watching. Peter and Jane were on the other side. The music was very rousing and I smiled until my ears and teeth hurt.

After an age we finally stood in front of Lady Mary and Lord William. They were also dressed in their finery. I just hoped that Winnie and Pooh were behaving themselves. I dare not look round. Lady Mary was smiling. She gave a long speech. I found it difficult to follow the gist, but it was obviously political. I think she was getting some mileage out of our marriage. She was talking about an alliance between Terranus and Earth. I could understand why with all the mind-boggling things that are going to happen in years to come. After her speech there was loud clapping and cheering. It was obviously a recording. I also noticed the cameras. They were like little flies silently hovering around us.

Then she began the marriage vows – not unlike the registry office wedding we had already been through. After the vows, we kissed with even more canned applause and cheering. Then we made a clever turn. Prudence was beaming and stepped aside. We stepped forward and Winnie and Pooh carried the cape with class and style and took up position behind us. We walked forward. The applause continued with some sort of music in the background. Richard smiled and waved. I thought his jaw might drop off. We climbed the stairs out of the conference centre and back into the reception area. I sighed with relief. It all seemed to go like clockwork. I dreaded having to do it all again in front of an audience.

Max was waiting by the desk with a large tray of glasses filled with champagne. Richard embraced me.

"That was perfect," he said. "You are a star." I kissed him; he was very happy and it made me feel good.

Richard gave me a glass of champagne. I sipped it. It was a strong apple cider. I took comfort in knowing where it came from.

The damn fly cameras had followed us but I ignored them with contempt. I took two glasses of cider to Winnie and Pooh. They were sitting in a very grown-up way on a leather sofa. I knelt in front of them.

"Thank you so much for your help," I said while I handed them the glasses. They showed their white teeth and took the glasses with amazing dexterity.

"We pleased you are a Lady," Winnie said.

"We look after you," Pooh said. They put their glasses on the marble floor and both embraced me. A lump appeared in my throat; I was ready to cry, but I subdued it.

"Thank you both," I said. "I look after you also."

I stood away and nearly fell over the cape. They showed their white teeth in animal amusement and went to sit on the rock near the pool, carefully clutching their cider glasses. I hope they were old enough to drink strong alcohol. I had no way of knowing.

I took off the cape. Prudence helped me and took it away.

Lady Mary and William joined us. Max offered them a glass of cider. Lady Mary looked very happy with herself.

"That went very well," she said. William nodded in agreement. "The film is being edited as we speak. It will be ready shortly. If all goes well, we may not have to repeat the ceremony. Personally, I think it was perfect. You all did so well. Later on we can all see it and decide."

The gathering turned into a party fuelled by nibbles and copious amounts of cider. Eventually we all went back to our rooms. I was happy to get out of the dress and relax my aching jaw after too much chattering and smiling. Richard and I had a shower and waited for the film show. I would be intrigued to see myself on film. I was not sure what she meant by not having to do the ceremony again. However, it would be good not to go through the whole rigmarole again.

Lady Mary summoned us all to her apartment. Horace and Prudence were there. They seemed to be very friendly with each other. My parents were also there with Winnie and Pooh sitting beside them. Lady Mary showed us the film on a large video screen concealed in one of the wooden wall panels.

I could not believe it. The film had been modified to show a crowd of people watching the ceremony. The editing was amazing. The audience was interactive and you would not know the difference. The film was highly detailed and three-dimensional. It was a product of superior technology. After the film had finished I could tell that Lady Mary was very happy with it.

"Well," she said, "I think that is absolutely perfect. I would not want to change anything. I do not think we need to repeat the ceremony."

I had mixed feelings about it. It was impressive. Winnie and Pooh had behaved beautifully. I did think it was a rehearsal. I now realised that she never intended to have real people watching. The film was just political spin and felt impersonal. Lady Mary was picking up my thoughts.

"Lisa," she said, "the marriage is quite real. Because of your lineage, it is legally binding for the whole system. It would have been impractical to invite all those people. It would take months to organise it. Because of your pregnancy we just do not have the time. All the people you saw in the film have been informed. They will be sent a personal copy of the ceremony. Please do not be upset. We do things differently on this world. You are now legally married on two different planets. It is my fault and I am sorry. I should have explained the situation. I don't give myself enough time these days."

"I quite understand," I stammered guiltily. "I don't know what I was thinking. It was a lovely ceremony. It was just a shock seeing the film."

"I just want you to be happy." She smiled. "It is wonderful to have you in the family."

Richard and I decided to stay at the complex for another two weeks. I wanted to understand Terranus culture and get to know the natives, especially my animal friends. My parents were to go back to Earth in Lady Mary's ship. Before they left, Dad gave me a list of places to visit, including natural history museums and musical venues for Richard.

As a wedding present, Lady Mary had given us Horace indefinitely for our own private use. Prudence was delighted. I think she was in love with him.

Curiously enough, Richard was just as ignorant about the Terranus culture as I was. We loved each other and it was very exciting to embark on a huge learning curve together.

CHAPTER 34

James was a very smart boy. His parents had to arrange for him to have private education suitable for a gifted child. When he was sixteen, he was studying for a doctorate in engineering, electronics and physics. Like his father, he had a passion for historic engineering. He had not inherited his father's musical abilities. His father's old Jaguar motorcar fascinated him. It was using a polluting fossil fuel. The museum of old steam engines was even worse. These days, modern cars were electric and powered by nuclear fusion. It was now becoming difficult finding petrol to keep the old Jag running. If you needed coal for the steam engines the only way was to dig it out of the ground yourself.

There were so many technological advances during his tender years, but he was embracing the new science as if by second nature. Power stations were being decommissioned. Houses and offices were now fitted with individual power generators fuelled by nuclear fusion. NASA was in the process of developing a new anti-gravity device that would revolutionise space travel and eliminate the need for the expensive hydrogen-fuelled rocket motors. Air travel was cheap and efficient. Since the discovery of harnessing the power of antimatter, NASA scientists were even claiming the possibility of travelling at the speed of light out in space.

James had a lively mind and these were exciting times for him. However, he sensed that something was not quite right. There was something odd about Prudence. Since Thelma's funeral, James realised that Prudence did not age. She seemed to have limitless energy.

Also his parents were away from home quite a lot. They always seemed to be so busy and any explanations he had from them did not seem to hold water.

James did not know about his origins, but one morning his life was about to be turned upside down.

He was up exceptionally early. Normally he would not be out of bed until at least midday. He walked past his parents' bedroom in search of a cup of coffee. It was only nine in the morning. Their door was wide open. Normally he would never bother to go into their room, but this time he peered round the door.

He saw his father walk off the balcony into a dark opening suspended in the garden. That was not right. He stood at the door frozen to the spot. His mother was making the bed and looked up in surprise.

"James!" she shrieked. "You're up early."

Richard appeared from the dark opening.

"Oh bugger," he said.

James quickly found his power of speech.

"What the hell is going on?" he said with wide eyes.

"Well, you would have to know sooner or later," Richard said. "I would prefer you to be a bit older but at least you are ahead of your years."

Richard walked into the bedroom and sat on the bed. Lisa stood with a guilty look on her face.

"I have a lot of explaining to do," Richard said. "Come and sit here and I will do the best I can." He patted the bed next to him.

James obeyed and sat next to him. He stared at Horace's interior in bewilderment.

"What is that in the garden?" he said, pointing at the dark opening.

"It is an intelligent interstellar space ship," Richard said. James dropped his jaw.

"I knew it," he said. "NASA have already invented space travel.

Why isn't it made public? This is another breakthrough in science. Why do you have this ship?"

"Hold on James. Calm down. You don't know the full picture." Richard got a feeling of déja vu. James was so like his mother.

"Although you were born on Earth, your roots come from another planet in a different solar system. The origin of this space ship is extraterrestrial. It was not developed on Earth. We use it to travel between planets. The technology this ship uses is very advanced. We are in the process of introducing the technology on Earth. In the meantime, Horace is top secret. Only a few people know of his existence."

"Horace?" James said with a confused look. "I thought he was Prudence's boyfriend."

"Horace is a synthetic biological living organism. He has natural intelligence. When he is not piloting the ship he can take on human form. Prudence is also synthetic. They have formed a friendship."

James looked even more confused.

"A synthetic biological living organism," he said. "Is that the same as the nuclear fusion controllers?"

"The programming is biological but not the same. For the moment do not worry about it," Richard said. "Prudence and Horace have their own intelligence. They are living beings. They come from a planet that has thousands of years of technological evolution that is far in advance of planet Earth."

"I always knew there was something weird going on," James said.

"I have some time," Richard said. "Come with me on a flight to the moon and I will explain the full picture. I will show you Planet Earth rising above the lunar surface. Your grandfather showed me this spectacle when I was twenty years old. You will understand."